SIPHON

JEAN DAVIS

Siphon

www.jeandavisauthor.com

ISBN-13:   (print) 978-1-962708-13-5
                  (ebook) 978-1-962708-14-2

First Edition: May 2026

Published by StreamlineDesign LLC

Also by Jean Davis

Sahmara
The Last God
A Broken Race
Everyone Dies
Destiny Pills and Space Wizards
Dreams of Stars and Lies
Not Another Bard's Tale
Spindelkin
Frayed
I9

The Narvan
One Shot at the Sphinx
Trust
The Minor Years
Chain of Gray
Bound In Blue
Seeker
Tears of the Tyrant

1

LAVINA SWIRLED her tongue over her faux canines, watching the crowd from the semi-flattering shadows of the club. The current iteration of this place wasn't particularly her scene—she much preferred the décor back in the seventies—but the food at Vadim's parties was always excellent. The music wasn't. In fact, it seemed to get markedly more irritating every time she came.

On the dance floor in front of her, three young women wearing next to nothing, were doing their damnedest to get Vadim's attention with their sexually explicit gyrations. Foolish little humans. He wasn't interested in what was between their legs. Like the others blissfully dancing away, they'd been invited for what flowed through their veins. For Vadim's actual guests.

Scanning the crowd in the flashing lights, Lavina spotted her ex. Vadim wore a pale grey tailored suit that fit his broad shoulders impeccably. His blond hair had grown out since she'd seen him last, now bound back in a flawless ponytail that trailed down his back. The ancient Russian—though he didn't appear a day over thirty—worked the room, shaking hands, making deals, renewing connections. Just as he had back in the days when she'd been at his side. Back when he'd been all dark and broody, full of a couple hundred years of tormented baggage.

Now he was smiling. Like actually good mood, friendly, hey-how-you-doing smiling. Lavina groaned. She'd ruined him.

She'd enjoyed his estate in Russia, his Mediterranean vacation home, and his flat in Paris for the seven years they'd been together. For a while there, she'd thought he was the one. But then he started talking about redemption and giving back to the community. She rolled her eyes again, just thinking about how earnest he'd been.

Fifty-three years ago, he'd have been making deals with his guests to keep their kind hidden, to increase their wealth in this ever-changing world, and delivering threats to keep everyone's feeding grounds separated. Now he was probably talking to the others about putting together a fundraiser for orphans or something equally banal.

A velvety hand slid over her wrist, yanking her attention back to her immediate surroundings. Gabriel Boros—one of Vadim's new favorites according to gossip she'd picked up during her social hiatus—pressed a drink into her hand. The young man appeared barely of legal drinking age. He leaned in close enough that she could hear his Greek accent over the throbbing music.

"You looked like you could use this." He nodded to the tall, fizzy pink concoction decorated with a paper straw and a skewer of artfully cut strawberries and pineapple.

It looked like something those idiot girls would have

happily sucked down. She sought out somewhere to abandon it, but there were no tables nearby. With a sigh, she clutched the condensating glass and attempted to appreciate what little chill it offered in the room full of too much body heat.

"Thank you." Not that she meant it.

As hungry as she was for dark memories, Gabriel was too...refined. He was well-dressed, clean shoes, pressed shirt, smelled good—all the things the blood bags on the dance floor drooled over. Yet, perhaps, under all that he harbored a little dark trauma that would tide her over until she found a long-term food source. She'd have to keep him talking, get to know him enough to learn what leading question would unlock a tasty memory morsel from his past.

He rubbed a manicured hand over his smooth chin and flashed her a charming smile. "If that's not what you're thirsty for, I could..."

A vampire nibbling on her neck was not at all what she had in mind. She took a deep breath and tried to clue him in so she could keep him talking.

"I remember how Vadim's parties work." Was that snippy? It probably came off that way.

Her social niceties might be rusty, but even as much as she wanted to sift through his head, her gut knew he wasn't her type. Lavina took a sip of the too sweet drink while narrowly avoiding stabbing her eyes with the stupid fruit skewer.

Gabriel gave her a hesitant side-eye. "You've been here before?"

Lavina threw a smile on her face, just barely exposing her fang dental implants. "It's been a few decades."

Since the Vadim disaster, in fact. Surely by now some

other drama had to have eclipsed the rumors that being with her had changed him. As far as she remembered, Gabriel hadn't even been in Northchester back then.

Damn Vadim and his delicious memories. Restraint had never been her strong point, but she'd made him last so much longer than all the others. That was progress, wasn't it?

"Oh, sorry, I didn't realize." He looked annoyed that he'd handed off his free drink prop to a fellow vampire instead of a blood-filled snack.

She considered handing it back. Most of the women in here were too drunk to realize someone else had already taken a sip, but it did feel more natural to stand with something in her hands, less out of place.

"I hope you find something more to your liking." She nodded to the gyrating crowd of sweaty humans.

"You too," he said absently. His attention wandered from her face to another of Vadim's favorites sitting at the corner of the dance floor, eyeing the human buffet.

In his defense, she did smell human, hot blood in her veins and all. Not that she was inclined to explain herself. He'd get over it.

Gabriel licked his lips, his tongue running over his very real fangs.

She wasn't jealous. Alright, maybe she was. Life would be so much easier if all she needed was to drain a human now and then. Sadly, feeding off their memories didn't extend her life and stop her aging like feeding from vampires did. If only she'd discovered that benefit before she'd crested the half century mark.

Gabriel offered her a semi-amicable nod and then wandered off to his buddy's table.

There had to be someone here who would take the edge off her appetite. She peered over the dance floor just as the lighting guy thought it would be a good idea to turn on every strobe in the place. It might not have bothered the true vampires, and the meat puppets cheered, but Lavina pinched her eyes shut and turned toward the wall.

A high-pitched voice cut through the thumping music, "Lavina Arendine? It *is* you."

Clearly the universe was punishing her for ruining such a tasty morsel as Vadim and daring to show her face in The Jackyl. Lavina gritted her teeth and turned to face the woman she could have gladly gone a few more decades without seeing. Ignoring the taste but needing the liquid tolerance to not cause a scene, she drained the rest of the drink Gabriel had given her.

Eveline closed the already too small gap between them, towering over Lavina in six-inch stilettos like a professional stilt walker. She rested her hand on Lavina's lace-covered arm without invitation. "What rock have you been hiding under? It's been so long." She smiled wide enough to show off her gleaming white fangs while taking in Lavina's outfit and then emitted a haughty huff. "Look at you. How very... bland. Fishing for a meal or a new man?"

Bland? Her ivory lace blouse flattered her cleavage nicely, thank you very much. Her sensible pair of black dress pants with the magical stomach-flattening panel was a much better choice than any of those short skirts on the dance floor. Not that she was going to get out there. And those high heels, she shook her head. Her arches hurt just looking at them.

She hated that people like Eveline could make her insecure. You're three-hundred and twelve years old, get a grip.

Lavina squared her shoulders and glared up at the beautiful old biddy. Rumor had it that Eveline was coming up on five centuries, though she looked to be in her mid-twenties. "Trolling for new toys? Or maybe a quickie in the back alley?"

Eveline snarled. "Good luck with your next fixer-upper, Grandma." She strutted her leather-clad perky ass onto the dance floor and proceeded to show up Vadim's fangirls in the choreographed dance the crowd was attempting to pull together.

Lavina resisted the urge to wipe off her sleeve where Eveline had touched her, like the woman had left dirt behind.

If that crone could fit in here, so could she. Maybe another drink or two would help her relax. Skirting the dance floor, she worked her way to the bar.

Vadim kept his club clean, and this private event meant a short line, both of which she appreciated as she leaned her elbows on the bar, waiting to catch the bartender's attention. He was a nice-looking young man, probably in his twenties like most everyone else here. The vamp-worshiping crowd tended to be a type. Once one got a family and sense, the idea of blood-sucking creatures of the night being attractive faded.

Under Vadim's rules, the feeder group was safe and his vamp crowd stayed in line. Feeding was fine. Killing forbidden. Violating the rules meant being banned for life. The easily available food source kept Gabriel and those like him on good terms with Vadim. The food all signed consent forms, just hoping for the opportunity to meet a real vampire. Most of them would by the time the party was over, but none of them would remember it, and yet, all would say they had. Foolish children, perpetuating the story just to pretend to be a part of it.

Lavina wanted a couple shots of tequila to wash Eveline away, but current company made her go with the safe bet of red wine. Easier to fit in that way. The vamps all liked to play up their roles. They'd tell the food that the wine was blood. It never was. Blood was preferred from the vein. She'd lived with enough of them to know.

"Hello, Lavina," purred a voice in her ear.

Lavina smiled and took a drink before turning to the young man she'd let go early in her life, the second vampire she'd been with. Back when she'd been smart enough not to get too attached to her meals. Too addicted.

"Hello, Fane."

He took the stool next to where she stood, one hand on his own wineglass. The other hovered only inches from hers. "Good to see you here, Lavina. We've missed you."

"Have you?"

He grinned, employing the charming dimple on his left cheek. "I don't know about the others, to be honest, but I have."

There was that honesty she'd brought out in him after one too many memory meals. Long ago, Fane had sustained her for a very enjoyable seven months and six days, not that she'd kept track even all these years later. She sighed, nostalgia washing over her.

The moment Fane had started to use words like honesty and truth, she'd cut him loose. One of her biggest regrets and best calls all in one.

Maybe, she considered, it wouldn't hurt to dip back into his pool for a night. Maybe even a week or two. They'd been apart for a very long time. He'd have slipped back into his dark ways a little bit by now. She just needed a little vampire snack, some deep terror to fill her stomach and stave off the natural aging process.

Lavina slid her fingers over his. "What have you been up to? It's been a while."

"Been home, visiting my family in Romania."

She gave him a dry look. "Isn't your family long dead?"

"Sorry, habit. Yes, they are. I *was* visiting though. It's nice to go back to my homeland. Out in the country, it's like time hasn't passed at all, you know?"

She squeezed his icy hand. "I do. You're cold. You haven't fed?"

"Not yet. I've only been here," he held up his barely touched glass, "this long."

"Ah. Well, you know the food here is clean and willing. Eat up."

He smiled warmly. "You always took good care of me, Lavina. Remind me why we parted again?"

In truth, because he'd begun to lose his flavor. But honesty was now his thing. It had never been hers.

"Because you like to go out, and I'm a homebody." She grinned. "I'm sure you've not been lacking for company."

"I didn't say that." He leaned in and kissed her cheek. "But I have been lacking *your* company."

Charming, attractive, and willing? Yes, please. Her mind took on the soft hum that signaled her abilities warming up to trance her meal into divulging delicious memories.

One night with Fane would be fine. She wouldn't slip back into him too deeply, wouldn't take too much. Most certainly wouldn't drain all his darkness and leave him clean and cheery. It wasn't like she was starving. Except, she was. She resisted the urge to lick her lips. There was far too much of that going on without her joining in.

"Then you should go get something to eat," she urged. "You're going to need the energy."

He laughed, eyes twinkling. Fane took a drink of his wine and set the glass next to hers. "I take it from your warmth that you've already feasted?"

Lavina nodded, waving him off. She'd been playing the dangerous game of pretending to be a vampire for two hundred and sixty years. If they got wind of her deception, she wouldn't just lose her access to life-extending meals, hers would no doubt be extinguished. Vampires, even the more vanilla ones, weren't known for forgiveness.

"Then watch that for me, would you? I'll be back shortly," he said.

"Will do."

She watched him melt into the crowd, not thinking at all about how he fit in perfectly with his black leather pants and the tumbled mess of soft dark curls on his head. He'd even embraced the stereotype of the white linen poet shirt. The color popped invitingly against his tan skin. How she'd managed to look into those big brown eyes and tell him she was leaving, she didn't know. And dammit, did she have the strength to do that again, as hungry as she was?

No way in hell. Lavina sighed. She emptied her glass and then his. She'd done poor Fane enough damage. Ditching him here might sting for a few minutes, but he'd be much better off.

She'd been seen tonight, reestablished contact with vampire society. That was enough progress for now. She'd find a human snack on the way home to tide her over, but if she didn't taste a vampire soon, her body's clock was going to resume ticking.

Lavina left the bar and ventured into the crowd that stood between her and the door. They'd spread out in the flashing rainbow of lights, masking any clear path. The fog machines were going full blast, lending a fitting ambience but also making her cough. She wove her way through the humans writhing to the beat in drunken bliss—made even easier and cheaper by the blood loss.

All the food was drug-free in accordance with Vadim's rules. Did that count as doing the community a favor? She supposed it did. One little good thing she could accept out of the damage she'd done to him.

Thankfully, she didn't spot Fane or any of her other exes in the crowd. She worked her way forward, narrowly avoiding the food who were busy taking selfies, draped over each other, doing their best vamp impressions.

With the advent of social media, many of the vampire crowd had elected to drop off the public face of the earth for their own safety and that of the race as a whole. The more social of them flocked in groups like this one, protecting each other with a legitimate cover. She'd witnessed a few reinventing themselves as their own children to account for their longevity.

Lavina had opted to use a smartphone for appearances, but she wasn't active on any media platforms. Email, text, or good old voice calls were her preferred modes of communication.

She found herself in an elbowless pocket and took the opportunity to pull out her phone to check the time. An update from her news app flashed a *Bloodless Body Found in Northchester* headline. She paused, putting her phone away. Someone wasn't following Vadim's rules. She wondered if he'd seen the headline yet and what he'd do about it. He was well-connected within the city, beyond the vampire population. Being wealthy had its benefits.

If she were the dutiful vamp she claimed to be, she'd seek him out and tell him about it just in case he was too busy enjoying himself to have noticed. But she wasn't.

The crowd thinned the closer she got to the door, mostly flirting couples and small groups with their robust laughter and slurred conversations. She was mulling over whether to go hungry another night or be disappointed with the tasteless memories of a boring human, when the stench of dead body and unwashed flesh hit her.

A tall, olive-skinned vampire stood just inside the door to The Jackyl, his clothes torn and stained. His mouth hung open enough to expose yellowed fangs, like an animal breathing in a mouth full of scent. Dark spatters on his face appeared to be blood. His narrowed eyes scanned the crowd, hunting.

He was positively feral.

Lavina's heart leapt. Even Vadim hadn't been this bad off when they'd met.

She couldn't wait to sink her figurative teeth into him.

Vadim was going to have a fit when he spotted this wild vampire in his civilized club. From the trajectory of a beeline approach, she gathered one of the bouncers already had.

She was closer. Thankful for her sensible boots, Lavina darted through the crowd. The bouncer was three people back to her right and still barreling through the milling crowd.

She clamped her hand down on the grungy vampire's arm, employing all the strength she could muster in her starving state to get her point across.

"Come with me if you want to keep your head on your shoulders."

Lavina didn't look back. She pulled the door open and yanked him through. As the door to the club closed, the decibels dropped to a tolerable level in the vestibule. The ravaged neck of the dead bouncer who had been posted there answered her question about how he'd gained entry. He certainly hadn't been on the guest list.

The irate vamp tugged at his arm, but she held tight.

"I'm trying to help you," she snapped. "Come on."

Lavina opened the door to the street and jerked him through it. Two more dead bouncers lay there. Their necks torn open like the one inside.

"That was unwise," she muttered, and yet her mouth was watering at the same time.

He growled something unintelligible, still trying to free his arm.

"I'll let go when I'm damned well ready. Let me think a moment."

But they didn't have a moment. She couldn't go home. Vadim would review the security footage and know she'd left with this new pariah. Good thing she had a backup apartment. She'd always loathed the idea of bringing her food home, at least not until she trusted them.

"We're going to have to lay low for a while. At least you're well fed. You'll need to be off the streets for a few weeks until Vadim calms down."

He bared his fangs and snapped at her.

Lavina spared fifteen seconds to spin him around, slam him up against the building, and bare her own faux fangs for all they were worth.

"You'll calm the hell down. Right now. Got it?"

He gasped, stunned. "Yes."

"Good." She pulled him off the wall, desperately hoping he had a host of dark memories to sustain her. While the element of surprise and a burst of adrenaline had served to establish her authority, she was now running on fumes.

With half an hour to go until the clubs closed, taxis were still trolling the streets for work, not yet overloaded with drunks. She sped down the sidewalk, towing her meal behind her until she spotted a cab near enough to them to take the valuable seconds to hail it and get inside. A mob of bouncers burst out of The Jackyl's door.

"Where?" he asked, seemingly capable of only one word at a time.

"My place is safe." She gave the address to the driver.

By the time the mob got close, the taxi was safely away from the curb and melting into traffic. Lavina settled into the seat, putting what little distance was possible in the back seat between her and the man in sore need of an hour-long scalding shower and a change of clothes. If nothing else, the smell of him would help keep her exhaustion at bay.

2

STEPHANOS KEPT a watchful eye on the woman in rich people clothes sitting beside him. He hadn't paid attention to clothes in a very long time. Or much of anything else, he considered, as the city flew by outside the taxi window. The bright lights hurt his eyes.

Gabriel was not going to be happy that the job wasn't done. Two days had seemed like plenty of time to walk into a club and take out one fancy-pants vampire. His sire had even given him the address and pulled up an internet search that provided a photo, hundreds of them actually, from every angle. Vadim should have been dead by now.

The driver glanced up in the rearview mirror every other breath, eyes darting to Stephanos, ignoring the woman altogether. He could easily take out the driver, but where would that get him? Another quick blood buzz, maybe, but he'd had his fill for the night. More than his fill, actually. The body he'd drained before attempting the job had sated him well enough, but then he'd topped off at the club. Gabriel hadn't mentioned that there'd be so much security between him and his target. The place had been packed, as promised, but security hadn't been nearly as distracted with managing the drunk crowd as expected.

Stephanos glanced at the enigma beside him. Not that he'd been over his head with the number of security guards between him and his target, but he wasn't exactly regretting getting pulled out of the situation. His sire might want to take over Vadim's hold on Northchester, but he could wait a week or two until a less daunting opportunity came up. However, Gabriel wouldn't see it that way. He sighed, relaxing into the seat. Tomorrow, he'd get an earful of shit, but for the rest of the night, he was looking forward to figuring out how this woman had been able to overpower him even as fully fed as he was.

Maybe she could be of use, and if not, he'd make sure she wasn't alive to thwart him again. The way her eyes were drooping, she wouldn't be up for pushing him around for a while. She must be one of the old ones. That and gorging herself on the humans in the club would explain why she was so strong. The boost from the blood wouldn't last. He knew that well enough from experience.

Stephanos smiled. Maybe she would be helping him whether she agreed to or not. Gabriel never said he couldn't bring in anyone else. His sire had never been one to get his own hands dirty, but Stephanos had more experience than he wanted. If she could distract the target, maybe he could one and done this mess and be on his way home sooner than later.

Their taxi came to a stop.

The woman reached into her pocket and came out with a wad of cash. She peeled off a twenty and handed it to the driver. "Keep the change. Sorry about the smell."

Smell? What was she going on about?

She got out and held the door open, giving him an expectant look. "Any day would be great."

He almost laughed, but then reconsidered, given how she'd slung him around before the ride. He got out and walked six doors down with her before heading up a set of porch stairs, where she unlocked the door with a key. She held the door open, giving him that look again. Shrugging, he went inside.

One hallway led toward the back of the building. A stairway next to it led upward. She took the stairs. He followed. Everything here was cleaner and brighter than he was used to. It made him more aware of how dirty he was. Not that it mattered. Nothing much did these days. Existing was easier when he didn't think about anything too much. Just do whatever Gabriel asked of him and feed, that got him through the nights. And when he couldn't do that anymore, the walking into sunlight option was always there.

At the top of the stairs, a hallway stretched out just like the one on the floor below. She walked to the last door on the left and pulled out the ring of keys again. With three locks taken care of, she pushed the door open and went inside.

The place was very far from the house Gabriel had left to him in Scotland, where he'd been blissfully oblivious to the world before his sire had shown up to summon him here two months ago. Since then, he'd been sleeping on a mattress on the floor in Gabriel's Northchester estate, wishing he was back in Scotland.

That wasn't going to happen until he fulfilled his task. The one he'd failed at tonight. Stephanos rubbed his forehead, not looking forward to the call he would surely get any minute. So far, the phone Gabriel had given him remained silent. Small blessings. He kept his hand on the plastic and glass rectangle, considering turning it off. The woman watched him out of the corner of her eye while she locked the door behind them and turned on the lights. Perhaps it would be wise to keep the phone handy in case he needed to call for help.

Her apartment wasn't overly filled with kitschy shit, but comfortable, and with actual furniture. She left the lights on a low setting that suited his eyes.

"You're safe enough here. There's no sunlight to worry about." She went to the one window he could see from three steps into the room and pulled up the blinds to show a bricked surface. "Lower rent with zero view."

"Handy."

"While I'd prefer to get right to business," she waved her hand in front of her nose, "you smell like God only knows what. The bathroom is right there. Use it. I'll find you some clean clothes."

"Sure."

No sense in being difficult until he'd figured out if she would be willing to help him take out Vadim. And really, a shower didn't sound horrible. He hadn't had one of those since Gabriel had informed him he'd need to be presentable to board a plane to get here.

The bathroom was suspiciously stocked. A basket with everything he might have required sat on the counter. How many men did she bring here? Maybe she liked to clean her victims first.

Stephanos set his phone on the counter and then peeled off his... Were they even considered clothes anymore? He dropped the rags into the trash bin. It was too small, but he figured that would earn him more points than leaving a filthy pile on the clean tile.

He cranked on the hot water and stepped into the shower. The little cube made him uncomfortable. Too tight. Not enough air. Too much like the prison he'd been confined to hundreds of years ago. He took a deep inhale of the steamy air and held onto the shower door. He wasn't trapped. Wiping away the steam, he kept an eye on the rest of the room while he went about washing with his other hand. As long as he could see the sink, the toilet, the light on the ceiling, he could do this.

The last thing he wanted was for the woman to sense his weakness, to have something to hold over him. Or to torture him with. Gabriel knew, but the idea of anyone he didn't trust having that knowledge made him snarl.

Washing the tangle that was his hair took both hands, and he hurried through the motions. Then he realized how matted it still was and washed it again. At least his host had the good grace not to provide any of that super fragranced shit that some of his victims reeked of. This smelled like soap. Like it should.

Anxious to get out of the confined space, he turned off the water and stepped out. Towels waited on a rack beside the shower door. They were soft and large enough to go all the way around him. Clean on the outside, he rummaged through the basket and found a toothbrush. Stephanos broke it out of its wrapper and put it to good use. By the third time he rinsed, his teeth finally felt smooth again. His victims never complained about his breath while he ripped their throats open, but he had the distinct feeling his host would. She'd not bothered to hide how she felt about much of anything else. That was a good thing, he supposed.

Upfront beat the hell out of mind games.

A knock sounded on the door. "Here are some clothes," she said.

He cracked the door and took the stack from her outstretched hand before shutting it again.

Stephanos dressed. Apparently, she had a wardrobe of men's clothes in his size on hand. The stuff didn't seem new, but it was clean and folded neatly. No bloodstains, but why the hell did she have clothes his size?

He opened the door, about to ask, but realized she hadn't given him shoes. He fished around in the trash, pulling out the ones he'd been wearing, then walked out of the bathroom.

She was standing right there, shaking her head. "No way, put those in the trash. You can take your pick from what I've got."

"Why?"

She rolled her eyes, which, given his day, just made him chuckle. He tried again. "This set up. Why?"

"You're not the first stray dog I've taken home." She waved for him to follow her into the next room down the hallway. "You'd be amazed what you can find at the local thrift shop."

"But it all fits." And it felt nice. Comfortable. Clean. There had been a time when he'd enjoyed those things.

"Yeah, I have a type." She smiled. "You can use this room."

The square bedroom contained a single bed, a wooden chair beside a squat three drawer dresser, a landline phone, and a little flatscreen TV on the wall. The closet stood open. True to her word, an assortment of shoes lined the floor, boots to sneakers, all black or brown. Clothes hung neatly on hangers and stacked on the shelf above them. She was prepared, but for what remained to be determined.

He took stock of her offerings and pulled out a pair of black boots.

"You're welcome to those, but you won't need them for a while. Vadim will have your face issued to all his hunting dogs by now. If you want to take your chances after you rest, that's up to you. For what it's worth, I don't recommend it."

"Why do you care?"

"I may have an interest in you. We'll see." She nodded him toward the couch in the small open living space that encompassed the kitchen and a two-person dining table.

"What kind of interest?" He was the one supposed to be using her, not the other way around.

"You tell me." She sat down at one end, giving him plenty of space at the other. Pulling her legs up underneath her and a square red pillow onto her lap, she turned to face him. "Start with where you came from and why you ate Vadim's bouncers."

"Out of town, and because they were in my way."

She seemed to be mulling those two things over. "In your way, how exactly?"

The way she asked, not accusing but intrigued, convinced him to test the waters of gaining her assistance.

"They were between me and my target."

"Target? Oh, you are going to be a tasty one indeed."

He noticed that she'd changed out of her club clothes while he'd been in the bathroom. She now wore black yoga pants and a baggy white cable-knit sweater that looked like it had been stretched too far in every direction. She looked comfortable.

And comfortable with him, an unknown in her place.

She didn't seem stupid, so maybe she was confident she could take him down again.

"I was sent to kill someone," he said, wondering if that would shock her into revealing anything.

"And it wasn't any of the bouncers, I'm guessing. If someone sent you, there must be a why." She leaned forward, her eyes taking on a captivating intensity.

He couldn't look away. He didn't want to. The words, *why someone sent you* bounced around in his head, softly bumping into thoughts, igniting memories he didn't want to think about, that he'd buried.

He owed Gabriel because... Memories spiraled out of control.

The never-ending darkness. The space just big enough for him with his arms wedged by his side. Unyielding iron walls. Everything stank like dirt. The heavy chains wound around him had been there so long that they had become part of his skin.

He couldn't move. He gasped for air even though he'd stopped breathing long before he'd been put underground.

His cries for help had long died out. They'd been muted by the metal mask the hunters had fashioned for him. It covered his face from the nose down, locked in the back. The heavy lock kept his head cocked at an angle that had become uncomfortable hours into the years he'd been there. The key was no doubt long gone.

His mind screamed. His bare feet kicked in the two inches of open space, legs only free from the knees down. Each movement brought further torment, only affirming he was still alive, for what little that was worth.

Leathery skin had molded to his bones, his lips drawn back from protruding teeth. Eyes gone dry. Bones broken, unable to heal without sustenance.

They could have just killed him, but they hadn't. They wanted him to suffer, to pay for what he'd done.

He had to get out. He couldn't be in the box again. He had to move. Had. To. Move. Now.

And then suddenly he was on the couch, his limbs free, surrounded by fresh air, and he wasn't alone.

A soft voice said, "You're safe here." Her eyes had lost their intensity, but her face was flushed.

The panic that had filled him only seconds before snapped and dissipated. He couldn't remember why he'd been so panicked. The burial had been long ago. He was safe now.

Safe. The word niggled at his brain. He shook his head, trying to clear the haze that seemed to be there even though the word told him there was nothing to worry about. "What did you ask?"

"Your name?"

"Stephanos Laskaris," he said, though he rarely gave anyone his full name. She'd got him out of the club, given him a place to hide out. He could trust her, couldn't he?

"Lavina Arandine," she said, holding out her hand.

He took it and squeezed rather than shook.

She smiled. "I think we're going to get along fabulously."

That seemed overly optimistic, being that they'd just met, but he felt a sense of calm here and he was in no hurry to let go of her hand. If she wanted to get along, maybe this was the time to see how useful she could be.

"What do you know about Vadim Lebedev?" he asked.

Lavina flexed her fingers as she studied him a moment. "Quite a lot. Care to be more specific?"

Subtlety had never been one of his gifts. He braced himself in case she was going to attack. "He's the one I'm here to kill."

3

LAVINA PULLED her hand out of his and clutched the pillow on her lap. The vampire in front of her hadn't just said he was going to kill Vadim, had he? She blinked once and then again, brain trying to cope with the words that had come out of his mouth and keeping her ass calmly on the couch. He wasn't giving off an enticing trauma smell, not like he'd been when he came out of the bathroom, freshly showered, no longer tainted by the overwhelming stench. There went her recourse to simply snack the murderous motivation out of him.

"Interesting. Why?" she said before he picked up on her unease.

"Does it matter?"

"Not really, I suppose. Just curious."

It definitely mattered. They might not be together anymore, but she'd lived beside Vadim for years. Despite ruining him in the ways that mattered to her, he was vital to the vampire community of Northchester. Not only the vampires themselves, but bridging the divide between them and the humans they fed on, especially in the last fifty years since his mental cleansing. No one was being exploited or hunted.

Stephanos pulled his long, damp mass of black hair over his shoulder, looking at it with a scowl. It had left a wet spot on his shirt. Hadn't he bothered to at least towel it somewhat dry?

His open annoyance started to focus on her instead. Quit staring and act more like a vampire, she chided herself. Humans were food. Higher and older vamps were to be obeyed or at least politely tolerated, everyone else could fuck off.

Vadim was old and socially elevated. Was Stephanos working for someone even higher and older? She wracked her brain for names that had come up in her years of living among the undead.

"Sorry, did I interrupt your killing spree then?"

"Yeah, you kind of did," he said with more amusement than malice.

"There was too much security between you and Vadim. You never would have made it close enough."

He grumbled something under his breath.

"You'll have to give it a week or two before he lets his guard down."

Stephanos nodded. "Not ideal, but necessary."

It sounded like he was rehearsing that line for someone else. She caught a whiff of anxiety, sharp and pungent.

He glanced around the apartment, eyes settling on the blind-covered brick window. "Anyone going to track us here?"

"No. Like I said, you're safe."

"I wasn't concerned about me."

For a second she smiled, but then realized it wasn't out of any form of fondness or consideration. He just didn't want anyone tracking her down after seeing them flee together because that would lead them to him.

"This is not my only residence," she admitted to put him at ease.

He nodded. "So, Vadim Lebedev, how do you know him?"

"All of us in Northchester do." That was the truth, even if she wasn't legitimately included in the 'us.'

His dark gaze drilled into her. "You said you knew quite a lot about him."

His attempt at intimidation put her on edge. She might have just fed off him, and he no longer stunk like a week-old dumpster in the summer sun, but he was still two degrees shy of wild. Unpredictable and angry tended to do crazy shit that she wasn't sure she could safely subdue. She had to give him a little something. Tit for tat and all that.

"It's been a while, but I used to go to Vadim's club a lot. It was the Moroccan last time I was there. The décor was better. And the music."

Stephanos chuffed. "That was what, fifty years ago?"

Lavina shrugged. So judgy for a man who'd worn rags only an hour before.

"Did you—" His phone buzzed in his pants pocket. Stephanos glared at it and let it ring twice more before taking it out to swipe the call away. He stood. "I should return that. He's just going to keep calling until I do."

As much as she wanted to fade into the couch and make him feel comfortable enough to take the call right there, they'd only just met. By the cagey way he was eyeing the bedroom she'd offered him, he was seconds away from making an escape to the private space.

"Go ahead." She waved him toward the bedroom as if she had zero cares. "The sun will be up soon. Might as well get comfortable."

Stephanos didn't hesitate. His long legs ate up the short path to the spare room. The door closed behind him.

If he'd been human, she would have crept over to listen outside the room, but he wasn't. One of the few things vampires had over her was their hearing. There wasn't enough trust between them to smooth over a possible eavesdropping discovery, and she wasn't willing to let him go after her first taste. Or finding out who wanted Vadim dead.

She might not want her tamed, more friendly vampire back long term, but there was nothing like an exposed assassination attempt with a target to go after to bring out the worst in a man. If she played this right, the revelation was sure to erase some of the excessive whitewashing she'd done on Vadim. That in turn would erase the rumors that she'd been the reason he'd changed. Win win.

Lavina eyed the closed bedroom door. No matter how much she strained her hearing, she couldn't pick up the conversation she was sure was going on inside. She'd have to bide her time and get a name by more honest means.

Honest. Lavina laughed to herself as she went into her own bedroom and double locked the door so she could pretend to vamp sleep the day away.

4

"WHERE THE hell are you?" Gabriel shouted through the phone.

"Somewhere safe."

"I'll send a driver for you."

"I'm fine here." Stephanos paced beside the bed, traversing the bedroom in five strides to turn and repeat.

"Where's here?"

"Doesn't matter."

The annoyed snarl Gabriel emitted said it did matter. "Vadim was supposed to be dead by now. You said—"

"You neglected to mention all the security. One might think you wanted me to fail."

"We're friends, idiot. Even so, why the hell would I fly you all the way here if I wanted to kill you? I could have easily done that while you were starving and weak back in Scotland."

Easily? Stephanos bristled. He'd been the soldier. Gabriel had always been the aristocrat. Through all their ages together, that dynamic had never changed. Even starved, Gabriel would have been hard-pressed to over-power him.

Not many could, yet Lavina had. However, she'd not attempted to use that against him. At least not yet. He found that intriguing.

"I never said you wanted to kill me." Bringing it up though, that made him wary where he'd never been before, not around Gabriel. "Was your intention to merely make Vadim paranoid?"

"No, I wanted him dead, as our agreement specified." Gabriel was back to shouting.

Stephanos held the phone away from his ear. The ass-hole knew the loud noise would get under his skin. He lowered the volume just shy of mute.

"Vadim's demise will have to wait, but I'll get the job done. I always do."

"I know. That's why you're here. You should have just barged in and made straight for him. He was all relaxed with his public, only his favorite security woman close by. It would have been easy. It would have been done!" Someone moaned in the background. "Lie still, dammit. I told you it wouldn't hurt if you stopped squirming. Do you want it to hurt?" Whatever he said after that was muffled.

Stephanos made out what sounded like a struggle. "I'll call back in a few days."

"Just give me a damned minute," Gabriel said. "Come home. I'll save some of this for you."

"I already ate. I'll be in touch." He hung up and turned off his phone, setting it on the table beside the bed.

By the stiffening of his muscles, he realized Lavina was right. The sun would be up soon.

As much as he didn't want to go to Gabriel's estate full

of vampire buzz addicted humans, being in the unfamiliar apartment made him uneasy. At least the bedroom door had heavy slide locks. He examined them and was relieved to discover that they were mounted into a solid door and a wall stud. The door wouldn't be opening without some hard work. If it did, there'd be nothing to stop anyone from taking his head.

He glanced at the phone. Gabriel kept dogs and a human staff, both of whom guarded him during the day. Lavina had nothing but locks, but if she was as old as he guessed, she knew what she was doing to have lived so long. No one would be looking for them here.

The mattress was firm but far more comfortable than the floor where he'd slept the years away. The room was not so small as to make him feel confined, even with the lack of a window. He stretched out on the bed atop the covers and got comfortable. For a long time, he listened to the sound of the traffic on the street below, muffled through the brick wall, but still clear enough with his enhanced hearing. Lavina made no sound he could pick up. She must have gone to her room to settle in as well.

He appreciated the privacy she provided. Gabriel had one saferoom they both shared at his estate. It was easier to secure, he claimed. This, his own space, tidy and austere as it was, was a welcome change. He didn't even miss the quiet solitude of his Scottish ruins. The muffled sounds relaxed him, made him feel part of the world without having to take part in it unless he chose to. For a few days, he wouldn't. Assuming he could get along well enough with Lavina. Or, more likely in his experience, assuming she didn't toss him out on his ass ten minutes before sunrise out of spite. Women, they were brutal like that.

5

LAVINA MARVELED at the quiet companionship she and Stephanos had fallen into over the past three days. He didn't speak much and stuck to himself in his room, but not in a way that made her concerned he was holed up in there. The times she'd wandered by his door on the way to the laundry room, pretending to need something there, it appeared he was playing a game on his phone. The look on his face when she'd offered to lend him a charger made her think she'd just gained a new best friend.

He'd emerged from his solitude an hour ago to sit at the opposite end of the couch where she'd been catching up on the news and rereading one aggravating email on her laptop. She curled her legs to make room for him. He sat in silence with his phone in his hands, lips pressed together firmly and a narrowed gaze with two fingers tapping the screen.

"What are you playing?" she asked after a while.

"Some stupid game," he muttered.

"The same one you've been at for three days?"

"Two. I tried a few before I found this one. Never understood the fascination with these things until now."

"Phones or games?"

"Both." He swore in something that definitely wasn't English and let out an angry huff.

"Lose?"

"Again." He tossed the phone onto the couch beside him. After a minute, he hauled his long legs up and planted his feet near her knees, taking up all the extra cushion space.

The couch hadn't seemed small until he was fully on it. He watched her like he was waiting to be told to get off of it. Lavina set her laptop on the coffee table and stretched her arms over her head before settling back against the pillow behind her. He seemed to relax a little.

"How often do you eat? Are you hungry?" she asked. Every vamp she'd encountered had a desired feeding schedule, even if they didn't always keep it.

"I've had more than I've eaten in years since coming to Northchester. I'm fine. You?"

She had everything she needed right here. Lavina smiled. "I'm good for a few days."

Stephanos nodded to the laptop. "Are we in the clear?"

"Not exactly." She chewed her lip, wondering how much to tell him. "A nosey friend has asked to see me. He's concerned for my wellbeing after I was seen leaving at the same time as a feral vampire."

"Feral," Stephanos repeated, entirely deadpan.

"That's how he appeared, yes."

She returned his unblinking stare. He didn't look so wild now, not in the same way, at least. He'd yet to utilize a brush, but he had changed his shirt today for the first time. That was progress. He spoke good English with a somewhat Gaelic accent, was fairly educated with technology if he could use a phone, and had made no move to attack her.

"Outside of current civilization, maybe," he conceded in a tone that didn't seem his own.

This being the first time he'd been conversational in three days, she didn't press to find out if those words had belonged to his employer.

"This concerned friend, would it be Vadim Lebedev?" he asked.

"No, though he sent out a blanket email to all the invited guests. He's very interested in knowing who you are."

Stephanos tensed from his shoulders to his toes. "Did you—"

"We wouldn't both be sitting here if I had."

He eyed the door as if waiting for someone to pound it down at any moment. Paranoid much?

"If I were going to hand you over, I'd have done it on day one. I don't plan to unless you give me a reason to need to be rid of you."

His gaze dropped to his knees, or maybe the phone between his legs where he'd tossed it. "What are you going to do about your friend?" he asked after several minutes of silence.

"I've agreed to meet him in a couple of hours. You can stay here. You *should* stay here." She hoped she was pressing that idea into his head enough without sounding like it was a demand.

"This friend—"

"His name is Fane. Do you know him?"

Stephanos shook his head. "I haven't been in town long.

Do you trust him?"

"I do." She trusted that Fane would pout and pitch a fit that she'd ditched him. He'd also want all the details on Stephanos because he was new and interesting, and Vadim kept Northchester so boring these days.

He opened his mouth, but she held up her hand. "I'm not selling you out to Fane either. He's a sweet man who has no interest in Vadim other than as a convenient means to trouble-free meals. Besides, he'd have no idea what to do with all of you."

His dark brows lowered. "All of me?"

Lavina reached down to pat his foot. "Indeed."

Stephanos stared at her hand on his foot. "What about you?"

"What about me?"

"Do you have ideas? For *all* of me?"

The way he asked would have been sexy if he hadn't sounded like he was trying out unfamiliar slang.

She chuckled, giving his ankle a squeeze to see what he'd do. "I might."

He just stared at her hand. At least he hadn't yanked his foot away or lunged at her for touching him.

"You'll be safe enough here. Do you want me to bring anything back for you? Takeout, if you will?"

Those big, dark eyes leapt to her face. "You would?"

"If you'd like me to. You're not a prisoner, Stephanos, but I'd feel better about your safety if Vadim had more time to forget about you. It does neither of us any favors if you're starving when you step out of here. The Northchester news team doesn't need another bloodless body to report on for several days straight. They're still going strong on that, in case you're wondering."

He had the grace to appear abashed, solving the mystery of who the killer was.

"Fuel for the big job?" she dared to ask.

He nodded.

"Right. So, would you like me to bring you a human snack when I get back?"

"Please?" he asked quietly.

"You got it." She tapped his legs to get him to move so she could get up. "I've got to get ready. Fane is used to me looking a bit more put together than sweats and a t-shirt."

She headed for her bedroom to change.

"You look fine," he called out just before she closed the door.

Lavina shut herself inside and grinned. She had ideas for him alright.

6

THE APARTMENT door closed behind Lavina, locks clicking one by one. Her footsteps, made more prominent by the heels she wore, tick ticked down the hall. She hadn't made him promise to stay inside, but it had been implied, heavily, and more than a handful of times.

His skin itched. He hadn't stayed locked inside for this long since leaving Scotland. Three days was a far cry from years, but it was the beginning of a trend he wasn't mentally prepared to repeat.

Lavina had been kind. So far, anyway. Most of them started out that way, but then the demands came. Tempers flew, and he'd be back at Gabriel's doorstep like always. Cursed, Gabriel called him.

One day he'd find someone like Isla had been. Melancholy settled over him at the thought of her. So far from the home they'd shared in Scotland, here in this new place, he couldn't allow himself to sink back into those times, the happy ones or the ones that had come after. He needed to stay alert. He had a job to do.

Lavina's footsteps ticked down the stairs.

Stephanos slid off the couch and slipped his bare feet into the boots Lavina had given him. He darted to the door, unlocked it and gently pulled it shut behind him as he hurried after her with whisper-soft steps. She wouldn't be pleased that he'd followed her, but he didn't plan on letting her know. Shadows were his territory, and Northchester had a lot of them. Even despite Vadim's efforts to work with the city management to make it a safe place for all.

Who was this Fane? Gabriel hadn't mentioned him.

She's going to sell you to Vadim, said the voice in his head.

She wouldn't do that.

Fane is setting her up to gain Vadim's favor. She'll be forced to turn you over.

The desiccated face of the woman he'd loved flashed in his mind. He shook his head, chasing the memory away.

He didn't want to see Lavina hurt on his account, like Isla had been. He'd follow, observe the meeting to make sure she was safe, and then slink back to the apartment ahead of her. She wouldn't know he'd left. He'd feel better for the fresh air. It would all work out.

Lavina walked confidently down the sidewalk, hands in the pockets of her long, open coat. Clouds sped across the moon, congregating until they blotted out the stars. A mist descended upon the city, collecting on his eyelashes and dampening his new, clean clothes. He squeezed the stupid phone in his pocket, wanting to crush it, but not daring. He should have used it to check the weather. So much informa-tion at his fingertips, if only he remembered to use it.

As if summoned by his touch, his phone rang. Cursing, Stephanos pulled it from his pocket to silence the damned thing, only to see that it was Gabriel. Who else would it be? No one else had the number. Keeping Lavina in sight, he answered.

Gabriel dispensed with any form of greeting. "Are you ready to try again? I've got an invite to a gallery tonight. Vadim will be there. One of his human pets has a show. Smaller crowd. Plenty of food, if you're feeling peckish by now."

"I've already fed." He didn't need Gabriel to provide for him like he was some newly fledged vampire.

"Good. Can you get to Sothams Gallery on Fifth in half an hour?"

"Sothams?"

"Yes. You remember how to use the map app on your phone?"

"I do, but—"

"Good. Half an hour then."

"I can't tonight." Stephanos wormed his way through a knot of oncoming inebriated pedestrians, straining to spot Lavina up ahead. She'd crossed to the other side of the street while he was distracted with Gabriel.

"Dammit, Stephanos, I didn't haul your ass over here for a vacation. Do what you're good at. Kill him and you can go back to dreaming of the good old days or whatever it is you do in that dank basement."

He waited for a gap in traffic and then hurtled himself across the treacherous street. Cars, as useful as they'd proven to be, were disconcerting in their bulk and speed. He didn't so much mind being inside one, but outside them, in close proximity, he could do without. One nearly crushed his toes before he reached the safety of the side-walk. The driver yelled something about using crosswalks out his window. Whatever the hell those were.

"I said I'd take care of him. Just not tonight."

"I'm already on the way to the gallery, dammit. I'll be seen. It will be easy. It's perfect. Just show up, rip his head off, and Northchester will be a better place. I promise, you'll be rewarded."

He'd been on the receiving end of Gabriel's promises since he vowed to make Stephanos live forever. His rewards always came through, but standing on a sidewalk in North-chester in borrowed clothes, hiding from an old, powerful vampire, Stephanos wasn't sure that he was better off for them.

Lavina's golden hair lit up under a streetlight. Seeing she'd stopped in front of a bar, he dropped out of the flow of people and found an unoccupied awning. He filled the shadow beneath it.

"Another time, Gabriel." He ended the call, switched the phone to silent, and dropped it back into his pocket.

A burst of loud rock music escaped the bar as Lavina went in. Colored flashing lights filled the front window. The silhouette of a woman with a guitar floated inside. He could just make out a drummer's arms flailing and a singer jump-ing up and down. What passed for music these days was boggling.

Stephanos lost sight of Lavina. He wiped a raindrop from the end of his nose. Knowing she was inside was one thing, but without seeing or hearing her conversation with Fane, he was no better off. He could have stayed warm and dry in the apartment.

She knows you followed her. She has people inside

waiting to take you down.

She might know. He hadn't yet ascertained how old she was or what talents she might have. He pressed his back against the damp window to huddle deeper in the shadows. The chill didn't bother him, but the sudden wetness made him shiver.

Would she be mad he'd followed her? He wouldn't give her the chance to know. He'd head back to the apartment and dry off before she arrived. She'd said she'd bring him someone to feed from. If she followed through, he'd know he could trust her. Stephanos took one step out from under the awning.

Lavina spilled out of the club with a slender man beside her. If this was her friend Fane, he didn't look happy. He said something to Lavina that made her visibly upset. They stepped away from the club, heading toward where Stephanos stood. If he stayed, they might spot him. If he left, he wouldn't know what they were talking about that made her look so hurt.

Fane told her she'd have to turn you in, or he'd do it for her.

She didn't want to. She'd said as much, anyway.

But what if she is forced to?

Then he'd have to kill Fane. He was the same height as Lavina but frail looking. Delicate. Like he'd rather run than mess up his expensive-looking outfit. He probably used a napkin when he fed from humans.

Fane was Lavina's friend. That's what she'd called him. She wouldn't take kindly to having him killed, and that would put him back on Gabriel's doorstep. If he wanted to piss Lavina off, he might as well catch a cab to Sothams Gallery and take a stab at Vadim. If he failed, the elder vampire would put him out of his centuries of misery.

The last three days hadn't been miserable though. He shook off his doubts. No killing. He'd just listen.

As the pair approached, he held his breath, standing as still as he did when waiting to grab his next victim. His tongue ran over his fangs, his thoughts making him hungry.

The rain persisted, but they didn't seem to notice, both wrapped up in tense conversation as they walked. Lavina held her arms crossed over her chest. Her hair glistened with raindrops. The other vampire reached out to her, but she pulled away.

Fane looked angrier the longer they talked and the closer they came. "Vina, I know you. You're hiding him. Admit it."

"You *knew* me. That was two and a half centuries ago."

"That rabid mongrel is dangerous," Fane snarled, his fangs exposed and eyes glittering in the streetlights.

Lavina planted her heels on the sidewalk and spun to face him, nostrils flaring. "So am I. Goodnight, Fane." She strode away with a peeved expression that made Stephanos regret sneaking out and chancing becoming the second victim of her ire.

"Lavina!" Fane called after her.

She was already crossing the street and paid him no heed.

In unfamiliar surroundings and considering the speedy pace she'd set, Stephanos' only hope of beating her back to the apartment was if she took the time to make good on her offer to pick up dinner.

Fane stood, getting wetter by the minute, staring at Lavina's distant form for far too long. There was no way Stephanos was sneaking past the other vampire without being noticed if he stepped out now. He'd just have to wait. Seconds ticked by with the sound of Lavina's heels in his head.

Fane pulled a phone from his pants pocket and made a call. "Hello. Yes, it's Fane. She says she isn't harboring him."

You should have killed him. You still can.

In the shadows, his fingers flexed. He didn't have any weapons on him, but he'd ended vampires without them before. Gabriel liked to watch as he tore them to bits with his teeth and hands, but he wasn't here to drive Stephanos into action.

Fane rocked from one foot to the other, like he was mimicking a toed dance step on the sidewalk. "No, and I don't appreciate being put in this position. Yes, I pressed her. Thanks to you, she won't be talking to me for a long while. You know how she holds a grudge for decades."

He listened to the phone, nodding now and then but saying nothing until he uttered a single, "Yes, fine." Fane hung up, and within a few minutes, had hailed a cab and left.

Stephanos fled, sticking to the shadows when possible, and having to walk at a normal pace amongst the humans when it wasn't. He managed to find his way back to the apartment with only one wrong turn. Dashing up the stairs, he was so distracted by the conversation he'd overheard that he didn't even think to be cautious when he slipped inside. He sighed with relief to find the room was just as he'd left it: empty, and one lamp on by the couch. He couldn't detect any other sounds inside beyond the perpetually running refrigerator and the grating motorized hum of the clock on the wall.

Needing to calm himself before Lavina returned, he headed for the couch to sit down. Just before his ass made contact with the pristine ivory colored fabric, he remembered he was soaking wet. In a panic, he checked the floor. Sure enough, he'd tracked wet footprints all the way to where he stood.

Stephanos shed his boots, dashed to his bedroom to hide them in the closet, and then grabbed a used towel from the basket in the laundry room. After using it to wipe up the mess he'd made on the floor, he contemplated what to do about himself. Back in the laundry room, he tossed the wet towel and other contents of the basket into the washing machine. Then he stripped and threw his wet clothes in too. Getting blamed for screwing up laundry seemed more innocuous than traipsing around town against her wishes. He plucked a detergent tab from the container atop the machine and tossed it in with the clothes. Hoping the last setting she'd used was the right one now, he pushed the start button and high-tailed his naked ass to the bathroom to jump in the shower. Wet was wet, but at least he'd be clean. Twice in one week even, a vast improvement over his recent record of months over years.

He heard the door open and two female voices talking. That was when he realized he hadn't brought any dry clothes in with him. Hoping he could pull off innocent, he dried off, wrapped the damp towel around his waist, and stepped out to face Lavina.

7

"YOU'LL LIKE him," Lavina assured Clarice, or Clarissa? Cindy? Something cute with a C.

The young woman nodded, looking nervously around the apartment. "This is nice," she said hesitantly.

"Thanks."

The woman smiled. "An hour for one fifty it is then. What do you want? To watch, or will it be all three of us?"

"I'll watch." Lavina headed for the guest room to get Stephanos.

Maybe Cindy rambled on about what she allowed and didn't. None of it mattered as long as she had blood in her veins.

The bathroom door opened, nearly hitting Lavina as she walked by to retrieve her tasty vampire snack from his room. She twisted aside, steadying herself on the wall, and got an up-close view of Stephanos emerging from the bathroom in nothing but a towel. Steam rolled out of the room like ethereal fingers reaching for him. She didn't blame the fingers one bit.

Clean as his hair might be, it was still a tangled mess. The rest of him, though, was tidy and delectable. Muscled in all the right places without being overdone. He'd been in fabulous shape when he'd been turned. One long white scar stood out amongst the dusting of dark hair on the multi-planed expanse of olive skin that was his chest. Startled, she dropped her gaze. Long legs with defined calves offered no chaste respite.

"Sorry, I didn't expect you back so soon," he said smoothly, as if she hadn't just staggered into the wall.

"I brought a friend for you." She nodded to the woman she'd picked up.

He smiled. "Thank you for that. Perhaps I should get dressed first."

His meal laughed. "Why bother? You've got fifty-five minutes and counting."

Stephanos glanced at the young woman, running his tongue over his fangs and then smiling. "Ah, one of those. Don't worry about the time," he said softly, suggestively.

The girl nodded in a daze.

Even though she'd seen a vampire trance a human hundreds of times, she still admired how quick and effective they were. Her thought suggestions worked similarly but vampires didn't blur memories like she did.

Stephanos walked towards the woman, perusing his meal.

"She's clean?"

"Clean enough with the things that matter. You may get a bonus high if you're susceptible to that. Some aren't." Lavina shrugged.

He pulled his assessing gaze from his meal to her. "Are

you?"

"No, but I ate on the way over. She's all yours." She hadn't. Her meal was staring her down as she spoke. Was he one of those private feeders? That would screw with her plan to gauge how safe he was to keep around longer term. It had worked for her many times before. She kept a smile on her face. "Would you rather take her to your room?"

"I don't like my food where I sleep."

"Me either." Except she totally did. Especially when they looked like he did. She found herself clearing her throat and stumbling over her words. "Would you...rather I—"

"You said you wanted to watch?"

He'd overheard that? If she'd been quieter, would she have caught him marching back to his room with no towel at all? She swallowed.

"If you don't mind? It's a thing I like to—"

Stephanos shrugged. "You don't have to explain yourself. I don't mind."

Lavina wanted to hug him for his easy acquiescence in light of the conversation she'd just had with Fane. The normally polite and elegant gentleman had shown his ugly side in the club. His demeanor hadn't improved after she'd stormed out with him on her heels. How dare he lure her there with guilt over ditching him at Vadim's party only to blindside her with an interrogation about the rabid mongrel that had attacked The Jackyl. Fane had never struck her as one of Vadim's lackeys, but she'd been out of society and things had changed. Changed without her.

She stood aside, letting Stephanos take control of the situation. The woman, blissfully under his thrall, stood patiently waiting, her countdown having been put on pause.

Stephanos circled his meal, "What's her name?"

Lavina settled onto the chair across from the couch. "Maybe Cindy? It starts with a C. I don't remember. Does it matter?"

"Probably not, but I find it makes them more relaxed."

As wild as he'd appeared when they'd first met, she wouldn't have thought he'd have given two shits about the condition of his food. "You like them relaxed?"

"Tastes better, don't you think?"

Not one bit, but she shrugged. "Vadim likes them drunk. Fane likes the sweet adrenaline of fear. Max liked them right after sex. I guess everyone has their own flavor preference."

He pushed the woman's hair back from her neck and looked over her shoulder at Lavina. "Max?"

"Long ago. Out of the picture. Last I heard he was haunting Vienna."

He addressed the dazed woman softly. "What's your name?"

"Charlene."

Ah, yeah, that was it.

"Charlene, why don't you have a seat with me?" Stephanos sat on the couch and held his arms out to her.

"I'd like that." She settled onto his lap, wrapping her arms around his shoulders.

Lavina wasn't jealous. She wasn't. She repeated that to herself a few more times. It didn't help.

She focused on the velvety fabric of the chair against the palms of her hands. On the calming scent of cinnamon oil that she'd put on the heat vent. On the warm air gently blowing through the apartment.

By the time she got her emotions under control and attempted a clinical distance, Stephanos had already sunk his fangs into Charlene's neck. She emitted blissful moans as her head lolled back on his arm.

Lavina wasn't wishing she was the one moaning. She didn't want to wonder how it felt to be pressed up against all that bare flesh. Was he warm now, having fed, or would he still be cold? Some gained full human heat, others barely got lukewarm. Someone in the room was definitely warming up, and it wasn't either of the people on the couch.

Then his eyes met hers. Nope, it was way too hot in the living room.

Lavina imagined shooting to her feet and shutting herself in her room until she'd cooled down or taken care of matters by her own hand. But would her sudden departure startle him, causing him to bite too deep and possibly kill Charlene? Could she trust him to feed responsibly on his own? He had drained someone dry only days ago, after all. Vadim wouldn't take kindly to another bloodless body showing up on his watch.

She settled in for the show, cataloging the way his toes curled when he drank, the quiet slurp of him feeding, and the way his long fingers were stroking Charlene's hair while he held her in place. Purely for reference of his feeding habits and evidence of him not being entirely feral. Wild, sure, but he had manners. She could keep him for a while...and she was building a defense. A defense of the man who was supposed to kill Vadim. Whom she didn't want him to kill.

Who the hell was she going to defend him to? Fane? He clearly had someone pressuring him to find Stephanos or he never would have pressed her as hard as he had. He'd never been aggressive before. Not with her, anyway.

She was already on the outskirts of vampire society. Getting caught harboring Stephanos wasn't going to help her slip back in with her preferred food source. So...she had to make sure she wasn't caught with anyone resembling that animal.

Yes, that's why she was sitting here observing him. To see what she had to work with to rehabilitate him, clean him up, and maybe give him a chance to change his mind about the job he'd been given. Maybe find a respectable place for himself in Northchester, a place she could maybe visit from time to time when she got hungry for one thing or another. Hungry like she was right now, in fact.

Stephanos pulled away from Charlene, licking up the last drips that escaped his bite and cleaning the wound. The woman sighed blissfully.

"You did well. You've been paid. You can go now," he told Charlene.

She nodded and disentangled herself from the vampire. Charlene took one sleepy look at Lavina before glancing back to Stephanos, who was now staring at Lavina like she was dessert. "I'll just..." Charlene wavered her way to the door and left.

"Did I pass your test?"

"Surprisingly civilized," she said as if she'd been making clinical observations the entire time. No sir, not at all worked up over any of that.

"I can be. Is that what you prefer?"

Not at all, but... "Civility will work in your favor for the time being. Vadim is looking for a rabid animal. If you stay fed, can you keep this up?"

"I didn't try to attack Vadim because I was hungry." He shifted around on the couch.

That towel was an accident waiting to happen. Don't look at it. Do not look at anything below his shoulders. His very broad, firm, perfect shoulders.

"I meant the appearance of not being who they're looking for. For now, anyway. Until such time as either I convince you not to complete your job, or you do."

He leaned back into the cushions, stretching his long arms along the length of the couch. Was he intentionally taunting her? That towel... Nope, don't look.

"It will help you not to get dragged down with me if I keep this appearance?" he asked.

She kept her dry swallow to herself. At least she hoped she did. "It would."

"Then I will try."

"Thank you," she said, meaning it wholeheartedly. "Perhaps you would like to get dressed?"

"Would that also help you?"

"It might," she said, sounding much like Charlene on her way out. Lavina cleared her throat. "It will, yes."

Stephanos chuckled. "I did just feed. I have plenty of blood flow if I could help you in other ways."

She couldn't help it. Her gaze dropped to the bulge trapped in the tenuous cotton shroud.

It had been a very long time since she entertained anyone else in her bedroom and one of the great things about sticking to vampire lovers was no fear of pregnancy. She'd never wanted that. One of her kind was plenty. Besides, Intimacy was another way to gauge what kind of man he was, wasn't it? Observing what he was like during and after, that was research.

He shifted forward and got to his feet. The towel started to slip but he caught the edge of it, questioning her with a raised brow.

Feeding would satisfy one hunger for her, but ruin the

mood for him on the other. She could eat after. Or tomorrow. Or next week. Hell, she'd gone years between full feedings, but not near as many years as what he was offering her now.

She stood and waved him toward her bedroom. Stephanos followed. The towel stayed behind.

8

WHILE HE'D had grand illusions of his stamina, it had been a very long time since he'd done anything useful with his penis. His day-to-day existence no longer required it, a useless appendage. Tonight, though, after being caught in Lavina's lust-filled gaze, he'd hoped to relive some of the glory of his human years. However, his brain and the borrowed blood flow weren't seeing eye to eye at the moment, giving him all of two embarrassing minutes before serving him a lackluster climax. Lavina had barely gotten warmed up, for fuck's sake.

"Give me a minute. I think I forgot how this is supposed to work."

Lavina chuckled. "Been a while?"

Was there a good answer to that? "Yeah."

Early after his transition, the human women he'd enthralled to please him hadn't offered the same thrill he'd enjoyed in his human life. Isla was different, but after her passing, he'd given up on sex. Given up on most everything.

No one had looked at him like Lavina did in a very long time. Not that he'd put much effort into being around humans except to eat and other vampires, well, other than Gabriel, he'd avoided their judgmental asses too. But this was fun. Maybe he'd just been introduced to the wrong vampires before.

Lavina relaxed into the pillow behind her and pulled the heavy layer of blankets over her naked body like she was actually cold. That struck him as odd. Temperatures hadn't bothered him since he'd changed.

"I like the weight," she answered the question that must have been apparent on his face.

"I'll give you weight, but in a few minutes."

"Promises." Lavina winked. "Take your time. We have a couple of hours before the sun rises."

"I could..." He wriggled his fingers and inclined his head to the heavy covers.

She shrugged. "I can do that on my own. It was more the thrill of having a partner for once."

For once? She'd listed off Fane, Max, Vadim, and he had little doubt there had been plenty of others by her non-chalance of dropping those three.

He settled onto his side next to her, marveling at the mattress beneath him that nearly provided the illusion of floating. He'd enjoyed the bed in the room she'd offered him, but this was a hundred times better.

"So, you and Vadim? Is that why you don't want me to kill him?"

"That was a long time ago, and no, not the reason."

"You have feelings for him."

"Not in the way you're implying."

"Good." If she didn't have feelings for Vadim, he might

be able to find an angle to get her to help kill Northchester's vampire leader. Enjoying a little more time with Lavina before he headed back to Scotland wouldn't be terrible either.

Back in his earlier life, he would have considered her well beyond her maidenly years. The light in her room was easy on his eyes, but caught on the sprinkle of silver threads in her blonde hair. She bore no marks of pregnancy, her stomach smooth but soft like the rest of her, full of delicious curves he wanted to taste. However old she might be now, she'd lived a pampered life before her change. No defined muscles, calluses, or scars. Yet, she'd proven strength hid under her soft exterior.

"Good?" Lavina eyed him suspiciously.

Enough with talking. His body was ready to try not to disappoint her a second time. She wouldn't be thinking about another vampire for a long while if he had anything to say about it.

Stephanos kissed her, swallowing anything else she may have wanted to say on the matter. Her momentary mumble of protest melted away, and soon after, the blankets were gone and her arms and legs were wrapped around him. And then she was moaning against his neck, meeting his every thrust with vigor.

One thing she'd said earlier stuck in his head, nagging him. *Max liked them right after sex.* He vaguely remembered feeding off the human women before lying with them to fuel his ability to perform at all. The more he thought about it, the more the need to bite grew. To feed. The urge kept distracting him, making him lose focus. Fuck, if he failed again, she wasn't going to give him another chance.

Would she taste sour like every other vampire he'd

ripped into? He'd bitten plenty, but never for pleasure. He'd never slept with one either. Humans had said they liked being bitten during sex, so maybe vampires did too. And hell, maybe a little sourness would offer a distraction so he could last longer. The more he thought about it, he wasn't opposed to her biting him back if she wanted to. He nipped at her neck to test her reaction. She pressed against him, moaning, breathing hard and fast.

His entire body was onboard with this line of attack, urging him to toss caution to the wind and just do it. Recklessness had served him well for hundreds of years. He wasn't about to argue now.

Stephanos bit into her vein, swirling his tongue through the sweet warmth in his mouth. Lavina was the most divine thing he'd ever tasted, not a single sour note. He groaned, taking a long draw of her blood. The taste ignited something deep inside him, sending jolts of energy coursing through his body.

Distantly, he realized she'd gone still beneath him. Like hell was he stopping now. He couldn't if he wanted to. His body was off and running while his mind was drunk on Lavina.

She wasn't resisting, not trying to push him away, but not vacant like a human when he fed. More like she was startled, waiting. There were no protests or angry rants flowing from her gasping lips, and after a moment, she relaxed against him. Stephanos licked her neck, cleaning the wound he'd made and cutting himself off. For all he knew, like his memories of alcohol, he might pass out from too much of this too.

Were all vampires so intoxicating during sex? Did it change the flavor of the blood so much? What had he been missing all these centuries? Why hadn't anyone told him about this?

The electric in his veins put him in the backseat as he spun Lavina round. He worked himself in deep and slow until she was again moving with him, urging him to go faster, gaining him a pleasure-filled shout for his efforts. He drove into her relentlessly until she'd gone all liquid and pliant two climaxes later. Only then did he allow the drunken haze to envelop him completely.

When Stephanos came back to himself, his body was still buzzing with blissful shocks but the frenzy had dissipated. He opened an eye to find Lavina resting against him, her head on his shoulder and her pile of blankets atop them both.

He knew he'd stayed too long by the heaviness in his limbs. Though, given his languid mood, he had no urge to leave even if his legs had been cooperative.

She picked up her head to look at him in the muted light cast by the stained-glass lamp beside her bed. "Do you want me to lock the bedroom door?"

"Bit late for that." He attempted to lift his arm to show her how stiff the motion already was but barely got an inch off the mattress.

Besides, if she was secure here, he would be too, whether the bedroom door was locked or not.

The sudden arrival of disappointment on her face was clear even in the shadows. Was she pulling away from him? Would she have felt safer with him locked out of her room even knowing neither of them could move during the day?

"Right," she mumbled. "We lost track of time."

Did she really want him gone? "I could try to leave."

"No, it's fine. The apartment is locked."

Her voice held a brittle cheerfulness that implied it wasn't fine at all. From what he'd witnessed, she'd been having just as much of a good time as he had.

Maybe his ability to gauge a partner's satisfaction was as rusty as his social graces. Not that he'd ever had many of those. Apologizing was his only recourse in this state.

"Are you angry? I should have asked before I tasted you."

"No, it's just... Why did you?"

How was he supposed to explain without sounding like the rabid mongrel Fane had called him? "Sorry, I shouldn't have."

Her voice was small, unsure, very not Lavina. "Why? Did I taste human?"

He shook his head, savoring the memory of the sweetness and already hungering for more. "Not at all. You're like nothing I've tasted before."

"Have you tasted other vampires?"

"Never. Why?"

"Just curious," she said, sounding more like herself.

"Have you?"

She stroked his chest slowly with one finger. He was impressed that she could do so considering how heavy his own muscles were.

"No, I haven't tasted a vampire's blood. You liked it?"

He would have kissed her if he could have moved. Stupid sun, making him have to talk instead. "Very much."

"If a little sip lit that fire, I'm definitely not opposed to you taking another. If you can keep this a secret between us."

"I don't exactly have anyone to go bragging to."

"Good, because I don't want to be the next bloodless

corpse headline when a bunch of horny vampires hunt me down for a pint."

"I have no intention of sharing your blood or how you taste with anyone else, vampire or not."

She kissed his shoulder and settled back against it, smiling.

Her smile made him quite pleased with himself. Maybe after all this time, he was getting better at not getting thrown out by women. Except...

"Dammit, I put a load of laundry in the washing machine. That's supposed to go in the dryer right away, isn't it?"

Lavina burst out laughing, jiggling the mattress. "You put the wash in while I was out? You. Did laundry?"

"I was trying to be helpful, but I didn't know what I was doing exactly. We were still mostly washing clothes by hand when I last made an effort to pretend to be human. Where I was staying before I..." He caught himself. She was too easy to talk to, or his defenses were down while his brain was still scrambled. "There was a staff that does that kind of work. I fit in more with them so I followed them around a little to see what all this new shit was about."

"That's almost adorable. Not feral at all." She nuzzled her cheek against him, smiling.

She seemed happier when he was talking. He had a while before daylight killed that too. Conversation wasn't exactly his strength but they were stuck together for the day now. At least she couldn't throw him out in the sunlight if he said the wrong thing.

Existence was easier back when he could just fall dead asleep after sex and no one cared. Now he had to wait for the sun to turn him off. Vampirism had its trade-offs. Several of them, actually.

Reckless had served him well with her so far so he asked, "How was the meeting with your friend?"

"Not great." Lavina sighed. "We were friends once. More than that for a little while. I thought, foolishly, it seems, that we were still on those terms. False pretenses led to accusations, and now I don't care if it's another fifty years until we speak again."

He might be playing a game of roulette but this could be the angle he needed to sway her against Vadim. "What kind of accusations?"

"I told him that Vadim's security footage shows me getting a dangerous, uninvited vampire out of The Jackyl. That I got him in a cab and away from Vadim's guests, and then I shipped him out of Northchester and told him not to come back. I was doing the asshole a favor. How dare Vadim accuse me of working with or harboring such a hazard to the balance he's worked so hard to attain for all of us?"

Stephanos knew how that conversation had ended, but for pretenses, he had to feign innocence. "And your friend didn't accept your answer?"

"No. He kept drilling me, and when I shut him down, he put his hands on me. I wanted to break them. I could have broken them."

Though she was still, he imagined he could feel her anger vibrating the silken sheets surrounding them. He was well acquainted with restrained violence. Vadim wasn't the only one with rules for the vampires under him.

"But you didn't."

"No, I left before I did something I'd regret, but he wouldn't leave me alone. He followed me out, still interrogating until I finally shut him up and stormed off.

"But you *are* harboring me."

"I am."

"And you didn't escort me out of Northchester or tell me not to come back."

"No, I did not," she said playfully.

"So, you're angry that your friend didn't believe your lies?"

"Yes! He should trust me, even when I'm lying." Lavina chuckled softly. "We've known each other long enough that he should trust that I'm managing the situation, whether he's getting the answers he was sent for or not."

"I suppose that makes sense."

She rubbed her cheek on his shoulder, the rest of her body still and heavy against him. "Go to sleep. You're keeping me awake."

"Sorry," he said, not regretting a thing.

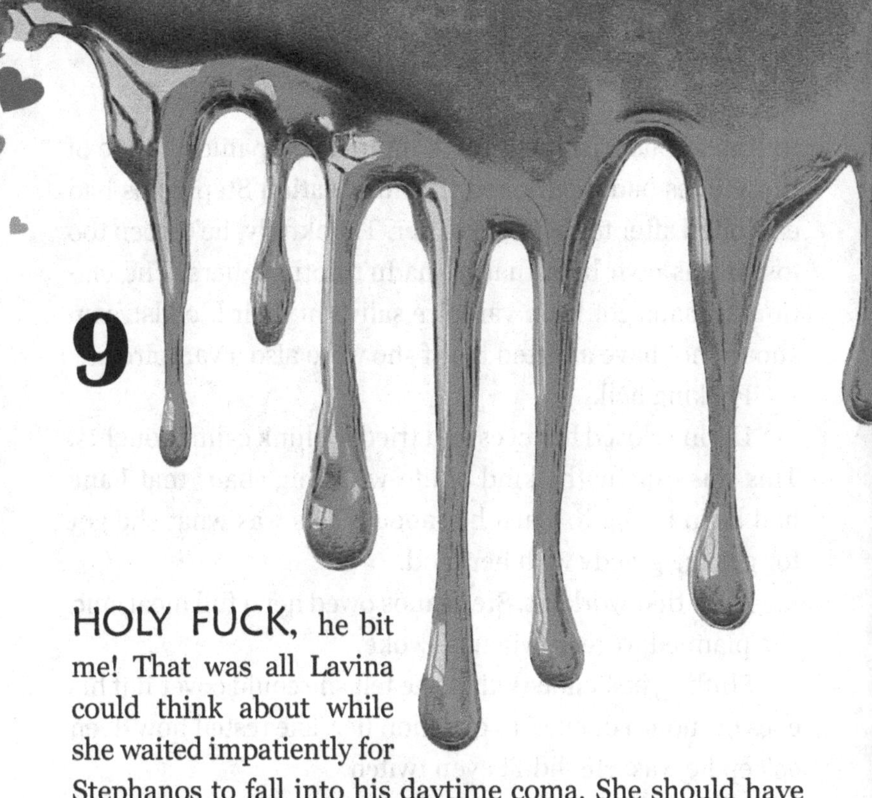

9

HOLY FUCK, he bit me! That was all Lavina could think about while she waited impatiently for Stephanos to fall into his daytime coma. She should have been exhausted enough to sleep the day away like usual, in keeping with pretenses. However, all she wanted to do was rub her hand over her neck, but she couldn't do that until he was unconscious because she wasn't supposed to be able to move either.

She'd always wondered what the humans felt while vampires were gleefully slurping them like blood straws. Now she knew. The thrall probably helped relax them even further, but she had to admit, the kids at The Jackyl were on to something. That was a high that made it worthwhile to stay off street drugs and play by Vadim's rules. Unfortunately, this drug was just as dangerous for her. If Stephanos told anyone, there would be disastrous consequences.

She'd heard of vampires exchanging blood, feeding off one another either to drain the other out of dominance or to transfer nourishment to an injured companion. None of those tales had mentioned the intoxication Stephanos had exhibited after taking a sip of her. Thankfully, he'd been too lost in his own high that he hadn't noticed hers. The elation humans got from vampire saliva in their bloodstream should not have affected her if she were also a vampire.

Fucking hell.

Lavina closed her eyes and tried to think calm thoughts. This was exactly the kind of life-wrecking chaos that Fane had been trying to warn her about. This was what she got for getting greedy with her food.

After that workout, Stephanos owed her a full meal, and she planned to get it when he woke.

Shifting just enough that she felt she could cover it if his eyes or mouth opened to question her, she tested how deep asleep he was. He didn't even twitch.

After making sure to note her position, she carefully slid out of the bed and ran to the bathroom. The woman in the mirror was flushed, eyes an extra shade of bright, lips still thick from his kisses. Despite being a couple ounces short of blood, she appeared very much alive and well. Almost a little younger even. Dare she say, happy?

Who knew that the cure to her fifty-year depression slump was a few hours between the sheets with an intoxicated vampire? A vampire with very bad hair, but who did laundry for heaven's sake? It didn't matter if he'd turned everything in that load bright pink. If he started vacuuming and dusting, she was going to have to marry him. Lavina giggled with the giddy woman in the mirror.

Then she sobered. Pulling her disheveled hair aside, she examined her throat. The two fang marks were already nothing more than pinpricks. In a couple of hours, they'd be gone entirely. She might not be a vampire in the same sense as Stephanos, but she healed like one.

Lavina washed her face and brushed her teeth. Those she could get away with. A shower, as wonderful as it sounded, would have to wait until morning. Giving herself a fangy smile in the mirror, she returned to the bed and repositioned herself against the big, not-so-scary, vampire and slept.

Lavina's dreams were filled with vampires finding out she was a drug to them, just as they were to her. Upon the fifth time of dying at their hands and fangs, she woke with a sob.

Stephanos stroked her cheek. "The sun has barely set. Go back to sleep."

"I can't."

No, thank you. She'd died enough times for one day. And did he have a hungry gleam in his eyes? What was to stop him from draining her while she slept? She was going to have to make sure he ended up in his own bed if he was still staying with her after what she was about to do.

"What was troubling your sleep? I could take care of it for you, if it was Fane or Vadim, or anyone else."

Was he being playful or serious? She was too out of sorts to tell. In a few minutes, she wouldn't be the only one.

"It was a lot of people." She slid closer to him, resting her head on his chest. "Talk to me so I can forget my dreams."

"About what?" His fingers stroked idly along her temple and down through her hair.

The soft hum of her abilities came alive, warming her from the inside out. She lifted her head just enough to look him in the eyes.

"Who put you in the ground?" She asked slowly, ensnaring him in her trance, dragging the memory to the forefront of his mind. Locked together in his head, she licked her lips and basked in his torment.

Hunger ate Stephanos, clawing at his insides, shadowing his every thought. Everyone in Argos knew his face after Gabriel had sent him to clean out the lingering Venetians, some of whom had been his friends. The Boros heir had sided with the Ottomans who had taken the city. He had new friends now.

Stephanos had died in the war that brought this governmental change. New rulers with new rules. Gabriel had given him a new life, given him food to hunt.

Stephanos tore through men's necks, their blood not coming fast enough to sate him. He feasted and gorged, but it was never enough. And now the Venetians were purged, and Gabriel wanted Argos quiet, wanted to gain favor with the new Ottoman government.

The half-dead slaves Gabriel gave him were tasteless. Animals he caught were even worse, no matter how large or wild.

Too many people had seen his handiwork with the Venetians. They knew him on sight and that he was no longer just a soldier, that he was a monster. They ran when he was near, barred their doors, shuttered their windows, and muttered prayers for their souls.

But he was so hungry.

Roaming the streets in his misery, he was delighted to see a woman slip out of a door and dart into the moonlit night. Just one more struggling human, and then he would behave.

They tasted so much better this way, wild and thrashing. He grabbed her. His fangs cut her scream short. She kicked and writhed for only a moment before going limp and sedate against him. Too fast, but still so good.

Lost in his meal, he never heard the men come up behind him until the iron mask slipped over his face. The lock clicked shut behind him just as he registered what was going on. He grabbed one of his attackers, flinging him aside to land with his neck broken. Another went flying into the wall of the house behind him. Chains dropped over his shoulders, pinning his arms. Another lock clicked. Stephanos screamed his rage into the mask over his nose and mouth. How could he feed? He was going to starve. Panic lit his every nerve on fire.

He spun, searching for Gabriel, for anyone who might help him, but he was alone with soldiers, some of whom had served under him only months before. They showed him no mercy, driving him into the dirt to kick and slice him. They broke his legs so he couldn't run and covered him with bruises and cuts. None of his wounds were enough to kill him.

The angry mob of men carted him out of the city. The clomping of a horse's hooves, creak of the cart, and a host of plodding footsteps went on. When they finally stopped, the moon was low in the sky. They rolled him out of the cart, and then the surrounding crowd divided, half grabbing shovels, the other standing guard around him.

This was his chance. Stephanos struggled against the chains, working himself bloody, terrified they were going to stand back and watch him burn as the sun came up. No matter how hard he tried, he couldn't get free.

He'd lost so much blood. Growing weaker and with no one to save him, he was left to the mercy of the men in the darkness. Darkness that was supposed to be his!

They kicked him, rolling him into a hole. Unable to catch himself, he landed face down in a metal box. Someone jumped down onto his back, cramming his legs into the tight confines. The weight was gone, but then a lid slammed down with a heavy, reverberating ring that overwhelmed his sensitive hearing. Try as he might to roll over, to thrust his back or shoulder against the lid, it didn't budge.

Dirt rained down on the lid. Within minutes, the world above became muted, distant.

Alone in the darkness that was once again his own, he was powerless, buried as if his childhood playmate had never given him new life. The panic and pain told him he was alive, but that meant little when he was weak and trapped, unable to move more than a few inches in any direction.

The mask muffled his screams.

Lavina swallowed all of his terror, leaving his memory of being buried alive blurred and distant. Like it should have been, rather than a heart-pounding horror that he kept reliving.

Like she'd just single-handedly polished off an entire Thanksgiving feast, her eyes wanted to close so she could digest all of that for a good long while. The hum within her quieted.

She stroked his chest, giving him a moment to come out of the feeding trance. Stephanos took a deep, gasping breath, nearly knocking her off of him as he started upright. She'd stayed in the memory too long, but it had been too good to let go.

"I must have fallen back asleep." Stephanos rubbed his face. "Sorry, what were we talking about?"

"I don't even remember. I think we wore each other out." She smiled, stretching languidly. "Are you taking a shower? I might doze a bit more."

"Do I need to take another shower?" He sniffed himself. "I don't think I've ever been this clean."

"Go." She waved him off. "And use some of the blue bottle on your hair. I'll brush it out for you after you're done, unless you can figure out how to detangle that mess on your own?"

"What's wrong with my hair?"

She pointed to the bathroom. Stephanos shook his head and left the bedroom. Lavina clutched the pillow he'd used to her chest and sighed. If only every day could start this way.

The buzzer at her entry door went off. Lavina dropped the pillow and sat up.

The buzzer went off again. She hadn't invited anyone over and no one was supposed to know she was here. Maybe it was a delivery guy with the wrong apartment number. Lavina grabbed a shirt and pants, threw them on, and went to tell whoever it was to get lost.

The screen beside the door did not reveal a misguided delivery. Lavina swore. How the hell had he found her here?

10

STEPHANOS STEPPED out of the shower and heard voices. Again. Lavina wouldn't have invited someone here for him to feed off already, would she? Maybe she wanted a repeat performance? He wasn't going to argue.

He pulled another plush towel from the stack, drying off, and then wrapping it around himself. Stephanos reached for the doorknob.

Lavina's cold voice made him freeze. "How the hell did you find this address?"

"It wasn't that hard when you have the right connections."

Stephanos stepped back, keeping his bare feet on the thick rug to stay silent. If he could have disappeared into a bathroom closet, he would have. Strangely, the thought of a dark, confined place didn't fill him with dread like it normally did. The conversation in the living room was doing that instead.

"Stephanos Laskaris, you will turn him over to me,"

Gabriel demanded.

"I don't have anyone here to turn over."

"You left The Jackyl with him."

"And as I told your spy, Fane, I got him out of the club before he caused more of a scene, and then let him out of the cab with a warning to get out of Northchester. Vadim should be thanking me, for heaven's sake, not sending you over here to harass me."

Gabriel's long pause was one Stephanos recognized. Where he would have been gauging his opponent to make a physical attack, Gabriel fought his battles with words.

"Fane isn't my spy. He was doing a favor for Vadim."

"And you being here, is that also a favor for Vadim? Since we're all bending over backwards to ingratiate ourselves, when are we going to see some benefits?"

"I seem to recall you enjoying last weekend's party and its benefits just as much as the rest of us," Gabriel said smoothly.

Stephanos tensed. What would Gabriel do to Lavina? Could she defend herself against Gabriel as readily as she had with him?

"Until the crazed wild vamp broke in, yes. Vadim's bouncers failed to subdue the situation so I took it upon myself to help him out. As I've said. Twice. So, unless you're the first vampire I've met that is hard of hearing, I suggest you apologize for disturbing me and get the fuck out."

Gabriel's voice dropped to the tone that made humans quake, full of Boros authority just like his father had used back when they'd both been human young men in Argos. "I'll leave when I'm ready." The hardwood floor creaked. "Why are you here in this hole rather than at your estate?"

Should he just step out of the bathroom and go with

Gabriel? If he'd been dressed and in the same condition in which he'd arrived at Lavina's, he would have. It wouldn't have been different than any other time Gabriel had reeled him in. Jobs did tend to make him not think clearly, to wander off, and do foolish things. Stephanos glanced at the mirror beside him. He was not the man Gabriel was looking for. Not this time.

"Why are *you* here and not at your estate?" Lavina's bare foot tapped on the wooden floor, slow and steady.

Was she signaling that he needed to remain calm and hidden, or was she showing Gabriel that she wasn't intimidated? Stephanos concentrated on the beat of her foot, letting his body sync with it.

"I'm going to search this place, and when I find Stephanos, I'm going to drag you to Vadim and enjoy watching him punish you." Gabriel headed for the guest room.

"While you do that, I'll just run over to your estate and search that while you're at it. You're friends with the feral, right? Longtime associates? Vadim knows that, surely?"

Gabriel's footsteps halted the same moment that Stephanos froze. How did Lavina know he worked for Gabriel? Had she known all along? Had he mentioned it? Stephanos manically scanned his memory for a hint that he'd slipped. He was positive he hadn't uttered Gabriel's name. That was the deal they'd had from the start of his life as a vampire: As long as Stephanos never revealed his connection, Gabriel would protect him from whatever trouble he got into. He'd always followed through.

But now the deal was broken. Stephanos ground his teeth together, fists clenching and unclenching. If he burst out of the bathroom to confront Lavina, Gabriel would take that as confirmation that he'd exposed their connection. He was already on thin ice for putting off his assignment.

If he waited until Gabriel left, he'd have to slink back as though he'd never been here. Like Lavina really had dropped him at the edge of Northchester, and then try to convince Gabriel that Lavina had put their connection together herself by whatever means. He didn't even know her other than from their cab ride. Yes, he felt the story coming together, he could make that work. He'd have to feed on a homeless person and steal their clothes and roll around in the dirt to undo all this cleanliness, but he could pull it off.

"Why would I be associated with a wild vampire?" Gabriel asked as though Lavina had just grossly insulted him.

"To do your dirty work, because god forbid you soil those pretty hands."

The floor creaked again. Which one of them was moving? Stephanos strained his hearing for a clue.

"You have no proof of such a wild allegation."

"It's no wilder than your assumption that I'd be hiding him in my little hole of an apartment. If I were trying to hide a blood-crazed vampire, wouldn't I do that in a place with more rooms to hide someone? Maybe an estate with a secure basement cell?"

Two sets of footsteps were on the move, circling each other. Stephanos reached for the doorknob, hand resting on the cool metal, begging not to be needed by either of them because he wasn't sure which one he should help.

Since the night Gabriel had sired him, he'd come after Stephanos whenever he'd gone off and done something unwise, taken one too many risks. He'd always brought him home, made sure he had someone to feed from, somewhere to sleep safely. Lavina had talked to him, had fed him from a fresh, healthy human, had also helped him, had given him a clean and safe place to sleep. But would she help him if he got into trouble? Would Gabriel help now that the connection had been exposed? And how had Lavina known?

Stephanos felt his more animalistic instincts rise. He opened his mouth wide and inhaled deeply. Fear. Danger. Threat.

"Lavina Arandine, you play a dangerous game."

"As do you. Gunning for Vadim's seat? That takes balls."

The beat of one set of footsteps stuttered. The other slowed as if to adjust to the change in pace.

A masculine hiss met her accusation. "I could rip you in half before you can reach that phone on the kitchen table. No one is coming to rescue you."

"What if that phone is on an open call to Vadim and he's heard every word?"

Gabriel's footsteps moved faster, speeding away from the bathroom. Something clattered to the floor. Glass shattered.

"No open call. Foolish woman." Gabriel stalked back toward Lavina, toward the bathroom.

"You realize you can't kill me, right? Vadim knows you're here. I'm a good little citizen like all the other city vampires. If he lets you off for laying a hand on me with no cause, he'll have a revolt on his hands. Infighting is punishable by death, as I recall. He'll have no choice but to put you down to keep the—" Her words ended in a garbled gasp.

Stephanos squeezed the knob so hard he half expected it to rip out of the door that his ear was now up against. His vision distorted from how hard his head was pressed to the sky-blue paint.

The thwack of a hand striking flesh drove Stephanos to turn the knob, his hand burning from squeezing it so tight, yet he kept it in his grasp, his body coiled and ready. Twenty seconds. If she didn't get free, he'd have no choice but to join the fight. Lavina wasn't going to die at Gabriel's hand until Stephanos got some answers out of her first.

"I might not be able to kill you, but you got mouthy when I questioned you. Some force was necessary to ascertain your innocence."

Another punch, this one louder than the last. Then a wall shaking thud was followed by a softer one.

"Get a good meal and you'll heal up just fine or limp to Vadim and cry. Up to you."

She might be free, but she wasn't speaking. The fact that Gabriel had been able to attack Lavina at all made him grateful he'd never directly challenged his sire.

Gabriel headed for the door. "If you breathe a word of your allegations to Vadim, you will have the misfortune of meeting the sun. Do we understand one another?"

Lavina coughed. "More than you intended. Scurry back to cover your ass, you rat."

The door slammed a few seconds later. Stephanos waited until Gabriel's retreat had faded before throwing himself out of the bathroom at the woman pulling herself to her feet.

His voice had lost any hint of civility. "How the hell do you know about me working for Gabriel?"

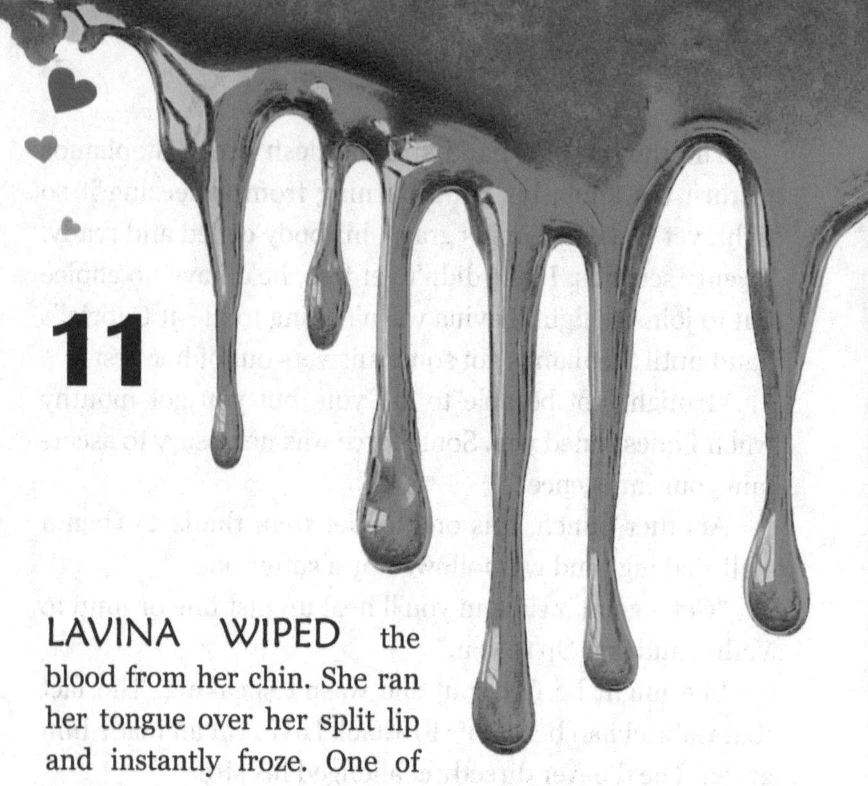

11

LAVINA WIPED the blood from her chin. She ran her tongue over her split lip and instantly froze. One of her fang implants was loose. Fucking Gabriel and his pretty hands. She rubbed her cheek while she tested the implant. It wasn't in immediate danger of falling out, but she would definitely need to schedule an emergency appointment to have it fixed.

As it turned out, staring into the rage-filled eyes of the very scary, towel-clad vampire rushing at her, the wobbly implant was the least of her worries.

Where she'd trusted her mouth to hold its own against the more refined vampire, she held no such misconception with this one. And knowing he was listening, she'd certainly not wanted to voice the knowledge she'd gleaned from his memories or the implications she'd drawn from them. Unfortunately, it had been the weapon she'd had, and it had kept her alive and whole, minus a little blood.

While seeming weak had worked to make Gabriel feel

he'd won so he would leave, Stephanos knew she wasn't. Acting cowed wasn't going to gain her any leniency. Full from her morning meal as she might be, an all-out brawl with him was not on her agenda.

"You connection to Gabriel was a guess."

She shifted her jaw left and right, hoping her healing wouldn't require another meal from the fuming vampire until he'd calmed down. Assuming he calmed down.

Lavina kept her voice level. "You said you were working for someone to kill Vadim. He showed up knowing your full name. You aren't from here, so why would you be known unless that was prior knowledge?"

Stephanos cocked his head, studying her with narrowed eyes. He paced in front of her slowly, keeping her against the wall Gabriel had thrown her into.

He'd thrown her with enough force to leave marks and a dent that she was now going to have to fix so she could get her deposit back. Because she was going to have to move now. What good was a secret hideaway if it wasn't secret anymore? Dammit, she really liked this apartment.

There was another knock on her door. Fucking hell, really?

Lavina glared at stalking Stephanos. "Do you mind if I get rid of whoever that is before you take your turn?"

He grunted, following close behind her.

"Hello? Everything alright in there?" a male voice called.

This building even had nice neighbors who normally minded their own business, but she couldn't fault them for being concerned over the loud thud of her whole damn body being thrown against the wall. She sighed.

"Yes, sorry, everything's fine. Thank you for your concern," she called out.

"Could you open the door, ma'am?" asked a woman. "We need to make sure you're okay, and then we'll be on our way."

Not a nice neighbor. A fucking cop. For as fast as they'd arrived, someone must have called as soon as Gabriel had raised his voice.

"Play along," she hissed over her shoulder at Stephanos.

He showed no sign of mellowing out or understanding, but she couldn't put off opening the door without chancing that they'd bust in to 'save her'. That would lead to her having to subdue them and maybe letting Stephanos drain them as a peace offering. If only she could think of a way to frame Gabriel as the killer so *he* would have the misfortune of meeting the fucking sunshine. How would he like it?

"Ma'am?"

With one more warning glance at Stephanos, she unlocked the door. "Sorry, we were getting a little rough. It got out of hand."

One of the officers slid her foot into the doorway, blocking Lavina from shutting the door. "Could you step outside here, ma'am?" She nodded to her partner and jutted her chin inside.

"There's really no reason to do that. Everything was consensual."

The male officer stared her down. Lavina refrained from rolling her eyes and stepped out into the hallway. She hoped Stephanos behaved. If not, she evaluated the female officer, noting her lithe build and where her hands were in relation to the gun at her side. Unlike a vampire, a gunshot could kill her.

"If you could please just come down the hall a little here, I need to ask you some questions."

Lavina let herself be led away, all the while listening for any sign that Stephanos wasn't playing nice. She answered the female officer's routine questions politely and succinctly in the hopes of getting back into her apartment before Stephanos killed her partner.

"Thank you. If you could just wait here, I'm going to go check on Officer Jeffries. I'll be right back," the officer assured her.

Lavina hoped she would. She seemed like a nice person just doing her job, as annoying as that was in this case. She let the woman get inside the apartment before approaching the door herself to peek inside.

Stephanos, now dressed—which was a shame—held out his hands while Officer Jeffries examined them. He glanced at the female officer and shook his head. She nodded but took a quick walk around the living room and kitchen area, pausing at the rounded dents where Lavina's head and right shoulder had hit the drywall.

The two officers kept their eyes on Stephanos but came closer to the door to confer.

"Not a mark on him. Doesn't say much," Jeffries said.

"She seems fine other than her cut lip and is adamant that she doesn't want to press charges."

Officer Jeffries nodded. "Bring her in."

Lavina stepped back, pretending to mind her own business until she was gestured inside.

The cops scolded them for making too much noise in the middle of the night and cautioned them against such rough play even if it was consensual.

On the way out, the female officer slipped Lavina her card and whispered, "You can contact me anytime if you need to. We have many resources available to help you."

"I'm good, but thanks." Lavina smiled and locked the door once they'd both left.

When she turned around, she balled up the card and threw it onto the floor. "What a fucking nightmare. I don't care what Gabriel is to you, that guy is a pain in the ass." She took a deep breath and exhaled slowly. "So then, where were we?"

Stephanos stood and was in front of her, too close, in seconds. "You hinged that whole accusation on a guess?"

His hands landed on her shoulders none too gently and gripped hard. He had very strong fingers, she noted. Clean now, but not neatly groomed like Gabriel's. A working man's hands.

Lavina winced. "Could you ease up a little? That officer might not have seen bruises on me, but they just haven't formed yet."

He did not ease up. "That was very risky."

"Yeah, I know, but it seems I hit enough nerves to make Gabriel leave without too much fuss."

Stephanos leaned down to get in her face, and not in the about to kiss her sort of way. "Hitting nerves makes him angry. Angry means that when I do contact him next, he'll probably add you to my task list."

Lavina went still. "The people to kill task list? Are you seriously Gabriel's hitman for hire?"

His dark eyes bored into her.

"You are." Somehow, the confirmation of her allegation wasn't all that gratifying. "And being a wild, feral vampire on the loose, it would track that you'd hunt me down for interfering in your attack on The Jackyl. That would keep Gabriel's hands clean. Vadim wouldn't question a thing."

Stephanos merely nodded.

"Can we go back to bed? I'm done with this night."

His fingers loosened their grip. "We? You want me to go back to bed with you?"

She picked up her phone from where Gabriel had thrown it to find it still powered on, but the screen was shattered. Her tastes might be dark, but asshole was not a flavor she relished.

"You can go back to your room if you'd prefer. I'm not actually tired. I just meant I'm having a shit day."

The only upside was that she'd covered the use of his memories because she didn't see that revelation going well if it did come to light. Speaking of revelations she didn't want discovered, Lavina checked her implant with her tongue. That was thankfully still hanging on.

Now that Stephanos wasn't drilling the hell out of her muscles, she eased herself out of his grasp. He let her go but still watched her with predatory focus. She eased her sore body onto the couch where he had been sitting before the cops left.

"Any suggestions for avoiding being added to your task list?" she asked.

"You made an enemy today."

"I picked up on that," she grumbled. "You're not being helpful."

He came closer to stand in front of her, glaring downward. "Why didn't you just tell him I was here and avoid all of this?" He gestured at her cut lip and the rest of her.

"If you'd wanted to be found, you could have come out of the bathroom at any time. You didn't. I was helping you."

He crossed his arms over his chest. "Why? You want me to owe you?"

Lavina rested her head on the back of the couch so she

could look up at him without getting a kink in her aching neck. She was going to have a bruise there too. Where Gabriel had choked her was no doubt red already.

"What? Owe me? No, you don't owe me anything. Though not killing me would be nice."

Did he just smirk? She wasn't sure, but the thin-lipped scowl had definitely slipped for a second.

"So why?" he asked with slightly less ire.

"Because you looked like you needed some help. Like what that police officer was offering me when she left." She nodded to the wadded-up card on the floor. "And Gabriel hunting me down when I clearly didn't want to be found pissed me off."

"And because he also didn't believe your lies."

"That too," she conceded.

"He doesn't like liars. Neither do I."

A shiver ran down Lavina's spine. Was he merely stating a fact, or did he realize she fed on his memories?

"Understandable. If you wish to go to him, I'm not stopping you."

"But what you said about Vadim, about staying out of sight for a while..."

"That holds true, but I'm guessing Gabriel put you up somewhere where you can do that. You can take care of yourself. I'm not your mother, and I have no interest in taking on that role."

Stephanos backed down and took the chair across from the couch. Lavina let herself relax a little.

He surveyed the apartment like he was a king upon a throne. "I like it here."

"Me too, but we're going to have to move this little party to my estate. Gabriel has already called me out for hiding here. If I have nothing to hide, I need to go home."

Stephanos nodded. "I'll stay here?"

She explained her plans to sell the space and the necessity of boxing up her personal things. "You can come with me, if you'd like."

"To your estate."

"That makes it sound fancy." She laughed. "It's not. It's mine." She gestured at her loose, baggy shirt and yoga pants combo.

"Is it condemned?"

Her brows rose. "Umm, no? Are you saying I should be condemned? I mean, I know I'm not in great shape, but—"

He shook his head. "Mine is."

"Oh." Her cheeks flushed. "Not big on home maintenance?"

"Didn't care."

She'd seen enough of his memories to pick up on that vibe. "So, knowing the choice is entirely yours, are you staying with me or going?"

"That depends."

"Yes, I will ask that you shower and at least occasionally wear clean clothes. No feeding from my staff and Vadim's general rules must be followed."

He waved that all off. "Can I taste you again?"

The hot flush on her cheeks flared. "Yes, but not tonight. We need to pack and be gone. I don't need Vadim showing up in person to verify Gabriel's report only to find you here." She tapped her chin, sorting the trains of thought barreling through her head. "First order of business, you need to not be the vampire Vadim is looking for when you arrive at my house."

12

THE CONCEPT of having to hide in another vampire's presence wasn't new, but he wanted to think that Lavina was different from Gabriel. "How do you propose to hide me?"

"Hide?" She shook her head. "I want you out in the open, subdued maybe, like me, but not hiding. Let's just build on this whole clean new you thing we've started, yeah?"

"I can do subdued."

"And you have." She winked. "Let's get your hair sorted out. That will help a lot."

Stephanos patted his hair. No one had cared about what he looked like in ages. Even Gabriel didn't, as long as he stayed out of sight from everyone else. "What about it?"

Lavina shifted forward, grimacing. She swung her legs off the couch and planted her feet on the floor. "We're going to need a comb, a scissors, a brush—"

"I'll get them. Sit. You need to feed so you can heal faster." He stood.

"Later. I'll be fine." She rubbed the side of her face, her tongue probing her right fang.

"Is it sore? I could pierce a feeder vein for you."

A pained smile brightened her face, and for a moment, he swore it looked like tears welling in her eyes, but she blinked and they were gone.

"That's sweet, but I'll get by for now. Thank you."

Stephanos retrieved the requested items from the bathroom and handed them to Lavina. She tossed one of the square pillows onto the floor in front of her and motioned for him to sit. Once he was settled, she went to work.

Fifteen minutes of gentle tugging and a few long strokes of the comb left him relaxed. He leaned against the couch, feeling Lavina's warm legs rubbing against his shoulders. She must not have been too hungry if she was still maintaining body heat. Confident she'd tell him if she needed anything, he let his thoughts drift off.

He couldn't remember the last time a brush had run through his hair. It took him a minute to realize it was moving in long, steady strokes. How long had he been sitting in a relaxed daze?

"Those curls are to die for, you know. I'm guessing they're even better after a fresh wash without all the brushing, but mmmmm," she uttered a pleased purring noise that made him chuckle.

He reached up hesitantly to feel what she'd done. His fingers met with smooth curls without a snarly matted knot. He'd been worried about the request for the scissors, but the length was the same. He turned around to check for the pile of hair he'd expected to find missing.

There was one, but not huge. "I only cut out what I couldn't untangle." She ran her fingers over his head, through his hair, her nails grazing his scalp.

How long had it been since anyone had done that either? If he'd have been freshly fed, he would have suggested they return to her bedroom so he could properly thank her both for hiding him from Gabriel and for this kindness. Alas, he was not, and she had already told him no biting tonight.

"Now we pack?" he asked instead.

"We do. Take whatever clothes you want. There's a suitcase under the bed. Pull your sheets, put them and the towels, and anything else you used in the laundry basket. Nothing that holds your scent can remain. Gabriel was too busy this time, but if he returns and investigates further, I don't want him to find you here."

"Got it."

Stephanos spent the next hour doing as she asked. By the time he was done, she had two suitcases of her own waiting by the door. The laundry basket full of linens and a bag of trash waited there too.

"I've wiped down the bathroom. Your hairball is coming with us." She nodded to the white plastic bag. "We should be clear enough for now. I'll have some of my people pack up the rest and get my phone screen fixed while we sleep the day away." Lavina bent stiffly to get the laundry basket.

"I'll bring it all down. Go."

She nodded gratefully and pulled the keys from her pocket. "Make sure you lock it up for me?"

There was no question about the tears in her eyes this time.

"I will."

Lavina started for the landing. Stephanos rolled the three suitcases out the door and then slid the heaped laundry basket and the bag with his foot. He glanced up to see her giving the door one last look before going down the stairs.

He fumbled his way through the keys to find the right one for each lock and then took everything down in two trips. Lavina waited by the curb with her broken phone in hand. "Our ride will be here in a few minutes."

The city was fairly quiet at this early hour. The crescent moon was heading downward, its view nearly blocked by the cityscape. Stars twinkled overhead.

As he stood on the sidewalk, the light breeze reminded him of the annoyance of having detangled, long hair. After the third time of swatting loose strands out of his face, Lavina fished around in her pocket and handed him a stretchy band.

He took it, stretching it experimentally. When he gathered up his hair into one long tail and slipped the band around it, the useless thing fell right out, landing by his feet.

"Let me." Lavina picked up the band, her movements less stiff than before.

She again ran her hands through his hair, gathering it up before slipping the band over it and tugging it around. The breeze hit the bare back of his neck. Stephanos shivered at the unfamiliar sensation. He reached up to feel the band wrapped around his hair several times. So that was the trick. He felt the thick knob of hair.

"Is this what they call a man bun?"

Lavina grinned. "It is. It looks good on you."

Was she mocking him?

"No, really." She patted his arm. "I like it. You look like one of those rugged models in some ad for expensive bourbon. Not at all like a filthy, rabid vampire who attacked The Jackyl."

"My disguise?"

She shrugged. "Or was the other your disguise?"

Stephanos pondered his clean hands and the fresh smell of the fitted dress shirt that looked like something Gabriel would have worn. His pants didn't have a single hole. He'd never worn denim before, but he liked it. There had been a time before he'd become this, when he'd worn clean clothes, that he'd brushed his hair and washed his face. Life hadn't always been good, but he'd been relatively happy.

"This is us," Lavina announced as a black car pulled up beside them. She took one of the suitcases and pulled it around to the trunk.

Wrangling the other two and the bag and basket, he followed. She had the trunk open and was hefting the case inside without much trouble. He fit the rest of their things in around it. She pulled the trunk closed and got in the back seat. He took the other side, giving her space. The driver, a grey-haired man with a short beard, didn't say a word. He just pulled away from the curb and drove. Lavina stared at her hands in her lap.

Not knowing what to say, he opted to remain quiet. He was used to quiet and not speaking for days. Weeks. Years, even. Yet, this silence felt heavy and left him discomforted. Maybe because there was someone else in the quiet with him.

He watched out the window as the heart of the city fell behind them. Tall buildings gave way to shorter ones and then to strip malls and sprawling masses of near identical houses. The car turned off onto another road and slowed to a stop before a large, black iron gate. The driver put the window down and punched a code into a box. Within seconds, the gate clunked and then retracted to each side. The window went up and the car drove on.

This street wound around, slowly going upward. Thick trees lined the road with occasional drives branching off and outward from the spiral. He caught glimpses of massive homes as they passed driveways. Others wove through wooded or heavily landscaped areas, hiding the view beyond.

The trees thinned, only dotting the roadside as they continued upward. The moonlight was brighter here. Off to the north, he caught sight of the bay and its shimmering waters. He'd only seen it from the plane when Gabriel had flown him in. The car turned down a driveway, threading between trees and shrubs as though the driver knew every bend by heart. Headlights danced over flowerbeds and broad boulders before flashing over a rock-faced three-story home.

While tall, narrow windows artfully dotted the structure, there were none of the wall-to-wall panoramic views like some of the other homes he'd seen here. It looked like part of a craggy hill, like it belonged here. The car pulled into an open garage.

When the big door closed, Lavina got out. Stephanos followed her lead. She did not retrieve the cases from the trunk, instead nodding to the driver and then going deeper into the garage to a door. They'd barely set foot on the step before it when it swung open.

"Welcome home," said a thick woman with a big smile. "We've missed you."

"Thank you, Trina. It's good to be back. This is Stephanos. He'll be staying with us for a while. If anyone asks—"

"You have a visitor. We don't know his name. But he is a handsome one." Trina winked at him.

No one had used any version of that word in... Maybe all these showers did have some benefits. While Trina seemed friendly, and he had to admit that he was enjoying the attention, he'd tasted plenty of humans. She'd taste nothing like Lavina. And the staff was off limits according to Lavina's rules.

"Welcome. We have a room ready for you if you'd like?" Trina said to him before glancing at Lavina.

He nodded. He'd had manners once, but he had a feeling his knowledge was far outdated. Gabriel had never expected them of him.

"Thank you, Trina." Lavina left the woman behind and gestured for Stephanos to follow as she made her way through the kitchen and past a dining room filled with a long table and twelve chairs. A big bouquet of purple and white flowers sat in the middle. He took a big sniff, enjoying the sweet scent that tickled his nose.

"I'll give you the quick tour, and then you can decide. There is a guest room above the garage if you'd prefer to be more alone. I'd imagine you were used to more solitary living. Being cooped up with me for days was probably not all that comfortable for you."

"I didn't mind." In fact, he hadn't been this comfortable in a very long time.

Lavina smiled and then launched into a quick run-through of her home. He'd spent months inside Gabriel's house here in Northchester, and he'd been in others over the centuries. None of them were as warm and inviting as this one. It looked like humans lived here: pillows askew on the couch, blankets on the back of a chair, one rumpled over the arm as if someone had just gotten up to answer the door. A cup of tea sat on the table beside it.

"Trina and Nathan live here. Rosa, my daytime house-keeper, has her own place. Her two young boys come with her. She's homeschooling them here between her duties. It works better with her hours and I don't mind them around. They are all very much off limits, do you understand?" She drilled in that declaration with a very stern stare.

"Got it."

"I hope you do. Good help is hard to find. I've got Trina for a while yet, but Nathan is nearing retirement. I'm not looking forward to having to replace him. He's been with me since he was nineteen."

"You keep them that long?"

"When I can. If they have families, a big move is a lot to ask."

"And when they're done serving, you dispose of them?"

"What?" She shot him an incredulous look. "No, I do not kill my staff! They get to choose where they want to live. I buy them a house. I finance their care until the end of their days, just as they've cared for me."

Gabriel would call her naïve. It seemed he didn't remember his human years, but Stephanos did. He wondered how different his life would have turned out if he'd served someone like Lavina instead of the Boros. Gabriel's family had owned his in life, just as Gabriel now owned him in walking death.

"That's kind of you."

Lavina shrugged "Yes, well, I'm not always an easy person to live with. They deserve it."

Stephanos shrugged too. "You seem pretty easy to live with."

She chuckled. "You've stayed with me for a few days. Give it a few months before you make any judgements."

A weight settled on him. He'd never be able to hide for months, no matter how much he'd like to. Gabriel would call soon, and he'd have to answer. He owed it to Lavina to clear her of any connection to him.

"Guess we better wrap up the tour. Nathan will want to know where to bring your suitcase so he can turn in for the night." She shook her head. "The third shift hours don't agree with his stomach these days. We've compromised on my getting a cab if I need to be out after three in the morning."

Stephanos felt his mouth drop open. "You compromise with your servants?"

"Help. We call them *help* these days, and we pay them a fair wage with benefits. Servants, slaves, owning people—all of that is a big no no."

He followed her up a carpeted stairway and then down a hallway papered with a muted green fern and brown bird pattern. She pointed to four doors, two on either side. "These are the interior guest rooms. There are others with windows for humans downstairs. I do have a room in the basement if you prefer a quieter space, or the room over the garage I mentioned earlier. Go ahead, take a look."

At her urging, he pushed the first door open to find a deep blue room that reminded him of the sea and his human home in Greece. He left centuries ago and hadn't been back.

"I'll take this one."

"You don't even want to see the others?"

"Until recently, I slept in a basement with the house falling apart around me. This is far better than I deserve."

"Then it's yours as long as you wish to stay here. Nathan will leave your suitcase outside the door. For their safety, the staff are under strict orders never to enter our rooms when we are here, even with our invitation."

Not that he planned to feed on any of them, but he saw the wisdom in her rule. "I've taken too much of your time already. We'll talk again tomorrow night?"

She nodded and headed back down the stairs.

Stephanos closed the door to the blue room and sat on the firm bed to call Gabriel.

His sire didn't bother with a greeting. "Where the hell have you been?"

"Walking. It's a very big city."

"I've been looking for you."

"I wasn't in the mood to be found."

"Vadim is being increasingly difficult since you showed up at The Jackyl. You need to kill him now."

"Tomorrow night. Tell me where he'll be."

"I'll text you when I wake. No more delays."

"Understood." He ended the call and dropped the phone on the thick satin bedcover.

Tomorrow he'd either taste Lavina for the last time or he'd convince her Vadim had to die so he could stay here. Here, in a house where people didn't own people. Where, for once in his life and death, he might be free.

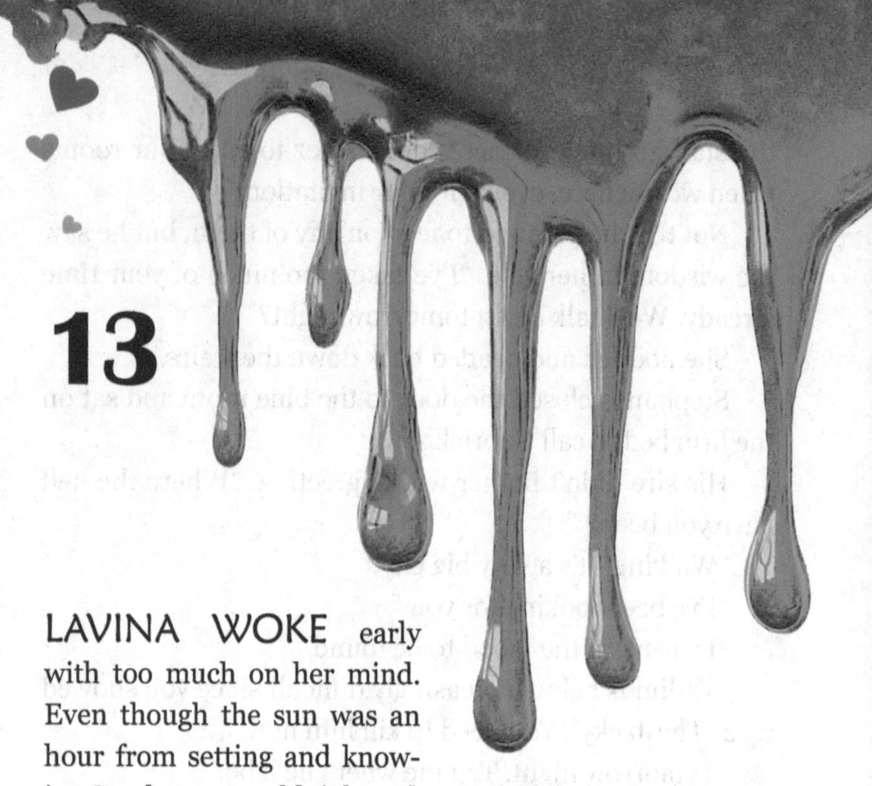

13

LAVINA WOKE early with too much on her mind. Even though the sun was an hour from setting and know-ing Stephanos wouldn't be a threat until then, she felt com-pelled to get up and check on Rosa and the boys. She threw on an over-sized black sweatshirt and grey knit pants with a pair of her favorite slouchy black socks. They might not currently be in style, but she didn't care. With her hair up in a messy bun, she unlocked her door and headed for the kitchen.

Rosa greeted her with a smile on her face and a spatula in her hand. "You're up early. I was just making brownies. Would you like one? They'll be about half an hour yet."

Though she could eat regular food, it didn't fill her like memories did. It was more a matter of appearances, but she didn't need to perform at home.

"That sounds delicious, but I'll donate my share to the boys. Are they well?"

"They're outside playing right now, so well enough.

Gregory knows to come in if he gets tired, and Eric knows to send him in if he looks like he's pushing himself too hard."

"The medication is working well enough for now then?" Lavina watched the boys out the window. They ran around laughing and kicking a soccer ball back and forth.

"Yes. We can do another blood transfusion if it comes to that." Rosa smiled. "We're grateful for the excellent medical insurance."

"Glad I can help. Children should be able to play and not worry about their bodies failing them. There's plenty of time for that when they get older."

Rosa chuckled as she put the mixing bowl in the sink. "That's what Nathan says."

The reminder of soon losing Nathan to retirement turned Lavina melancholy. She stared at the children surrounded by long shadows. The early evening sun had already vanished behind the trees.

"Will your guest be dining this evening?" Rosa asked.

"Not by conventional means. Do we have any reliable blood donors on call? I don't normally entertain my guests here. Sorry to expose the boys to this."

"It's your house." Rosa scrubbed the bowl, avoiding Lavina's gaze.

"Still."

Though she'd avoided general vampire society for decades, humans weren't sustaining in the longevity sense. The few vampires she'd tided herself over with had been relegated to the apartment. Trina maintained the upkeep there, but it had always been after guests had vacated. Lavina sighed. Her evening housekeeper wasn't going to be happy with all the packing duties on top of having a houseguest here to clean up after. Granted, that's what she was paid for, but... Trina hadn't even been hired yet when Vadim had stayed here. She'd only had to stock the apartment and arrange for blood donor delivery from a distance. Nathan was the only one fully experienced with her taste in men.

"Trina showed me how to use the donor app on my phone this morning." Rosa nodded to Lavina's phone on the counter. "Yours is all fixed, by the way. The app seems fairly straightforward. I'll get that set up and Nathan can retrieve one. What time would you like that served?"

Trina must have briefed her well. For never having to deal with a vampire herself, Rosa didn't appear as unnerved as Lavina had expected. Then again, her staff was used to turning a blind eye to her unusual lifestyle. She paid them well for it.

"Anytime between sundown and midnight will be fine. Just text me a time."

"Yes, ma'am. I've prepared tonight's meals for Nathan and Trina. We already ate. The house is cleaned, and the laundry will be folded before I go. Will you need anything else today?"

"No. Thank you, Rosa."

Lavina left her to her baking and went to sit in the living room under a worn quilt sewn for her by her previous housekeeper. There were days she missed Shantel's lined face and sharp wit, gone forty-one years now. With Stephanos sleeping upstairs and Gabriel out for blood, she needed to channel some of Shantel's energy for the call she had to make.

She stared out the window, basking in the relative quiet of two young boys stuffing their faces with chocolaty goodness in the other room. Moments after the sun set, she dialed Vadim's number.

"Arandine. About time you surfaced," Vadim groused. "You weren't home. I checked."

"Sometimes a girl wants some quiet time to lick her wounds."

There was a pause before he proceeded with less annoyance. "You were hurt?"

"You saw what that monster did to your men. He wasn't exactly friendly."

"Lavina, you're okay though?" How quickly he slipped into concern. She'd made him too soft.

"I'm fine now. I've fed. All better. What I don't appreciate is you sending Boros over to hunt me down. Keep that asshole away from me if you want to keep your peace."

"He said you were less than cooperative," Vadim's smooth voice chided.

"He's not a good listener, and he plays rough."

Vadim chuckled. "You like it rough, Vina."

He thought this was funny? Would he be laughing when she vanished without a trace thanks to Gabriel?

"I like rules, Vadim. If he's not going to follow them, neither will I. Is that clear enough for you?"

"Come to The Jackyl tonight so I can read you."

Lavina groaned. Not this reading people bullshit again. She'd hoped that fad had passed.

"Sure, I'll be there at opening and then I'm going home to be left alone in all this. You've made me regret doing you a favor. Don't expect my help again." She ended the call.

"Who was that?" Stephanos asked.

Lavina did her best to cover her startlement. She'd been too focused on Vadim and covering her ass to hear him come in.

"Vadim is demanding that I show up for a reading tonight so he can clear me."

Stephanos stood still as a statue, silent, yet she could almost see his thoughts swirling.

"A reading of what?"

"Me." She rolled her eyes. "He went through a mystic phase a while back and got it in his head that he can see the truth of people. Funny thing is, most of them believe him, and it keeps them in line. The power of suggestion." She shook her head. "It's ridiculous."

"What if it's real?" he asked as if studying the idea, not out of concern that it might be true.

As rough around every edge as Stephanos was, he wasn't stupid, just out of touch. Like he'd been away from civilization but had been given a crash course in current society that had skipped all the finer points. Though she supposed he was here only to operate smoothly enough to kill Vadim, not fully integrate into Northchester.

"It's nonsense. Consequences of hanging out with a crowd of mystics who thought he was charming. He thought they were tasty, but even with all their supposed divination, they never figured that out."

"Still, aren't you at all concerned that he won't accept your lies either?"

"Vadim likes me. It will be fine." She peered toward the kitchen. "Rosa and the boys will be leaving soon. When they do, I'll have Nathan take me to The Jackyl. Will you be alright here on your own?"

"Yes, but will *you* be alright on your own? What if he doesn't believe you? What if Gabriel is there?"

"I'd rather he weren't." If she'd known what a pain in the ass he was, she never would have talked to him at the party. She certainly wouldn't have considered tasting his memories. Though if she had, perhaps she would have uncovered his desire to remove Vadim from power.

Stephanos shifted from conversational to suddenly predatory. He stalked closer. "So you can warn Vadim that I was sent to kill him?"

Knowing Rosa and the boys were too close by to escape to a car if Stephanos did attack, Lavina shot to her feet and blocked his view of the kitchen. As alluring as the thought of enjoying years of satisfying meals from his mind was, he was dangerous. And he would be for a good long while before the effects of her eating altered his personality. Damn, she really didn't want to cut him loose so quickly.

"I plan to mention Gabriel's intention to have him killed, yes. However, I was going to leave you out of it."

"If you breathe a word of his plans to Vadim, I will be sent after you. Do not doubt this."

She was relieved that his attention was focused raptly on her and not the easy meals in the next room. "I don't doubt it. What you don't seem to understand is that Vadim is good for us, for Northchester. Hell, he's even good for the humans. I may have only met Gabriel Boros twice, but he's none of those things."

Stephanos scowled. "And Vadim *is* good for you?"

"In that I can live here, relatively in the open, go about my life without the fear of being persecuted by humans, and have clean and willing food? Yes. Me personally? No. We went our separate ways a long time ago."

"I see. And you think Gabriel would not maintain these things for the vampires here?"

"If he is going to keep things as they are, there would be no reason to take Vadim out, would there?"

"What if he were to make Northchester better?"

Lavina noticed there wasn't much conviction in his question. Her answer was certain. "He won't. You think he's your friend. Maybe he is. You've seen the aftermath of his actions. You tell me. After he's used you to kill off his opposition, is there peace and prosperity for those around him?"

"Those close to him, yes."

"Really? You're close to him. How much peace and prosperity have you personally seen, dressed in rags and living in a moldering basement?"

He grimaced. "That was my choice. He gave me Isla and the house was nice when he gifted it."

She couldn't hide her disdain. "He gave you a woman. Good people don't own people, Stephanos."

"In our time, they did." He shrugged. "The humans he's had deals with live long and do well. He's had alliances with other vampires too." His determined gaze drifted aside. "I've dropped in and out of his life too many times to know if he's maintained them. It's not my business."

She wasn't going to start a fight over his sire. Not yet anyway. She needed more memories for proof first. "If you say so."

Stephanos studied her face, blinking slowly. "I will go with you. Not to your meeting. I need to meet with Gabriel. If I'm with him, he won't be with Vadim."

"You'd meet with him as you are now?" Lavina nodded to the clean, neatly dressed and groomed man in front of her.

He smirked. "No. I will need a shower when we return."

"Be a shame to make a mess of all this." She reached out to run a hand down the front of his shirt.

"I would not ruin these things you have given me. I will find other clothes."

"I wasn't only talking about the clothes."

Stephanos captured her hand and held it. "I've seen the bathroom. There's plenty of room for two in the shower, if you want to make sure I've fully returned to this state later."

Nope, she was definitely not ready to cut him off so soon.

"I've already ordered a meal for you, so this night might go well indeed."

He grinned.

Lavina checked her phone. "Steven will be here in half an hour to provide for you. Let Trina know if you like him. He's willing to be a regular."

She hoped he did like Steven, because she was far less likely to be jealous of Stephanos feeding off a male. At least in theory. The thought of reenacting the night in her apartment in about an hour made her want to skip the meeting with Vadim, but she needed to stay in his good graces.

"Feed, change, get dirty, whatever you need to do. I have to dress for The Jackyl. We'll meet back here in an hour?"

He nodded and reluctantly let her hand go.

She reluctantly took it back.

Lavina left him on the couch with his phone to go to her room to change. While she would have happily left the house as she was, Vadim would hate it. He'd always liked her to appear far more high-maintenance than she was.

Hair done and make-up on, bejeweled and dressed in high-waisted black slacks, heels, push-up bra, and a silver sequined tank top, Lavina went to collect Stephanos so they could get to The Jackyl and back at a reasonable hour. A handsome young man with spiked platinum blond hair and a septum piercing sat on the couch next to Stephanos. The boy's dreamy, dazed smile and Stephanos' contented gaze in her direction let her know that the transaction had been completed.

Confident that Trina would see Steven was paid and provided with transportation, she nodded for Stephanos to follow her to the garage.

"Nathan is ready to go. I thought you were going to change?"

"I'll do that when you drop me off."

"But you don't have anything with you to change into."

He let out an amused snort. "Nothing you provided is adequate for this meeting. I'll find something suitable on the streets."

"Oh. Right. I see." Of course she hadn't provided him with rags like he'd worn when they'd first met. Seeing him as he was now, she wasn't looking forward to his regression. She did like dark and damaged, but also with good hygiene.

They got into the car and after a moment of polite small talk with Nathan, they were on the way back into Northchester's heart. Five minutes into the drive, Stephanos cleared his throat quietly.

"Would you consider distracting Vadim so I could complete my task?"

"So your sire can take over Northchester? We covered this already. No way."

He sucked on his lips and dropped his gaze to the phone in his lap. After a moment, he turned to her again. "If I told you I had to choose between two tasks and you were one of them, would you help me complete the other one?"

Lavina swallowed. "Hypothetically, right?"

"At the moment, but this would all be so much easier if

I could do this one thing."

"This one thing, being ruining Northchester for every-one."

"Not for me, I don't live here," he mumbled.

She took a wild leap. "What if you did? If you stayed with me, or got a place of your own? You'd do well here. Vadim values people like you."

"People like me? Vampires? Killers?"

"Enforcers. People who know how to get things done and motivate others to fall in line."

"I do that already. For someone else."

She nodded. "But look at you now, and you're barely in Vadim's shadow. Compare that to how you were when you were fully in Gabriel's."

He went silent for a few minutes.

"You said you've moved before. If I complete my task, you could move again, be happy and safe elsewhere if you don't like what Gabriel does with the city."

"Stephanos, I'm not moving, and I don't want Vadim dead. What I do want is for you to enjoy the benefits North-chester has to offer, whether that's with me or not. You deserve to be happy too."

"You are too kind for this world," he said quietly, star-ing at his phone again.

"I'm really not." Guilt urged her to get him out of the car and let him go, to let him do what he must before she ruined him.

But looking at him there, all deliciously broody, made her mouth water. It wouldn't hurt to hang on to him for a few months. Or a year. She'd just neaten him up a little inside and then cut him loose.

He looked so forlorn. She cast about for a topic to bring

him back to life. "How was Steven?"

"Fine, but he wasn't you."

Warmth crept over her cheeks. "Shall I tell Trina you'd like him again?"

His gaze focused on her neck. "I'd like you again."

"After we get back to the house. You need your head clear for your meeting."

"I do." He sighed. Stephanos shifted closer and then glanced at the back of Nathan's head before turning back to Lavina. He reached one hand around to cup the back of her head. "May I... instead?"

Her mouth watered for an entirely different reason. Lavina nodded.

When her lips met his, she no longer sat in the back of a car speeding down the highway. The driver disappeared. Her stomach wasn't in knots about the meeting, and her stupid bra wasn't cutting into her shoulders. All of it fell away in the hungry rhythm of his lips against hers. His hand kneading her scalp like a contented cat making biscuits. She could almost imagine him purring. Or maybe she was purring. Lavina grinned.

Stephanos took her open mouth as an invitation, his tongue darting inside to take the lay of the land. She met him in the middle, giving what she got. A pleased rumble worked its way up through his chest and against her lips.

She held tight to his shoulders, encouraging him, knowing she was taunting trouble since he'd just fed and had plenty of fresh blood coursing through his veins.

Trouble had its own allure.

His tongue swept over her teeth, pausing, and then coming to a sudden halt. Stephanos pulled back.

"Your tooth. It's loose! Did Gabriel do that?"

Her appointment was tomorrow to get that fixed. It couldn't come soon enough. Lavina nodded, clenching her lips together so he couldn't see the faulty fang.

"Why hasn't it healed with the rest of you?"

That was a very valid question, and she didn't have an answer that she wanted to share. "It will be fine," she mumbled.

"You shouldn't go into this meeting weak. Feed first."

His concern would have been endearing if it weren't for the part where blood wasn't the problem. "I will after we drop you off. Where is Gabriel?"

His entire countenance shuttered. He sat back, running a finger idly over the face of his phone. Alright, he wasn't going to share that information.

"Where do you want me to pick you up then?"

"I'll meet you outside The Jackyl. Just down the street. There's a bread shop."

"A bakery."

He shrugged. "Same thing."

At least he was still in relatively good spirits. "Sure, that works. Just be careful and don't get too close. If you'll be looking like you were before, his employees may recognize you."

Stephanos nodded and turned his attention to the window beside him. After five minutes and thirty-seven seconds of silence—she may have been watching the time to calm herself—he tapped the window.

"Let me out here. Be safe, Lavina." He leaned over to land a kiss on her cheek as Nathan dropped out of traffic and slowed. Stephanos barely waited for the car to come to a stop before slipping out the door and into the night.

14

THOUGH LAVINA was used to traveling alone—other than the driver—the car felt empty without the large vampire to fill the rest of the seat. She sat back to touch up her make-up and fix her hair. She'd just put herself back in order when Nathan announced that they'd arrived at The Jackyl.

Lavina took a deep breath and exited the car.

"Shall I wait here for you, ma'am?"

"I don't anticipate being inside long. Please do."

The silver-haired man nodded and rolled up his window. She glimpsed the sci-fi novel on the passenger seat, a bookmark near the halfway point. Getting paid to read whatever he wanted surely made up for the shitty hours. The interior light over his seat clicked on.

Standing outside in the chilly night air wasn't accomplishing anything. Lavina regarded the line by the door. Good thing she was expected. The humans, however, were subjected to contracts, pat-downs, and a quick blood test.

Those took time. Sucked to be them.

She gave her name to the doorman, someone new, considering Stephanos had killed the three men who normally did the job.

The tattooed thirty-something in a t-shirt stretched tight around his thick muscled arms scanned his list and smiled. "The boss will be happy to see you. Head on inside."

"Thank you."

Lavina used the narrow door beside the larger one to the main lobby where the pat-down and finger prick were happening to two leather microskirt-clad girls of questionable legal drinking age. She hoped Vadim's people weren't getting lazy while short-staffed. But really, not her problem.

Inside, she looked for a table swarming with young people because that's likely where Vadim would be, smiling, schmoozing, posing with the admirers to make them feel special while his friends shopped the crowd.

Sure enough, he was chatting up three college-aged girls and two young men, taking selfies with them, his smile never quite wide enough to reveal his fangs for photos. He'd perfected the whole downplay of vampires. The fangs were all in fun, a quirky subset of club society. A kink for some, fantasy play and escape for others. There was little judgement here on anyone's reason for hanging out at The Jackyl, both for those who played victim and vampire, and the true vampires who fed on them all.

A few of Vadim's usuals were stationed around the room, surveying the humans. Being a weeknight, the crowd was thinner, and most of the vampires in attendance were of the dress-up human variety. The low lights helped sell the ruse for those who made a decent effort.

Lavina approached the table. Vadim caught sight of

her and smiled, his fangs making an appearance that made the three girls titter. He turned away from them when they picked up their phones, likely to take more photos.

"Lavina, you made it. And so soon after opening, even. You weren't kidding."

"I rarely am."

She accepted his polite hug and kiss on the cheek routine. Before she'd devoured too much of his darkness, he never would have done such a thing. Or smiled. Or let anyone take a photo of him. Ugh, it was such a shame.

"Let's go to my office where we can talk."

He held out his hand as if to usher her in the right direction. As if she didn't know where the damned office was. They'd had plenty of fun in there during their years together.

As much as she wanted to retort about being able to talk out here just as well, it was a lie. A gaggle of older women were heading his way, all batting fake eyelashes over creased eyelids spackled with eye shadow. Their age-spotted tits on display in low cut shirts.

To the clear dismay of the oncoming cougar squad, Lavina let Vadim escort her out of the fray and down a quieter hallway guarded by a thick bouncer with a neck that seemed wider than his shaved head. He pushed the door open with his other hand and held it as she entered.

The office had undergone a remodel since she'd seen it last. Small, glimmering midnight tiles threaded with silver covered the long wall, otherwise bare of ornamentation. The other three walls had been painted grey-blue. Black framed photos of Vadim with various guests, a few of whom she recognized as semi-celebrities, hung in a neat row along the other three walls. Her gaze was drawn to one in particular. The one she was in. New Year's Eve, six days before she'd walked out of Vadim's life. She stood by his side in a form-fitting deep blue dress, diamonds around her neck, her hair piled artfully in curls on top of her head, scarlet lipstick accentuating her big smile. Her fangs had been more of a pain in the ass back then, before cosmetic dentistry. The glue had tasted terrible, and she'd almost swallowed them a few times when they fell out unexpectedly.

The Vadim who stood beside her was reminiscent of his original self, at least on film. Back before he'd embraced the change she'd wrought upon him on the inside by becoming the charismatic socialite he was today. Black suit, red and gold brocade vest, hair long and swept back from his face to hang loose over his shoulders. The eyes gave it away though, having lost their glint of darkness, given way to mirth instead.

They looked happy. It was a lie.

"Have a seat, won't you?"

He offered her one of the two tall-backed wooden chairs with silvery-grey velvet upholstered seats that sat across from his minimalist black desk. A slim laptop, an ornamental-looking dagger with a blue gem in the hilt on a wooden stand, and a crystal vase filled with curly bamboo sat on top. He took the black leather chair behind it.

Lavina sat, keeping her purse on her lap. No one had patted her down or searched her bag. Vadim's rules kept them all relatively safe from one another, or, more accurately, the penalty for violating those rules. She supposed he had the dagger in case anyone was willing to risk it all.

Not that her purse contained any weapons. This time. She preferred to carry some protection against unpredictable humans, but needed Vadim's trust.

"Let me first say, Gabriel Boros sends his apologies."

Like hell he did, but she nodded and smiled.

"We were concerned about you, Lavina. *I* was concerned about you."

"Thank you, but as I said, I'm fine now. All better." She held up her bare arms as if to illustrate this point.

"That feral, have you seen him since you dropped him off?"

"I have not."

"He killed three men, Vina. Ripped them apart, sucked them dry. What kind of animal has an appetite like that?"

One she hoped to enjoy in bed in a few hours.

"I have no idea."

"Good gods, woman, what possessed you to take matters into your own hands? You could have easily been killed too."

"Your staff are not vampires. You should get them steel collars if you don't want to risk them again."

He leaned back and sighed. "You're still angry with me."

"You sent that Boros asshole to my private hideaway. Not to my estate. If I'm not at home, it's because I don't want to talk to anyone. Now I have to sell my happy place and move all my shit and no, I'm not happy about it."

He frowned. "You don't have to do that."

"It's discovered. Violated." Her fingers clutched her purse for lack of Gabriel's neck to strangle. "You could have just called."

"Vina. I'm sorry. I overreacted, but only because I care about you. You were gone for so long, and I respected your need for the space you asked for. Then you attended my party. I thought you were ready to join us again." He met her gaze with such sincerity that it tied her stomach in knots. "To join *me* again."

You've got to be fucking kidding me. As if the decades apart hadn't scabbed over his wounds even a little? Did he really think she only wanted some space for five freaking decades? She'd really scrambled his brain.

"Vadim, I—"

"I know you said we were done, but look at us, Vina." He pointed to the photo on the wall. "We were so good together. What you and I started all those years ago, look where it led. People are happy, both ours and theirs. We're safe. They're safe. You and I did that."

"That was all you, and you're right to be proud of it. I'm proud of you. However, me coming out of seclusion, it's not to rush back into your arms. I needed some time away."

"Yes, space. You made that clear," he said earnestly, as if he'd read the instructions on the assignment a hundred times and followed them to the letter.

"Distance. Separation." How the hell could she be clearer without pissing him off?

He nodded. "I let you be just like you asked. No calls, no visits. No guilt."

"You did." For fuck's sake, did he want a pat on the head?

"Lavina, you were good for me. Without you, none of this would be possible."

She raised her hands to her face to scrub away the frustration, but then remembered at the last minute that she was wearing makeup and put them back down. One deep breath in and out and then another. She prayed for patience.

"I'm glad everything has worked out so well for you. I'm happy to see that it has. If you need to talk anything through, things I can help you with, I'd be happy to do that, but I can't go back to how we were."

His nostrils flared, and his eyes narrowed. "I've done everything you asked. I waited for you."

"I didn't ask you to wait." Her patience frayed until it was a single thread. "I thought I was quite clear that we were separating."

His mouth dropped open. "For a while. That's what you said."

Had she? Had she softened the blow too much?

Not wanting to make him angry was one thing, but she didn't want to mislead him forever either. *Rip the bandage off, Lavina.*

"Come on, it's been decades. We can be friends, I hope, but we're not getting back together."

"Friends?" He looked at her as though she'd just offered him a dead rat to feed on. "You ask me to wait all these years and then just want to be friends?" Vadim stood, the chair shooting out behind him to smack into the wall. He ripped the picture of them from its nail and threw it at her like a throwing star aimed at her head.

Lavina dodged aside, but the sharp corner of the frame caught her temple. The picture fell to the hardwood floor. Glass shattered, covering the wood in razor sharp glitter.

She did not attack or leap from the chair. Instead, she remained seated, purse still on her lap. She opened it.

Vadim rushed toward her and grabbed her arm, yanking it from the bag to reveal a tissue in her hand. Lavina pulled her wrist from his grasp to dab at her temple.

Open wounds for everyone, she grumbled to herself. "I'm sorry if you misunderstood me when we broke up. I thought I'd made myself clear. You have women throwing themselves at you out there every night. Go enjoy yourself."

He let out a huff. "I do. We were on a break, I believe they say these days."

She covered her snicker with a hand to her mouth to brush away non-existent glass particles. However, they were all over her heels and on top of her feet. Reaching down, she carefully removed her shoes and wiped her feet off before turning aside to a less glass-strewn zone to put them back on.

"Exactly that. I'm happy for you. Continue to do so."

"I'd rather not join Lavina's Cast Off Club."

That got her full attention. "What club now?"

"Fane started it." Vadim glared at the closed door.

The music outside thumped. Flashing lights cast colored shadows in the crack under the door. The club night had begun in earnest.

"And who is in this club?"

"Fane and Max. I've never met Max in person. Fane looked him up. We all chat online now and then."

Lavina was glad she was sitting down. If her exes had joined forces, were they also comparing notes? Would they connect the blurred memory dots that led back to her? Her deodorant was suddenly not doing its job.

"And how long has this club been going on?"

"Probably since you dumped Fane. You know how he is with all the melodrama. He enjoys knowing he's not the only one." Vadim backed off and slumped into his chair. "We had a bet, Lavina—his bar tab now going on year forty-seven—that when you popped back up as you always eventually do, I'd be joining the club."

"Why would you take that bet? We were separated for goodness' sake."

"Because I believed in you, that you'd come back to

me. You weren't supposed to be gone so damned long." He slammed a fist on the desktop.

The water in the vase sloshed, but the bamboo remained standing. The dagger, however, bounced out of its wooden cradle. He scooped it up and regarded the glimmering blade.

"He's going to rub this in my face for a century or more. You know he will."

"That's on you and you can't do anything about it. You have rules."

"I know." But he didn't sound happy about them.

"If it was an honest bet, you'll have to honor it."

"I know!" he growled. "He's racked up quite the tab. I needed him to pay it."

Lavina checked the blood on the tissue. It was still flowing. Damn head wounds. She fished around in her purse for another tissue but came up empty. "Surely, you're not running on such a shoestring budget as that around here. Look at this place, it's packed even on a weeknight."

"Favors and goodwill are expensive." He placed the dagger back on the stand, watching her, as if issuing a dare to grab it.

Her hands were busy, and she wasn't feeling that stupid. "Do you have a napkin or something? I don't want to get blood on my shirt."

"Yeah, hold on." His dare retreated.

Vadim walked out into the hallway, closing the door behind him. For a moment, she considered leaving, but nothing had been fully resolved yet and taking off would only bring on another outburst, one that would likely be far worse and on her doorstep. Other than flinging the frame, Vadim had been manageable so far. Confident she could get things straightened out amicably without any further bloodshed, Lavina sat tight.

It was ten long minutes of staring at the void in the neat row of photos before Vadim returned with a handful of cocktail napkins. "Sorry about that." He pointed to her head. "Sometimes my temper gets the best of me."

As it had far more often when he'd first met. His volatile moods had been worth it then.

"It's nothing compared to Gabriel's invasion."

He grimaced. "I'll have a talk with him about that."

Boros hated her enough already without Vadim chastising him on her account. "I'm sure he was just doing his best to get you the answers you desired. As to this, I'll grab a snack on the way home and be fine by morning." She took in her vague reflection on the tiled wall. "Your finances, are you in trouble?"

Vadim returned to his seat and planted his elbows on his desk, leaning forward. "There's a lot of overhead, and I'm financing two charitable organizations to maintain good optics. I'd like to say it's all worth it, but Vina, I'm one big bar tab and three family bereavement benefit packages away from hitting zero." He wagged a finger at her. "Not a word of this to anyone. I've always trusted you. Don't make me regret it now."

Her shoe ground on the glass underfoot as she shifted in the chair, searching for a more comfortable position. As pretty as they were, they had nothing on her recliner at home.

As if he could see the dollar bills adding up before his eyes, Vadim winced. "Could you please not do that? It's going to scratch the floor."

Lavina slid over to the second chair where there was

less glass. Their smiling faces stared up at her from the broken frame. "I'd help you if I could, but my finances aren't secure enough to carry all of that. Maybe you could lean on a few of your regulars to chip in for the charities? You shouldn't be expected to foot that all on your own. Tell them you're grooming them for a support position within Northchester."

Vadim tapped his chiseled chin. "Perhaps. See, this is why I need you, Lavina. We can talk about these things."

Like she was some sort of consultant or therapist. Lavina snorted softly. "We're friends, Vadim. We can still talk. However, this hurts." She held up the bloody napkin. "If you don't mind, I'd like to go get something to eat so I can start healing."

"You always took too long between feedings, let yourself run dry. You would have healed already if you took care of yourself."

She got to her feet, purse in hand, ready to be out of the office and outside where she could stop pretending such nonchalance over the cut on her head. It really did hurt like hell and was still bleeding. "Yes, well—"

Vadim was out of his seat and in front of her before she could take a step. He gripped her upper arms firmly. "Before you go, as friends and all, I will need some financial compensation to cover what Fane owes me. I don't expect it all right now. We can arrange a payment plan. You're a responsible woman, I'm sure you have steadfast investments you can draw from. This situation I find myself in is your fault, after all."

It was, she supposed, but not in the way he was implying. "I didn't make that bet."

His fingers squeezed tighter.

Okay, not the time for snippy replies. "I'll see what I can do to help."

"I'm going to need more than that before I can let you leave. Make some calls or whatever you need to do. I'll get you an account number for a direct transfer."

"I said I'd help, and you said you trust me. Give me a couple of days to free up some funds."

Fond of the darker Vadim as she was, the fang-filled smile on his face now made her go cold. Apparently, she hadn't erased all the blackness after all. Not that this was the time or situation she wanted to make that vindicating discovery.

"I can't afford any misunderstandings between us this time. No decades of waiting patiently. If you want my forgiveness, for us to remain friends, you'll sit back down and make the calls. You're not leaving until you do."

She eyed the dagger on his desk, not that she wanted to hurt him, but she would have felt better with a weapon in her hands all the same. Sadly, he was closer, and he noticed her line of sight.

Vadim pushed her back down into the chair. He held on with one hand and used the other to brush her hair away from the wet napkin she still held to her temple. "So much wasted blood." He shook his head, staring at the blood smeared on his fingers.

Blood. Her blood that had made Stephanos high. She could... No, she quashed that thought. Packaging her blood to sell as a drug to vampires was a terrible idea. Her nightmares from the other night played vividly in her head. She did not want to end up a dried up husk, another bloodless body headline.

"Nathan is so much older than I remember," he said offhandedly. "Those good looks and strapping youthful body all gone in a blink to the rest of us."

Lavina went still.

"He sends his plea for you to do as I've asked so he can get back to his book with both eyes intact."

No question, she hadn't erased all of the old Vadim. While that eased her conscience a little, dragging Nathan into danger negated any relief.

"I'm going to go wash my hands and check in with the staff. When I return, I expect you to have some money ready to move."

"It's after banking hours. You know humans don't operate on our schedule."

"I'm sure you'll figure something out." He patted the top of her head and left. The door lock clicked behind him.

15

S T E P H A N O S **MEANDERED** down the street, seeking an alley likely to be harboring someone near his size that wouldn't mind being removed from this earth as long as they were given a pleasurable exit.

A beggar sat against the brick wall of a shop with a sign hanging off kilter. An empty display window revealed a few overturned metal racks inside the vacant building. The cup in his lap contained a few dollars and change. He wore a black knit cap pulled so low that it covered his eyebrows. His coat had seen better days, covered in stains and torn in several places. The rest of him was more of the same. A scraggly beard kept his neck warm, but his too short pants revealed no socks and thin legs. The soles of his shoes couldn't have gotten much thinner without his feet showing through.

Now that Stephanos was clean, the smell of the man before him was revolting. The tang of old sweat and smoke nearly made his eyes water. Had he smelled that bad? No wonder Lavina had wanted him to shower when they'd first met.

"Are you having a good night?" Stephanos asked.

The rheumy-eyed man scowled. "Drop a dollar or fuck off."

Stephanos glanced around. Another homeless person sat further down the street, a blanket pulled up around their shoulders, head tipped forward onto knees that were pulled up in front of them. Close enough to being alone. He sat down next to the elderly man.

"How about I help you out?"

The scowl melted into a more interested squint. "Whaddaya got?"

"A way out of here. To a better place. At least, that's what people tell me."

"Can't be worse than here." The coins clinked in the cup as he sat up straighter. "What do I gotta do? I only have a few bucks."

"Just sit back and relax. I'll take care of it."

He leaned away. "Uh, I ain't into that."

"You will be."

Stephanos lunged, grabbing the man's head and shoulder, bending one away from the other to bare grimy skin. His fangs sank in, puncturing deep. Though he'd fed from Steven before they'd left, he'd always had a raging appetite. That was part of his problem. Or maybe his whole problem, and why he was better off away from humans. It was safer to starve himself than sink into an over-indulging bender that Gabriel would have to rescue him from yet again.

Hot blood surged into his mouth. Drinking deep, he pulled every last drop from the tired body sagging against him. He met with no resistance. Only one quiet sigh, and then he was gone.

The other person down the alley must have been asleep or they were really minding their own business. They never moved.

With deft hands, Stephanos stripped the body of its threadbare clothes and removed his own. Once he'd folded his new clothes into a neat stack and dressed in the disguise, he gathered up a handful of dirt and rubbed it over his face, hands, neck, and into his hair. He grabbed the knit hat and pulled it on. After stashing his nice clothes out of sight, he headed off to meet Gabriel.

The pants were too tight, the waistband biting into his hips as he walked. The shoes had been too small. His bare feet slapped on the concrete with each determined step. The sooner he got this meeting over with, the sooner he could get into Lavina's bed and sink his fangs into a much more pleasurable meal, one that would keep him inside and out of sight from any humans on a vampire hunt.

Following the map on his phone, he tried to decipher whether he was going the right way or not. The damned dots kept moving as if he were walking backwards. Gabriel had been adamant about the wonders of this new technology, but Stephanos found most of it frustrating. After one more wrong turn, he gave up on the fucking dots and just watched the red pointy thing that signified his goal. Just go forward to that. It should have been easy, but there were roads, and nighttime traffic, and four rowdy young men who yelled obscenities at him from the windows of a slow-moving car. One threw an empty bottle at him. Stephanos grabbed it out of the air and threw it back. The glass hit the back window with a gratifying crack. The car sped away.

The red point brought him to a lot that was empty but for one shiny black car. The window went down.

"You're late," Gabriel said. "Get in."

"I don't have a car," Stephanos grumbled as he slid into the passenger seat and closed the door.

"You wouldn't understand how to drive one. It's complicated. Besides, you're here to do a job and then you'll be headed back home, right? What good would having a car do when you let everything around you fall to ruin?"

It couldn't be that complicated, could it? Stephanos took a moment to glance over all the gauges and the lighted display in front of Gabriel. Okay, yeah, it looked like a lot.

"Use the money I put in the account for you. Remember how to do that on your phone? All you have to do it tap it. You could take a cab or take the bus. Use one of the ride services if you can figure that out, though they probably wouldn't want you dressed and smelling like that." Gabriel's nose wrinkled.

Maybe he'd ask Lavina to show him how the money worked. Gabriel had shown him when he'd given him the phone, but there had been so much to learn.

The air was warmer inside, and it smelled like sandalwood. Now that he was seated and out of sight of humans, he leaned back and exhaled loudly.

"There are too many people here. How is Northchester so big?"

"There are cities way bigger than this one, my friend."

Stephanos shuddered. That sounded horrible. He couldn't wait to go back to Lavina's house, away from all of this.

"The world is full of so many more people than it was in

our day. The numbers are staggering. If you stayed in touch with civilization for more than a few months at a time every few years, you'd be able to keep up with all this much more easily."

"I don't want to."

"You do know that Isla would have wanted you to enjoy your years on this earth, right? All this moping on her behalf isn't going to bring her back."

How dare he bring up Isla? It was his damned fault she'd died. They should have had many more years together.

"Do not speak her name."

Gabriel held up a hand. "I'm just saying, it wouldn't kill you to live a little. You've got endless youth, enjoy it."

"I never asked for this."

"So you keep telling me, but I recall that night differently. Something about begging not to die."

While that might have been true, going on endlessly to watch everyone else die wasn't what he'd had in mind. Isla was the last one he'd let himself care about. Now existing was just being around people long enough to do what Gabriel asked of him. Except Lavina.

Stephanos studied his clean fingernails in the faint interior lighting from the dashboard. He should have gotten dirtier.

"Good god, man, would it kill you to bathe now and then?" Gabriel waved a hand in front of his face. He pushed a button. The window beside Stephanos went down.

"Sorry."

"So, are you ready to do this?"

He hoped that by taking his time getting to Gabriel, Lavina could finish her meeting and not be present when he showed up, but checking his phone, he guessed it was still too soon. How long could he drag this out before Gabriel's patience ran dry?

"Where is he?"

"The Jackyl."

"I can't get to him there. Too many people."

"Get comfortable, my friend. We're going to wait until the club closes. No public. No staff. No more delays."

"Sure."

What would Lavina do if he wasn't there to meet her where she'd dropped him off? How long would she wait? He absently rubbed at a smudge of dirt on the back of his hand. He wanted them clean again.

Gabriel pushed a button. Music flooded the interior of the car. He thumbed a control on the steering wheel, turning the volume down. The sad, slow song hung in the air like fog, filling the space between them, bringing Stephanos back to his youth in Argos. He'd loved when musicians played in the square, when he'd dance with the girls. When his mother and sister would laugh and whisper about which one he should marry. His father would try to coax his mother to dance, but her leg was twisted from an accident when she was young, and she didn't like the way she had to move. His father had never cared.

They worked in the fields for the Boros. Eirene served in their house and Stephanos trained with the other young men of the city to be a soldier in place of the Boros heir, a donation to the city guard so the newly changed Gabriel could stay safe at home while tensions grew outside the city.

Gabriel interrupted his thoughts. "Don't you agree?"

He'd not been listening. Gabriel hated that. And not agreeing. "Yes.

"Good."

What had he just agreed to? He grimaced.

"I can't believe she had the gall to drop you at the city line. And the mouth on her?" Gabriel gripped the wheel, his knuckles turning white. "Try to frame me, will she? Make sure you do her slow. We'll get her after we wake up tomorrow."

"Tomorrow?"

"I swear you'd never have made it a day after I turned you if I didn't watch out for your distracted ass." Gabriel let out an exasperated sigh. "Are you listening this time?"

"Yes."

"Alright then, I'll spell it out slowly so you can follow along." He held up three fingers. "One. We're waiting here until the club closes. Two. When we get to the club, you'll kill Vadim and leave his body out for the sun so we can be sure he's gone. Three. We go back to my house to sleep so you don't get lost again before we take out that Arandine shrew."

"Got it."

How was he going to get out of killing Vadim with Gabriel right there with him? If he could manage to keep her alive, Lavina was going to be so angry. She'd never let him back into her house.

They sat listening to quiet music, watching traffic go by and the moon travel overhead. Stephanos tried to relax, to wipe his thoughts clean so he could focus on the problem of defeating an older, likely more powerful vampire, but he kept thinking about Lavina. She could handle herself. She'd be fine, annoyed that he kept her waiting for sure, but she'd give up on him after an hour or two and go home. He checked his phone. No calls. Then it occurred to him that she didn't have his number. Useless fucking thing. He was about to drop it on the floor when he remembered he had a game he could play. That would pass the time and help his mind unwind. He settled back and matched colored blocks until the car's engine startled him out of his trance.

Gabriel pulled out of the lot and onto the road. "We'll get the car parked outside The Jackyl so we don't stand out."

"Okay."

"You'll want to charge that." Gabriel pointed to a cable snaking out from the compartment between them.

Stephanos plugged the phone in and set it down. Not that he'd have any use for it since he didn't have Lavina's number either.

Traffic was light at this hour, most people having to get up for work in the morning. Gabriel glanced over at him repeatedly as he drove.

"You could stay here when this is done. For a while. If you want."

"Why?"

He watched a red light, chewing on his lower lip until it turned green. "You don't have to go back to that house by yourself. It's not good for you."

"Since when do you care what's good for me?" He'd been doing jobs like this on and off for centuries.

"I may not have always been the best friend, Stephanos, but I remember us before. Don't you?"

They'd played together as young boys, while his parents had been in the field, while Eirene learned her first job as a kitchen girl. A playmate for the Boros boy. That's what Gabriel's mother had demanded. And so there he was, in the yard with a boy he could never win against, never talk back to, or his parents would suffer.

"Yes, I remember."

"You took my place with the city guard. I haven't forgotten that. It could have been me bleeding out in the street instead of you."

"The sun would have taken you first."

Gabriel nodded. "You saved me, and so I save you."

"Maybe I don't need saving anymore."

"Look at you. You definitely do." He pulled into the half-filled lot across from The Jackyl. After backing into a spot that offered a good view of the place, he turned the car off. "Tomorrow, when Vadim is gone, and this city is mine, there will be plenty of room for someone like you."

"Plenty of work, you mean." Of course, that's what he meant. He needed a strong arm, and that was what Stephanos did.

"That, yes, but also, I need someone at my back that I can trust. We could get you cleaned up. Find you a nice place. Maybe even a car," he added with a wink. "There would be steady work." He nodded toward the club and the bouncer standing at the door in the shadow of the overhang.

What would it be like to have something to do every night? A reason to get up. People to talk to. A simple job unless other tasks came up. He mulled that over and wasn't immediately opposed to it. Given enough time, and assuming he could find a way out of killing her, Lavina might forgive him or at least allow him the chance to explain why he'd done what she'd asked him not to. And if Gabriel did just as good of a job as Vadim, maybe she'd be agreeable to letting him have a taste of her sweet blood now and then.

"Taking over for Vadim, you think that will be easy? No one else will to try to step in?" Stephanos asked.

"If no one else has had the balls to take him out after all this time, they won't be a problem for me either."

That seemed optimistic, but who was he to argue? He hadn't lived here and moved among these vampires. Not knowing their strengths and territories or what duties they performed to retain Vadim's favor, he had little information to work with beyond what Lavina had given him.

No line of eager humans stood outside this time, though the colored lights and thumping music were still going. The windows revealed a scattering of people still inside. To pass the time, he tried to match the people with the cars outside. The big bouncer probably drove the giant white pickup truck. A blonde girl and a redhead staggered out the door. He placed his bet on the blue, boxy car covered in daisy stickers. Wrong. They walked two cars further down to a red minivan. So much space for two small women. Lights flickered on the back, and it pulled out of the space, straight back into the car across from it with a loud crunch. He winced and noticed Gabriel doing the same.

"Someone's gonna be pissed. That's a nice car," Gabriel said.

If he might have a car of his own one day, Stephanos supposed he should pay more attention to them. What made a car nice? He glanced around, spotting one that was sleek and black, shiny in the parking lot lights. And familiar. Lavina's car. Shit, what was she still doing here? She should be home fuming about him not meeting up with her.

Gabriel checked his phone. "Twenty minutes until close. Give the staff another forty to clear out, and then you can get to work."

16

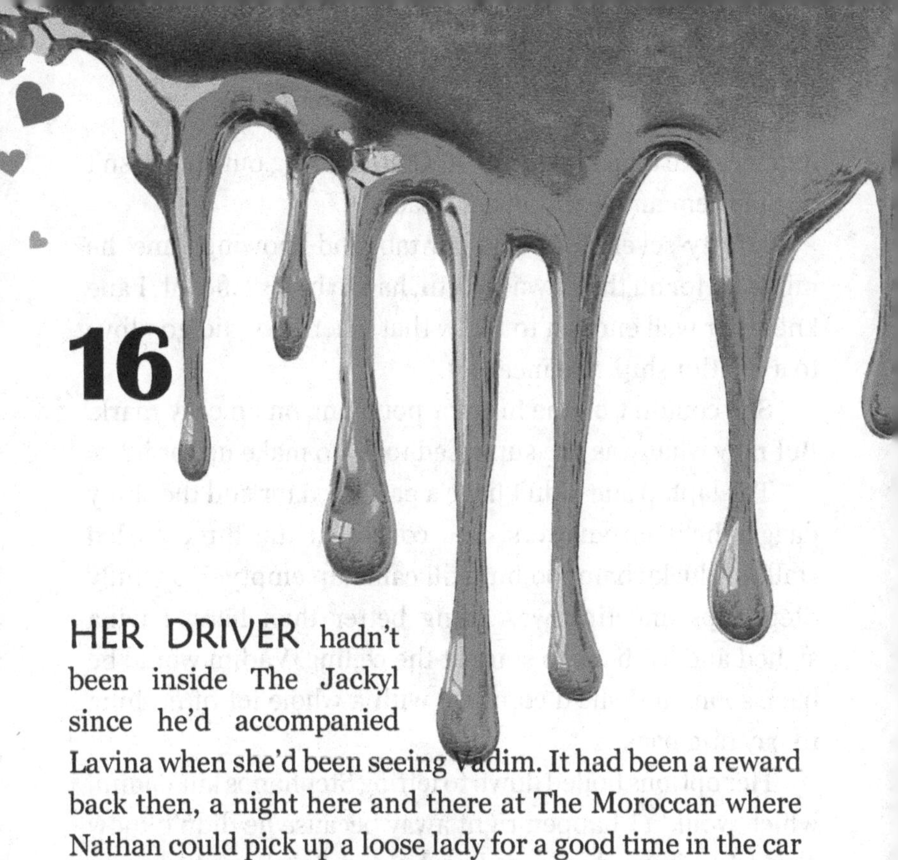

HER DRIVER hadn't been inside The Jackyl since he'd accompanied Lavina when she'd been seeing Vadim. It had been a reward back then, a night here and there at The Moroccan where Nathan could pick up a loose lady for a good time in the car while he waited to drive Lavina back home. She'd bought his drinks and aimed pretty girls his way. He'd been a handsome young man who had turned into a dignified gentleman, and he deserved his retirement and as many books as he could get lost in before his eyes shut for the last time. How dare Vadim drag that poor man into their little spat.

Fuming, Lavina planted herself in Vadim's chair with her feet up on his desk. She considered smashing his laptop out of spite, but he'd probably expect her to pay for that too.

Stupid men and their idiotic bets.

Though she lived a comfortable life, she did so by investing and being conservative with her spending. A good deal of her funds were in separate accounts for her staff. Those funds were not tied to her in case something bad should happen, like a fucking Cast Off Club figuring out she wasn't one of them and wanting her dead.

A forty-seven-year long bar tab, and knowing Fane, he milked it for all that it was worth, had to be significant. Fane knew her well enough to know that when she said goodbye to a relationship, she meant it.

She couldn't blame him for pouncing on an easy mark. But now what was she supposed to do to make up for it?

The laptop she didn't have a password for and the shiny dagger held no answers. She consulted the three curled stalks of lucky bamboo but still came up empty. Hopefully Stephanos' meeting was going better than hers. Lavina sighed and sat back to stare at the ceiling. Vadim would be back soon, and she'd come up with a whole lot of nothing to pay him back.

Her options boiled down to letting Stephanos kill Vadim, which wouldn't happen right away because he didn't know about her immediate need and she didn't have his number. Why didn't she have him listed as something vague like Wild Man in her contacts for emergencies such as this? Then again, even if she could figure out how to make it out of the club alive, she'd be driving herself because blind or dead Nathan would be of little use.

The thought of being without the faithful man made her sniffle. Damned Vadim better not harm him.

It had been a long time since she'd driven a car. All the high speeds and haloed headlights made her anxious as hell. Day driving was one thing, but she wasn't often out during the day, being a faux vampire and all.

The other option was to bleed some more and let him taste it. And pray that it had the same effect on him as it did Stephanos. Then maybe she could talk high Vadim into letting her go and figuring out his financial situation on his own. As long as he didn't remember what made him high to begin with. Stephanos had remembered with hungry clarity.

Unless...she could convince Vadim that the results weren't because of her blood. The blood was just a carrier for a drug, something she'd ingested before coming here. Yes, she could make this work.

Lavina plucked the dagger from the stand and dumped the lucky bamboo and water into the trash. Letting Stephanos bite her was a spontaneous choice. She had no urge to offer Vadim a go at her neck, especially not in his unpredictable mood.

Using the dagger, she cut a short vertical slit in her left wrist, catching the flow in the now empty vase. The sight was kind of funny, she considered distantly, the sight of her own blood making her lightheaded. Once she had a shot glass worth of blood in the vase, she pressed the remaining napkins to the cut.

Deciding not to antagonize the situation any farther, Lavina left the vase on the desk and returned to the silver chair with less broken glass around it. A quick scrounge around inside her purse yielded two hair ties that she slipped over her wrist to hold the napkins in place. She kept her hand elevated against her chest and looked everywhere but at the blood until Vadim finally came back.

"So, what do you have for me?" he asked her back as he walked in. His steps slowed as he approached his desk. "What's this?"

"Something better than money. Go ahead, take a sip."

He picked up the vase, tipping it side to side, and then holding it up to the light.

"Lavina, are you trying to poison me?" Vadim laughed and started to let go.

If he dropped her offering on the floor with the other shattered glass, she was going to be so angry that she might go for the dagger to stab it into his heart after all.

"Do not drop that!"

His other hand came up to steady his grip on the vase.

"What is it that has you so pale, Lavina?"

"Blood, you idiot. Specifically, a new drug that affects vampires. How long has it been since you were able to get high? Like really high, not just the mild buzz off a drug-ridden human?"

Vadim placed the vase delicately on the desk and sat.

"Tell me more."

"Take a sip. That will tell you all you need to know."

He kept his hands close to the vase but made no move to pick it up. "This blood came from your veins."

"Yes. The drug is in my system. It can be transferred in blood."

"You do not seem under any influence."

No, she did not. She swore silently. Thinking fast, she glanced around the room for inspiration. As before, nothing helpful popped up. Was there anything useful in her purse? She opened it, peering inside. Nothing there inspired her either. Nothing... Oh! There we go.

"It hasn't kicked in yet. I took it in pill form when you walked out. I take it a lot, so it doesn't hit me quickly anymore. It's totally safe though, I swear."

Vadim watched her for a moment. "Where did you buy it? Why haven't I heard about it?"

"Not in Northchester. I have a supplier who flies it in from Greece. My connection," she said firmly. "I've been keeping it to myself for years. I could share it with you now and then, when I can spare a little."

"Share it with me. Just me." He eyed the blood before him. "Intriguing, but that doesn't help my finances. Let's test this first before we talk business."

Yes, let's. Lavina, on the edge of her seat, waited for him to toss back the shot of blood. She'd know in seconds if it hit him like it had Stephanos. She was already working on how she'd talk her way out of his office and past the beefy bouncer he'd no doubt ordered to keep her back here.

Vadim pulled his phone out of his pocket. He made a call. "Yeah, Onriel. I need to see you in my office. Yes, right now."

No! If he had someone else to watch her while he sampled the blood, she couldn't work her magic to get Nathan peacefully released so both of them could walk away. Maybe she could take on one of the bouncers, but he picked the big ones who wrestled drunk humans into submission on a regular basis, and they'd be expecting her to fight. There'd be no element of surprise on her side like she'd had with Stephanos. When the doorknob turned, she twisted around to see what fate had dealt her.

A pretty blond-haired man with an elfin face and build walked into the office. Oh hallelujah. Lavina grinned. He wouldn't be any trouble at all.

"What can I do for you?" Onriel asked.

"I have a blood sample I'd like you to try. Take just a taste to be safe. I've been told it's not tainted, but you can't trust anyone these days." Vadim glared at Lavina.

Her grin vanished. This wasn't going how she'd wanted it to at all. What the hell was she supposed to do now?

Apparently Onriel didn't have any trust issues because

he dunked his finger into her blood and stuck it into his mouth with zero hesitation. He licked the blood-coated finger like it was a rare delicacy.

"Smooth, rich, and oooooh, what's this? Oh! Oh my." Onriel's bright blue eyes grew even brighter and his grin wider. "This is fantastic."

Hoping to salvage the situation, Lavina revived her grin, making it match Onriel's. "See, I told you. You really should try a taste."

Vadim gave her a disdainful look. "I don't dabble in recreational drugs these days. You'd know that if you'd been around."

He used to be fun. Hoping to maintain the ruse, she kept her annoyance to herself and went with a lighthearted giggle.

"May I?" Onriel licked his lips as he eyed the remaining blood in the vase.

Vadim nodded. "Please do."

The waifish vampire downed the shot with glee. He spun around, arms wide, nearly hitting Vadim in the head. His exuberance earned him a hard glare.

"Get out of here. Go enjoy that on the dance floor." Vadim shoved him toward the door.

Onriel threw his head back and let out an uproarious cackle. He fumbled with the knob a moment before managing to exit, laughing all the while.

"How much of that can you get me?"

Lavina feigned good-hearted confusion. "You just said you don't want it."

"No, I said I don't want any for me. I do want to sell it. How much can you get me?"

Well fuck, that hadn't been her plan at all. "I'll have to

talk to my supplier and get back to you."

"Leave whatever you have on you, and I'll let you take Nathan with you tonight."

"I can't leave him here. He's human. An old man. He needs to sleep."

Vadim held out his hand. "Then hand over what you've got."

"I only had the one I took."

"Vina." He tsked. "Just when I was starting to trust you."

What the hell was she supposed to do now?

"Let's go, dump it out." Vadim pointed to her purse.

Thank the heavens she hadn't packed any weapons, or anything else of worth, for that matter. Lavina opened her purse and dumped the contents onto his clean desktop.

Nail clippers, brush, the last wadded up tissue she'd been hunting for earlier, cosmetics, a few loose dollars, a quarter, and two dusty pennies. She gave the purse one last shake. Nothing else fell out.

"Guess I'm keeping Nathan. Clean that up, and then you can go. I'll see you back here tomorrow. Same time. Don't be late."

"Sure." Frustrated beyond measure, she barely kept up her act, helped only by being able to shove everything forcefully back into her purse rather than look him in the eyes that she wanted to spit in.

"Can I get the key from Nathan?"

"He's already tucked in for the night by now. Let's not disturb him."

A chill ran through her. What did that mean?

"You shouldn't drive while under the influence anyway. The cops wouldn't like it. Be a shame if they pulled you over and kept you in one of those nice cells with a window while you sobered up."

Thinking back to his comment about favors being expensive, she had a feeling he had policemen in his pocket. Would he be that big of a dick to call the cops on her? As erratic as he'd been tonight, she couldn't rule it out.

With her belongings scooped back into her purse, and the haphazardness of their order grating on her nerves, she headed for the door, making sure to wander a bit like Onriel had.

"I'll see you tomorrow night then." She waved and headed into the hallway, shutting the door behind her. The burly bouncer gave her an unamused, flat stare. Who farted on his dinner?

She gave him a wide berth and entered the gyrating chaos of the dance floor. It wasn't as shoulder to shoulder as it had been the night of the big party, but she got elbowed and hip-checked several times before she made it to the door. The chilly night air offered no relief to the fire burning in her chest.

The line of humans was just as long as it had been earlier. The door guy paid her no mind. She was the same as his boss, allowed privileges and a blind eye in most things.

He had better be treating Nathan well. The two of them had been on good terms back in the day. Lavina glanced up at the three-story building that housed The Jackyl. The upper floors were apartments, all owned by Vadim. Nathan was likely in one of them.

She pulled out her phone and called him. He answered before the first ring ended.

"Don't do anything foolish, ma'am. I'm well enough."

"Well enough, meaning unharmed?"

"As long as you cooperate, according to the muscled cretins who brought me to this room."

"I'm working on it. Get some rest. I'll have you out and back behind the wheel by tomorrow night."

"That would be much appreciated, ma'am. Enjoy the rest of your evening." He ended the call.

Lavina shook her head. She wouldn't enjoy a damned thing until he was freed and he knew that. One of her favorite things about the old man was his calm head. Whether he was withholding any harm he'd taken on her account in favor of keeping her calm too, was a revelation for another day. There would be consequences if that was the case. She gave the building a long glare, as if it would give Nathan up to appease her, but it did not. Hoping for the best, she turned to the street and hailed a cab. Maybe Stephanos would have some ideas for how to get out of this mess when they met up. Hopefully he wouldn't keep her waiting long with the meter running.

Now she just had to figure out how to explain the wound on her face and arm to him. And why she looked even worse off than she had before despite her promise to get a good meal tonight. How many lies could she juggle?

17

THE LAST customers had been herded out the door. The Jackyl was closed for the night, the front door locked. Five of the staff had already left, and only a few cars remained in the parking lot.

"There are always a few here overnight," Gabriel assured Stephanos. "People too drunk to drive. The last two guys should leave out the back soon. They're parked back there."

"What if Vadim leaves too?"

"He won't. He lives upstairs. The third floor is all his."

"You want me to break in and take him out up there?"

Gabriel nodded. "Keep it quiet. There are tenants on the second floor. We'll use their entrance in the back. They should all be sound asleep by now if they don't already have earplugs in to sleep through the club music."

"Quiet. Got it." Whatever the hell earplugs were.

Ten minutes later, the front of the club lights went out. One light was still on in the back. It stayed on.

Lavina's car was still in the lot. If she was upstairs with

Vadim, he was going to have some tough choices to make. It was one thing to attempt screwing up the job to buy some time to figure out what he wanted to do, but if Gabriel was right there with him, that would be impossible. And if Lavina was there too? Gabriel would demand that he do them both. His stomach twisted into a tight knot.

"Let's go." Gabriel reached up to hit a switch and then opened his door. No lights came on.

Reluctantly, Stephanos got out of the car.

Gabriel was already halfway across the parking lot. Stephanos hurried to catch up. They walked around the building to the back.

"Doesn't matter if we're on the security cameras. I'll erase them when you're done."

"Security cameras?" When he'd arrived in Northchester, Gabriel had stuck him in a room with a television for three nights with instructions to watch everything and learn. Compared to the last time he'd had to touch society, it was an easy way to pick things up, but there had been so much. Everything moved so quickly, and though he'd relearned English several times, there were more new words than ever before.

"Never mind. I'll take care of them. Come on." Gabriel led the way to a covered entrance at the back of the club. He pulled out a key and put it in the lock. "I've been waiting for this. Picked up a key months ago off one of the bouncer buffoons and made a copy. He magically found his key the next day, so Vadim didn't change the locks." Gabriel grinned as he pushed the door open.

They walked into a room similar to the front of the club. A locked, heavy-looking set of glass doors with metal running through them protected the inner club. A lit stairway on the left revealed the way to the second floor.

Gabriel slipped the key back into his pants pocket and started up the stairs. Stephanos stepped quietly behind him. They made it to the landing without incident.

As they turned the corner and headed up to the third floor, Stephanos scrambled for a plan. Could he nudge Gabriel into joining him in the fight with Vadim to give Lavina a chance to get away? There weren't enough stairs to give him more time to think.

At the top, a long, wide, window-lined hallway led off in either direction. The inside walls either way were solid. Ah, so that's how he maintained appearances and safety. Light shown in from the parking lot across the street and the stairway, but the space was otherwise dark.

"You'd think this access was harder to get, but it turns out it just took an invite up to see a painting I was interested in purchasing from his collection. Sometimes being civilized and friendly has benefits," Gabriel said over his shoulder with a meaningful gaze.

"That's what you do. Get me inside so I can do what I do."

Gabriel entered a code on the panel above the knob. It clicked. He pushed the door open. "He's all yours."

This was not the time for hesitation. If the older vampire had heard the click, he might be waiting to pounce. Stephanos rushed into the suite. Gabriel waited by the door but in full observational view. No backing out now. Sorry, Lavina.

Stephanos slowed as he walked further into the wide, open space of the main room. Paintings lined the walls, like a gallery, but the lighting was too dim to make them out. In the middle sat a scattering of chairs, two couches, and a few low tables, one topped with a tall vase filled with lilies that were too sweet. They made his nose itch. A hallway in the middle of one long wall drew his attention. It had a door at the far end. The rest of the suite was likely behind it. Hopefully it wasn't also locked.

He approached the door with caution, listening. No voices. Maybe he was fortunate, and Vadim had left with Lavina in his own car. Maybe they were off enjoying the rest of the night somewhere, and Gabriel would have to wait for another time.

Stephanos desperately hoped that was the case when he wrapped his fingers around the knob and twisted it. The door opened. Dammit, why couldn't it be locked so he'd have to make too much noise, giving Vadim and Lavina time to flee? Or fight back? Or...

Vadim burst from the darkness before him, bowling Stephanos over with the elder vampire on top. He didn't see the gun before he heard it and felt the bullet enter his chest, but yep, there was a gun in Vadim's hands. Good thing Stephanos had blood to spare.

The pain grounded him, making him forget about not trying to kill the vampire who was taking aim for another shot. At least he could say it was a fair fight if Lavina asked. If she would speak to him after this.

Stephanos twisted his hips, knocking Vadim off balance. The shot went wide, hitting the tile next to his shoulder. Knowing the gun could hurt but not kill him, he surged up, grabbing it from Vadim's hands. He threw it toward Gabriel. Maybe his sire would kill Vadim so he wouldn't have to. Lavina already didn't like Gabriel.

While he did pick up the gun. Gabriel just nodded to Stephanos as if urging him to get on with it. Sure, he wasn't the one bleeding.

Stephanos made a grab for Vadim, but the other vampire was light on his feet and danced away. He backed up, retreating further into the unknown as if drawing Stephanos in. Gabriel was watching. Resolved to see this job through, Stephanos took the bait.

Once through the short hallway, the space opened up into a living room, still large and similarly decorated, but not as expansive as the gallery. A kitchen and dining room lay off to the right, another hallway to the left, this living suite running perpendicular to the entire gallery room.

Aware Vadim was heading to the kitchen where numerous pointy weapons would be available, Stephanos lunged for him. He got his hand around Vadim's ankle, hauling the other vampire back from the brightly lit room.

Vadim kicked with his loose foot, catching Stephanos in the nose. More blood gushed from his face. With determination, he crawled up Vadim's flailing body, finally pinning his arms down with his thighs. Stephanos glanced over his shoulder. Gabriel wasn't inside yet.

He leaned in close to Vadim's ear only to get a fang in his cheek for the trouble. "You're not going to like this, but I don't want to kill you. Play along, and maybe you'll live."

Vadim stilled. When Stephanos pulled back, he was met with a confused gaze.

"Thank Lavina if you're alive tomorrow," Stephanos whispered.

Gabriel's footsteps came closer.

Vadim bucked, fighting to get free. Stephanos slammed his forehead into Vadim's nose. A satisfying crack gave him a little retaliatory satisfaction. While Vadim was momentarily stunned, Stephanos reared back, baring his fangs. He grasped Vadim's chin, wrenching it to the right to give him room.

Knowing this was Gabriel's favorite part, he met his sire's gaze before tearing into the flesh beneath him. He made a messy job of it, as he always did, playing the feral part well. Ripping flesh away with his teeth, clawing deeper with his dirty hands. He spat the sour vampire taste out.

Vadim was not playing along, or maybe he was, but Stephanos couldn't blame him for instinctual self-preservation. The elder vampire clawed at Stephanos' face and chest, making every effort to pry him away. Sour blood dripped from his mouth onto Vadim. It puddled on the floor around him, flowing freely from the gaping wound in his neck. He'd torn half the meat and muscle away. The white of his spine peeked through.

"Stephanos, not too much," Gabriel cautioned.

If he beheaded the vampire, that would be that, but Gabriel never allowed an easy end. He liked the sun to finish them, to destroy the body, erasing the vampire from the world as if they'd never been. He liked them weak and on the verge of death, helpless, begging. The hard way would give Vadim a chance.

He leaned in for another bite. "Where is your phone?"

Vadim struggled weakly, the blood loss taking its toll. For a moment he didn't think the dying vampire understood him, but then he felt something hard against his leg. Stephanos let go of Vadim's other hand and took a big bite out of his chest while he pocketed the phone. He spat out the glob of flesh and stood.

Wiping his mouth on his sleeve, he turned to Gabriel. "Enough?"

His maker grinned and nodded. "Just right. Such an

animal. That's your gift, Stephanos."

Was it? He wasn't the one leaving vampires out in the sun to die. Well, not the one ordering it, anyway.

"Bring him down." Gabriel checked the time. "We've got about an hour to get home."

"Give me a minute. I want to make sure he didn't have anyone else up here that might cause you trouble tomorrow."

"See, that's why I want you to stick around." Gabriel came closer, gleefully standing over Vadim. "Tomorrow, Northchester will be mine."

Vadim glared up at him and bled profusely, too weak to do anything else.

Stephanos left Gabriel to his gloating and darted down the far hallway to find two bedrooms and a bathroom. All of them were empty. He wasn't sure if he was relieved or more concerned. With only moments before Gabriel would come looking for him, he took out Vadim's phone and scrolled down to Lavina's number.

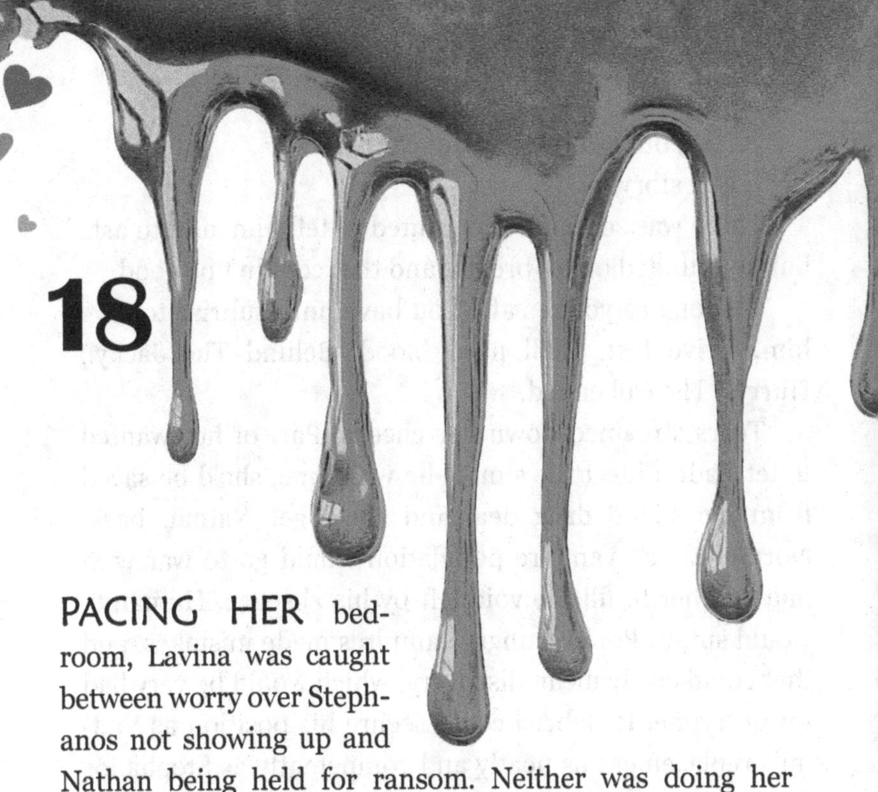

18

PACING HER bed-room, Lavina was caught between worry over Steph-anos not showing up and Nathan being held for ransom. Neither was doing her nerves any favors. She should be exhausted, but she was too tired to be tired.

Her phone rang. Vadim's name flickered to life on her screen. This close to dawn? That couldn't be good news. Praying he wasn't calling to tell her one of his meathead bouncers hadn't accidentally done Nathan irreparable harm or that they had seized Stephanos, she steeled herself and answered.

"Lavina?"

Stephanos' voice took her aback. "Why are you calling from Vadim's phone?" The answer her brain supplied a sec-ond later made the floor fall away from her feet. She sat on the edge of her bed. No wonder he hadn't met up with her.

"Stephanos, please tell me you didn't kill him," she begged.

"Close, but no. Why is your car here?"

"Long story."

There was so much she wanted to tell him, and to ask, but he sounded out of breath, and that couldn't be good.

"As long as you're safe. You have until sunrise to save him. Drive fast. He'll need blood. Behind The Jackyl. Hurry." The call ended.

Tears streamed down her cheeks. Part of her wanted to let Vadim meet the sun. If he was gone, she'd be saved from her blood drug deal and she'd get Nathan back. Northchester's vampire population would go to war with one another to fill the void left by his absence. Humanity would suffer. Power-hungry vampires made mistakes, and that could easily mean discovery, which would be very bad for everyone. If Gabriel could secure his position as Vadim's replacement as neatly and competently as Stephanos hoped he would, that would minimize the risk, but could she hinge everything on Gabriel after dealing with him herself? He likely wanted her dead whether he assumed power or not.

Rescuing Vadim would put him in her debt, hopefully voiding his threats. One thing that was guaranteed was that he'd want to retaliate against Gabriel, and he would not want Lavina dead. Saving Vadim it was then.

"Trina!" she yelled. "We need your car."

She threw a hoodie over her t-shirt and a pair of sweats over her boxer shorts. Rescuing vampires did not require a bra. Shoes in hand, she ran out of her bedroom and into the kitchen.

Trina was already on her feet, scrambling for her purse. "What's the emergency?"

"Get some towels. Maybe a tarp. Yes, a tarp. In the

garage on the shelf by the side door. Hurry!"

Without question, Trina hurried into the garage with her purse on her shoulder and keys in hand. Lavina was hot on her heels. With the folded tarp in her arms, Lavina slid into the backseat. Trina took the front and hit the garage door opener. They were on the road within five minutes of the call.

Breathless, Lavina watched the sky with worried eyes. The darkness was already retreating. "Faster!"

"Getting pulled over is only going to delay us."

"It's a matter of life or death. Drive!"

Trina's car sped down the highway. Thankfully they were ahead of the commuters who would be clogging every road into the city once the sun was over the horizon. She clutched the tarp.

Vadim would need to feed right away. Like hell was she going to let him take one sip from her and discover she was the drug he sought. That left one trustworthy option.

In light of her yelling, she tried to phrase the necessary question more calmly. "How do you feel about providing an emergency meal for a wounded vampire?"

The grimace on Trina's face in the rearview mirror revealed her true answer, but she said, "If it's necessary."

"I'll see that you're compensated. Or he will."

"Thank you, ma'am."

Her thoughts wandered to Nathan. Hopefully the poor man was safe.

"Thank you, Trina. I don't say that often enough." Her staff deserved every perk she could provide.

They pulled into the back lot of The Jackyl with seventeen minutes to spare. Nothing seemed out of place. Where the hell was he?

Panic rising, she jumped out of the car and frantically searched the lot. Then she spotted blood drops. A thick trail of them. She followed them to the space between two cars in the tenant spaces.

"Over here!" She waved her hands, catching Trina's attention. "Bring the tarp."

Trina gasped at the sight Lavina was trying desperately to avoid looking at. Her peripheral vision told her he'd been nearly decapitated. Half of his neck was missing. Wounds, bite marks, her brain informed her, covered him from chin to chest. What kind of animal had done this? Her brain informed her of that answer too. She shoved it away, not wanting to acknowledge it right now.

"Help me get him into the tarp. We need to cover him before the sun rises."

Trina unfolded the tarp alongside the unconscious vampire. Together they rolled his limp, bloody body into it.

"Hurry, bring the car over here." Lavina gently pushed Trina away.

She covered Vadim's body and looked into the face she'd once loved. "You were a dick tonight, but you don't deserve this."

His eyelids moved. They lifted only halfway before slipping closed again.

The car roared to life and backed up toward them. "I take it you can hear me."

His eyelids quivered.

"Good. I'm taking you to my place. I don't suppose you can tell me where Nathan is?"

His mouth opened, but nothing came out. Which wasn't a surprise, considering several inches of his esophagus were missing.

One hand moved inside the tarp. She pulled the edge aside so he could raise his arm. He pointed upward and held up two fingers, then four.

"Thank you."

His hand landed on hers and squeezed weakly.

"Yeah, you're welcome. We'll call ourselves even as of now." She put his arm back inside the tarp and covered him completely.

"Trina, help me get him in the trunk."

Trina got out of the car and opened the trunk but looked hesitant. "Can't we put him in the backseat? If I'm to feed him, I mean?"

"Sorry, you'll have to get in with him. The sun will hit him in the back seat."

"But..."

"He'll make it worth your while." She squeezed the tarp over his shoulder. "And he'll only take what he needs to hold him over until we get home. We'll get another feeder who's more agreeable once we get there."

"Yes, ma'am." She said the words, but her heart clearly wasn't in it.

Trina helped Lavina lift the limp vampire-filled tarp into the trunk. Vadim wasn't a small man, and as dead weight, it wasn't an easy task. Compact cars didn't have six foot tall vampire sized space with the spare tire, jack, and Trina's go bag.

Lavina pulled the bag out and checked the horizon. Too much pink. "I'll put this up front to give you more room. Hurry up, get in."

"Are you okay to drive? It's a stick, do you know—"

"Trina, I was driving when all cars were manual. I think I can handle it." Sure, it had been a while, and no, she didn't like it, but she'd muddle her way through. Like riding a bike, right?

Trina had never met Vadim, so she had no knowledge of the man she was about to curl up beside and bare her neck to. Introductions were the least she could do in the few minutes they had before the vampire could potentially combust. "Trina, this is Vadim. He owns this building. We used to be a thing. Vadim, this is Trina, my... well, she does a lot. If you hurt her, I will put you back outside to burn. Am I clear?"

The tarp rustled. Good enough.

She gave Trina a hand to get inside and then closed the trunk over them. Glancing up at the building, she considered grabbing Nathan, but assuming he truly was unharmed, he'd be sound asleep for a while yet. She had the threat to him with her and Vadim needed the safety of a sunless room with from Gabriel's grasp.

She tossed the bag in the back seat and then she sat in the front, taking a minute to remember what her hands and feet needed to do. It took only two tries before she got the car out of the parking lot and onto the road. Lavina rolled down the window and enjoyed the sunrise with the cool breeze flowing around her.

Once he recovered, Vadim would take his revenge on Gabriel. She'd repaid her debt, Gabriel would be dead, Stephanos would be free. Everything would be good. She got on the highway and headed home.

19

GABRIEL WAS already up and moving. Stephanos wished the day had been longer. Endless would have been ideal. He wasn't prepared to see Gabriel lose his mind when he learned Vadim was still alive. Nor was he anxious for Vadim to show up to exact his revenge. Stephanos may have spared the elder vampire, but he'd been none too gentle about it. Assuming Lavina had saved him. Uncertainty left him feeling unsteady.

A finger poked him in the arm. "Get up already. We have work to do."

Stephanos sat up on his stiff mattress on the floor of Gabriel's safe room. Not his own room. Not a bed. This had never bothered him before but having enjoyed Lavina's hospitality, these details now grated on him.

"We? I did my job."

Maybe it would be best for him to leave town. Surely Gabriel could book a flight for him tonight. If he left now, he wouldn't have to deal with any of the fallout. He could go back to the house he'd shared with Isla and sleep as long as he wanted.

"I'm done. I'm leaving."

Gabriel pouted. "I was hoping you'd stay. We work so well together."

Did they? It seemed like he was the one who got shot and bloody last night. Like he was the one who carried the heavy, bloody body down the stairs and out into the parking lot.

"Can I ask you to stay for a few days at least? Help me get established, and then you can go on your way."

There was only one kind of help he was good for. "You have more bodies that need to be taken care of?"

"I might. We'll know in the next few days." The way he said it, like it was something he thought Stephanos would be excited about, made him even less willing to agree.

"I'll think about it while I take a shower."

"Oh, thank the lord. Yes, go. I'll have a feeder waiting for you by the time you get out."

Stephanos nodded. They'd arrived just before sunrise and hadn't had time for any of that before they slept. At least the worst of his wounds had healed overnight with the blood he'd enjoyed at Lavina's. Steven. He'd appreciated the young man's company and the reciprocal nature of their transaction. So much better than a scared-stiff slave.

Gabriel owed him for a job well done—at least until he'd learned that it hadn't been done. "I'd like a willing one."

His maker laughed. "What do you think this is, The Jackyl?" He paused, tapping his chin. "I'll tell you what, you take what I give you tonight and once we get the club open under my management, assuming you stick around, you have my permission to dine on all the willing you can find there."

That was more concession than he'd ever been given before. He didn't want to say yes until he found out if Vadim still lived. "I said, I'd think about it."

"You'll say yes," Gabriel said confidently.

Now he wanted to decline out of spite, but there were too many unknowns to make a decision yet. "Where might I find this shower?"

"Oh, right. You've never used it," Gabriel said dryly as he opened the door and spoke to the slave outside. "Andrew will show you the way. He's also offered to feed you, haven't you, Andrew?"

The boy was maybe fifteen. Most of Gabriel's slaves were young. Kids he'd picked up off the street who were at first awed by his generosity and then too scared to leave. Stephanos had watched Gabriel drain a girl dry in front of them because she'd gone out in the yard—too close to leaving for his liking. When they behaved, he provided them with food, clothes, entertainment, and rooms in his giant house. At night, they fed Gabriel and enjoyed the drug-like benefits. It wasn't a terrible arrangement, considering how the Boros had treated their slaves in his human years.

Andrew kept his gaze on the carpet. "Would you like to drink now or after?"

"After. You don't want to be near me like this." Vadim's dried blood covered his tattered, already pungent clothes.

Andrew merely nodded and led the way to a modest bathroom. It had all Stephanos needed, but from the limited space and generic furnishings, it was clearly not the same one Gabriel used. It was probably for the kids.

"Get me something clean to wear."

Andrew nodded. "I'll be right outside."

Stephanos peeled off the disgusting clothes and dropped them in the trash. Then he took a long, hot shower, remembering to wash his hair. After drying with the thin towels, he opened the door to find Andrew waiting with clean clothes.

Eager for answers so he could decide to stay or go, he dressed, ran a comb through his hair and even brushed his teeth to get the sour taste of Vadim out of his mouth. Feeling somewhat refreshed, he stepped out.

"Where can we sit?" he asked.

"Sit? You can drink here if you'd like."

"I'd like to sit," he said firmly.

Andrew, still averting his gaze, nodded and brought Stephanos into a room just down the hall filled with chairs, a giant television screen, and numerous game consoles. Right, he was one of the slaves too, not welcome in Gabriel's spaces. Sadly, he had more in common with these kids than his sire. Except he no longer had to avert his eyes. He'd given that up after Gabriel had made him. They were friends just like they'd been for years, but not exactly equals. He'd never be that.

Once Stephanos was settled in a wide recliner, the largest seat in the room. Andrew stood fidgeting beside him.

"Just sit here with me already."

The boy sat stiffly on the arm of the chair, holding his head cocked to give Stephanos access. He bit gently, drinking and savoring more once Andrew relaxed. His saliva sent Andrew off into his bliss. Stephanos drank deeply and then stood, settling the boy into the chair where he could comfortably enjoy his reward.

He'd just found his way back to Gabriel's room when his sire met him in the hallway. "Holy shit. I haven't seen you... like the old you, in so long. It's like going back in time." He clapped Stephanos on the back. "Let's go celebrate at The Jackyl with a little private party, shall we?"

"What if we're not welcome there?" Going a day or two without injury sounded nice after getting shot the night before.

"Who's going to stop us? Besides, I can't wait to see that parking spot filled with nothing but ash."

"The men who worked for Vadim might have something to say about your walking in and taking over."

Gabriel chuckled. "That's why I have you beside me."

So much for an injury-free day. Stephanos sighed. "Then let's get this night over with so we can both sleep easier tomorrow." For more reasons than Gabriel was aware of, and that he wisely kept to himself.

"That's the spirit. Really, my friend, Northchester looks good on you. I hope you'll stay."

He looked like he meant it, and maybe he did, but he'd been just as charming with others and then asked Stephanos to kill them days later.

When they arrived at The Jackyl and parked in the back, Gabriel got out, scowling at the filled spot with Vadim's name on a sign. "That spot is mine now. I'll have to find his car key and move that monstrosity."

The monstrosity in question was an orange sports car that sat low to the ground with absurdly thin tires. Stephanos crossed that off the list of kinds of cars he should want.

It did not surprise him one bit when Gabriel jogged over to the spot where they'd left Vadim the night before. Both of the tenant's cars were gone, but a dried bloodstain remained.

He bent low, peering around. "I don't see any ash."

"Wind probably blew it away already. It's been out here

all day."

"True." Gabriel grinned and help up his key. "Let's head inside and see what fun awaits us."

"Sure."

Stephanos was more than happy to let Gabriel go before him. After all, he had the key to the back door. And if anything unpleasant, say a revenge-filled vampire and his ex-girlfriend, waited for them, Gabriel would meet that first. He'd pick a side when he got the lay of the land.

Once through the back door, the rear club door was already open. The waitstaff was busy pulling chairs off tables and preparing for the night's business. A few over-eager humans had already lined up outside to be the first to get in when the club opened in an hour and a half. Fools.

One of the tall, muscled men noticed them and hurried over. "The boss isn't down yet. I can let him know you're here, Mr. Boros."

Gabriel put on a friendly smile. "That won't be necessary. I'll be in his office if he should show up." He fluttered his fingers at the interior of the club. "Carry on. Looks like it's going to be a profitable night."

The man nodded without comment and returned to helping a woman stock the bar.

"I love that they know not to question us. Vadim trained them well." Gabriel headed for a hallway along the wall, past the bathrooms.

The door marked private wasn't locked. They went inside. Shattered glass and a photo lay on the floor in front of one of the chairs across from a black desk. Gabriel sat in the chair behind it and flipped the laptop open.

"They think he's still upstairs, so they've not checked the security footage. He's got to have access on his laptop or maybe his phone. Did you see his phone upstairs last night?"

"No, I was kind of busy." And when he'd carried Vadim outside, he'd slipped Vadim's phone back into his pocket in the hopes of gaining a little favor in case the elder vampire did recover.

"Right. Let's see if I can get this to work for us." Gabriel's fingers danced nimbly over the keyboard.

Stephanos scowled. He'd been feeling accomplished with his leap into current technology and managing to get his finger on the correct tiny letter on his phone one at a time. Using both hands at once was confounding.

Gabriel laughed. "What a simple man, he used the same code as his door upstairs. I'll just go in and delete that from the cloud so no one can access it remotely."

Sure. Whatever the fuck any of that meant. Seeing Gabriel had that under control, Stephanos pondered the gap in the row of photos on the wall and the broken frame beside his feet. The photo of Lavina and Vadim made his mouth go dry. Was that blood on the corner of the frame? He picked it up and discreetly took a lick while his sire was occupied with the computer.

The hint of a rush that lit in his veins confirmed his fears. She'd been hurt. Had something happened to Lavina? Was that why her car had still been in the lot the night before? At least he knew she was alive since she'd answered his call.

"I need a drink. I'll be right back. You want something?" Stephanos asked.

Gabriel's quizzical stare made him pause. How quickly he'd fallen into relaxing around Lavina, feeling halfway human again. But he wasn't around Lavina now.

"No, but thank you. Send someone in to clean that up

while you're at it." Gabriel pointed to the glass on the floor.

"Sure."

Stephanos dropped the broken frame in the garbage can beside the desk. Was that blood on the tip of the dagger on the desktop? It looked like it had been hastily cleaned. The water in the vase next to the dagger held a pink tinge. He spotted blood drops on the desktop, some smeared, having been wiped over, but others near the laptop had been missed. Three stalks of drooping bamboo sat in the blood-tinged water. His concern for Lavina surged. He shouldn't have given Vadim's phone back. Then he could have at least called her to make sure she was alright. Maybe if he thought hard enough, he could recall the number that had been on the phone screen when he'd dialed the night before. Try as he might, all he could remember was that there was a two and a seven. That got him nowhere.

He left Gabriel to his clouds and remotes and wandered back into the club. The staff glanced up at him but then went back to work without the disdain or insults he was used to whenever he was near humans. As he passed by the mirrored wall filled with glass shelves of liquor bottles, his reflection answered his conundrum. Ah yes, he was clean and dressed in nice clothes, like one of Vadim's guests.

What he did not actually want was a drink from behind the bar or from one of the humans. He wanted to stare out the front window and not see Lavina's car in the parking lot, to know she'd made it home with or without Vadim.

He made his way closer to the front wall, quickly giving up all pretense of a leisurely wander so his muscles could hopefully relax. There were six cars out there now and none of them were black. Lavina had left. Wherever she'd been the night before when he'd called her from Vadim's apartment, she was safe. Or at least not here and in immediate danger from Gabriel. Hopefully, his sire had other things on his mind than the mouthy female vampire who had called him out on his plans.

"Looking for someone?" asked a woman wearing a cut off t-shirt with The Jackyl's logo on the front and a pair of skin-tight leggings. Her curly brown hair was pulled up into a ponytail on the top of her head, baring her neck for all to see. Stupid human.

"Not really. Just waiting for him." He nodded toward the back hallway where the office was.

"Can I get you anything?"

Now that he knew Lavina wasn't here somewhere, his nerves could use a little something to take the edge off, especially in light of the taste of Lavina still tingling on his tongue. He needed to keep his head straight until he figured out what he was going to do with Gabriel, Lavina, and possibly Vadim—assuming he was still alive.

"No, thanks." Not like he had money...but Gabriel had said he did, on his phone somehow. "Wait." He turned on the phone screen and pointed to the square picture of a V on the screen. "Can I pay with this?"

She smiled widely. "Yep. What would you like?"

"I don't really know. It's been a long time."

"Most of the boss's friends like wine, but," she looked him over with a critical eye, "you look like a bourbon man."

He smiled, remembering Lavina mentioning something about that too. "Maybe?"

She giggled, touching his shoulder. "The boss likes it."

If Vadim liked it, it couldn't be that bad. Unless it was like his car. "Sure, I'll have that then."

Stephanos sat on a stool at the tall table in front of the

window. The girl returned in minutes with a short glass with one large round ice cube surrounded by brown liquor. He could smell it before she set it on the table in front of him.

She waited while he took a tentative sip. The pleasant oaky flavor washed the tingle of Lavina away. The taste of plums and honey followed as the warmth trickled down his throat. Not the thick heat of blood, but satisfying in a different way.

"What do you think?" she asked.

"I like it."

She flashed him a beaming grin and held out a black rectangle. "Just open your app, tap your phone there, and you'll be all set."

He must have looked lost because she did whatever opening the app was and tapped his phone for him. "Let me know if you want another. I'll be right over there." She pointed to the bar where a cutting board, knife, and a clear container of limes waited.

Alone, he sipped his bourbon while the opening crew bustled around him. Hundreds of years had passed, and still people went about the same things: eating, drinking, and serving others. The workers chatted with one another, laughing and joking. They all looked healthy. None of them seemed scared, or like they were here against their will. Would that continue once Gabriel took over?

The man who had first greeted them said something to the others about the boss being late. He eyed the back entrance where the stairway was. Stephanos finished his drink and returned to the office.

Catching sight of the scowl on Gabriel's face, he stayed in the open doorway. "They're saying Vadim's late. Odds are they'll start looking for answers soon. What should we tell them?"

"We?" Gabriel looked up and closed the laptop. "I'll take care of it. Why don't you go upstairs and clean up the mess you made. I might stay in my new apartment tonight."

Stephanos nodded and took the scrap of paper with the door code number Gabriel offered. Lingering in the hallway, he hung back while Gabriel addressed the workers.

He clapped his hands once, gaining their attention. "Vadim was called away on business. I'll be supervising tonight. Carry on as usual."

Confused, Stephanos waited until Gabriel returned. "I thought you were going to take credit for Vadim's murder?"

Gabriel's entire face scrunched. "Why on earth would I do that? He's gone. I'm taking over. That was the plan. The plan was not to incite an investigation or get arrested. Smooth, my friend, that's the way to do it. Just stepping in to help, and then maybe a family emergency causes Vadim to settle back home in Russia."

"Oh."

"Leave this to me. Go clean and when you come down later, find a pretty one and take her upstairs for some fun. You deserve a night off. The spare room, mind you."

Gabriel had an entire estate. Part of Stephanos had hoped that the apartment might be his, the place of his own Gabriel had mentioned. On the other hand, if Vadim might still be among the living, not being the one claiming ownership to the place might be the better move.

"Sure." Stephanos headed up the back stairs to the third-floor suite. He found a bucket and a scrub brush under the sink and got to work.

20

TRINA HELPED Lavina carry Vadim through the garage and into the house. Ideally, she would have housed him upstairs in one of the guest rooms, but Trina was wobbly on her feet after feeding Vadim in the trunk on the way home. There was no way the two of them would make it up the stairs with the dead-weight of the helpless vampire.

"We'll put him in my room."

At least feeding from Trina had healed him enough to stop his grievous wounds from bleeding, but there was still a lot of oozing and seeping from the gaping holes in his neck and chest. Lavina shuddered. Vadim had a lot of healing to do, and from the looks of the carnage, it wouldn't miraculously happen in one day.

Lavina pulled her nice linens off the bed and into a pile on the floor. After spreading out three towels, they hoisted Vadim off the tarp and onto the mattress. Trina brought in an older blanket from the linen closet to spread over him. Not that he would care about the temperature, but it masked some of his wounds. For that, Lavina was thankful.

She got him as comfortable as one missing most of their neck might be and stepped back. He opened his eyes a crack, just enough to confirm he was alive.

"Sleep now and heal. You're safe here."

Wanting the full story before she let her anger get the best of her, Lavina pulled out her phone and dialed Vadim's number. Ringing under the sleeping vampire made her swear.

Why had Stephanos given the phone back? How was she supposed to yell at him for what he'd done? If she ever saw him again, she would... Hmm, maybe that's why he didn't keep the phone. Maybe he didn't want to talk to her. But he'd called. He'd given her the information she needed to save Vadim. Chasing her thoughts in circles wasn't helping anyone.

She closed the door and stepped away from the room with Trina beside her. "Go to bed, my dear. It's too late to get a feeder over here tonight. Vadim will be out until tomorrow evening. I'm going to drive back and get Nathan before anything else goes wrong, and then when we're all back safe under one roof, I need to sleep."

As if she could think about sleep with her emotions running rampant.

"Yes, ma'am. Thank you." Trina stumbled off to her room.

The drive back into Northchester took twice as long now that the work commute was in full swing. When she arrived, everything was quiet in the rear parking lot. Thankfully.

Using the key she'd taken from Vadim, she opened the back entrance door and headed up the flight of stairs to the second floor. For all his faults, Vadim was a good landlord. The hallway was well lit and the floor tile clean. The mostly unmarred walls were painted a calming shade of pale green, not too minty, more mossy. She approved.

At the door marked with a painted ornate number four, she knocked softly. "Nathan, wake up," she called through the door loud enough that she hoped he could hear her without being obnoxious to the paying neighbors.

From the heavy, uneven footsteps inside, she gathered he'd heard her. The door opened to reveal a blinking Nathan. "Ma'am?"

"I'm here to bring you home. There's been a situation. Vadim has voided our arrangement. You're free to go."

"Very good. The lighting here was horrendous for reading in bed."

She chuckled. Little ruffled the old man. He'd seen too much in his time working for her. "So glad to see you're well. I'd be quite upset if he'd harmed you."

"The boys downstairs were a bit rough, but they let me bring my book and they gave me a nice dinner. I'm ready for my own bed though, if you don't mind."

"As am I. You have the car key?"

He pulled the fat key from his coat pocket and held it up.

"I'll meet you there. I borrowed Trina's car." She headed for the stairs.

Nathan grabbed his book and then gently pulled the apartment door closed and followed.

"Don't be alarmed when you get home. Vadim will be staying with us for a couple of days. He's currently using my room."

Nathan's bushy white brows rose. "Are you getting back together, ma'am?"

She took to the stairs. "Oh, no. No. Just, well, treat him

nicely while he's with us, yes?"

"Of course, ma'am."

"Thank you, Nathan."

Just as she opened the door to the parking lot, he reached out to tap her arm. "Thank you for coming for me. I was afraid that you might have suffered at his hand. I'm glad all is well."

It was far from well, and she had suffered, but sometimes vampire business was better left unexplained to humans. His concern warmed her heart and further confirmed that she needed to treat him well in his later years. Perhaps even spoil him a little. She smiled to herself as she got into Trina's car.

Pulling around the building, she waited to watch Nathan make it across the street and into the car in the lot before getting to the street herself.

When she arrived home, she greeted Rosa and informed her of their houseguest, warning her to keep the boys away from him. Then she checked on Trina, finding her sound asleep and no worse for wear after having fed Vadim. Nathan arrived minutes later. She locked up after him, shooing him off to his room next to Trina's. She considered taking one of the guest rooms upstairs, but really, she wanted her own bed after the whole ordeal. It didn't even matter who was in it with her.

Lavina quietly opened her door and gathered up the bed linens she'd piled up earlier. She spread them out on the side of the bed not occupied by day-coma-sleeping Vadim. Already in comfortable clothes, she locked her bedroom door and tunneled under her blankets.

Her sleep was fitful, interrupted by urges to check on Vadim, to worry about Stephanos, and to wonder if Gabriel would come after her when the sun went down. When she finally felt Vadim stirring, she gave up the pretense of sleeping. The only benefit of spending the day in bed was that her temple and arm had healed. Small blessings, she supposed.

Before he fully woke, she went to use the bathroom. Funny how all these years later, she sank right back into the routine of hiding her humanity under the noses of vampires as if she'd not taken a hiatus at all.

She emerged from the bathroom, freshly showered, teeth brushed, and an excuse ready so she could get to her appointment to get her fang fixed in forty minutes. Getting the last appointment of the day had been fortunate. She didn't want to chance missing it because of traffic.

Vadim held out his arm, but was otherwise unmoving.

"I'm right here. What do you need?" She realized that was a stupid question the moment it came out of her mouth. "Besides the obvious, I mean."

Looking at him was a stomach-turning endeavor. She tried to focus on his eyes and nothing below them. He pointed to his mouth.

"Feeding. Yes, I'll get someone ordered up and have Trina bring them in. I have to run out for a bit. I'll check on you when I return."

He held out his phone. It was dead.

"I'll charge that for you. At least you can still text people, right?"

His eyes narrowed.

Okay, probably not the time to be lighthearted or look for the bright side when he was in so much pain. "Sorry. I'll be back."

After making extra sure to close the door so no one

else had to see that horror, Lavina handed the phone off to Trina with directions to charge it and order a feeder for Vadim. Nathan, privy to her calendar, was waiting with the car ready.

The appointment went smoothly and with her faux fang back solidly in place, she felt more confident about her vampire disguise. Lavina returned home.

Trina was waiting for her in the kitchen, her face and stance tight. "He's been fed. He's asking for you."

"Asking? He's talking already? That was fast."

"No, ma'am. Texting. I know we're not supposed to go in, but with him like that... I escorted the feeder inside and gave Vadim a charging cable. He's been at it since he was at two percent. On the bright side, he was considerate with the feeder so you'll get no complaints there."

"That's one good thing." She sighed. "I can't wait to see what he has to say. Thank you, Trina."

Nathan came in, sitting with Trina at the counter bar. They launched into a discussion about whatever book he was reading. That apparently, they both were reading, if she overheard their discussion correctly. She chuckled. The had an employee book club.

She opened the door to her bedroom to find Vadim propped up in her bed, her nice pillows behind him. At least he wasn't bleeding on them. "What's got you all in a mood, other than the obvious?"

His gaze snapped to her, his lips drawn into a tight line. The feeding had helped. His neck was slowly knitting back together, but it was a long way from done. Vadim tapped on his phone and then held it out to her.

She came closer until she could read the lengthy note-pad file labeled: **Lavina.**

Thank you.

How many people know I'm here? Who drove us here if Trina was in the trunk with me? It was day.

Lavina didn't look any farther down his list, her gaze locked onto the second item. "It wasn't day yet. Close. You needed blood. Trina was the option I had. I drove. We made it back just as the sun was coming up. No one but my household knows you're here."

His brows lowered further. He took the phone back and scrolled down to type more and then held it out.

That was reckless. You could have killed us all if the sun came up while we were on the road.

"Yes, well, it didn't." She shrugged and took a seat on the edge of the bed. "We didn't have time to get another driver and still make it back in time."

Should have stayed at my place.

She shook her head. "Where you were attacked? And you call me reckless?"

Gabriel Boros.

"I know. Stephanos, his..." What was he? Henchman? Assassin? Thug? "His whatever, called me to get you."

You know his name, the one who attacked me? Killed my men at the club?

How did she want to answer that? "We talked when I extracted him from The Jackyl, when I drove him out of the city. I gave him my number in case he needed help getting further away, like out of the country."

He said he wasn't going to kill me because of you. Lavina, a man doesn't do that because you offered to help him get a plane ticket.

Whatever Gabriel had ordered Stephanos to do, he hadn't gone through with it because of her? Warmth blossomed in her chest. Aww, he did care.

"He's not a bad guy, Vadim. Gabriel Boros, though. I have nothing good to say about that one. I can't believe you befriended him. I thought you could read people? Couldn't you see he wants all that you have? Surely you weren't blind to that."

Vadim scowled so hard his nose creased, and she swore his left eye twitched. He typed madly, glanced up at her, and then shook his head the fraction his half a neck allowed. Wincing, he typed again.

Not a bad guy? He ate my fucking neck, Lavina!

"Okay, fine, there's that, but come on, Vadim, you're no angel either."

His eyes about bugged out.

You slept with him? The feral? WTF

Perhaps Vadim could read her a little too well. "I'm a single woman. I can sleep with whoever I want. And really, you should thank me. He didn't kill you, did he?"

Vadim grimaced, squeezed his eyes closed, and then let out an empty huff. He held his phone out with the list back at the top and pointed to number one.

"Yeah, you're welcome." She read further. Her mouth dropped open. "He had the nerve to show up at The Jackyl tonight like he could just step in for you? Seriously? The balls on that one!"

He nodded, more of a rocking backward and forward than moving his head.

"What do you want me to do about it?"

Already texted Juanito. They'll roll with it to keep the doors open for now. Need the money. Hell to pay when healed.

"I bet. Can you do me one favor, since you owe me for

risking the sun to save you?"

He blinked once. Twice.

"Do your worst to Boros, but leave Stephanos out of it? He's only following his sire's orders."

Have you seen my neck? I'm going to pull his fangs and wear them on a necklace for the rest of my days.

While she was happy to see the old, vengeful Vadim was alive and well, just perhaps buried deep, she did not approve of this particular target.

Lavina stood and thrust her hands on her hips. She leaned in close to his face. "If you pull his fangs, he'll die, and I will be very angry. Am I clear?"

His stare-down lasted so long she thought he'd fallen asleep with his eyes open.

"Fine, mess him up a little. He did tear you up pretty badly. But nothing permanent, and no fang pulling."

He typed again and held the phone out. Gaze steady, he watched her read.

New deal: The life of one feral vampire for twenty doses of your drug a week in perpetuity.

"A week?" She panicked. Handing over two pints of blood a week? Her body couldn't sustain that. "Ten, and as I said, you can mess him up a little, but nothing he can't heal from."

Thirty.

"Now you're just being a dick. I can't do twenty, for fuck's sake, and you want thirty? You know what? Get out of my bed and my house. And good luck wrestling your life back from Gabriel Boros!"

She grabbed his phone and tossed it onto the far side of the bed. Angry as she was, she wasn't heartless enough to smash it like her temper wanted to do. Life was about compromise, like placing it out of reach where it would hurt like hell for him to grab it.

Lavina stormed to the door and pulled it open with every intention of slamming it shut.

He clapped loudly.

She spun around. "What?"

He held up ten fingers.

It was a shitty deal and Stephanos would owe her, but she took it. "Fine. You have a deal."

21

GABRIEL HAD assured Stephanos business at The Jackyl would pick up after ten, but it hadn't. No one enticed him to take them upstairs to enjoy the use of Vadim's guestroom, where he'd spent the last few nights. There was only one woman he wanted to see, and she wasn't here.

Tiffany, the waitress who had elected herself as his personal server since he'd chatted with her about bourbon three days before, approached his table.

"Are you sure you don't want another?" She batted her long lashes and flashed her dimples.

"I'm sure." Two drinks took the edge off the flashing lights and noise. Three removed him too far, leaving him with only thoughts of all the shitty things in his long life. Four did not bring things around. It just made him want to lie in bed and stare at the ceiling until the sun came up. He was starting to long for his dank basement in Scotland where he could do all of those things without spending any of Gabriel's money, possibly further indebting him to his sire.

Rather than go away, she leaned against his table. "You said your business here would be done in a few days. Will you be heading home soon?"

He cursed the lack of a crowd to keep Tiffany occupied. She was always chatty before they opened and sought him out when she was on break. Like he was her new best friend. He wasn't.

"I may leave tomorrow."

He really needed to talk to Gabriel about that. He was sick of sitting around the club with nothing to do. The staff didn't need his help. No one had caused any sort of ruckus over Gabriel stepping in for Vadim during his supposed business trip. The couple of vampires that had come in looking for Vadim had met Gabriel in the office with Stephanos lurking behind them. They'd accepted his story with only a few questions.

Not that he'd hoped to have to bloody his hands, but he was bored and not needed.

Tiffany pouted. "I'll miss talking to you. You're a great listener."

He was great at occasional nodding and tuning out the jumble of conversation he only half understood. The first night he'd gone upstairs early to watch the television with the intention of learning more of the words these people were using. Fifteen minutes into it, he realized it didn't matter if he was going home soon, so he went to bed to stare at the ceiling.

In fact, that sounded good right now too. He'd talk to Gabriel and then go enjoy the soft bed because his sire was going to get bored with this club and the apartment soon enough and want to go back to his estate. Stephanos had no desire to sleep on the floor again.

"Goodnight, Tiffany."

Her smile wavered. "Look, I know English isn't your first language, but in case you didn't pick up on it, I'd be happy to go upstairs with you. They don't need me down here tonight. It's dead and the tips aren't worth it."

Was that why she kept talking to him? He looked her over. If she worked for Vadim, she was safe to feed from. He hadn't eaten in days, but he wasn't starving. Maybe after he'd fed, he'd be in the mood for all she was offering.

"I need to talk to Gabriel first. I'll find you when I'm ready?"

Tiffany nodded enthusiastically. With a light step, she took his empty glass with its lonely ice ball to the bar and struck up a conversation with the young man working there. Stephanos caught her pointing at him and grinning during her conversation. He sighed. Might as well get this talk with Gabriel over with so he could decide he was taking anything on the flight with him tomorrow night beyond the newer, nice clothes on his back from Vadim's closet. The man had better taste in his clothes than in his car.

Stephanos knocked on the half-open office door.

"What now?" Gabriel called out.

He slipped inside. "I was thinking I would maybe return home tomorrow."

Gabriel glanced up from the laptop. "Home as in my estate? Is the room upstairs not to your liking?"

"Home to Scotland. You don't need me here."

His sire spun the laptop around and pointed at the screen. "Look at this."

Stephanos peered at the columns of numbers. The rows and sums meant nothing to him.

"He was nearly broke! Can you believe it! I was supposed to be stepping into a fortune here. Instead, I'm going to have to do a complete overhaul of his business model." Gabriel continued ranting, waving his hands in the air and pointing at various numbers on the screen.

The two drinks Stephanos had enjoyed were doing their job but not helping him understand a damned thing that might get him past this conversation and on a plane. He sat in the chair across from the desk and stared at the empty nail on the wall just over Gabriel's shoulder.

"And no one is interested in taking on more responsibility or stepping into a city leadership role to cut bribery costs. It's fucking ridiculous. Why wouldn't they? It's not like I'm asking them to give up anything. They'd benefit, for heaven's sake."

Nodding was only going to get him so far. "Aren't city jobs during the day?"

"Don't be a smart ass," Gabriel grumbled. "I'm not sending you back to Scotland yet. Fane is coming in tonight, and that bitch, the one who can't keep her mouth shut. I may need you to take care of them first."

"The one who pulled me out of here?" he asked, all thought of Tiffany erased from his mind.

Gabriel nodded. "We'll see if she'll come around now that her pal Vadim isn't here to back her up. The little weasel Fane will do whatever doesn't get him dirty, but if she doesn't cooperate, we'll take her out to the dumpster and leave the lid open to the morning light."

"When?"

"Any time now. Why don't you go watch for them by the front door? Bring them back yourself."

Stephanos nodded. He left the office and headed for the front door.

Tiffany stopped him, running a hand over his chest and smiling. "Are you ready to go upstairs?"

"I don't—"

"Don't keep the girl waiting. Do you have somewhere else to be?" Lavina stood with one eyebrow raised and her arms across her chest.

Stephanos froze. She shouldn't be here. He didn't want to take care of Lavina the way Gabriel wanted him to.

Tiffany turned to glare at Lavina before tugging at Stephanos' shirt and taking a step toward the back of the club. He gently pried her hand away. She was a nice girl, even if she talked too much. He didn't want to see her hurt either.

"Change of plans. You should probably head home for the night. It will be safer there." He gave the waitress a push toward the back door.

Fane came up behind Lavina, the two of them of similar height and build. While he had no idea if Fane could put up any physical resistance, he knew Lavina could. One of Vadim's rules Gabriel had agreed with was not to make a vampire scene in front of the blood bags.

"Gabriel is waiting for you." He held out his arm, inviting them to head toward the back hallway.

"Fane, go ahead. I'll be along in a minute."

The male vampire did not go ahead. He took three steps away to allow them a modicum of privacy and waited with a scowl firmly planted on his delicate features.

Stephanos was vaguely aware of the eight girls laughing and dancing on the dance floor to a robot-sounding high-voice singing over a throbbing drumbeat and screeching sounds. All of it grated on his nerves. If it weren't for the impending meeting with Gabriel, he would have invited

Lavina to talk outside or upstairs, or anywhere far from this club.

"You didn't have to tear his throat out!" she hissed over the music.

He couldn't meet her eyes. "It's what he expected me to do. What he likes me to do."

"You're not his rabid beast on a leash."

She'd seen him before, filthy, in rags. "Aren't I?"

"Break the chain, Stephanos. He doesn't deserve your loyalty."

What was she going on about? "He made me."

Lavina shook her head. "He *made* you miserable." She eyed the back hallway. "I'd assure you that Vadim sends his thanks, but I'd be lying. He has agreed not to kill you...for a price. You can thank me later."

"How is he?"

"Angry. Very, very angry. I wouldn't recommend going into that office right now."

"What?" He spun around to find Fane blocking his way.

With the music thumping, he couldn't make out any sounds from the rear hall. Was Gabriel yelling for help? Was Vadim already inside exacting his revenge? His body went cold from head to toe. Was he already too late?

"I'd recommend staying right where you are," warned Fane.

Stephanos knocked the male vampire aside. Lavina's hand landed on his shoulder briefly, but he wrenched himself away and rushed toward the office. Two of the brawny bouncers burst from their post by the rear door to block his way.

Stupid humans. He grabbed one by the neck. The other beat him with fists while the one in his grasp flailed, trying desperately to dislodge his hand.

"Let him go, Stephanos," ordered Lavina. "Gabriel Boros does not deserve your sacrifice. He's been using you for centuries."

Let him go? He couldn't do that. They'd been together since they were children. Gabriel was the one constant in all his existence. His friend.

Stephanos squeezed harder. The bouncer's face turned red. His pounding on Stephanos' arm grew weaker.

A fist hit his face with an impact that made him sidestep and drop the man. Lavina rubbed her knuckles and glared at him. "Ouch!"

Fane appeared beside her again. Stephanos had gotten close enough to the office to make out the sounds of a fight going on inside. He had to get in there.

The noises were suddenly wet. His gut screamed at him to join the fight, to protect Gabriel.

With single-minded focus, he rushed Lavina and Fane. Knowing which side was weaker, he shouldered Fane hard, separating their wall just enough that he could use his momentum to wedge through. The blood-spattered walls in the office brought him to a sliding halt on what appeared to be intestines.

Gabriel, on the floor, near torn in half, opened his mouth, reaching out, screaming silently for help. His throat had been sliced by the dripping dagger in Vadim's hand. He turned toward Stephanos.

"Perfect timing," Vadim rasped. His throat was still missing skin, bright pink and raw, muscles moving in plain sight. The rest of him appeared fully recovered. Unfortunately.

"Is Fane outside?"

Was Vadim asking him? Was he not going to attack? Had his mercy or Lavina's deal gained him such a boon?

"Yes?"

"I can't exactly yell for him." Vadim gestured to his throat. "Do you mind?"

Stephanos glanced down at the entrails under his shoes. Rather, Vadim's shoes—a fact Vadim also seemed to be realizing.

"Seriously? Is that my shirt too?" Vadim growled. The hand holding the dagger rose, making a slash in his direction.

With the floor a bloody mess, Vadim was forced to advance slowly lest he slip and fall.

Stephanos put all his weight on the foot still on blood-less floor and backed away until he bumped into another body. Peripheral vision informed him it was Fane. He grabbed the smaller man and pulled him forward.

"Here." He shoved Fane into the gore-strewn office.

Gabriel made choking noises. His hands trying to press his neck back together like it would help him talk.

"Get a garbage bag and scoop that up," Vadim rasped, nodding to what remained of Gabriel.

Stephanos wanted to flee. But Gabriel was helpless, his arms and legs all akimbo, throat cut, stomach ripped open. He'd need weeks to recover, and he'd never get that chance if left here with Vadim. Maybe he'd be easier to grab if Fane was allowed to do as Vadim ordered. Which meant he was left standing in the doorway, uncertain if he was about to be gutted next.

Fane grimaced at the mess. "This will ruin my shoes."

"Buy new ones," Vadim rasped.

With a groan, Fane leaned out into the hallway and

yelled for someone to bring him a big garbage bag.

Lavina was at Stephanos' back a minute later, with a black plastic bag nearly as tall as her.

"It would be in your best interest to get in there and help him clean up," she suggested in his ear as she handed him the bag.

"Gabriel will think I've betrayed him."

"Is that better than ending up like your friend on the floor?"

That was debatable, but with a bag in his hand and a dagger-wielding madman in front of him, he didn't have time to mull it over. This was going to require a lot of explaining once Gabriel recovered.

22

VADIM WAS not at all recovered, but anger had fueled him enough to channel the part of him Lavina had thought long gone. Decades of misplaced fears flew out the back door. She hadn't ruined him at all. Well, certainly filed down the rough edges, but look at him, all murderous rage from head to foot.

He may have gone good on the exterior, but his dark, gory center was fully intact. She nearly grinned to see it, but the pure misery on Stephanos' face dialed back her glee.

Lavina locked gazes with Vadim, her brows raised in question. Their deal had allowed for some physical retribution against Gabriel's weapon, but Vadim didn't appear to be making a move to collect on that for the moment. Not that she was eager to see Stephanos bloodied. She rather liked him whole and clean. He looked good in Vadim's high-end clothes. Far better than he had in her thrift store finds.

She stayed in the doorway, blocking the view without having to go in and get filthy like the three men were. She could almost see dollar signs adding up over Fane's head as he calculated the replacement costs of everything he was wearing. He pulled off his watch and slid it into his pocket along with his two rings and a gold bracelet. He probably would have asked for gloves if he could have without being ridiculed.

"Do they need any help in there?" asked a bouncer from the end of the hallway.

"We've got everything under control, but could you maybe bring a mop and bucket? There's been a spill. Thank you."

Fane and Stephanos picked up Gabriel's broken body. While it looked like Stephanos had intended to use the bag as a stretcher, Fane opened it with one hand and tipped Gabriel's legs into it. With both hands free, he pulled the bag up, enveloping all that Stephanos helplessly held.

"You can't..." he protested.

"Toss that into the dumpster where it belongs," Vadim ordered.

"Don't. You can't do this. He needs help," Stephanos pleaded.

Fane yanked the bag from his bloody-handed grasp. The Gabriel-filled bag sloshed through the gore on the floor as he pulled it toward the door. "Bag open or closed?"

"Sun or buried unfed in a landfill?" Vadim tapped his chin. "How would you like to go, Boros?"

Taking pity on Stephanos, Lavina suggested, "Landfill."

If she slipped Stephanos the information on how to track Gabriel's phone, he might be able to rescue his sire. Eventually. If he were so inclined. She hoped he wouldn't be.

Stephanos sent her a grateful, albeit helpless and lost, glance. His gaze seemed fixated on the bag.

"Help him carry that out. No blood on the club floor," Vadim ordered.

No doubt hoping for a chance to get a few words in to Gabriel, Stephanos cautiously made his way across the floor to help Fane. They disappeared down the hallway.

Hearing the screech of wheels behind her, Lavina turned to find the mop bucket had arrived. She pushed it into the office doorway and left it there. This wasn't her mess. The men could deal with it.

Vadim was already kicking the worst of the gore into a pile. Was that one of Gabriel's fingers? And there was another one. She turned away, focusing on keeping anyone from getting too close. A waitress came back to use the bathroom but ventured no further down the hall. That's when Lavina realized the music was quieter and the only conversation she could hear was from the employees. Chairs slid onto tables. Someone called goodnight to the others and walked out the back door.

Fane and Stephanos had been out there too long. How long did it take to heft a bag of liquid vampire into a dumpster? Did the bag split open? Those damned things were so thin these days. Anything to save a few production cost pennies.

A dropped or burst bag would make quite the mess in the parking lot...that one of the human employees had just walked out into.

"I'm going to check on them." Lavina closed the office door and headed outside.

A pair of brake lights and the sound of a car's engine at the far end of the back lot revealed the human's location. The back lot lights illuminated Fane's outline. He stood facing the tenant parking spaces and he no longer held the bag, but he was holding something. She did not see Stephanos.

Heart beating wildly, she hurried over to Fane.

"They won't kill him," Fane's deadpan voice informed her as the sounds of a fight reached her ears.

She realized he held the shirt and shoes Stephanos had been wearing.

Lavina ran into the dark corner opposite the dumpster, where the sounds were coming from. Where multiple arms were swinging. Where legs were kicking. Stephanos lay on the asphalt, covering his head, knees drawn up.

"Enough. Get away," she screeched, shoving the nearest attacker aside with no regard for hiding her strength.

He staggered two steps and toppled sideways, landing on the ground. Now in the light, she recognized him as one of Vadim's vampire regulars. These others likely were as well. He'd called in reinforcements. And here she'd thought she had the situation under control, having agreed to pulling Fane in to assist. Vadim had planned to hurt Stephanos after all, just mercifully, not in front of her. How kind of him. She cast a disgruntled look over her shoulder at Fane, who had to have been in on it.

"All of you, inside. Help Vadim clean up," she ordered as if she had full authority to do so. One of them listened, helping the one she'd flung aside to his feet. The other one did not, he kicked Stephanos in the head one more time before snarling in her direction. She didn't flinch.

Looking disappointed, he followed the other two. They joined up with Fane and went inside. She knelt beside the groaning vampire.

"Can you get up?"

He unfurled slowly, wincing as he did so. Bone protruded from one forearm. One eye was already swelling shut. He might have been bleeding, or it could have been Gabriel's blood.

On his knees, he wavered for a moment before getting one foot under himself and then the other. He stepped into the light. She gasped. They'd stabbed him repeatedly all over his chest and back. While he was upright with his entrails safely encased inside, they had no doubt been perforated multiple times.

The deal had been honored, but he'd be in pain for days. Just like Vadim had been. Fair play, when it came down to it.

"Come on. Let's get you in the car. I'll have Nathan come around. You're not getting far on your feet." Standing close in case he needed to hang on to her, she texted Nathan.

"Get him out," Stephanos said through clenched teeth.

Her canned answer of not being strong enough on her own to do that didn't make it past her lips. He knew better. But she still couldn't help him. She had to go with the honest answer instead.

"I can't risk crossing Vadim right now. He's already got me over a log to keep you alive."

Bless his heart, the big bleeding vampire looked concerned for her.

"Yeah, you're welcome, for what it's worth." She grimaced, seeing all the blood trickling from the stab wounds on his bare chest. "Does Gabriel have his phone on him or at least in the bag?"

Stephanos shook his head. "It was on Vadim's desk."

"Do you really want to get that asshole back at some point? Gabriel, I mean, out of the landfill. You'd be wise to never touch Vadim again."

"Agreed, but I owe Gabriel."

"Now you're going to owe me. Dammit, I just got this phone's screen repaired from that asshole throwing it in the apartment he made me give up. Do you know what a pain in the ass it is to get a new phone set up just like the old one?" She grumbled, going over to the dumpster. Leaning in, she untied the knot on the bloody bag.

Gabriel's eyeballs caught the light, making her jump back. "Fuck me, you're a scary ass sight!" She gathered her wits and handed him her phone.

A bloody hand missing two fingers grabbed it.

"Protect that with your life if you want us to find you when it's safe to show your face on the surface again. And you better believe you're going to owe me too."

With great relish, she tied the bag shut, shuffled a couple other bags on top of him, and closed the dumpster lid. Hopefully any dumpster divers wouldn't dig too deep.

Her car pulled into the back lot. She waved Nathan over and spread her coat over the back seat before Stephanos slid in.

"No bleeding on my seat," she warned, getting in the other side. "I was looking forward to having a houseguest-free evening, but I suppose, for you, I'll make an exception."

"Thank you, Lavina," he whispered.

She reached up to tap Nathan on the shoulder. "Have Trina order me a new phone right away, please. I seem to have thrown mine out with the trash."

"Of course, ma'am. Right away."

Lavina sat back and sighed. Why did the best meals take so much work?

23

STEPHANOS WOKE in his room in Lavina's house. Misery filled him instantly. Not only was he in pain everywhere, but Gabriel hadn't believed him when he'd said he'd had nothing to do with Vadim's attack, not even after he'd been attacked himself. If his sire stayed buried until Stephanos had healed enough to retrieve him, there would be hell to pay. If he left Gabriel buried, his conscience would eat him alive. He had to decide pretty quickly because Lavina's phone wouldn't stay charged forever.

Someone knocked on his door. Since Lavina had said the staff weren't allowed to enter, he got up and hobbled to the door to answer it.

Trina stood in the hallway with Steven. The kid gasped, backing away a step and coming up short against the housekeeper.

"We thought you might appreciate a meal."

His face hurt, so he merely nodded. That hurt too.

"Ms. Arandine asks that you feed in the sitting room.

We have one on this floor so you don't have to go far."

The sturdy housekeeper didn't flinch at the sight of him and looked like she'd put up a fight if he didn't agree. He wasn't up to fighting.

Stephanos nodded and stepped out of his room, closing the door behind him. It felt wrong to leave his bed unmade in such a tidy house. He had a feeling that when he returned from dining on Steven, the room would be put to rights, probably with fresh sheets since he'd bled on the other ones despite his best efforts to clean himself after they'd returned home. He'd stopped leaking blood now, but nothing was healing quickly. There was just too much damage, and despite it being evening, he was still sluggish and tired.

His steps were halting, but he slowly made his way to the seating area Trina led him to. Steven looked back at him sympathetically, but stuck close to the housekeeper.

"Come downstairs when you're done, both of you. Ms. Arandine would like to speak to you, sir."

Stephanos grunted his agreement as he lowered himself gently onto a small sofa with his one good hand. The other, he kept close to his chest and tried not to look at it. He'd had plenty of injuries in his long life, but the sight of bones jutting through flesh was a sight that still made him queasy.

He would have rather stayed in bed where he didn't have to move, but Lavina had requested this and he needed to heal to rescue Gabriel. Who was buried. Underground.

Memories of being buried in the box fell around him, blocking out the room and Steven standing before him with concern etched on his youthful face. Distantly he heard Trina calling for someone. Then it was all gone. Only blackness remained. He pounded on the walls, screaming to get free. For once he wasn't terrified, but he was still trapped. The panic probably just hadn't hit him yet. It would. It always did.

He had to get out. Stephanos clawed at the iron box, at the mask over his face, at the chains digging into his flesh. He opened his mouth to yell for help, but the mask muffled everything.

Sweetness filled his mouth. That wasn't right. Where did that delicious nectar come from? Energy raced through him, electrifying every nerve until he was sure he could feel air. Fresh air...on his skin. Outside the box. Tears ran from his eyes at the joy of being free, from the bliss running down his throat. His body felt so far away. There were no aches, no pains, only warmth and the sensation of floating. He couldn't drink enough fast enough. He needed more. Needed it now.

"Get him off!" yelled a woman's voice. "Help me pry him off!"

Somewhere far away, hands tugged him. They pushed. They pounded. His skin tingled. None of it mattered. He drank deep.

The electric tingle grew, rising until it screamed inside his head. He couldn't move, couldn't drink. He pulled back, screaming as new pain registered across his chest as though he'd been struck by lightning.

"Get her away from him!" Trina shouted.

"Did you just tase a vampire?" Steven asked in an awed voice.

"Ms. Arandine said to take every precaution. This is one of them. If you don't have one, get one. Having seen this, I hope you'll protect yourself just in case. I know you feeders think this is all fun and games, but sometimes it isn't."

Stephanos shook his head slowly. Or maybe it just felt slow. The whole room seemed like it was underwater, if the water was thick jelly. Stephanos' arms and legs felt like they were asleep, tingling and sluggish to respond.

"More," he begged.

"I don't know as I'm comfortable..." Steven said.

"Wise of you. How about you wait downstairs for now until I get this situation sorted out?"

Lavina on the floor registered in his vision. The bloody bite marks on her neck caught his attention seconds later.

He tried to call her name, but his tongue wasn't cooperating.

She wasn't moving.

He wanted to wipe his lips, to confirm with his conscience that he hadn't caused the jagged tear at her throat, but the blissful taste on his tongue knew the truth.

Getting his good arm under him, Stephanos awkwardly wedged himself up to a seated position against the sofa. He was still so hungry, but Steven had gone downstairs. Feeding from Lavina's staff was against her rules, and he'd already fucked up. Even worse, he owed her for whatever she'd done to save his life from Vadim's vengeance.

Trina rushed into his field of blurry vision, pressing a towel to Lavina's neck. A first aid kit sat by her side. The housekeeper glared at him over her shoulder repeatedly while she worked, as if keeping an eye on him.

"If you can move, go back to your room. Then I'm going to do us all a favor by locking you in there until Ms. Arandine can speak to you. And after what you did to her, that might be awhile."

After what he'd done. No avoiding the truth when there were witnesses.

The best thing he could do was to comply. Stephanos got to his feet. His steps wavering, he used the furniture and walls to prop himself up to get back to his room. He did not close the door but went to the bed and collapsed there. Maybe if he cooperated, Trina would leave the door open. She wouldn't lock him in. He wouldn't be enclosed. Trapped.

Stephanos stared at the ceiling with his one eye that wasn't swollen shut. Lavina wanted him to be like Vadim, like Gabriel, but she was wrong. This was the disguise. He really was just an animal.

24

LAVINA BLINKED, confused at finding herself sitting on the loveseat in the guest floor living area. Trina sat beside her, frowning at the door to Stephanos' room.

"I don't want to say I told you so, but you know what I'm implying," Trina said.

"I'll give you that one." The burning pain in her neck was only slightly offset by the buzz from the vampire saliva. He must have ripped into her pretty deep for the pain to rule out that high. She gingerly touched the bandage she discovered on her neck. "How long was I out?"

"Only a few minutes. That was gruesome." She gestured to the blood on the carpet.

That was going to be a bitch to get out. She sighed. "I'm fine now. Better start on that before it sets."

Trina nodded and headed downstairs for her cleaning supplies and a bucket of cold water. Lavina had seen plenty of blood in her life, but it had never been hers. Her hand hovered over the bandage while her gaze darted to the door that had remained cracked open.

He'd been terrified, and lost in the delicious moment, she'd fed. When his arms started flailing, she'd tried to hold him down, but she'd made the mistake of getting too close to his gnashing fangs. One drop and he was the one who was lost. Once the vampire saliva high hit her, she'd no longer been able to subdue him. The bliss and blood loss had been too much. Note to self, neither of them were at their best when they were feeding.

Trina returned and began blotting the blood with a thick pad of paper towels. The first few presses turned them red all the way through. "He should leave," Trina muttered as she worked.

The image of Vadim's chewed-through neck permeated Lavina's mind. "Tell me truthfully, Trina, did that mess happen before or after you tased him?"

"After," she admitted darkly. "When I had to dislodge his fangs from you because he sure wasn't letting go on his own. He would have drained you dry."

She didn't want to think that Stephanos would do that, but high on her blood? He'd seemed still relatively in control when he'd done it the first time, but sex might not have been as distracting for him as it had been for her. Though it certainly seemed like he'd been enjoying himself. Then again, she'd been blissing off his saliva. Maybe she wasn't remembering all of that with full clarity.

"Is Steven still here?"

Trina tossed a wad of splotchy red paper towel aside and started in with blotting water. "He's downstairs." She scowled at Stephanos' door. "I told him to close it. That you'd lock him in until you were ready to talk to him. He didn't even do that."

He might not have closed it, but he wasn't hovering at

the door either. In fact, she couldn't hear him at all. She got to her feet and took a tentative step. Not too shaky. Healing must be going fast thanks to the meal she'd just enjoyed before it all went wrong.

"I'll check on Stephanos and then have a chat with Steven."

"Yes, ma'am."

Trina might have sounded polite enough on the outside, but Lavina sensed her disapproval. "You handled the situation well. Thank you."

The housekeeper nodded, still scowling.

Lavina couldn't blame her. Humans were never meant to deal with vampires like this, to live in their darkness. They were creatures made for sunshine and laughter.

Passing the open door, she spotted Stephanos on the bed, flat out on his back, arms by his sides, unmoving as though he were sleeping. From what she'd gleaned from their conversation and his memories, shutting down was his default reaction. Or maybe she was reading too much into it, and he was just basking in the high of her blood. Whichever it was, he didn't appear to be an immediate problem. She went downstairs to deal with the human.

Steven sat at the dining room table with a glass of water and a plate of cookies in front of him. He hadn't touched either.

"Rosa's cookies are the best. You're missing out." At least that's what Nathan and Trina always told her. Her tastebuds weren't as enthusiastic, but neither had they been repulsed.

The young man smiled weakly. "I'm not hungry, but thank you."

"Sorry about that. Wounded creatures can be unreliable. We didn't mean to put you in danger."

His gaze focused on the bandage on her neck. "Are you okay? He bit into you really hard."

"I'll be fine."

"Forgive me for asking, but it was my understanding that you didn't feed off one another?"

Right. That. So many lies to manage. "We don't. He wasn't in his right mind." She put on her best reassuring smile, confident again now that her faulty fang had been fixed. "So that we can get him more himself again, would you be opposed to doing a manual feeding? For, say, an extra hundred?"

Steven mulled over her offer.

"We'll pay your base rate regardless, and I'm sure Trina will provide a glowing review."

Trina had walked her through the new feeder app, portrayed as a dating site to connect faux vampires with humans. Not that she needed it, but sometimes the guests at her apartment had. Having it on her own phone also helped to keep up pretenses. Not that she had a phone right now thanks to fucking Gabriel.

"Yeah, I can do that, I guess." Steven picked up a cookie and took a bite.

Money had a way of relaxing humans.

"Great. Trina will get you set up as soon as she's finished upstairs. Enjoy the cookies.

After the first bite, he took a second with more relish. Maybe they really were good. Lavina shrugged and went upstairs. The spot on the floor was mostly clean now. Trina was working on the blood spatter on the loveseat. She looked ready to question the wisdom of Lavina entering Stephanos' room, but Lavina went in before she could.

Humans didn't understand how drawn to the broody, violent thoughts she was. It was almost magnetic. Even though she'd just fed from him, the flavor he emanated now was even more enticing, like an endless plate of the best cookies ever made.

In the back of her mind, the thought of getting hurt again begged to be regarded. Hunger overruled it, dulling the burning in her neck.

She'd taken two steps into the room when his still form spoke. "Stay back."

Lavina couldn't feed from here. She was too far away. She needed to be closer, to look into his eyes. Windows to the soul and all that. A window to the buffet that was Stephanos. She shivered with anticipation.

"You won't hurt me again," she assured him, as if declaring it made it true. That little voice in the back of her mind called her brazen and foolish. She crept closer.

"Lavina, I don't *want* to hurt you again."

"Then don't." She reached the side of the bed.

His good hand fisted the blood-stained sheet, and his eyes squeezed shut. The wounded vampire remained still but for his panting.

"Hungry," he said through clenched teeth, his nostrils flaring.

Same, buddy. Same. "I'll make you a deal. Steven is downstairs right now, ready to donate a pint of fresh, hot blood for you. I know it's not as good as straight from the vein, but it's safer for everyone right now."

He nodded. The cords in his neck pulled taut.

His restraint reaffirmed her choice to approach. Told you so—she squashed the little voice of caution. He wasn't the animal he thought he was. That, no doubt, Gabriel had convinced him he was.

"You said this was a deal. What do you want in return?"

"I want you to look at me."

He shook his head. "I hurt you. I didn't mean to."

"I know. That's not why you need to look at me."

"You're going to make me leave. After Steven's blood. After I heal a little, I'll go. I promise. It's just this hand." He held up the badly broken forearm. It had started to repair, but it hadn't gotten far yet. "It's useless."

"Stephanos, just open your eyes."

Brows crunched low, he peeked his less swollen eye open a slit as if he were expecting to see a cleaver coming down to behead him. Confusion played over his face when no such thing happened.

"You thought you were trapped earlier. Confined. Tell me about that."

"Underground," he whispered. "Buried in an iron box."

"You're free now. No one is going to bury you."

He averted his gaze. "If I get out of hand. If I don't heed the warnings. All it takes is an angry mob and I'll be buried again."

She leaned in to rub the back of his uninjured hand. "I won't let anyone bury you again."

"Why would you help me? You have everything here. I'll only bring trouble. I always do."

Lavina wedged herself onto the edge of the bed to sit beside him. "Is that what Gabriel tells you?"

He finally looked up at her.

The hum in her mind ignited. "Tell me how you got out of the box in the ground."

Endless darkness surrounded Stephanos. Every night he woke to the same pain. No hope of healing, only hunger that seemed to eat him alive. The chain had long ago worked its way into his skin. He no longer felt the weight of the mask on his head. It was just part of him. Part of his existence and misery.

A shuffling noise caught his attention. Was it his feet moving against the box? Was he walking in his half-sleep?

The noise came again. He hadn't felt his legs move. Even the night vision he usually employed had lost its usefulness down here. Everything was just black.

He tried to move his head to make sure the noise wasn't the lock at the back of the mask swinging against the metal walls of the box, but he was too weak. Useless. What good would he even be if he ever got free of his bindings? He'd never make it out of the box. It would have been more merciful to have taken his head rather than lock him underground. But mercy had never been part of this. It was punishment for the lives he'd ended.

How long ago had that been? He'd lost all track of waking and sleeping. Everything blended together, even the pain. At one time he'd been able to discern his broken bones, to know his broken toes, his left leg from the shattered knee, broken ribs, his shattered shoulder. Now the pain was all one, just an endless throbbing that wore away his sanity until all he knew was hunger and the stench of decay.

As much as he prayed for it, his body wouldn't die. As long as he kept his head on his shoulders and stayed out of the sunlight, he would live forever. Forever in absolute misery.

The noise grew louder. It was outside the box. A sound. Outside the box. Getting louder.

Stephanos rocked his body, working up momentum

until the iron mask and what was left of his moldering boots alternated in thudding and clanking against the metal walls. Unused to any sound after so long, his ears rang from the racket. Something struck the box with a metallic clunk. Stephanos tried to yell, but all he could manage were weak moans. His tongue had long since dried into a shriveled mass in his mouth.

More clanging outside the box. The ring of chains against metal. A rasping, ringing racket surrounded him. He wanted nothing more than to clamp his hands over his ears, but with the mask in place and his arms bound to his sides, it was impossible.

The box shifted and then rolled, tossing Stephanos sideways. Unable to brace himself, his head knocked against the side. His broken, desiccated body bloomed with new bursts of pain. The box rolled again. A grating clicking noise echoed through the metal. He wanted to scream, but could not. His prison tilted end to end, his feet hitting the unforgiving metal wall and then his head, the rest of him sliding helplessly back and forth, adding weight to each blow.

With a heavy clunk, the box stopped moving. The chains clanked away, falling silent after a dull thud. Faint clicking came from outside, and then the top of the box opened.

Stephanos winced, sure sunlight would burn him any second. Someone was probably expecting a chest full of treasure, surely something of value in a locked box. He was anything but that.

Fresh air rushed in, warm against his skin. The mask held his own stink close, though he longed for the scent of anything else. Moonlight, blessed moonlight, shown down from above. To see the sky once more, to feel the air on his body, to be above ground—it was all he'd prayed and pleaded for.

The silhouette of a man blocked out the moon. Chained and weak, all Stephanos could do was brace for the blow that would sever his head from his shoulders.

Except there was no blade in his hands, only a key.

Stephanos moaned as the man rolled him onto his side. A set of hands held him there. More clicking and another thump. And then again.

The hands let go, returning him to the ground before pushing him upward. Another person stood in front of him, pulling his shoulders upward. He groaned, trying to get away from the pressure being put on his shattered shoulder.

"Be still, my friend," said a familiar voice, one he'd been sure he'd never hear again.

Stephanos spotted an approaching shadow. Gabriel came to stand before him. Dressed in fine clothes and a long, lightweight cloak that swirled around him, he looked as he always had: aristocratic. Tall boots gleamed in the grass as if they'd never had to walk through a field or along a muddy bank.

"Pull the chains away carefully," Gabriel directed the men around Stephanos. "Then the mask."

Each link pulled from his body both relieved pressure and felt like skin being torn away at the same time. He couldn't decide whether to sigh with relief or to cry out. In the end, he focused on Gabriel's face, praying to never see the inside of a box again, and remained absolutely still.

When the men pulled the mask away, tugging so much skin with it, he couldn't help but whimper.

"You've looked better, Stephanos." Gabriel shook his head. "You must be starving after all this time."

He was beyond starved, but he was too weak to even lift his arms. All he could do was groan miserably and look at his maker. If the person holding him up let go, he'd flop back to the ground, his muscles having lost all strength.

"Put that all in the wagon. Yes, even the box. There are three of you, surely you can manage," Gabriel ordered. "Set him down gently."

Stephanos watched as the moon floated overhead until he came to rest in a nest of grass that tickled the back of his neck. Stars twinkled as if he'd only blinked and not been underground for what seemed like an eternity.

He could smell the freshly broken blades of grass beneath him, the turned earth they'd pulled him from, the sweat of men laboring. The pulsing of the blood in their veins as they hefted the box made him bare his fangs and beg his muscles to pick his body up, but they didn't listen. How was he supposed to feed if he couldn't even lift his damned head?

Footsteps moved away. A horse whinnied off to his right. One of the men swore. The scent of fresh blood on the air drove Stephanos mad with frustration.

When the men returned, they gathered up the chains and the mask. Shovels clanked together. Three sets of footsteps again retreated toward the horse. He'd never fed from a horse before, but he was ready to sink his fangs into anything with blood. Wriggling in the dirt, he managed to move a few inches toward the noise.

Gabriel stood over him. "Patience, my friend. They're almost done."

The moon was still high overhead, but how was he supposed to find cover if he couldn't move? If he couldn't feed? Stephanos continued to struggle toward the wagon Gabriel had mentioned. He'd gained nearly a foot when the glint of a blade made him freeze.

"I'll be right back. Conserve your strength." Gabriel tucked the dagger under his cloak and headed for the three men.

Stephanos had rolled himself over enough to at least be able to see his goal, though he was nowhere near it. The men were busy securing the box and chains in the wagon. They paid no heed to Gabriel's approach.

He came up behind one of the two men on the ground to drive the blade between his ribs. He caught the second one in the stomach as he spun around. The third tried to jump from the wagon, but Gabriel was fast, darting in front of the man before he could flee into the night. He sliced the man's throat. Keeping as much distance as he could, Gabriel grabbed the arm of the dying man and dragged him over to Stephanos. With the gushing throat in front of his face, Stephanos summoned the strength to lift his head and drive his fangs into the bloody flesh to capture the last gushes pushed forth from the fading heart. He drank, pulling all he could until the blood stopped flowing. By that time, his muscles had gained enough energy to propel him gracelessly toward the other two bodies.

Stephanos fell upon the wounded men, gorging himself until he could drink no more.

"Finished?" Gabriel asked, standing over him.

Stephanos nodded before testing his newly whetted tongue. "How long?" he rasped.

"Sixty-seven years. You were not an easy man to find." He motioned to the bodies. "Throw them in the hole. Grave robbers deserve no better."

He'd had nothing to steal. Stupid men. Stephanos

basked in his returning strength. Knowing his body would heal soon, he shambled his way back to the hole one dead body at a time, and rolled all three men into the pit. They'd dug down quite a way to find him and the hole was wide. With the job done, he stepped away from the edge, never wanting to go down there again.

Returning to the wagon, he pulled himself up inside the open bed beside the box. Gabriel sat on the bench at the front with the reins in his hands.

"You're going to like my new house, Stephanos. So much land and so many bodies to run it. Life is good here. As long as you control yourself, you can enjoy it with me."

"I will," he promised.

"Good. I prefer not to dump any more bodies in holes in the field. Let's get you healed up and then we'll see what you can do to repay me for all the time I spent looking for you."

As long as he could enjoy the wide open and the night air, he'd do whatever it took to repay the debt.

25

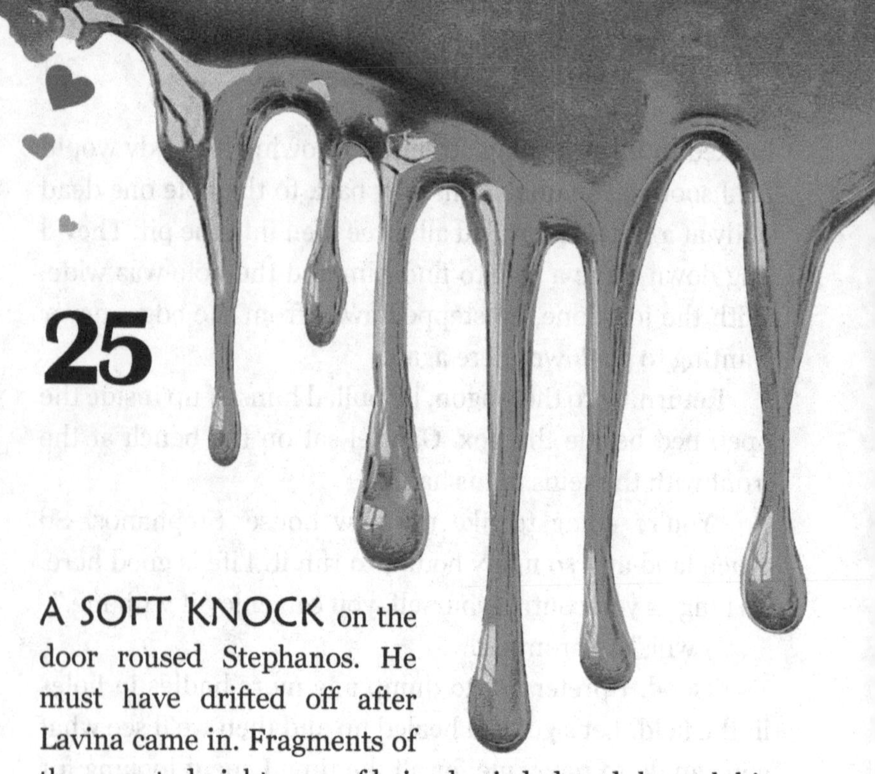

A SOFT KNOCK on the door roused Stephanos. He must have drifted off after Lavina came in. Fragments of the repeated nightmare of being buried played through his mind. They didn't hold the terror he usually felt upon waking, which often left him weak and nauseous.

Lavina sat beside him, rubbing the back of his hand. Her presence calmed him, making even the pain of his barely healed wounds less oppressive. The edge he'd been on before, the feeling that he was about to slip out of control and attack her again, had faded. Instead, there was only guilt and shame for having attacked her at all. She'd helped him. Repeatedly, and asked for nothing.

She brushed the hair from his forehead with a tender sweep of her long fingers. "What are you thinking about in there?"

"Thanking you. How to do it."

Lavina laughed lightheartedly. "I have ideas, but you're going to need to feed first."

He liked where this was headed. As long as his wounded

body would cooperate. "Gladly."

"I'll be right back. Don't go anywhere," she tossed over her shoulder with a wink.

Despite the distant pain, he chuckled. He'd never felt more human than he did with Lavina. He didn't even need to water down who he was like he'd done with Isla.

The wildness in him retreated into the shadows of his mind. It could stay there until Gabriel needed him again. He liked this much better. This bedroom, this house. The woman who was now entering the room with a plastic bag filled with blood that his fangs ached for. He held out his hand, knowing his face was begging but too proud to say the words.

Lavina held the bag away as she approached. She was going to make him plead for it, demand promises, deals. She'd said something about a deal earlier. He licked his lips. He needed that blood. Needed it now.

"Stephanos, calm yourself." Her mild scolding drove him to avert his eyes.

"So hungry," he whispered.

"I know, and you're going to want to sink your teeth into this, and then you'll waste half of it on my nice sheets."

Her hand was on his chin, warm and soft, lifting his head so he had to look at her. The brighter light in the hallway lent her an ethereal glow, catching the gold in her hair and making it shine. For a second he forgot all about the blood, but then the hunger raced back in, flooding his thoughts.

"I want you to drink like this." She illustrated how to turn the tiny knob over a protrusion at one end of the bag. "It's like a straw. If you know what a straw is. Just put your lips around it and suck." Her lips quirked into a silly smile

that made her eyes sparkle. "If I had a nickel for every time...
Nevermind. Here. Don't make me regret this by making a
mess."

He took the warm bag, disheartened that it wasn't hot,
but hungry enough that he'd drink it anyway. Who was he
kidding, he'd have cut open a corpse and licked up whatever cold, sludgy fluids were left. With shaking fingers, he
put the hard nub in his mouth and then turned the knob.
Sweet Steven flooded into his mouth. He sucked and gulped
until the bag was empty.

Lavina plucked the bag from his hand and set it on the
bedside table. "Now that we've taken the edge off, how do
you feel?"

"Better." Far more alive all over his body, in fact. He
shed what little he'd been wearing. "You have too many
clothes on."

She grinned. "I'll just lock us in and then we'll take
care of that." Lavina shut the door, returning his room to
calm darkness. Fabric shuffled and rustled. A weight at the
end of the bed let him know she'd joined him. The weight
shifted closer.

Though Steven's blood was pumping through his body,
working wonders on his injuries, he didn't want to tempt
disaster. Rising up on his knees, he used his good arm to
intercept Lavina, gently pushing her down onto the thick
bedcover.

It had been so long since he'd had women in his bed, not
since Isla. Inspired by the ghost from his past, he pressed
his lips to her knee and slowly kissed his way upward,
scraping his fangs along her soft skin as he went. Lavina
shivered beneath him, her breath coming faster the higher
he went. When he reached where he expected to find a nest

of curls, his tongue instead slid over smooth folds. Confused, he explored further, only to find more of the same. Had women changed so much in a couple hundred years?

"Don't stop," Lavina pleaded breathlessly.

His nose finally encountered a trim patch of curls assuring him female anatomy hadn't changed entirely. Her fingers in his hair guided and encouraged until she gasped and went stiff against his face. Stephanos grinned as Lavina relaxed, her plump bottom falling into his hands. Hands that might be wounded, but he didn't much care at the moment.

Lavina sat up, her fingers searching until they brushed his chest and then his neck to pull herself closer. She kissed him hard and long until he was lost in the caresses of her tongue against his. She worked herself into his lap, where her full breasts rubbed against his chest with every movement, driving him mad. He palmed one, working her nipple into a hard nub.

Straddling him now, she pulled away just long enough to say, "Bite me."

Maybe he was imagining her saying that because he really wanted to. Very badly, in fact. "You're sure?"

"Don't make me ask again."

With her neck so recently ravaged, he didn't want to inflict pain. Instead, he kissed his way down the unblemished side of neck and onto the breast he held. He sank his fangs there, close to her heart. Where Steven's blood brought energy and healing, Lavina's induced euphoria—much the same as his saliva did with humans.

Lavina moaned, throwing her head back. With one warm hand on his shoulder and the other deep in his hair at the base of his skull, she held him close. He could stay like this forever and be perfectly happy.

She shifted upward just enough to slide him inside, and then she began to ride him. No, he amended, he could stay like *this* forever.

He pulled his fangs from her flesh and basked in the high that was this glorious woman. Grabbing her wide hips, he guided her up and down, harder and faster until they were both covered in sweat. Until she cried out, and he followed a second later. She slowly melted off of him and onto the bedcover. Stephanos held her close, his chest to her back, basking in the heat they'd created. Specks of light continued to dance in his vision, and he couldn't stop smiling.

"I could drink you in forever," he said against her ear.

Lavina wiggled in closer, her soft curves pressing against the hard muscled body that had served him well as a soldier so long ago. He didn't want to think about that, or Gabriel, or even Isla. Stephanos pressed his face to Lavina's shoulder, breathing her in, anchoring himself in the present so the past couldn't drag him away.

After a while, Lavina sighed. "I suppose I should get moving. There isn't much of this night left, and I have a deal to honor."

He held on tight, not letting her go just yet, but talk of the bargain on his behalf dimmed his blissful state.

She pried herself from his grasp.

"What exactly is this deal?" he asked.

Lavina sat up and clicked on the lamp on the bedside table. She held up the blood bag. "I have to fill one of these and deliver it to him every week."

A bag of blood didn't sound so bad. She had plenty of feeders on call. She'd said so. "So have Steven fill another one before he goes."

"Steven will be off for a couple of weeks. He should have been off already. Humans are supposed to wait a month before giving that much blood again. It weakens them."

"Oh." That was unfortunate. He liked the taste of Steven, virile and sweet. "You have others, though."

When she averted her gaze, that normally bowed for no one, alarms went off in his blood-hazed head.

"The deal was for a bag of my blood."

"Your..." The dots connected in a flash of understanding that overruled the haze and ignited anger instead. Of course, Vadim wanted her blood. Who wouldn't? And yet, he felt betrayed somehow, even though she wasn't his. Hell, he'd barely known her for what, a week? "He's tasted it too?"

"Only the other night. I had no idea my blood had the effect it has on you. Or that it would have on others, for that matter. We don't feed on one another. It's never come up." She shrugged, still not meeting his gaze.

"Why did you let him taste it then?"

Her shoulders slumped. Her eyes seemed locked onto the hands clasped in her lap. As his gaze traveled down her body, he paused on the already healing bite marks on her breast. His marks. Not Vadim's.

"He imposed an unexpected and large debt on me. I had nothing else worthy enough to offer as payment."

Seeing Lavina subservient made him even angrier than the idea of her giving her blood to someone other than himself.

"I was desperate. He was holding Nathan as collateral."

Lavina's love for her pet humans was one of the things he admired about her. One of the things that set her so far apart from his sire.

"Where did he drink from?" The words flew out of his mouth before he realized he'd spoken aloud. He hadn't noted Vadim's mark on her body, but had it healed before he'd seen her again? The thought of another vampire's fangs in her flesh...

"Stephanos," Lavina snapped. "You don't own me."

Nor did he want to, at least not in the way she was implying. All he knew was being owned, and he wouldn't put that on anyone. "I know," he assured her.

She shook her head, her hair sliding over her bare shoulders. He could still smell the hibiscus scent of it from when she'd been comfortable in his arms. Before she'd been upset with him, like she was now.

"I didn't let him taste anything directly from me. He doesn't even know that it's my blood that is the intoxicant. He thinks it's because of a drug that I buy and consume, that it was in my bloodstream at the time because I took a pill."

"But Gabriel said Vadim was serious about keeping drugs out of the vampire food chain. Why would he want your blood drug?"

It saddened him to watch Lavina stand and walk to the end of the bed to retrieve her clothes. She began to dress. "Humans on drugs aren't healthy. They can have diseases that weaken vampires. Not to mention, the drugs they take have little effect on us in any enjoyable sort of way. But you showed me that my blood does affect you. That it's different for whatever reason, and that makes it valuable."

"Can you give him a bag that often? You said Steven had to take weeks off."

She finished dressing, and he couldn't help but notice

that she was busy straightening her clothes rather than looking at him. "I'm not like Steven."

While that was true, he had a bad feeling about the details she was leaving out. In an attempt to make her smile, he joked, "You could have struck a better deal. Maybe he wouldn't have had his men attack me."

Lavina turned away. "I tried. He asked too much." She hurried to the door and unlocked it as though she couldn't get away fast enough.

And she didn't because he was at the door and pushing it shut before she could escape. It bothered him that she looked worried. Did she think he was going to attack her? Was she hiding something that might cause him to? He suddenly wished he were dressed in case he needed to leave. That bothered him even more because he really didn't want to leave. He liked it here.

"Lavina, did you know what was going on in the parking lot?"

"I thought he'd changed his mind, that he was going to let you go. He distracted me, or I would have been out back looking for you sooner."

Changing his mind meant she knew he was going to be attacked, just not when. Would she have warned him? Betrayal began to gnaw at his gut.

"Did you condone the violence against me?"

He kept his hands on the door rather than on her because controlling his temper wasn't something he was used to having to do. Filled with wild rage was where Gabriel liked him.

She glanced between his hands holding the door shut and his face and then exhaled loudly. "I had to give him something, dammit, you nearly chewed his neck in half. He has a right to be angry about it."

"He should be grateful I stopped at nearly and called you to get him. I was supposed to kill him. Gabriel was right there. I took risks, Lavina. I took them because of you."

"I know," she said softly. "And I thank you, but still, he's rightfully angry. For what it's worth, you're here, in my house relatively whole and fed, and Gabriel is in pieces in a landfill."

"True." Yet, he couldn't help feeling that he shouldn't trust her quite as wholeheartedly as before. "I should get dressed. You'll show me how to find Gabriel now?"

"Do you really want to find him?"

"I have to. I told you that." Was she hiding the truth again? "You said you would help me."

Lavina scowled. "I said I'd show you *how* to find him. Digging him out is not part of the deal. I'd rather that rat rot for an eternity."

Gabriel had wanted her killed. He supposed that would flavor her feelings for his sire. "Alright then, you show me and I'll go with you to deliver your blood to Vadim. I don't trust him not to change the terms of your deal."

Her scowl faded. "I'd appreciate that, actually. Thank you."

He backed away from the door, letting her leave. Maybe he'd go take a shower to continue to improve her mood. Hell, he might even put together a clean outfit if they were going to visit The Jackyl. Wishing he had some of Vadim's clothes to wear just to annoy him, Stephanos headed to the bathroom.

26

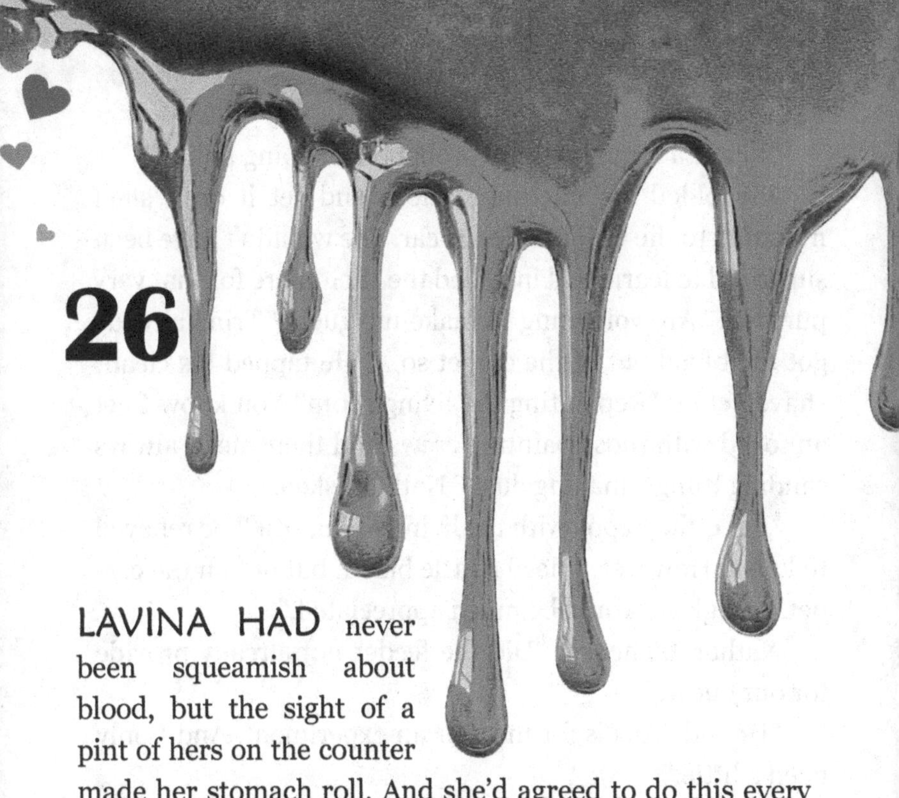

LAVINA HAD never been squeamish about blood, but the sight of a pint of hers on the counter made her stomach roll. And she'd agreed to do this every week. Indefinitely. How the hell was she going to keep that up? She might not be fully human, but her body was more so than vampire. Maybe she could dilute her blood with regular human blood to make it go farther. Inspired, she grabbed a shot glass from the cupboard and went to find Nathan. While Trina would have been her first choice, she had fed Vadim recently.

She found Nathan in the garage, wiping down the car. He took great pride in her automobiles, keeping each one spotless.

"Good evening, ma'am. Good to see you in such a fine mood."

Her fine moods had been few and far between since she'd ditched Vadim. They'd vastly improved since finding Stephanos.

"I have a request you're probably not going to like."

He folded his microfiber cloth and set it on a shelf mounted to the wall beside the car. She wouldn't have been surprised to learn he'd installed the shelf there for that very purpose. "Are you going to make me guess? Trina already got the blood out of the carpet so..." He tapped his clean-shaven chin. "Repainting the living room? You know I get annoyed with those painting crews and their mess, always sanding things, making dust." Nathan tsked.

"I'm quite happy with the living room, you'll be relieved to know. However, I need a little blood, but not on the carpet. In a glass, would be much appreciated."

Nathan blanched. "Did the feeder not already provide for our guest?"

"He did. This is for me. For an experiment. And I only need a little."

"Very well, ma'am." He didn't look excited about it, but he followed her into the kitchen.

"Have a seat. I'll get Trina to draw it for you."

She'd been fortunate to find a housekeeper with a nursing past. While Trina hadn't clicked with her intended profession, her skills came in handy from time to time. Being able to claim to have a nurse on hand for the boys had been part of the reason she'd been able to rope Rosa into employment despite Lavina's eccentric lifestyle.

"Please. No offense, ma'am, but skills with a needle of any sort are not your best quality."

"Agreed," she said with a chuckle.

Her adopted mother had attempted to teach her the skills most girls learned back in those days. As much as she tried to mask herself as normal so she wouldn't be burnt as a witch like her mother had, needlework had not been her friend. She'd had to rely on feigned obedience and her wit until she'd been old enough to venture out on her own.

Lavina located Trina in the library where she was sitting with a rectangular box beside her, a phone in her hand, and a determined look on her face. The housekeeper glanced up and offered her a pained smile. "I hate setting up these things. Almost done though. I hope you don't mind white. We can get a case for it tomorrow."

"As long as it works, that's all I care about."

"If you could not throw this one out for a year or two, I'd be most grateful." Trina pressed a few more buttons and swiped at prompts on the screen. "There."

She took the phone and verified all the usual apps were in the usual places. The weight of the phone felt wrong. Was it even thinner than the last one? Why couldn't they keep these darn things one uniform size and weight?

"Thank you, Trina. I'm afraid we need a little more blood drawn tonight, if you wouldn't mind." It needed to happen whether she minded or not, but Lavina attempted to pose it as a request. "Not yours," she clarified.

"In that case, lead me to the vein that needs poking."

Lavina pocketed her new phone. The slippery, damned thing was definitely going to need a case. She went back to the kitchen with Trina.

"I need to fill this glass with half me and half Nathan."

"Easy enough." Trina opened a cupboard and pulled the supplies Lavina insisted be kept on hand for emergencies.

Within fifteen minutes, she had the glass full of the half and half mixture and both of their arms adorned with a cotton ball and tape.

Stephanos arrived a minute later, looking quite delicious, freshly showered and dressed in clothes that reminded her of Vadim. She laughed to herself. He'd done that on purpose, no doubt. Unlike Vadim, who kept his hair short and neat, Stephanos let his long curls drift over his broad shoulders. Now that he was keeping it clean and tangle-free, she wanted nothing more than to run her fingers through the silken strands.

Oh, was he saying something? She paused her ogling. "What?"

"The blood? What is this?"

"That. Right. If you wouldn't mind, could you drink it and let me know if it has the same effect?"

"I'm going to hope that it doesn't if we're going to The Jackyl now because I'd prefer to be in my right mind."

He had a point, but still, she needed to know before she delivered a full bag of potent blood. If she could get by with cutting it, it was best to do that from the start. She could play off the instant high Onriel had experienced by saying it affected him differently or had interacted with whatever he'd been drinking that night.

"Please," she prompted, sliding the glass toward him.

He eyed it warily.

"If it works, this means more for you and less for him."

Stephanos picked up the glass and tossed the contents down his throat.

Jealousy did work wonders.

The dazed look he usually got didn't make an appearance. She started to sweat. What if mixing her blood with human blood did something bad? What if she'd just poisoned him?

He cocked his head, looking at the three of them watching him. "Are you sure your blood was in there?"

She'd watched Trina draw it and empty the syringe into

the glass. "Yes."

"Sorry, I don't feel anything. The blood tasted a little off, not sour, like vampire, but weak, maybe? Like the blood of someone who is sick."

Trina leaned over the counter to grab the glass. She put it in the dishwasher. "You can taste sick?"

Stephanos nodded. "Not that it does much good, but yes. I used to drink a lot of... Well, never mind."

"Can all vampires do that?" Nathan asked.

Stephanos looked at Lavina. "Can you?"

"No." She'd never heard of such a thing, so she had no idea how she was supposed to answer. Better to be a deficient vampire if it was a widespread thing than to say yes and be put on the spot to prove it.

"Gabriel can't either. Maybe it's just me." He shrugged.

Nathan cleared his throat. "You can't, by chance, tell what kind of sickness you're tasting?"

Lavina reached out to pat the back of his age-spotted hand. "It's probably because we mixed our blood, not that you're sick, dear."

"Blood has different flavors. I suppose it could depend on the disease. I've never thought about it much. Most of my food has been sick in one way or another. I don't get to taste healthy blood very often. Steven's is perfect."

Trina reached for her supplies. "Now I gotta know. Do me next!"

Lavina shot her a glare.

"Taste my blood," she amended, holding out a sealed needle, tourniquet and collection tube. "Lavina, would you mind? A bit of practice wouldn't hurt, anyway."

Normally she would have declined, but she was also curious. "As far as you know, you're healthy?"

Trina nodded. "Just had my annual physical with blood-work last month. Not to say the doctors wouldn't miss stuff, though. It's not like they can test for everything."

It had been a long while since Lavina had bothered with medical supplies, not since her time with Vadim when she'd had to have blood on hand for keeping up vampire pretenses. Having just watched Trina draw her blood and Nathan's, she figured she could muddle through. The tourniquet was more pliable and easier to use and the needle, when she unwrapped it, was so much thinner. Trina pointed out the vein to use and silently coached her through guiding the needle in.

"Oh, that was so much easier than it used to be."

"Medical advancements for the win." Trina winked. "You just need to pop the collection tube into the holder, and we'll be good to go."

Feeling victorious, Lavina did as Trina instructed and finished the blood draw. Popping the filled tube from the holder, she examined it while Trina removed the needle and did her cotton ball and tape application. The blood looked like any other blood she'd ever seen. She handed the warm tube to Stephanos. He eyed it hungrily.

"Go on. I want to know," Trina urged.

He carefully popped the rubber top off and tossed back the contents. His blood-tinged tongue licked his lips. He smiled. "Quite healthy," he announced.

Trina grinned. "Good to know I didn't waste my copay payment. What we need now is a true test." Her eyes lit up. "I know just the subject. We'll do this again tomorrow night."

"Who do you have in mind?" Lavina asked.

"I'll take care of it. Go on and get that bag delivered so

you can enjoy what's left of the evening."

Enjoying was asking a lot, but business before pleasure. Or, well, pleasure, then business, followed by hopefully more pleasure.

"I'll just go change a minute. I'll be right back," Lavina announced.

Trina's abrupt bark of laughter made Lavina stop and turn back around. "Something funny?"

"You, taking a minute to change." Trina shook her head. "Go on. Nathan and I will keep an eye on this fine gentleman until you return."

Lavina almost burst out laughing herself when Stephanos discreetly double-checked to see if there was someone else nearby. He might be cleaned up, but he still had a wild air about him, as if the feral side could make an appearance at any moment.

Now that she knew the warning signs, she hoped not to fall victim to that side again. As long as no one got hurt, she quite liked his wild side.

She hurried to her room and changed into a clean, loose white silk shirt and a pair of dark grey leggings. She paired the outfit with a long silver necklace and calf-length black leather boots with a short heel. Getting an inch on Stephanos would be welcome. She preferred men of similar height, but he had several inches on her.

Fully intending to stride back to Vadim's office to slap the blood bag on his desk and then leave, she didn't bother with anything more than a bit of foundation, a dusting of blush, and a quick layer of mascara. She ran a brush through her hair and called it presentable enough. With a smug smile, she headed back to the kitchen within ten minutes.

Hearing hushed voices, her confident stride slowed to a crawl just before she burst in.

Trina and Nathan stood on one side of the kitchen island with Stephanos on the other. His head was bowed and shoulders hunched. Her staff appeared serious, standing side by side.

"...better never have to clean blood out of the carpet because you lost your shit again, do you hear me?"

Stephanos mumbled something she couldn't make out since his back was to her.

Nathan's steely tone caught Lavina by surprise. He was always so mild-mannered around her. "If you ever hurt her again, the sun will take you. I don't care if I have to jackhammer a hole in the wall to make it happen."

Touched by his protectiveness but also to save Stephanos from further chastisement, Lavina tapped her heels on the tiles loudly as she entered the room. "Are we ready to go?"

A smile reappeared on Trina's face. "That was fast." She busied herself with putting the medical supplies away and then quickly vacated the room.

"I'll get the car ready, ma'am." Nathan grabbed the key from the cabinet by the door and headed to the garage.

Once they were alone, Lavina brushed her hand over Stephanos' shoulders. "I hope they weren't too rough on you?"

"Nothing more than I deserved." He stared at the bag of her blood on the counter. "You're fortunate to have people who care about you."

"I care about them too. It goes both ways." She picked up the bag. "Shall we get this over with?"

He nodded, following her into the garage.

The ride passed in companionable silence. After all the drama that had gone down in that damned club, Lavina would have been happy to not step foot in the place for a long while. Now she was supposed to visit once a week? Maybe she could have Nathan drop off the blood. The idea of avoiding the obligation and Vadim rankled even worse than having to make the weekly trip. Feeling her mood worsen with each passing minute, Lavina scooted closer to Stephanos.

He regarded her uncertainly, but when she didn't retreat, he wrapped one arm around her. Lavina smiled. The heavy weight of his arm comforted her in light of the impending meeting.

It occurred to her that she probably wasn't the only one not excited to go back to the club. "Are your wounds healing?"

"They've closed. They just ache now. Still healing on the inside."

She leaned her head on his shoulder. "I'm sorry you were attacked."

"I'm alive," he said sullenly.

Okay, not quite forgiven for that yet. She kept her mouth shut for the rest of the trip.

When they pulled into the parking lot, it was mostly empty already. It was barely midnight.

"If you don't mind, ma'am, I'm going to lock the doors while I wait," Nathan said.

"A wise choice. We'll do our best not to take too long."

"No rush. Enjoy yourself." He held up the book he'd been reading. "I have three chapters until the end that I'd like to get through."

With no one waiting outside, they walked right in. The

tall, burly man working the lobby door waved them inside.

"He's in the back," he said.

Lavina nodded, holding her purse close to protect the blood inside. Stephanos stuck beside her, holding the inner door open.

A grating voice called out, "Woo Grandma, look at you with the fine piece of flesh in tow."

"Fucking hell," Lavina grumbled.

"Who's that?" Stephanos sounded far more intrigued than she liked.

Lavina didn't bother with a smile. The little trash vamp couldn't meet the sun soon enough. "Eveline, you're still single. Who would have guessed."

The mini-skirt wearing, bubble-boobed twit dragged her French tips over Stephanos' sleeve. "Not single, but available for tonight if you're interested."

Stephanos watched her fingers. "Available for—"

"Transmitting diseases most likely." Lavina faced down the female vampire who appeared half her age.

Eveline's bright pink—good lord, was that glitter lipstick?— lips parted with a disbelieving huff. "Such a bitter old biddy. Why don't you go find someone your own age and leave the young, pretty ones to me?"

"You want pretty? Give Fane a call. You wouldn't know what to do with this one." Lavina grabbed Stephanos' wrist and pulled him away from Eveline, heading for the back hallway with determined steps.

When she reached the closed office door, she turned to tell him to behave, but his fangy grin caught her off guard. "I didn't think facing the man who had you beaten would put you in such a good mood."

"It doesn't. Seeing you like that does." He jutted his

chin toward where Eveline was standing by the bar talking to a man who had to be well into his thirties. Must have been slim pickings for the tramp tonight.

"The nerve of that woman, calling me Grandma. I could just—"

Stephanos' lips ate her threat. He had her pressed up against the wall with just enough pressure to make it fun without worrying her that he was devolving from the fine catch of a man he appeared to be tonight.

While she gladly indulged in putting on a show for Eveline for several minutes, they were here for a reason. The sooner they got that taken care of, the sooner they could get back in the car and continue this. She tapped his chest.

"We're here on business, remember?"

"Just taking care of this business first." He flashed that delectable grin again. "She does not look happy, by the way."

"Good. Remind me to thank you for that later." Despite having to talk to Vadim in that damned office, she felt lighter.

Lavina knocked on the door.

"What?" Vadim barked.

"I have a delivery for you."

The lock clicked, and the door opened twenty seconds later. "That was fast."

"Getting this out of the way so I can enjoy my week." She strode into the office but did not sit down.

Stephanos, as if attached to her hip, stood beside her.

"And you." Vadim frowned. "At least you're not wearing my clothes this time."

Lavina took the bag from her purse and set it on the desk. She noted that the bamboo was back in the vase and looking healthy. Leave it to a vampire like Vadim to have a damned green thumb. Was there anything he couldn't do?

Stephanos remained silent, though her peripheral vision informed her he was in deadly, feral mode. Maybe she should have pushed his kiss away in favor of uttering a warning to behave.

Vadim looked him up and down. "You're looking quite healthy for what I heard my boys did to you. How's your hand?"

"Quit baiting him. You had your fun. Here's your delivery, as we agreed."

"I think I shall revise our agreement. Your new friend doesn't appear to regret his actions against me. Two bags next week."

A low rumbling next to her made Lavina turn to Stephanos. Was he growling? Way to offset the civilized appearance.

Vadim rubbed his throat but kept his level stare. "Two bags next week."

"That wasn't the deal," she said tightly. Didn't he realize that he was poking the bear here? While she was grateful to have Stephanos with her, keeping him leashed was going to be a challenge if Vadim kept this up.

"If you want him upright and above ground, then the price has doubled."

Stephanos lunged at the desk, slamming his fist down. "No."

Vadim sat back, hands gripping the arms of his chair, putting as much distance between them as the office space allowed. "Keep that up and I'll make it three."

"I told you I can't get two. How do you expect me to make three magically appear? Don't be an idiot. You'll get your single bag next week and not another drop." She bumped Stephanos aside with her hip, pleased to find he took a step back.

Lavina took his place, planting her palms and leaning over the desk. "If that's a problem, I'll be sure to let everyone know how you change your deals and why. You think you have financial issues now?"

Vadim shot up from his chair. Stephanos was instantly back beside her. Violent energy crackled all around him like an electric charge.

Vadim bared his fangs. "If you breathe one word of what we discussed to another soul, you'll both enjoy a bright and sunny morning."

"Tough words for a man who waited fifty years for me to come back to him." Her gaze flicked to where her picture had hung, only to find it replaced with a framed stranger's face as if she'd never been there.

"You made it very clear we're over and that you've moved on." Vadim waved his hand at Stephanos.

Leave it to Vadim to be petty about being dumped now that he finally figured it out. She couldn't afford to do the same. It wasn't her habit to burn bridges, not when vampiric longevity meant living with the same people indefinitely.

Stephanos straightened, flexing his strong fingers and flashing his fangs. "Maybe I should finish what I started."

Lavina's voice rose. "Could we all take a breath and be adults here? One bag next week. I maintain my silence on your financial crisis. You keep your throat intact. Stephanos comes home unharmed with me. Everyone agreed?"

"Not on your—" was as far as Vadim got before Stephanos leapt over the desk and threw him to the floor.

Lavina grabbed the glass vase, bamboo and all, and flung it at the offending new photo on the wall over their heads. Water and shattered glass rained down on the two snarling vampires.

"E-fucking-nough already!" She grabbed the back of Stephanos' shirt and tugged him backward. "We're leaving."

He snapped at Vadim, who clutched his throat. "I could take—"

"No biting." She loosened her hold on his shirt to take his hand instead. His fingers entwined with hers, making her smile.

"Take your dog and get out," Vadim shouted.

"We'll see you next week." She was definitely getting a courier for the next drop off. Never setting foot in the club again was her new goal. She had no place here any longer.

They walked to the front, past the few remaining customers, mostly humans. Eveline had left. Thankfully.

"Hey, Stephanos," called a perky female voice.

Lavina halted and turned to face this new annoyance.

"Tiffany." He nodded his greeting but didn't appear overly friendly about it.

The waitress smiled widely, standing tall to proudly display her wares beneath her thin, tight-fitting uniform t-shirt. Black lace bra, how predictable. And uncomfortable. Lavina grimaced.

"I've missed our chats. I thought you were leaving town?"

"Change of plans."

"That's wonderful. Sorry, I didn't see you come in. Would you like your usual?"

He had a usual? And was apparently quite the chatterbox with Ms. Tiffany of the perky tits? He'd settled in quickly during Gabriel's short Jackyl reign.

"No, thank you. We were just leaving," he said.

"Don't be a stranger." She flashed her smile one more time and sealed it with a little wave.

"You have a fan," she remarked as they walked out the front door.

"She's very young."

"And very willing," she muttered.

"She wanted to go upstairs." He shook his head.

"And did you? With her?"

"No."

They crossed the parking lot and quickly spotted her car by the reading light inside.

Lavina squeezed his hand. "Let's go home."

"I'd like that." He nuzzled her neck, fangs scraping lightly over her skin. Goosebumps rose over her entire body.

She wiped the glass dust from his shirt. "Maybe I should have let you devour him."

"I'd rather devour you instead."

Lavina knocked on the car window, startling Nathan. He unlocked the doors, and they slid inside. "Home, and as fast as possible, please."

"Yes, ma'am."

27

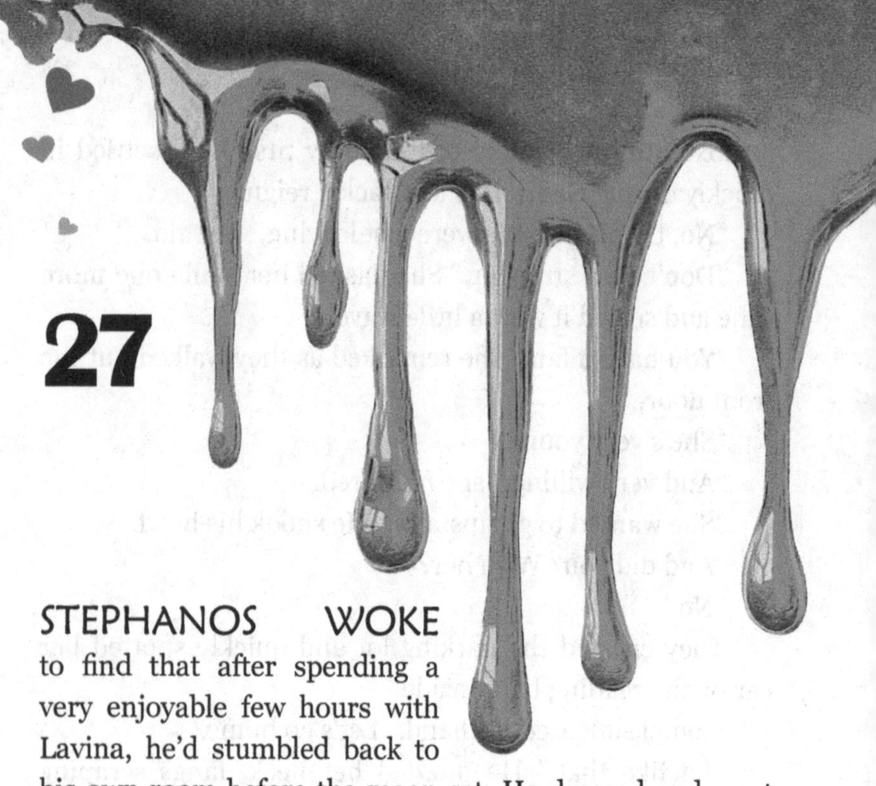

STEPHANOS WOKE to find that after spending a very enjoyable few hours with Lavina, he'd stumbled back to his own room before the moon set. He dressed and went to find her. She'd promised to show him how to track her phone to find Gabriel.

He tried the kitchen first, but it was empty, as was the living room. The house felt quiet, and he was loath to disrupt the peace. The feeling of being alone, but with people nearby, was a comfort he hadn't enjoyed in a long time. He was well fed, dressed, clean, and dare he admit, happy.

Stephanos opened the back slider door and stepped out onto the deck overlooking the yard. Cool night air welcomed him into the grassy expanse. The moon lit his way as he ventured out to take in the flowerbeds. Some blossoms had closed for the evening, but others remained open, their colors muted by moonlight. Distant memories reminded him what daylight flowers looked like, all bright and cheerful.

His mother had loved flowers. Red poppies had been

her favorite. How long had it been since he'd seen one? Her face, blurred and softened by his memory, smiled sadly. She'd long ago turned to dust, along with his father and sister and everyone else owned by the Boros, even the Boros themselves, except for Gabriel. Being the only child, the line had ended when he'd been turned, unable to sire any living offspring of his own. He'd maintained the family's fortune, grown it, and lived off it still.

Stephanos tipped his face up to the stars, wondering at the different constellations than those he'd grown up with in Greece, and those he'd shared with Isla in Scotland.

Far in the distance, down the hill, light filled a window here or there, but most of the homes through the trees were dark. The humans were sound asleep, enjoying their dreams or tossing and turning. Nothing like the vampire's dead sleep that stole his days. Whether he dreamed and just forgot them or never had any at all, he couldn't say. One thing he'd surely never dreamed was living in a place like this. Or being with anyone like Lavina. He left the night to its mysteries and wonder and went inside to find her.

Nathan sat at the kitchen table with a book in his hand.

"You finished the other one?" Stephanos asked.

The old man stuck a finger between the pages and closed the cover. "I did, yes. Perfect timing last night. I'd just turned to the about the author page."

Whatever that was, but the old man seemed pleased. "Have you seen Lavina yet?"

"I'm afraid not. Trina went to check on her. She's usually up by now."

Stephanos nodded and pulled out a stool at the island, giving the human some space. He took out his phone and started the game he'd been playing.

"I scheduled a doctor appointment," Nathan said.

"I'm probably wrong."

The old man shook his head. "No, I don't think so. Lately, I've been tired, more than usual, and nothing I eat sits quite right. I've been downplaying it for a while now, wanting it to be just a passing bug, but yesterday was the kick in the pants I needed to get myself looked at. I hate doctor appointments. All those nosey questions," he confided.

"I've never seen a doctor, but I'll take your word for it."

"Lucky you."

"Maybe. Maybe not."

Stephanos slid his finger over the screen, matching colored blocks without really seeing what he was doing. The reflection the bright kitchen lights sent back at him was of a young man who should have died hundreds of years ago, before doctors who took the time to see old men, blood in plastic bags, phones, houses that could have sheltered enough people to fill a small village, and cars that traveled farther and faster than horses. He did his best to keep up with it all, to pretend to understand it, it fit in, but there was so much and most of it was mind-boggling.

Nathan broke the long silence filled only by turning pages and a tapping finger. "You could find a book in the library if you want a break from your phone."

A book. Isla had taught him to read but doing so for enjoyment wasn't something he'd ever considered before. Would he understand enough of the words for it not to be a chore? Languages changed just as much as everything else.

The stool wasn't that comfortable. A walk wouldn't be so bad. He put his phone away and followed Nathan's directions to the library at the other end of the house. He spotted

Trina in Lavina's open doorway and detoured join her.

Whatever they'd been saying came to a sudden halt at his arrival. Was he intruding? He peeked inside to find Lavina still in bed.

"I'll be up in a bit," she assured him with a smile that didn't light her face.

Worry niggled at him, but he left the women to their conversation and went into the library. Unsurprisingly, the walls were lined with books. There was a window, however, and it had no sort of window dressing at all, which he found odd. What if she lost track of time in here? At least all the other windows in the house had blinds or heavy curtains. Why allow this unnecessary risk?

He looked out over the front yard with its towering boulders and plantings. The view reminded him of when he would wake to find Isla sitting by the front window with the shutters open to the night sky. She would tell him about the sunset he'd missed and all the colors that had faded from his world as they talked the night away by candlelight. She would always fall asleep first, her frail human body desperate to maintain its natural rhythm, and he would tuck her into her bed so she could wake up first to enjoy what daylight was left to her. He'd listened to her talk for hours about what she saw outside, of the nearby village she walked to for supplies, of the animals in the woods between here and there, the flowers in the fields and passing seasons. She'd had a beautiful voice.

"Do you need help finding anything?" Trina's voice startled him. "Lavina has her own system for organizing them."

"No, I was just looking around."

"Stay here too long and Nathan will have you reading half of these."

Would Lavina let him stay that long? How difficult would Vadim make her life if he did stay, given the chance?

"That doesn't sound so awful," he said.

She regarded him thoughtfully. "It's not. He's got good taste. At least, I think so. Might be a bit too tame for you. You look like a serial killer biography and thriller kind of guy."

He shrugged, not knowing what either of those might be in terms of books.

"Lavina likes them all arranged by color." Trina shook her head. "Don't ask. She's a good boss, so we forgive her quirks."

His brain spun, quickly trying to define quirk with what he'd seen and heard on the television. "What she likes in bed?"

Trina laughed. "Those are kinks. Quirks are odd things she does. Things that make her, well, Lavina."

He filed that away. "I see."

She perused the spines on several shelves. "You don't get out much, do you? Around people, I mean."

"No."

She handed him a book with a blue cover. "You're getting better at it."

"Thank you." He took the book. "What is this one?"

"Vampire romance. Nathan likes to throw me a bone now and then. I liked it. Figured you should start with something you know." She winked.

"Is she alright? Lavina?"

"Yes, but I think she'd be better if you crawled into her bed for a while. In whatever capacity keeps her in bed." Trina tapped the book in his hands. "I'd say she's sick, but I've never known Lavina to get sick, so I'm thinking the blood draw weakened her. One pint shouldn't have affected her like this if she were human, but she isn't."

"She should feed."

"Maybe you could convince her to take care of herself, hmm?"

Stephanos nodded.

"Before you jump into her bed, could you take a quick taste of two blood samples for me? I collected them a few hours ago. Hopefully that's still fresh enough to work?"

"We'll find out, I guess." The only time he'd dealt with blood from a glass and not a vein was in this house, but he was willing to try if it might endear him to Lavina's people.

Trina brought him back to the kitchen. He set his book on the counter. Nathan again marked his page with his finger and then asked Trina what they were doing. While she explained, she pulled two sample containers from a cupboard. These two had tape around them with names written on them.

"Who are Gregory and Eric?" he asked.

"Taste first. Answers later." Trina urged him to pop the rubber top off one of the tubes. She watched raptly while he took a sip of Gregory.

"It tastes off."

"Try the other one so we know if it's the storage time or something in his blood."

After tasting Steven and Lavina, he wasn't so hungry that he was compelled to drink the whole tube. Gabriel wouldn't like that he'd become pickier about his food. He took a smaller sip of Eric.

The pleasant, sweet taste of healthy blood landed on his tongue. He tipped back the tube and downed the rest. "This one is good."

Trina and Nathan both stared at him before exchanging a knowing nod.

"Can you describe how the other one tastes wrong?" Nathan asked. "Does it taste like mine did?"

"No, this is too thick and sharp. Yours had a vinegar aftertaste."

"So illnesses do have different flavors." Trina bounced on her heels. "This is so exciting."

"It is?"

Nathan nodded. "A diagnostic vampire. Who knew?"

"It's good," Trina assured him, almost as if she knew he was about to ask what diagnostic meant.

Despite her harsh chastisement of his behavior yesterday, he quite liked her. Nathan too.

"Answers now?" he asked.

"Rosa's boys. Gregory has aplastic anemia."

"Sick blood won't harm you?" Nathan asked.

"It never has before."

Trina grinned. "Imagine a vampire just sitting at a desk sipping blood samples all night to let humans know if they have an illness that needs to be tracked down."

"That would be magnificent. I would imagine it would also provide significant goodwill from the humans it helps as well."

Stephanos shook his head, backing away. "They could never know how it was done. I would never expose us. Not only would that be foolish of me, but other vampires would punish me."

"Alright, no one outside of a trusted circle would need to know. Seriously, Stephanos, this is huge. You could help so many people, and you'd never go hungry."

That part did sound good. It was the trusted circle of

humans he was hesitant about. He was just starting to accept the two living in Lavina's house. More was asking a lot. Humans were unpredictable in their reactions. The book cover caught his eye. A handsome male vampire in outdated clothing held a petite woman with big pink lips that reminded him of Eveline. They gazed longingly at one another.

"This is a story. It's not real." Humans had put him in the ground for sixty-seven years.

"Talk to Lavina about it. See what she thinks," Nathan said.

Trina gently shooed him out of the kitchen. "And make sure she rests."

28

THE KNOCK on her door was too heavy to be Trina. Nathan never knocked. He just called his questions through the door or texted her.

"Come in."

She'd been dreading the worry she now saw on his face. As it turned out, not being human meant she had different criteria for what was a safe size blood draw. Clearly, a pint was too much. And she was supposed to do this every week? Lavina sank back into her pile of pillows.

"If you have your phone with you, we can figure out where Gabriel is. I'm not up to a field trip to get him, but I can have Nathan drive you. He's usually up for an adventure as long as it's before midnight."

"Sure, but are you alright? Are you sick?"

"Just tired." She patted the mattress beside her. "You wore me out last night."

The smile she'd hoped to elicit didn't appear. Instead, he looked quite serious as he sat beside her. "This is because of the blood you had to give him, isn't it? Because of the deal you made on my behalf?"

No need to soften the blow he'd already laid out. "Yes."

"Why hasn't Trina provided a feeder for you?"

That was a valid question she didn't have an immediate answer for. She was too tired to think fast. "The feeder will be here soon."

She'd just have to excuse herself somewhere without him to pretend to eat. This was all so much easier with Vadim, who was busy with his club and had his own place. They'd shared each other's homes, leaving her plenty of opportunities to pretend to feed when they were apart. If she asked Stephanos to stay elsewhere, he undoubtedly would. But after the threats they'd all put on the table the night before, she wouldn't put it past Vadim to make some sort of accident happen or to kill Stephanos outright and take care of her next. Together they were more of a force to be reckoned with.

Since he was here, and in her bed, and she did need to feed, she got comfortable next to where he sat up against the headboard and looked into his eyes.

He chuckled.

"What's so funny?"

"For a second there, you looked like the woman on the cover of the book Trina gave me to read."

"What color is the spine?"

"Blue."

She ran through her internal book catalogue. "His Dark Secret by Mia Silverman?"

From his amazed expression, she had guessed correctly. "You have them all memorized?"

"I spend a lot of time in there."

"Then you should cover the window."

She liked the natural light when she was up during the afternoon hours—when she wasn't in full faux vampire mode.

"I'm careful." No, you're getting sloppy, she chastised herself.

"You better be." He kissed the top of her head.

Lavina almost felt guilty as she prepared to feed. The hum activated within her. She gazed up at him and prompted, "Why did Gabriel make you a vampire?"

His eyes took on a dazed, unfocused gaze, and his head tilted back against the headboard. His muscles relaxed into the feeding trance.

Stephanos went into the house kitchens to see Eirene, as he did every evening after working in the field with their father. He was an adult now, and though he had no family or home of his own, he didn't want his mother to have to cook for him every day. Someday soon he'd meet the woman he'd make his wife, but he'd yet to find her. Eirene teased him endlessly that he never would, even though she was years older and had yet to find a husband.

Eirene was busy getting the food together for the Boros family's evening meal. The plate she often left on the counter for him was right where it always was. He wasn't allowed any further into the house unless Gabriel took him inside. Nor was he allowed to eat their food, but Yianna, the cook, knew he was Gabriel's friend, and that earned him his silence. Stephanos ate quickly so he wouldn't get Eirene or Yianna in trouble.

They were all surprised when Gabriel's mother ran wild-eyed into the kitchen yelling for help. Stephanos nearly choked on the strip of lamb in his hurry to hide that he'd been eating. He tried to look busy doing anything that would explain his presence.

"My son has fallen ill. He will not wake. Yianna, please, you must help him!"

All eyes in the kitchen went to the old cook. Yianna handed her spoon to one of the helpers. "Stephanos, you come too. He's on the floor, and I can't lift him."

Stephanos followed Yianna through the house to Gabriel's bedroom. Gabriel's father was already there, holding his son's head. Gabriel stared blindly at the ceiling, his body limp in his father's arms.

"What happened?" Yianna asked, wiping her hands on her apron and regarding the fallen Boros with a scowl.

"He complained of a pain in his head."

"He's been complaining about that for weeks," Stephanos said. "He's been in a sour mood."

"Lying around here all day, too much wine, too many girls in his bed." His father huffed. "Spoiled boy, always complaining about something."

"He's your only son," exclaimed Gabriel's mother.

"You coddle him too much," he grumbled. "Now look him. He's weak. Fainting like a woman."

Yianna knelt her substantial self beside Gabriel, poking at his face and neck. She lifted his hand and watched as it fell. Then she turned his head side to side. After leaning close to him with her ear over his mouth, she hefted herself back to her feet.

"He is weak but not faint. His soul will leave his body soon. I have heard it," she proclaimed.

Sobbing, Gabriel's mother begged them to put her son on the bed where his dying body would be comfortable. Stephanos lifted the legs of the young man he'd grown up playing with. Now, at twenty, he was dying. Gabriel Boros might be the spoiled boy his father called him, and he wasn't exactly kind, but Stephanos did live a better life than others for having been his playmate, suffering his jests and pranks.

Gabriel had barely had a chance to live. It all seemed very unfair. Stephanos prayed to the gods, saying so.

"Is there nothing you can do?" his mother begged.

"There is one who might help, but there will be consequences."

At the mention of consequences, Stephanos went stiff. He swallowed hard, begging to be small and forgotten in the room.

Yianna tapped his arm. "You, fetch the one called Diodoros. You know where he lives?"

He nodded reluctantly. According to his parents, the windowless house on the outskirts of town was one to be avoided. Only the desperate went there when they wanted to forget their troubles. They were marked on their necks, shunned by respectable folk. The mere thought of having to venture to that house filled him with terror. He didn't want those marks on his neck, for his parents to disown him, for Eirene to despise him.

"It's dark enough. He'll come," said Yianna. "Be sure to tell him you're with the Boros when you enter so he will not mark you."

"Take a horse. Go quickly," Gabriel's father instructed.

Excitement over getting to take one of the fine Boros horses almost overwhelmed his terror at facing Diodoros. Almost. He flew through the house and out into the stable, where he pulled the horse Gabriel often rode from his stall and avoided waking the stable boy to saddle it. He mounted the horse bareback and galloped through the streets.

When he reached Diodoros' house, he rushed inside, out of breath. A single candle illuminated the front room, where a grey-haired man sat in a chair holding a teenaged girl in his arms. He looked up from her neck at the sudden interruption. The girl's head lolled drunkenly when he pulled away with blood dripping from his lips.

"Explain, boy, or you'll pay dearly."

"Boros," Stephanos panted. "Gabriel Boros is ill. Yianna sent me to fetch you. She said you can help him."

"Help him, eh?" Diodoros shifted off the chair, setting the girl in his place. He licked his lips clean, smacking them loudly. "They'll pay dearly for this."

Hoping the old man meant with money and not blood, Stephanos nodded. "I was sent to fetch you. That's all I know."

"Off we go then, boy. Best not to keep the Boros waiting."

Stephanos' skin crawled where old Diodoros held onto him from behind on the ride back. They could not get there fast enough.

Leaving the horse in the stable, he rushed Diodorus to Gabriel's room. Gabriel's parents stood beside the bed, arms around one another. Stephanos had never seen them that close. The situation must have been dire indeed.

Diodoros glided to the bedside, rubbing his hands together. "Does he still draw breath?"

Tears rolled down Gabriel's mother's cheeks as she nodded.

"If he drinks from me, he will be infected as I am for the rest of his days. No sunlight can touch his skin. He will no longer eat as you do."

"He is my only heir. Do what must be done to save him," declared the elder Boros.

Diodoros bared pointy fangs with a mad smile. "There is the matter of my price."

"Two servants, yes. You will be paid," he snapped.

Stephanos jumped when the old man sank his fangs into Gabriel's ashen neck. He realized this was what he'd walked in on when he'd retrieved the old man, that this creature fed on the blood of others. And now Gabriel would too. Revulsion flooded through him.

The old man pulled back and used his bloodied fang to puncture a vein in his wrist. He pried Gabriel's mouth open and dripped blood into it, holding his wrist just above Gabriel's lips.

Stephanos grew hopeful when his friend opened his eyes and color returned to his cheeks. All the rumors of Diodoros being some sort of monster conflicted with the miracle taking place before his eyes. It was like watching Gabriel come back to life. But then he grabbed the bleeding wrist and latched onto it like a suckling babe.

His mother shrieked. His father clapped his hand over her mouth and pulled them both back two steps. Stephanos stood rooted against the door, his hand out, ready to flee. Though candles lit the room, it seemed darker than it had only moments before, the shadows heavier. Gabriel slurped at Diodoros' bleeding wrist. And then the old man pulled his arm away.

"Enough, young one. Rest now."

Stephanos marveled at the tenderness in the old man's voice, almost like he cared deeply for the man on the bed. The hard door against his back assured him the wall was real, but his mind desperately wanted this to be a nightmare he'd wake from at any moment.

Diodoros went to stand before Gabriel's parents, speaking again in the soft, calm voice. "I will take my payment on my way out. You will not argue my choice. We will not speak again, for you will not thank me for what has been done this night."

They nodded.

When the old man approached Stephanos, he pulled the door open, unsure if he should run or just get the blood drinker out of the house as quickly as possible.

"Get them out of the room and bar this door for the rest of the night unless you wish to become your friend's first victim. He will need to feed tomorrow night, but he must be discreet or he will end up in pieces when the city rises up against him."

Stephanos nodded and then found his tongue. "Don't touch the kitchen servants, they are needed here."

"We all need to eat, don't we?" Diodoros chuckled and then headed off down the hallway at a leisurely pace.

Torn between protecting Eirene and everyone from Gabriel, he darted into the room to politely beg the Boros to leave so he could bar the door. They seemed dazed and didn't argue. Surprised at his good fortune, he took care of the door and then hurried down to the kitchen. Yianna and Eirene chatted over dough they were kneading. They were safe. He hung in the background, adrenaline pumping through his body, wanting to make sure Diodoros left before he went to his own bed.

The elder Boros barged into the kitchen. His angry gaze snagged on Yianna but then honed in on Stephanos. "You. Not a word of this to anyone. You'll take my son's place with the city guard. If you do well, your family will remain safe.

You now represent the Boros family, boy. Don't disappoint me."

Stunned, Stephanos nodded. He knew nothing of fighting, but he'd heard the rumblings of an invasion coming—a war. One he had no desire to take part in. He was a strong back in the fields, not a soldier.

Tomorrow everything would change.

29

STEPHANOS WOKE to find he'd nodded off next to Lavina who was still sleeping against his chest. He checked the time to find he'd lost an hour of the night. Lavina might need to sleep, but he needed to find his sire. He shook her gently.

"You said you'd show me how to find Gabriel."

She nodded sleepily and reached for her new phone. "Here's the find my phone app. Just follow the map. Nathan can take you. I'm not going anywhere tonight."

"You said you would feed. Don't forget."

Lavina nodded and tapped on her phone. "Go on. I'll eat while you're off saving that asshole."

She did sound more herself and color had returned to her cheeks. He slid to the edge of the bed and got to his feet. "Rest."

"I will."

"You can't do this every week, Lavina. It takes too much out of you."

"I know."

She sounded defeated and it saddened him. Firey Lavina was far more fun.

"We'll figure something out," he assured her. If she wouldn't alter the terms with Vadim, he would. His safety wasn't worth draining her to exhaustion.

Stephanos closed the door behind him and went to find Nathan. He and Trina were eating at the table. The smell of their food turned his stomach, but ignited vibrant memories of Eirene sneaking him meals fit for the Boros. He smiled, remembering the good times they'd enjoyed, needling each other about their uncertain futures over a stolen plate of food.

"She's sleeping again." He informed Trina. "When you're done there, I need a ride." Stephanos held up the map on his phone to the location Lavina had given him.

"Ah, yes, the treasure hunt." Nathan dug into his dinner with great enthusiasm.

Though he had no desire to eat human food any longer, it brought him joy to watch the two of them savor their meals, chattering about the books they were reading and what seasonings Rosa had used for their dinner.

He played on his phone, flipping back and forth between his game and the blinking marker on the map that indicated where Lavina's phone was. If only Gabriel had had such a thing when he'd been underground. He could have been rescued in a matter of days instead of decades.

Nathan was suddenly too close, startling Stephanos. He'd been getting caught up in his memories too much lately. Yet, for all their refreshed vibrancy, they didn't drag him down as they always had before.

"Are you ready?" Nathan asked.

"You'll make sure Lavina eats?" he asked Trina.

She nodded, smiling warmly.

"Then yes, I'm ready."

The drive out to the landfill took forty minutes. Nathan pulled to a stop at the edge of the road near the gated entrance. "I'll wait here for you then. There's a shovel in the trunk and a tarp should you be successful. I do hate a mess in there."

"Thank you." At least a shovel was a tool he was adept at using.

"There will be a guard at the gate."

That was absurd. "Who guards garbage?"

"It's more about keeping foolish people out of the garbage. Mind the open flames. And where you step. My back isn't what it used to be and I wouldn't be much good for pulling you out."

The garbage was on fire? What kind of hell did these people live in behind their giant houses and smooth roads? All Gabriel had to do was send three fieldworkers out to dig him up. Now he was expected to dodge security, open flames, and a treacherous mountain of stinking trash single-handedly?

"We should probably exchange numbers in case anything bad happens. They do seem to happen since you joined us."

"Sorry." He handed Nathan his phone so he didn't have to stumble through figuring out how to add another number into it.

"All set. I took the liberty of adding Ms. Arandine as well."

"Thank you."

"Off you go then. I've got my book." Nathan reclined the

seat, turned on the interior light, and found his page.

Stephanos walked up the road, turned up the drive, and approached the front gate lit by the soft glow of a phone screen. Everyone spent way too much time on those damned things. At least Nathan was reading a book.

As the old man had warned, a tall fence lined the entire perimeter. Stephanos really didn't want to rip up his nice clothing on the wicked-looking wire by going over the top. The gate was closed. The guard in the booth seemed the neatest way.

Stephanos tapped on the glass, making the man inside jump. He fumbled his phone, sending it crashing to the floor.

"Shit! What did you do that for?" the man yelled at him.

"Sorry."

The guard bent down. "Hope I didn't crack another screen. Shit, Brenda's gonna kill me."

Stephanos pulled the door open and swooped down to bite him. Not to rip him apart, he reminded himself, just to get a little fresh blood and to daze him a bit.

"I'll just slip inside, yeah?"

The guard nodded, a smile plastered on his face.

Stephanos pushed the labeled gate button and walked inside. Lavina would be proud that he'd not ripped anyone to pieces. He wasn't being reckless. He was in control. Head held high, he marched up the dirt and gravel drive that spiraled up a scene straight out of an end-of-the-world movie. Flames burned from black pipes, surrounded by discarded appliances, building materials, boxes, bags, and rotten food. He grimaced. As long as he stayed on the road, he'd be fine.

A quick check of Gabriel's location told him he'd be

walking for a while. He headed up the spiraling road, dodging deep tire tracks that zigzagged in all directions. Then it started to rain. Grumbling, he traveled upward.

He reached a plateau where the phone indicated he was close. From there, he'd have to travel inward on the ragged landscape. Raindrops soaked his clothes and hair. The water brought out a deeper level of rotten stink that reminded him of the damp earth and his clothes decaying when he'd been buried. His steps slowed, anticipating panic to set in any second. When it didn't, he took several shallow breaths of the fetid air and, using the shovel as a walking stick, felt his way forward. With each slip in the thick mud, he prayed he wouldn't snap his ankle. Crawling down this trash mountain before sunrise would be a challenge.

When the phone notified him that he'd arrived, he looked around. So many black garbage bags. Why did they all have to look the same?

"Gabriel?" he called out several times but received no answer.

Lavina had shown him how to use the phone as a flashlight. Now that he was far from the gate, he touched the light app and aimed the bright beam over the tumble of debris. With no help for it, he dug around, opening every black bag he came across. Several times he had to use the shovel to lever a heavy object off the next layer of bags. Discouraged at finding nothing, he checked the time. Sunrise in two hours and by now, the guard at the gate was back to himself and probably wondering why his phone was cracked and his neck was sore. He was running out of time.

Stephanos shuffled forward, pushing at the bags with the shovel to feel what was inside. His foot snagged on something. He reached down to untangle himself and found a slimy, empty bag. A black bag bigger than most of the others. He held it open and used the flashlight to look inside. It was wet and smelled atrocious, like rotten flesh. There was a ragged hole torn open on one side. At the bottom of the bag, he spotted Lavina's phone.

He wiped it off the best he could on whatever slightly absorbent thing he could find other than his soaked clothes and slid it into his pocket.

Somewhere, Gabriel was free. And angry. And hungry. Damn, that couldn't be good at all.

30

LAVINA SAT on the couch, her legs drawn up underneath her. Trina had gone to her room an hour ago to read until Rosa arrived so they could chat for a few minutes as they usually did over breakfast. Sunrise wasn't far away but Stephanos and Nathan weren't back yet.

The memories of Stephanos' parents, and even Gabriel's, had dredged up vague recollections of her own past. Her father was a faceless man with blonde hair and long legs in her mind. He'd been thrown from their horse and cracked his head open when she was five. With him gone, her mother had no choice but to venture into the village for the things she couldn't make on her own. The crowd had come for her before a year had passed. The flames danced behind Lavina's eyelids even to this day.

Believing she could be saved, a childless couple had taken her in. Maybe it was only because they needed help and she was an extra pair of hands for chores, but they'd given her a bed and food and prayed over her. What little good that had done. Lavina sighed, remembering the years of hunger, barely daring to feed from her adopted parents or anyone else in the village for fear of ending up on a pyre.

She glanced around her own house with its warmth and comfort and people who cared about her and was immensely thankful.

The garage door opened. She sat up, bracing herself. Stephanos, dripping and dirty, wasn't smiling as he made a beeline for her. Nathan came in and went straight to his room.

"You didn't see Gabriel?" Lavina asked, attempting to keep her joy to herself.

"I yelled for him, but he didn't answer. He has to be hiding there somewhere. There's no one close by for him to feed from. It would be a long way down to the gatekeeper for the shape he was in."

"Well, you tried. What happens to him from here is out of your hands."

The stench rolling off his clothes was making her eyes water.

"I need a shower before sunrise. I'll go out again tomorrow to look for him."

"Either he'll turn up or he won't. Why don't you let be what will be?"

"I can't do that."

Of course he wouldn't. Like it or not—and she definitely didn't—those two were linked together. Bound by centuries of guilt and obligation.

"Suit yourself."

He started to depart, but paused. "Are you feeling better?"

"Yes, and thank you for asking. Now, go get cleaned up

before you get stuck sleeping in those stinky clothes. Bag them up and set them in the hallway for Rosa or your room will stink too."

He nodded, heading up the stairs.

Relieved that he was home and safe, she allowed herself to relax. He wasn't running off with Gabriel. He'd come back to her instead.

What she really wanted was for him to sleep in her bed, where she could find a better memory to feed from. The one she'd asked for hadn't been nearly as dark as she'd hoped. She'd barely gleaned any substance from it, not wanting to dull the memory of his sister. He deserved to hang on to what he had left of the ones he'd loved.

She took a small amount of satisfaction in guessing how horrified Gabriel's parents must have been when they realized what the life they'd bargained for their son truly was. It would have been kinder to have let the brat go. They could have adopted a son who would have been grateful, who may have actually made them proud. Then again, she'd never had children. Maybe her callous reasoning made that a wise choice.

Lavina untangled herself from her blanket and made her way to her room on stiff legs. She waited there until the sky turned pink and then blue. Once she was sure Stephanos was fast asleep, she emerged to find Rosa and Trina in the kitchen, talking over tea. Gregory and Eric were eating breakfast at the table, tossing dry cereal bits at one another.

"If you get that on the floor, you'll be cleaning it up. I hate when those nubbins stick to my socks," she warned them.

Their cereal fight abruptly ended.

Rosa laughed. "They woke up full of the dickens."

Yet another reason Lavina was relieved to never have had children. She had little patience for their mischief.

"I was just filling Rosa in on Stephanos' blood tasting." Trina briefed Lavina on the experiment they'd done the night before.

"Fascinating." Her mind started whirring with how she could use this. Or maybe, she stopped herself, how *he* could use this.

If he could find something of worth to do on his own, maybe he'd stop doing Gabriel's dirty work. He had a head for learning. He could be so much more.

Good god, was she really fixing another one? Lavina sighed heavily, garnering wary looks from both Trina and Rosa.

"I'm going to read for a while before I turn in. See if you can rustle up another selection of blood samples for Stephanos to try, would you?"

"Yes, ma'am. Anything else before I turn in myself?" Trina asked.

"No, get some sleep, dear. We both deserve it."

Trina smiled warmly.

"Did you need anything from me, Rosa?"

"A few bills that need paying. I'll leave them in the library for you later."

There were always bills. Hundreds of years of paying them. The recluses who lived off the grid might be on to something. If only she weren't a creature who loved her comforts.

"Good day then, ladies." Lavina headed for her room, but not before glancing up the stairs where a freshly showered vampire slept. Sometimes those loved comforts were people.

The urge to climb into bed with him, even as totally asleep and cold as he would be, hit her. But how would she explain how she'd gotten there? And she would inevitably have to get up and use the bathroom at some point. Her bladder wasn't as on board with large holding capacities as it had been when she was younger. Real vampires had no need for such things.

The one time she'd gotten up the nerve to covertly taste Vadim's blood to see if it would change her, nothing had happened. It seemed her brand of nightmare creature didn't mix with theirs in that way. And the sour taste, she gagged just thinking about it. No, thank you.

She spent half an hour in the library, organizing the new books Nathan and Trina had put there for her to read. Trina had left a sticky note on one of them that read: I dare you to read this one.

Well, she couldn't turn down that challenge. In the light of morning sun, she dove into the world of a centaur prince falling in love with a surprisingly experienced young woman who laughingly failed at posing as a virtuous maiden by page eight. Just one more page turned into two chapters. She glanced at the clock, knowing she needed to go to bed. She'd just take the book with her in case she couldn't get to sleep right away, because really, she was curious to find out how the sexual mechanics of that relationship were going to work. Hung like a horse, indeed.

Lavina's alarm went off far too soon. However, her curiosity in all things centaur were assuaged. She got in and out of the bathroom for all the necessary non-vampire things with ten minutes to spare. The mirror said she hadn't slept at all, but she'd had at least three and a half hours... which wasn't nearly enough. She groaned.

After getting dressed and checking to see that the sun had set, she crept out of her room and went straight to Trina's door.

A bleary-eyed woman answered her knock. "What is it? Is something wrong? What did that pretty stray do now?"

"No, this is all you." Lavina dropped the book at her feet. "This stupid book kept me up all day, you horrible person."

Trina threw her head back and laughed. She pumped her fist in the air. "I knew you wouldn't be able to resist. Nathan owes me ten bucks."

"Look at me, I'm exhausted and for no good reason," Lavina whined. "What am I supposed to tell him?"

"Tell me about what?" Stephanos asked as he knelt to pick up the fallen book.

Trina held her hand out for it. "The blood she wanted me to get for you to taste. I didn't get a chance to get a verified pool of samples together so we can try to start narrowing down the different tastes of diseases."

He shrugged. "We can do that tomorrow. I need to look for Gabriel tonight." Then he seemed to get a good look at Lavina. "You fed just last night. Why do you look starved again?"

She couldn't even manage being fake offended over being told she looked like shit. "I was just going to take care of that. No worries."

She retreated from Trina's doorway. Stephanos followed right beside her, crowding the hallway.

"It's still the drain from supplying Vadim, isn't it? I'll have a talk with him while I'm out," he said darkly.

She wrapped herself around his arm and smiled up at him. "No. No need for that. I'll take care of myself. Really."

"It's no trouble. I planned to talk to him anyway. If

Gabriel is on the loose, he should know. Assuming you still want peace between us?"

Dammit. She did, and that was a thoughtful gesture. If he went to Vadim unsupervised, could she trust them not to devolve into a schoolboy tumble within minutes?

"He doesn't know he's dealing my blood, remember? And he can't." She clutched his arm, drilling her earnestness in with brute force. "If he learns this drug is from me, he'll toss me in a room and drain me dry."

"I won't let that happen," Stephanos vowed.

"No, you won't. Because you won't tell him anything about me or my blood. Do, however, let him know that Gabriel is back on his feet. Coming from you, that would go a long way to seal the rift between you and Vadim."

He nodded. "Gabriel won't appreciate it, but I hope it will make things easier for you."

"Oh, you sweet, sweet man." She relaxed her grip on him and kissed his cheek. "Please be careful."

"Please rest and feed. For real this time. Don't lie and tell me you're well when you're not."

She nodded. She would feed well when he returned. Until then, she'd take a nap and not pick up another book for a while. She hoped Trina enjoyed her ten dollars. Troublemaker.

Stephanos rewarded her with a kiss that left her dizzy. Yep, she was going to keep this one around as long as she could without cleaning him up too much. She wouldn't make the mistake she'd made with Vadim. Stephanos already had a fine line between civilized and wild rage. She wouldn't be responsible for sending him out into the world as randomly unhinged as Vadim turned out to be.

31

NATHAN PARKED in what was becoming his usual spot at The Jackyl and resumed his reading. Being a Friday night, the lot was filling up fast. Stephanos followed Lavina's instructions to bypass the long line and go straight to the man at the door. The human recognized him before he even got close enough to speak and nodded him inside.

At least he hadn't been banned from the place after Gabriel's short takeover. Then again, maybe his association with Lavina had negated some of that.

Vadim stood at a tall table with two women who were seated, one of whom was human. The other was the female vampire Lavina didn't like. They waved him over.

"Stephanos, what a surprise! Would you like a drink?" Vadim asked with an unsettling amount of hospitality. He didn't seem drunk, and he'd made it clear that he didn't partake in recreational drugs.

"Sure?" He had a feeling he was going to need a drink to occupy his hands and settle his nerves. Instinct made him want to punch the guy for Lavina's condition and what he'd done to Gabriel. Who was he kidding? Instinct wanted to do far more than punch him. Claw him, rip him to pieces. He bared his fangs but quickly converted his warning into a smile.

"You remember Eveline? And this is Marci with an i." Vadim gestured to the women.

Eveline leaned forward over the table, exposing more cleavage than was already spilling from her shirt. "Alone tonight?"

"For now, yes."

"Not for long, is what I'm hearing." Marci giggled.

Eveline shed a patronizing smile in her direction before whipping her focus back to him. "Wore the old lady out? Looking for a younger model more your speed?"

"Lavina isn't old."

Eveline laughed. "She could be your mother. Or mine. Hell, she's even older than our handsome host." She batted her eyelashes at Vadim.

"Not by a long shot," he said, "but I do accept handsome host."

"Her body is older, I mean," said Eveline.

Vadim shot her a look and inclined his head toward the human at the table.

Eveline caught herself. "Right. Anyway, younger, more limber," she ran her hands over her breasts and hips, "everything where it belongs. You know, if you're into women your own age."

"I bet he's into a lot of—" Marci started to say before Tiffany trounced over and knocked her hip into Stephanos.

"Hey stranger. Your usual?"

"Yes."

She glanced at Vadim, who nodded, and then she winked at Stephanos. "On the house, lucky you."

He was starting to wonder why he was here. He would have rather been home in bed with Lavina. Except Marci did look tasty, and a vampire needed to eat. By the way she was ogling the three of them like she'd won the social lottery, Marci with an i wasn't going anywhere. Business first.

"I really just stopped by to talk to you about a matter you might find alarming."

"Oh?" Vadim fussed with the cuff of his purple dress shirt. It was a nice color, like sunset on grapes. He'd have to look for one like it.

"Our mutual acquaintance is not where he was expected to be."

Vadim's brow furrowed. "You looked?"

Damn the women at the table, making him have to dance around the plain words he wanted to say so he could leave. "I did. Signs show that he left of his own accord. He must be quite determined."

Tiffany picked that moment to show up with his drink. He downed half of it, hoping his task would be done in minutes so he could eat and run. Or hell, if it meant getting out of here faster, Trina could order someone in for him when he got back.

Vadim cast an alarmed glance at the nearest bouncer. The man hurried over. They had a hushed conversation. The bouncer nodded and went to speak to another employee.

"And you came here to tell me this?"

"I don't like being on both sides, but being with Lavina," he shrugged, "here I am."

Eveline watched them both raptly, no doubt trying to collect gossip. Oblivious Marci kept attempting to engage her in conversation but was completely ignored.

"So, she sent you," Vadim said.

"No, I'm here on my own because I find myself in the middle. I helped you as much as I could before, and that's what I'm doing now. I'm not Gabriel."

"You've cut your allegiance with him then?"

"I didn't say that." He took another sip of his drink. He was definitely having Trina order someone in. Being in this conversation was making his head hurt.

"The middle is a precarious place to be, my friend."

They were friends now? The still tender muscle and bone in his arm didn't agree. Couldn't they just not be enemies?

"I've said what I came to say. I'll let you get back to," he waved at Eveline and Marci.

"Before you go, perhaps you would be interested in making more friends?" Vadim offered smoothly, stepping away from the table and nodding for him to follow.

Stephanos expected their direction to be to the office where bad things happened, but Vadim led him to a low table near the bar where two men sat. He recognized Fane, but not the other one.

Fane stood. "He's joining already? That was fast. Hardly even counts by our standards."

"Not quite yet, but I feel he should be informed. I happen to know firsthand that Stephanos has quite a penchant for violence. We can't have that running amok in Northchester when the inevitable happens."

Stephanos glanced between the three men. "When what happens exactly?"

"Think of this as a support group," the man with short, blond, curly hair said. Light freckles dotted his cheeks and narrow nose. His cream-colored, thick sweater did little to make his fair skin appear more lively.

All three were vampires.

"You may have met Fane, who was Lavina's second love and founder of our club. This is Max, who is visiting North-chester for the first time in person. He usually attends our meetings virtually. You were... I forget?"

"Fourth, and maybe sixth if you count when we got back together briefly," Max said, holding out his hand.

Was he supposed to shake it? What he wanted to do was back away, all the way out the door. But Vadim was right beside him. If he ran now, this would be one of the embarrassing moments that haunted him forever. Better to shake hands with Lavina's exes and then make an orderly retreat.

"I, sadly, was not informed of my number by the lovely Lavina Arandine, but we were together for far more years than these two can lay claim to," said Vadim.

Stephanos drained every last drip of liquor from his glass. The round ice ball smacked against his teeth. This was going to be a two drink night for sure. Where was Tiffany when he wanted her? "What is this?"

Fane held out his gold brocade sleeved arms and wiggled his fingers. "The Lavina Cast Off Club."

Max joined him in the finger wiggle.

Vadim rolled his eyes. "Don't mind these two clowns. We are your source for all things Lavina. You have questions or feel you may go off the deep end and tear up my town, you come here first."

"Why don't the three of you just work out your problems with Lavina? She seems to like to talk things out."

Fane sat down and kicked out an empty chair, nodding him to it. "She's a talker for sure. Have you noticed what she talks about"?

Nothing in particular stood out to him. "I don't know. We just talk."

Max glanced at Vadim. "You want to take this one, since you have more experience? We've never had an intervention for a current victim," he said to Stephanos.

"Victim?" What the hell were these three going on about?

"Have you ever seen her taste the blood of another?" Max asked.

"No? It's not like she stands over me when I feed. Why should I watch her?"

"None of us have seen her feed," Fane stated.

"So she doesn't like eating in front of others. What of it?"

Vadim took the last chair and waved Tiffany over. "Don't you find that odd?"

"Not really." He didn't watch Gabriel feed either. It was a private thing as far as he was concerned. Humans tended to get quite relaxed. They deserved privacy in return for their blood.

The one time she had watched him, she'd clearly had other motives, and he'd not been opposed to them.

"How do you think she eats? One cannot live without blood." Stephanos considered his own questionable well-being at several points in his life. "Live well enough to look human, anyway. Lavina does."

Vadim, having caught Tiffany's attention, pointed to the table and then returned his attention to them. "That is the million dollar question, my friend."

Max tapped his pointed chin. "Perhaps you, being on the inside, could find an answer to this nagging question."

"Which brings us to the second question." Fane raised his brows, glancing at Vadim.

Vadim leaned in closer. "Have you noticed memories fading? Getting duller?"

"Particularly the bad ones?" added Max.

Stephanos stared into the drink that appeared in front of him. "Would it be so bad for nightmares to lose their grip?"

"Not of itself, no." Fane sipped the wine Tiffany offered him. "But why does this happen around Lavina? To all of us... around Lavina?"

He looked into the now serious faces of the men at the table. "Is this also a question you wish to have answered?"

"Drinks on the house in perpetuity if you do," Fane offered.

"I didn't offer that," Vadim clarified. "But I could find a position for a man capable of getting answers in ways that don't require a bloody mess."

The second drink tasted better than the first. Maybe Vadim did have a few redeeming benefits. "Sadly, bloody messes are my specialty."

Vadim shook his head. "Not in my city, they're not."

"We don't want Lavina hurt," Max said.

"Good, because neither do I."

Fane raised his glass. "To answers." Max and Vadim raised theirs. Stephanos, at their expectant stares, lifted his as well, clinking them all together.

The four men drank.

Tiffany visited their table twice more. Whatever she served him there was far more potent than what she normally gave him. He blinked at his phone, trying to decipher the time.

"Not a big drinker either, I take it?" Vadim asked, eyeing the other two men who were blathering like giddy girls in a slurred language Stephanos didn't understand. "Someday, she'll cast off someone with a tolerance I can hang out with."

"No." Stephanos closed one eye and tried to find Nathan's name on his contact list.

"Would you like an escort out to the car? I'm assuming old Nathan is waiting patiently out there for you?"

"Maybe." At least that's what he meant to say. It sounded just as slurred as whatever Fane and Max were speaking.

"We'll call this an advance. A little taste of what life could be like if you can come through for us." Vadim snapped his fingers at Marci. "Would you mind helping Stephanos out to his car? It will be the one with a light on inside, parked in the front lot. And don't worry, the driver is quite discreet." He winked.

Marci grinned, throwing a victorious look at Eveline, who sat alone at the tall table. "I'd be happy to help."

"Stan," Vadim snapped his fingers again. "See these two get safely outside without bowling anyone over, please."

Stephanos stood unsteadily. He couldn't remember the last time he'd been drunk. Yes, he could. He just didn't want to. Isla.

If Lavina really could dull memories, maybe she could do that one for him.

"Hey, stay with me, okay? We're going to have a good time outside." Marci held tight to his arm, guiding him toward the door.

Stan, one of the lumbering bouncers, walked in front of them, clearing the way.

They made it outside with only knocking into one empty

table. The cool air felt very good on his face. He gulped it in.

"You're not going to be sick, are you?" Marci asked.

One benefit of being a vampire was that he'd never thrown up. "No."

"Good. I don't care if you're drunk and rough, but I don't like vomit breath."

The cars in the lot all blurred and then doubled. Now he remembered why he didn't drink heavily anymore.

"Hey, hold up." Tiffany shot out from the shadows. Had she come from around the back?

"He's mine." Marci glared at the waitress under the too bright parking lot lights. "Vadim said so. Back off."

Tiffany held up her hands. She had something in one of them. "Don't tell him I gave you this. Promise?"

Stephanos closed one eye so she was more in focus. "Gave me what?"

"The drinks I served the three of you, they were spiked. Vadim said." She sneered at Marci. "He likes his guests relaxed, but I know you don't drink much. You'll feel like hell tomorrow unless take this as soon as you get in your car. Whatever you do, please do *not* drive."

"He has a driver," Marci bragged.

"Good." Tiffany pressed a gelatinous packet into his hand. "Rip the corner off and drink it all. Got it?"

Stephanos squeezed her hand and slurred his thanks.

Marci shooed her away.

Tiffany shook her head. "Make sure you use protection with that. It's been around."

"Don't listen to that jealous bitch." Marci licked his cheek.

What the hell was that about? He wiped his face on his shoulder.

"You're all mine," she said.

The light of Lavina's car drew him like a blessed beacon. "This one."

Marci reached for the door just as Stephanos stumbled into the side of the car. His were pleasantly numb.

Nathan popped out of the driver's door. "Do you require some assistance, sir?"

"Oh, fancy!" Marci grinned. "He drank a little too much."

The pulse in her neck, so close to his face, called to him. "Didn't drink enough."

"Oh, hun. You did. Mind taking us home?"

"Us?" Stephanos and Nathan said simultaneously.

Marci pouted. "Or you could maybe give us a little privacy in the back seat for a bit?"

"I fear you'll make a mess in this condition, sir."

Marci giggled. "I hope so."

The vein pulsing beside him was the only thing in focus. He pressed his body against Marci's, holding her against the side of the car.

Nathan cleared his throat. "I'll uh...just leave you to it then, shall I?"

The sound of his door opening and closing dimly registered.

Marci's hands ran up his chest and over his arms. "Yum."

He leaned down to nip at her neck. She melted against him, wrapping one leg around his and arching her back.

Perfect angle. He sank his fangs into her and drank deeply.

Marci went limp in his arms, moaning softly. They were not the moans he wanted to hear.

Once he had his fill, he set dazed Marci on the hood of the car next to Lavina's and got in.

"All set?" asked Nathan.

"Yes."

"Very good." The old man started the car and pulled out of the lot.

Stephanos fingered the pouch in his hand. Maybe he'd take that later. Right now, fully fed and pleasantly drunk, he wanted nothing more than to fall into bed with the woman waiting for him at home.

Home. He liked the sound of that.

32

LAVINA, DRAWN by the noise, met Stephanos and Nathan in the kitchen. "Are you drunk?"

"Sort of," he slurred.

"Very much so, ma'am." Nathan shook his head. "Will you be needing anything else this evening?"

Stephanos hung onto the countertop, leering in her direction. Or, more accurately, over her right shoulder.

"I think we'll be staying in for the rest of the night, thank you. Do check with Trina, though. She may need blood samples retrieved."

Nathan nodded, hung up the key, and headed toward Trina's usual haunts.

"I didn't think vampires could get this inebriated. Do you need to lie down?"

"With you, yes." He stumbled closer but then paused, holding up a clear plastic square filled with liquid. "Tiffany gave me this. Should I take it now or after?"

Lavina plucked it from his hand. "Who's Tiffany?"

"The waitress. She said Vadim spiked us."

"Put something in your drink, you mean." Vadim really was drifting back to his old ways. "Why did Vadim drug you?"

"Me and Fane and Max. I'm in their support group now," he slurred proudly.

Her stomach plummeted. Don't freak out. Don't. Freak. Out. "Max? He's in town?"

Stephanos nodded. "Silly fellow."

He certainly hadn't been silly before her. "This is a support group for what, exactly?" Was her voice squeaky?

"You." Stephanos wrapped his arms around her. "Did you feed?"

All moisture had left her mouth. She managed a vague nod.

"You need all your blood." He held up his hand and blinked at it a few times, waving it back and forth. "I don't need to bite you tonight."

"You don't *need* to bite me any night."

His face lit up with a big, sloppy grin. "But I like to. You're delicious."

In any other angle of this conversation, she would have eaten that up, but not when he'd hung out with the Lavina Cast Off Club. She slipped the plastic square into her pocket. Drunk, high, whatever this was, he was talkative, and she needed answers and to actually feed. Clarity on his part could wait.

"Shall we?" She nodded toward the stairs. If he was going to pass out at some point or get sick, she wanted him in his own bed.

He bent down as if to scoop her into his arms. She jumped back. "Hey now. How about you concentrate on getting your own staggering feet up the stairs? I'll follow."

As though she'd smacked him on the wrist and called him bad, he gave her a forlorn look and started for the stairs. His emotions were as high as he was. She planted a smile on her face and took his hand to walk beside him.

At the top of the stairs, he stopped, turning to her and taking her other hand in his. "You do like me, don't you?" he asked quietly and more clearly than he'd spoken before.

"I do." She meant it. But she'd also meant it with Fane, Max, and Vadim until she'd had to let them go. "What did your support group tell you? That I didn't?"

He shook his head enthusiastically, sending his hair tumbling into his face. A big, deadly puppy, this one. She pulled one of her hands from his to smooth his wayward locks back. Stephanos leaned into her palm. "I fed. Do you want to..." He raised his eyebrows and glanced at his door.

Screwing the endearing, deadly puppy would level him out a little. Maybe. It was an enjoyable means to her goal of feeding, for sure.

Lavina leaned in to kiss him but caught a whiff of cloying perfume. "Is that glitter on your cheek?"

Stephanos scowled and wiped his face. "Sorry. Dinner had the wrong idea."

First, some waitress was doing him favors, and now a bar tramp wanted to fuck her vampire? "And you ate her up."

"Not like I'm going to eat you up." He grinned wickedly. Within seconds, Lavina found herself inside his room and on her back on his bed.

His enthusiasm smothered her jealousy, especially after her clothes were stripped off with great efficiency. His followed quickly thereafter. The packet would have to wallow in her pocket for a while. She had other priorities at the moment.

His body hovered over hers. He lowered his face to whisper in her ear. "They said you make our bad memories go away."

Her breath caught in her throat.

"I have far too many of those. You can make them all go away if you want to."

"I don't—" panic ate the rest of her words. She scrambled out from under him and off the bed. Her breath came in gasps. The walls, like the truth of her existence, closing in on her.

Lavina grabbed her clothes, pulling her long, baggy shirt over her head. She dug into the pocket of her pants and tossed the packet at him. "You should take that and then go."

"Go?" He looked at her like she was speaking gibberish. Maybe she was.

"Leave. Please."

She felt behind her blindly for the door. Her mind spinning. She was going to have to move, to change her name. Good god, Vadim knew. They all knew. Had they followed Stephanos here? Were they circling the house, readying their lynching? Where the fuck had she put her go bag? It wasn't in the trunk. She knew that for sure.

"Leave? Lavina, what are you doing?" Stephanos slid off the bed in a beautifully fluid motion, all naked, flexing muscles. She would have much rather been drooling over that, but she couldn't find the damned doorknob. She didn't dare look away to make her escape. Like facing off with a wild animal, breaking eye contact would signal weakness, and she was definitely weak, as underfed as she was.

Filled with fresh blood, the speed at which he advanced, pinning her to the wall beside the door, was gloriously terrifying.

His hot breath blew over her face. He sniffed her hair, her cheek and then her neck. "Why do I smell fear, Lavina?"

"Let me go." Her voice held no authority, and it pissed her off. This was her house. It was her life that he was endangering. He should be the one who was scared. Yet, she couldn't make her heart stop pounding.

"I don't think so. They wanted answers." He sniffed her again. "And now so do I."

She stilled as if by doing so she might become invisible to the predator holding her captive. "Answers to what?"

He didn't move. Was she even speaking out loud?

What if Vadim wasn't coming for her at all? What if he'd triggered this beast of chaos to do his work for him? Her legs started to shake.

"I want to watch you feed, Lavina. Now. Downstairs. Prove that they're wrong. I *want* them to be wrong."

She did too. Very much.

Could she get Nathan and Trina out of the house under the guise of picking up a feeder for her? If they were away and safe, could she overpower Stephanos?

He grabbed her wrist.

"Ouch, you're hurting me."

His iron grip did not ease. Like a wild beast scenting the air, his mouth hung open the slightest bit.

"So much fear. What would you taste like now, hmm?" He cocked his head, regarding her with narrowed eyes.

If she didn't get control of this situation, she and everyone else in the house was doomed. "Stephanos, let go."

He pulled the door open. "You choose. Which one will

you taste for me?"

"I can't feed from Nathan or Trina." Giving it her all, she tried to wrench her wrist out of his grip. All she got out of it was a future date with bruises and some ice. Damn Vadim and his blood demand, weakening her.

Maybe she could reason with him. Talk him down. "It's too soon for either of them. Trina fed Vadim after your attack. Nathan fed you. If you want me to drink blood, we need to get a feeder."

"No. Now. Use me. Prove them wrong so I can vouch for you."

Tears welled in her eyes. Now who was suffering from high emotions? She wanted to kick herself, but everything felt numb. Could she drive her fake fangs through his skin and suck a mouthful of blood in a convincing manner? She'd never had to bite anyone before. How was she even supposed to line up a bite in the right spot for fuck's sake?

"Don't make me do this," she begged, not even sure if she meant the bite she was sure to fail at or proving the Cast Off Club right.

"Why?" he demanded.

"Because I can't." Her world crumbled in those three words. It had been a good run, her life far extended beyond her natural span. The lie had been spread too thin for too long.

Fight ran out of her with the control of her muscles. As much as she wished she could, she did not pass out or faint to spare her the ripping and gnashing of fangs that was sure to be set upon her at any moment. She'd seen first-hand what he'd done to Vadim, and that had only been at a command from Gabriel. Vadim hadn't done anything to Stephanos. He hadn't fed from him, or sheltered him, or slept with him.

He hadn't lied to him from the moment they'd met.

Stephanos shoved her limp body hard against the wall. "What do you mean can't?"

"I'm... I'm not a vampire," she whispered.

"What?"

She knew his hearing was not at fault. The truth was.

"You lied to me? Lavina, you lied?" He let go of her to slam his hands open-palmed on the wall beside where her head had been seconds before she crumbled limply to the carpet.

"All of this? It's all lies?" He threw his hands at the wall again, harder this time, shouting.

She nodded mutely.

"They were right." He shook his head, backing up a step. "Your fangs?"

"Fake."

"All the times you told me you fed?"

"I did, just not blood."

He dropped to a crouch, still naked, but there was nothing sexy about it. He was a feral vampire about to rip her apart. Stephanos' head swiveled, tilting, sniffing her, fangs exposed, lips drawn in a snarl.

His voice took on the hypnotic tone vampires sometimes used on unwilling humans. "What did you feed on, Lavina?"

The tone had never worked on her, but she'd already lost. Lying wouldn't save her.

"You. I fed on you."

"This is how you dull memories? You feed on them?"

"Yes."

She stared at her knees drawn up before her, her arms

wrapped around them. This is how it ends, half naked on her bedroom floor? How pathetic.

Stephanos shot to his feet. He grabbed his clothes in a wadded pile in his arms and strode naked out of her bedroom. Heavy footfalls, like he was taking two stairs at a time, followed seconds later.

If he wasn't going to hurt her directly, would he take out his anger on Trina or Nathan? Lavina rocked there on the floor for a moment, clutching the hair at her temples, tears running down her face. She couldn't let him hurt them.

Lavina worked herself up to standing and then stumbled blindly out onto the stairs. She couldn't hear any screams or sounds of a struggle, no raised voices. No cries for help.

Maybe he'd struck that fast.

Expecting to find a puddle of blood and a body at any moment, she crept through the main level.

"Lavina?" Trina called in a hushed voice.

She found Trina in her favorite chair in the living room, still under a blanket draped around her. A huge wet spot covered the front.

For a second, Lavina forgot to breathe. Then she noticed the fallen teacup on the floor in front of the chair.

"Where is he?" she whispered.

Trina's voice gained strength with each word. "He strode in here naked as can be. Scared the ever-loving piss out of me and then walked out the front door. Lavina, what happened?"

"We had a falling out." To put it mildly.

Exhaustion flooded through her. She fell limply onto the couch. The feral vampire she'd taken in had walked out the front door without spilling a drop of blood.

At least not yet. He'd also been drunk and drugged.

Who was to say that he wouldn't return, fully enraged, once he was sober?

Or even worse, that he had Vadim's number and had filled him and the rest of the Cast Off Club in on the truth? The weight of dread made it hard to breathe.

"You should probably leave. Wake Nathan. You two should take the car and head into town. Get a room somewhere nice and sleep well. I'll text you when it's clear to return. Your bag is already in the car. Go on."

"Lavina, I don't want to leave you here alone. You look pale as a ghost. This blanket needs washing, and besides, Nathan is likely sound asleep by now."

"I'm not." Nathan walked into the living room, looking annoyed. "Who can sleep with all the wall pounding upstairs?"

Trina shot him a glare that immediately had Nathan looking contrite. "Sorry, ma'am."

She found enough lifeless air to say, "It wasn't the fun kind of pounding, I assure you."

"They had a fight," Trina clarified.

Nathan's lips thinned and his jowly jaw went tight. "Did that vampire hurt you, ma'am?"

"No." He had not, other than the sore wrist that she now rubbed. In the grand scheme of things, a few bruises were far less than she deserved. "The wall suffered more than I did."

"He left." Trina answered Nathan's next question before he got a chance to give breath to it.

"Shame. I was starting to like that one," he said quietly. He turned back toward his room.

"Me too," Lavina said under her breath. "I'd like the two of you to head out for the night as a precaution. No arguing.

Take the car. I won't be needing it."

Trina stared her down for a moment but ultimately stood and went to the kitchen to get the car key. Nathan went to his room and returned with a bag. The two of them paused at the door to the garage as if waiting for her to change her mind. She did not.

Once the sound of the car faded, Lavina locked all the doors and windows and then went to her room to put on some pants. If she was going to get murdered tonight, at least she was going to go out fully dressed.

33

SHE'D LIED. All of it had been a lie. The cold asphalt under his feet barely registered. There were too damned many streetlights in this safe fucking neighborhood. Stephanos ripped open the packet and sucked the gooey, bitter contents down his throat. If he was going to be out wandering unfamiliar territory on his own, he needed his wits. His rage was scrambling them enough without help from whatever Vadim had fed him.

The quarter moon overhead was barely enough to light his way. Sticking to the plentiful shadows, he worked his way down the hill of luxury homes. Near the bottom, he veered off the road toward the trees.

Before he entered the branches and uneven footing, he put on his pants and shirt. He hadn't grabbed his shoes. The dirt and leaves under his feet felt more natural anyway. This was his home, not the fine estate atop the hill with its safe walls and comfortable beds.

A buzzing in his pants brought him out of his fuming.

He halted his downward, determined pace to answer his phone.

Gabriel's hoarse voice greeted him. "Where are you?"

"Nowhere. You?"

"It took a lot of feeding, but I'm home. You were supposed to help me, Stephanos. Why didn't you help me?"

A lot of feeding didn't sound discreet. It sounded like a trail of bodies. Vadim wasn't going to like that. In fact, when finding bloodless bodies, the first name that would likely come to mind would be his, not Gabriel's. Fuck.

"I did come for you. You were already gone."

"You were too slow. I couldn't wait there indefinitely."

Standing alone in the middle of the trees, Stephanos peered through the bare branches to see the stars overhead. He inhaled the damp night air. How long had *he* suffered underground without such luxuries?

"Too slow? It took you sixty-seven years to find me."

Gabriel scoffed. "I didn't have a cell phone to track."

Unhindered by the terror that normally accompanied every thought of his years trapped underground, Stephanos, for the first time, pondered his rescue. And his capture.

"Are you there?" Gabriel snapped.

Had he gotten too wild after the war? Gabriel had sent him out hunting night after night until all he could think about was the taste of blood. And then he'd been commanded to stop. To go back to the sick slaves who barely had enough breath to go about their own lives let alone sustain his. If they didn't let him feed, Gabriel whipped them. They lost blood either way. At least the high Stephanos offered gave them a short release from their miserable lives.

"You knew everyone in Argos who would have known where they buried me. Did you not ask?"

"Of course I did. What are you going on about? Stephanos, come home."

Had he been an unruly cur, to be leashed out of sight until he was needed next? A dog, given a bed on the floor? To be fed scraps?

How many times had he been captured or beaten? Had he narrowly escaped meeting the sun, only to be freed by Gabriel at the last moment? Always Gabriel.

Yet his sire had never been caught, wounded, and chased out of town until pink edged the early morning sky. His sire had always known where to find him.

Had it always been...Gabriel?

"Stephanos," Gabriel snapped. "We need to take Vadim out for what he did to us."

Lavina had given him a home. One with comfort, good feeders, had made him feel human again.

She'd also lied and used him.

Vadim kept this city safe, clean, and fed the vampires under his care. Hell, he even helped the humans in a way. He'd also drugged him and quite possibly sent him back to Lavina to do his bidding.

Even so...

"Vadim did nothing to us that we did not deserve."

"Are you out of your mind?" Gabriel screamed in his ear.

"When you called me away to America to gain your footing here, when you promised you'd have someone look after Isla, did you?"

"What are you prattling on about? Get to the house, Stephanos. We'll talk when you've regained your senses." His sire ended the call.

Stephanos closed his eyes and sat in the leaves and

underbrush. His senses hadn't been this clear in his life. For all her lies and using, Lavina had given him this.

He settled into the forest detritus, burying himself and, for once in his vampire life, wasn't terrified.

Tonight he would simmer in his anger. Tomorrow he would act.

34

LAVINA DID not sleep. The night passed in utter silence. Staring into the darkness of her living room, rooted to the couch, she waited. Waited for Stephanos to storm back in once he'd sobered up, or for Vadim, Fane, and Max to pull up and confront her. If Stephanos found Gabriel, would they come at her together? She prayed not.

She'd given Stephanos her secret. By now, he'd no doubt told everyone who would listen. He certainly didn't owe her allegiance after all her lies.

If Vadim knew what she was, there was no use in running. He had too many connections now, was too embedded within Northchester. He could have the police after her, people watching for her at the airport. Who knew what calls he might make. At least her people were safe.

The front door opened. Rosa and the boys spilled in with the morning sunshine.

"Hello?" Rosa called.

"They're elsewhere. I thought Trina would call you. Sorry. I should have texted. Please, take the week off."

"Don't be silly. We're already here and there's cleaning to do. Trina never unloads the dishwasher because she claims she doesn't know where anything goes, and Nathan can't make a bed. They're hopeless. Not to mention our guest who goes through bath towels like he's never reused one before."

A sharp pain lanced Lavina's heart. He'd smelled so nice right out of the shower. Not at all like he'd been when she'd found him. Now he was gone.

"My guest has departed. Truly, it's not safe for you and the boys here. Please go. Don't worry about the pay." Lavina shooed her toward the door. "Go on. I'll take care of things for a bit and call you when the coast is clear."

Rosa wrung her hands, concern rolling off her. "Boys, go gather up your school things and be back in five minutes. Change of plans." She came closer instead of going away. "Are you in trouble? Is there anything I can do? Should I contact the police?"

"They won't help me. Not with this. I fear I've made a mess, and it's up to me to deal with it." Lavina worked herself to her feet, keeping the blanket around her shoulders. "This may well be a cut and run situation, Rosa. If you don't hear from me in seven days, please assume that it is and don't return here. Keep in contact with Trina and Nathan."

Looking solemn, she nodded.

"Hurry, grab what you need and go."

Rosa went into the kitchen and started filling bags with food items and a few personal things. "Don't want any of this going to waste," she called out as if she suspected Lavina might think she was stealing.

"Go ahead." It wasn't like she was going to eat the meals Rosa had prepared. At this rate, she wasn't going to eat anything at all for a while.

Once Rosa and the boys had departed, Lavina dared to leave the living room. She couldn't stay there forever. She was going to have to go back to her bedroom and confront the memories she'd made there.

Filled with trepidation, she crept to her room and took one step inside. Tears filled her eyes and spilled down her cheeks. He'd wanted so badly to help, to believe in her. Lavina rubbed her sore wrist but couldn't summon the will to be angry about it. He could have done so much worse, as the hand indents on the wall beside the door illustrated. Even furious, he hadn't hurt her.

She climbed into the bed, wrapping herself in Stephanos scented sheets. It struck her that she'd never been heartbroken when she'd ended things with Vadim, or Fane, or even Max. Sad, sure, but she'd been more concerned with how many of their memories she'd glossed over, how much she'd changed their personalities. Caring about them, but not suffering the loss she felt now. And she'd only known him a short time. Her sweet, feral vampire, who was polite and did laundry. She cried harder.

Her phone rang.

Mid sob, she wiped her eyes enough to make out the number. It wasn't him.

She set her phone down. It continued to ring.

The number also wasn't Vadim or Fane. It was unknown. What if something had happened to Stephanos? What if this was someone trying to contact her because he needed help?

Lavina wiped her face on the sheet and answered the

phone.

"What the fuck did you do to him, you witch?" Gabriel spewed into her ear.

A witch, just like her mother. It had taken three hundred years, but that accusation filled her with terror just the same. She could feel the flames, smell the burning flesh. Lavina drew a ragged breath and attempted to pull herself together. She was not going to the pyre bawling and begging.

At least if Stephanos was with his sire, she could be assured he wasn't off causing chaos on the streets of Northchester. Gabriel was an asshole for sure, but in the few days he'd held Vadim's position, he'd proven himself to be a stable sort of evil. He just wasn't the type of vampire she wanted near her home or all of Northchester for that matter.

"He's with you?" she asked with a fairly steady voice.

"No, you meddling vampire whore, he's not where he should be. What the fuck did you do to him?"

If he hadn't run back to Gabriel... She didn't want to think about what dangerous Stephanos might do when he was as angry as he'd been when he'd left. Grasping for a more positive spin, she considered that maybe he'd had just enough memory dulling to break the hold his sire had held him under for centuries.

"Fuck off, you manipulative bastard. You should have stayed in the dump where you belong." Lavina ended the call and blocked the number.

She put the phone on silent and pulled the blankets up. Closing her eyes, she gave herself over to sleep.

Pounding on the door brought Lavina awake. Shaking and fumbling, she untangled herself and made her way to the living room window, where she could see the front door. There was a car parked in the drive but it was too far back for her to get a good view. It was not one she immediately recognized.

Lavina cautiously made her way to the door and peeked through the hole. Fane. As far as threat levels went, he was behind Stephanos, Gabriel, and Vadim. If she had to face someone, he would have been her choice. She opened the door.

Fane looked her up and down and scowled. "Woman, you look like hell. Those are breakup clothes, aren't they?" He stepped inside without invitation, but neither was it a threatening manner.

She started to push the door closed, but a foot stopped it.

"Way to make me feel welcome." Max stepped in behind Fane. He closed the door for her.

At least she hoped that meant Vadim wouldn't be joining them.

"What..." Annoyed at how ragged her voice sounded, she cleared her throat and tried again. "What are you doing here?"

"You weren't answering your phone," Fane said.

"And neither is he," Max added.

"Ah yes, your little club bonding party." Lavina grimaced. "Lose touch with your newest member already?"

Fane reached out to pat her shoulder, but she dodged aside. "We didn't mean to chase him away."

"He seemed like a nice guy, despite what Vadim said," Max added.

He had been. At least to her.

"Why are you here?"

"I was in town and wanted to see you," Max said. "This one was worried about you, even though I tried to convince him that you were perfectly capable of taking care of yourself. You dealt with all of us, after all."

Fane glared at Max over his shoulder. "You didn't see what that *nice guy* did to Vadim." He turned back to Lavina. "I had visions of walking in here to find pieces of you all over the place. Good lord, woman, I know you have a type, but when did a death wish become part of it?"

"I don't. The death wish part." She retreated to the living room and plopped back on the couch with Trina's favorite blanket.

The two men followed, Fane sitting across from her and Max standing. He peered out the window at the front lawn.

"This is nice. Big step up from the old days, huh?"

"I saved my money instead of blowing it on continuous travel."

Max shrugged. "If I'm going to live forever, I might as well see the world. And for your information, I do go home sometimes. I have one of those too."

"I know," she conceded.

Max smiled and sat. "Oh, Lavina, you softy, you did check up on me."

Why did they have to gang up on her when her tears were barely under wraps? She was Lavina without a care in the world, sensible, sarcastic. Not this sniveling emotional wreck.

Fane coughed quietly. "So, my dear, do you have any idea where Mr. Nice Guy went? Vadim is concerned that he ignited the fuse to a problem he was trying to avoid."

"Whatever he means by that." Max rolled his eyes. "We were just having a few drinks together, getting to know the guy. You do kick us all to the curb eventually. Vadim and his ulterior motives deserve whatever he gets."

"Speak for yourself, visitor." Fane grumbled. "This could be very bad." He shook his head. "I don't know what Vadim said to him. We were all drinking a lot. Stephanos was very fond of you. That was quite clear."

"We all were at some point," Max said.

Fane glared at him again. "Some of us still are."

"Okay, fine, yes, we still are. Or we wouldn't be here," Max sighed. "I don't know how you do it, but you make us better, and if the price for that is heartache, then so be it."

Was he kidding? He looked sincere. She glanced at Fane. He nodded. A tear streamed down her cheek, followed by a cascade of others.

"Look what you did." Fane cursed. "You broke her."

Max hopped up and came to sit by her side. He wrapped his arm around her. "What do you need? A hug? A drink? Us to leave you the fuck alone?"

Lavina cried harder. Why did they have to be nice after what she'd done to them?

"A shoulder to cry on. Got it." Max rubbed her back while she sobbed.

"I hate to interrupt this pity party, but we did stop by for important reasons. You're safe and whole. Max has the comforting thing taken care of. Now we need to address the missing vampire who likes to tear people apart."

"He doesn't like it," she said between sobs. "Gabriel makes him."

Fane tapped his chin. "But Gabriel is taken care of."

Lavina shook her head. "He escaped the landfill."

"Well, that's a problem. I need to make a call." He stood and walked into the kitchen.

"Vina, dear, did you have a fight, or did he leave? We had some good fights, remember?" Max chuckled. "But the one thing the club agrees on is that you do the leaving. Was he the first?"

Lavina caught her breath and wiped her face on her sleeve. "He was angry, and he walked out the door."

His arm stayed around her, comforting, fingers slowly rubbing her shoulder. It reminded her of the good times when they'd been together so long ago.

"Did he pack his things? Like he left for good?"

"Naked, with the clothes he'd been wearing in hand."

Max whistled. "Must have been one hell of a fight."

She hadn't really fought. It was more of one giant confession. One he'd walked away from.

"Do you know where he'd go?"

"If he's not at Gabriel's estate, then no. Back to Scotland?"

"What on earth is a Greek doing living in Scotland?"

"I think there was a girl involved in that relocation at one point."

Max nodded. "That would do it. You lot tend to make us do all sorts of illogical things."

She met the gaze of the man she'd once loved. "What did I ever make you do?"

"Behave." He kissed her forehead. "Now, I'm just a washed up reformed bad guy."

She tried a tenuous smile. "Washed up? You are rather clean."

Max grinned. "That's not what I meant, and you know it. But it made you smile, so I'll take it." He dropped his arm and stood. "We should be off. We have hunting to do."

Lavina jumped to her feet. "You're not going to hurt

him, are you?"

"Gabriel. As long as Stephanos remains in Vadim's good graces, he's safe."

"Thank you."

"Anything for you, Vina."

Feeling her lips tremble along with everything else, she wrapped her arms around Max and hugged him. "I'm sorry about the heartache part."

"Me too." He cleared his throat and went into the kitchen to find Fane.

After a quick promise to feed and get some rest, they left her alone in the big house. Lavina returned to the couch where she sat listening to the furnace run. She couldn't remember a time when her home had ever been so empty.

35

WHEN STEPHANOS woke in the dirt, he sat up slowly, letting the soil roll off him. His body relaxed. He stared up through the branches and marveled at the ease that had settled over him.

He pulled out his phone to find the battery nearly dead. Nowhere to charge it in the woods. He scowled. If he was going to stay in touch with humanity, he needed the stupid phone. Or he could catch a flight back to Scotland and go molder away in the basement for another decade or two. He pondered the escape plan for a few minutes, but it didn't hold the allure it once had.

Which fire should he attend to first? Vadim or Gabriel? He stood and brushed the dirt from his clothes. Both of them were a long walk away. Where was Nathan when he needed the charming old man? Oh yes, attached to the woman who had been lying to him.

Stephanos started off through the woods, skirting around people's yards until he connected with the road. As he walked, keeping his body busy, his mind poked the open wound that was Lavina. She'd been strong enough to subdue him before, but she'd put up no resistance this time. Nor had she yelled or belittled him, only provided answers to his questions. Answers he hadn't wanted to hear.

His strides grew more determined. Before he realized how far he'd traveled, Stephanos blinked to find he'd left the houses behind and was now down the long stretch of road that separated the hill homes from the clusters of less grand dwellings and shops. It would take him most of the night to walk back into town. He eyed the phone. Gabriel had mentioned an app for rides.

Forty minutes later, the ride service dropped him off in the parking lot across from The Jackyl. Vadim may have drugged him, but he'd suffered nothing more than companionship and relaxation. His conversation had also opened Stephanos' eyes to the truth of Lavina. He'd promised a job and had demanded nothing.

Stephanos crossed the street and bypassed the short line of humans, his mind busy comparing what he knew of Northchester's leader to his sire.

Had Gabriel drugged anyone, it would be to cause them harm. He never gave anything without something in trade. Even when they'd been human together, he'd never allowed himself to relax around Gabriel. One wrong word or action and the Boros would make his family suffer. When they spoke now, it was so his sire could assign tasks. For all Gabriel's talk of being friends, Stephanos could not recall a time when they'd laughed and joked like Max and Fane.

The man at the door waved him inside. Stephanos went in search of Vadim. He was ensconced at a table of humans who were doing shots and shouting over the music at one another. Vadim held the same drink but didn't consume it.

Stephanos thought back to his drinks with the Cast Off Club. Had Vadim been drinking then? He couldn't remember seeing him empty or refill his glass. As Stephanos watched from a distance, lurking in the crowd, he realized Vadim was good at directing the conversation and then watching it happen, listening. Gabriel preferred to be the center of conversations, basking in the attention.

Tiffany found him in the crowd. "How are you feeling?"

"Fine. Thanks."

She nodded. "Anytime. I take care of my favorites."

She considered him a favorite, like he'd thought of Isla? Like Lavina thought of Nathan and the rest of her staff? He wasn't sure what to say about that. "Does Vadim do that to his guests often? Spike their drinks, I mean?"

"Without them paying for it and him approving it first? Tiffany shook her head. "Only his closest friends get that for free when he's feeling generous. But you're new and knowing you don't drink nearly that much normally, I had a feeling you weren't realizing what he was offering. You had a good time though?"

He shrugged. He'd thought so, but what had come after had tainted the night.

"Are you thirsty?"

"No. I'll just wait until he's done there."

"Oh, I can get him for you if you'd like."

The night did have limited hours, and he also had Gabriel to deal with. "Sure."

She bumped her hip into him and winked, then sashayed her way over to Vadim's table. While he wasn't blind, Stephanos was not in the mood for feminine wiles. He'd left a whimpering puddle of one last night, and that was still ripping him to shreds inside. He'd yet to decide if he was angry that she'd lied to him or if he was angry at Vadim for exposing her deception. He'd been happy for the first time in so long.

"You wanted to see me?" Vadim asked, startling Stephanos.

Damned overwhelming thoughts. "Yes. Gabriel called. He's back at his estate."

Vadim scowled. "What? How?"

There was no use in lying when he needed support. "Lavina did me a favor by slipping her phone into the bag with Gabriel so I could track him later. That's how I knew he was gone. Guessing he used Lavina's phone to call for help. She doesn't use a lock screen."

"I should have cut his hands off." Vadim swallowed the remains of his drink but didn't appear anymore relieved by the influx of alcohol.

So, he was actually drinking, yet he seemed clear-headed. Maybe he did really have the high tolerance he'd alluded to. Stephanos waited for Vadim to say anything else before he decided how he wanted to proceed.

Vadim also seemed to be waiting for further information. "And you again came here to tell me this of your own accord?"

"I might not want to return to his side." Even saying the words out loud felt like betrayal. His gut twisted, but his mind said it was the right move.

"Might?" Vadim clenched his empty glass, eyes searching for someone to summon to refill it.

"It depends on what you can do for me. I like it here."

"I'm glad to hear it." Vadim set the glass down and studied Stephanos.

Feeling like he was back in Argos under the eyes of the

Boros, the man before him silently determined his worth and usefulness. Stephanos stood tall, shoulders firm, and feet planted wide.

"Gabriel Boros is your sire."

Stephanos nodded.

"But you would turn against him?"

"I have served him well all my life. I gave my first life for him, and what do I have to show for it?"

Vadim nodded. "And what would you do for me should I give you more?"

"It depends on what you ask of me and what you would give."

Vadim grinned. "No blind devotion then?"

"I'm walking away from that."

He motioned to a nearby empty table and went to sit down. Once Stephanos was settled across from him, he asked, "And Lavina?"

"What about her?"

"Do you have any answers?"

That Vadim would be better for him than Gabriel was no question, but what about Lavina? He might be willing to throw Gabriel to the wolves, but did she deserve the same? Gabriel hadn't ever given him truths or tears.

"Not yet."

"No?" One brow cocked, Vadim looked suspicious. "Fane said you walked out on her. That doesn't sound like you're looking for answers. It sounds like you found them."

Stephanos wasn't comfortable betraying what she'd given him. "We had a fight."

"Men don't leave Lavina. She leaves them."

Because she helped them, made them better, more human. Even Vadim knew it.

He liked how he'd been with her, how she made him feel when he hadn't felt anything for so long. She dulled the things that had made him want to turn everything off. Being with her had allowed him to see Gabriel clearly, had helped clear his mind to many things.

Did Vadim deserve the truth? What would it gain him?

Lavina had been willing to pay for his safety in blood. A perpetual agreement for blood, for that matter. And he hadn't even been present when she'd made that deal. She might not be a vampire, but that didn't make her an enemy to be handed over.

"She drank from me."

Vadim went still. "She's real? Like us?"

Stephanos nodded.

Vadim signaled for a drink for both of them. "Well, I'll be damned."

Weren't they all?

He pulled up the ride app again and put in his next request.

36

WITH THE house empty
and her hunger growing,
Lavina got off the couch to
at least wash her face. With
that little step toward normal accomplished, she felt up to
brushing her teeth and then changing her clothes. After
that much progress, she was exhausted. She went to bed to
stare at the ceiling.

Sleep refused to come. She wasn't tired, just exhausted
with reality. She picked up her phone. No messages. Nothing from Stephanos, but neither was there anything from
Vadim.

She pulled up Stephanos' number and started a text.
Can we talk? Her finger hovered over the send button.

What was there to talk about? She'd said what needed
to be said. It was up to him to accept it or act on it.

She stared at the words for a minute longer and then
deleted them. Tossing the phone aside, she sank back into
the pillows.

When the doorbell rang, she swore loudly. Couldn't
anyone let her wallow in peace?

Annoyance flooded her deflated body with enough energy to pry her out of bed. She stomped to the door to peek through the hole. A stranger stood outside.

"What do you want?" she yelled through the door.

Glass shattered the side windows as a deafening rain of gunfire filled the foyer. Panic froze her on the spot. A hand snaked through the broken window to reach for the knob. Another round of gunfire sent her to her knees with her hands over her ears. Windows shattered in the living room. More shattering as her mind supplied the inventory of a lamp, her curio cabinet, and a vase as likely victims of the attack. The arm became a shoulder and then a head with eyes looking directly at her.

Lavina got up and ran.

Shouts confirmed that the man in the foyer wasn't alone. Men called from the back door, the living room, and the foyer, all passing word that one had seen her and the direction she'd taken.

With her heart in her throat, Lavina bolted to her room. Closing the door behind her, she grabbed her phone and ducked into her closet. She reached behind the shelf full of shoes to hit a latch that released a hinge. The shelf wall swung open, revealing her panic room—more of a panic closet in reality. She crawled in, pulling the handle behind the shelf to close herself in. To the left of the entrance, she felt for the light switch, but didn't flip it. She sat on her knees, hunched over in the cramped space, panting. *Quiet, you idiot.*

She breathed shallowly, growing more lightheaded by the minute, her panic doing her no favors as she tried to suppress the urge to take a deep gasping breath. *Just slow the fuck down, and you'll be fine.* But thinking and doing were two very different things. Curling up on her side, she closed her eyes and did her best not to exist.

At least she'd vacated her staff from the house. If only she'd left with them. But then she would have endangered them wherever they were now.

Even as miserable as she was, she didn't have a death wish. Lavina blocked out the sound of her panicked breaths to listen for footsteps.

A pair entered the bedroom, slowly coming closer. Calls of "clear" sounded in the rooms nearby, muddling her tracking of the invader's approach.

"She can't have gone far," someone yelled. "Let's get this taken care of so we can all go home."

One man chuckled. "Like some middle-aged lady is going to be a problem to kill. She's probably shaking under a bed."

Lavina glared in the darkness. She was not under a damned bed. Whether she was shaking or not was up to interpretation.

As long as she stayed quiet, they wouldn't find her. They'd give up and leave. Wouldn't they?

She listened hard, hoping to catch some whisper of Gabriel or Vadim so she'd know who was directing this witch hunt. None of the voices were familiar.

Footsteps entered the closet. Rustling on the other side of the shoe shelves indicated they were moving clothes around, likely looking for a bolt hole just like the one she was huddled in.

A distant voice yelled, "A house like this likely has a panic room somewhere. Tear it up. No one is leaving until the job is done."

She went still, though every instinct begged her to press

up against the back wall of her hiding hole as if she could get further out of sight. If they got the door open, there was nothing to hide behind. One sweep of a flashlight and it would be over.

The phone in her pocket vibrated. Thank goodness she had the volume off, but even the buzzing seemed to echo. Gritting her teeth, she silently begged the notification to go the fuck away. She didn't dare to pull the phone out and possibly drop it, considering how badly her hands were trembling—okay, they were definitely all out shaking—to see who was trying to call.

"Did you hear something?" asked a voice that was far too close for comfort.

"Yeah, where the hell did that come from?"

"Somewhere in here."

The banging around of things being pulled off shelves in the closet rose to a frenzied state.

Far from her bedroom, a man screamed. The sound was cut off by a wet choking racket.

What was going on out there? Had the call been from Fane or Max, warning her that Vadim was sending thugs her way? Had they come to help her? Neither of them was fond of getting dirty these days, but having known them before her feeding had tamed them, they had it in them to be quite the menace to society. Lavina silently begged the well-dressed duo to be her saviors.

Gunfire erupted, not nearly as muffled as her senses would have liked it to be. Did bullets travel through drywall? How many walls were between her and wherever hell was breaking loose? She pressed herself flatter against the floor.

Her terror spun out of control. What if this wasn't a rescue at all? What if it was Gabriel and Vadim fighting over who got to kill her? Or worse, capture her and drain her dry now that Stephanos had told them both her secret. Or worse worse, her hot feral vampire had gotten over any feelings for her and now he was here, feeding on her attackers so he could be the one to rip her apart like he'd done to Vadim.

Somewhere close there was a wet gurgle and then two guns firing. A man yelled, "He's over there."

Lavina was breathing so hard she was sure the hunters in the closet would hear her. She clamped one hand over her mouth.

Cursing outside the bedroom brought the two men in the closet to a halt. They muttered indistinctly to one another, and then one set of footsteps departed.

A gun rapidly fired before going silent.

A loud thud hit a wall somewhere to her right. In the hallway, her scrambled brain supplied seconds later.

Scuffling, and then meaty thwacks and grunts reached her ears. A man cried out and then there were only wet, gagging noises.

A single pair of footsteps thundered through the house, upstairs and then back to the main floor. Her phone buzzed again.

"Lavina!" yelled Stephanos.

Worse worse it was then. She gulped dryly, giving in to the urge to press herself as far back as she could get.

All she could make out was the steady beat of one person rushing through the house. They came closer again, and then back into the bedroom.

"Lavina!" He sounded more desperate this time.

Her phone vibrated again and again. Get the fucking hint, whoever it was! She pressed her free hand over her pocket as if her palm could further muffle the noise.

The shelf door was wrenched open. Light from the closet flooded into her dark hiding hole. She blinked and held up her hand. Lavina desperately tried to will herself away, but that didn't happen, so she faced whatever was about to transpire with all the grace and dignity she could muster. Which wasn't much.

Stephanos, crouched low, leaned into the compartment, one empty hand outstretched. "Are you hurt?"

"No," she said in a breathy squeak that made her cough.

"They're gone. Come on, let's get you out of here and somewhere safe."

It was a trick, surely. She stayed put.

While her eyes slowly adjusted to the light, his heavy breathing registered. Still backlit, she couldn't make out his face to know if it was merely exertion or if he was salivating over the idea of sinking his fangs into her.

"Lavina, please. Come out." His hand wavered and then so did the rest of him. He pulled his arm back, using it to steady himself instead. Sitting back on his heels, he blinked heavily, his head lolling to the side.

He didn't appear very threatening now. Or maybe it was an act to lure her out. Though, really, she considered now that she had a moment to think, if he had wanted to grab her, all he had to do was lunge forward and do so. It wasn't as though he couldn't fit inside if he wanted to.

Lavina slowly crept forward until she reached the entrance. He hadn't moved. Now that she was out in the light, she realized it wasn't just shadow darkening his face, but blood. So much blood. His shirt was soaked with it.

"Are you hurt?" she asked, her voice barely a whisper.

"Too many bullets," he muttered.

They'd all had guns. He only had teeth and his bloody hands. Yet, he was here, and they were likely all as dead as the mangled body lying next to the tumble of sweaters on the floor.

She pulled herself out of the hiding hole and crouched beside Stephanos. "Are there more? Alive, I mean?"

"No, but Gabriel will send more if they don't report back soon. Or send the police, which, considering the condition of the bodies, wouldn't be in our favor either."

Our favor. She turned that over in her head a few times. "You're sure Gabriel sent them?"

"I was headed to his place after talking to Vadim, but when I saw the vehicles filled with armed men heading out of his driveway, I followed them instead. Figured I owed it to Vadim to let him know if there was trouble to deal with."

"What do you owe Vadim?" She shook her head, trying to keep up.

Stephanos waved her question away with one hand while clutching his side with the other. Blood seeped between his fingers.

"I followed them here. I tried to warn you. To call you. You didn't answer." His feet went out from under him. He rocked back onto his ass on the jumble of shoes and the wire rack he'd torn off the door.

A different kind of fear hit her raw nerves. If Gabriel called the police on her, if they walked in and saw the ripped open bodies and the man sporting the fangs that matched the wounds, nothing good would come of it.

"What do you need?"

"To feed. I didn't dare when everyone had guns, and I couldn't find you. Vadim will be here soon. Or he'll send Fane and Max. He knows I'm here. Called him too."

Should she get him up or let him sit? The blood loss and bullet wounds wouldn't kill him, but he was weak and unable to defend himself should anyone unfriendly arrive to finish her off. He needed blood, but there was no one else alive here.

His eyes met hers, pleading. The last time he'd been hurting, and she'd gotten too close, he'd violently taken without consent. She edged away.

"Lavina, please."

Could she trust him after last time?

He had come back to help her even after learning the truth of what she was. He'd also said he'd talked to Vadim. After she'd told him what she was. Her stomach churned. "What did you mean by owing Vadim?"

"For wounding him. I don't know him well, but you trust him, and he's treated me better than my sire. He certainly didn't need to after what I did."

A killer with a conscience. No wonder she liked the taste of him so much. "If I let you feed from me, I will need to feed too. Are you willing?"

"You're asking now?"

She shrugged. "You know what I am. You asked me, so I will ask you. Keeping it fair."

He chuckled weakly. "If we're going to be fair about it, do I get to choose what memory you take?"

"I don't take them, just dull them, gloss them over, consume the feeling from them."

Stephanos watched her intently. Blood leaked from his side, dripping onto the ivory carpet. Trina was going to have a hell of a time cleaning all of this.

"Yes, fine. You can choose. Feed me and I'll feed you. Deal?"

He nodded. "Her name was Isla."

Lavina leaned in close and got comfortable. Her mind hummed as she captured his gaze. *"Tell me about Isla."*

Flashes of a dark-haired waif flitted into her mind. Her smile, twinkling eyes, laughter. She was too thin, her clothes hanging from her.

What part of Isla did he want her to take? Surely it wasn't this bubble of sweet fondness. Unlike when she usually prompted a memory, he seemed to be holding on tightly. Maybe because he was aware of what she was doing. She needed to get in closer, to pry it from the grip that held the pain close.

"Who was Isla to you?"

Lavina gasped when she caught the hazy sight of a well-dressed Stephanos, clean and smiling, reflected in Gabriel's eyes.

"You've earned it. I told you I'd get you a house of your own. There's no one here to bother you as long as you stay out of the village. Isla will keep you company and provide blood. Treat her well and she'll live another forty years."

The house was large for the time: five rooms maybe, two stories, two windows in the front and a solid door. An overgrown garden sat alongside the house, and a couple of goats stood behind a fenced square with a lean to. A flock of chickens pecked and scratched through the grass. Beyond that, nothing but rocks, tall grass, and the occasional tree. Sweet happiness flavored all of it.

"Promise me you'll stay here, that you'll be here should I need you again, and this is all yours."

Stephanos nodded. "You have my word."

"I have a contact in the village who will let me know immediately if you misbehave. Is that clear?"

"No killing the villagers."

"Good. Isla has served me well. She's earned her rest here too. Savor her. I won't send another."

The thin woman with hollow eyes and stringy long hair watched them both. She seemed afraid. Everyone feared him but Gabriel.

He would make her comfortable here, maybe even happy. If she'd served the Boros, she hadn't had an easy life. He knew that well from long experience. He would be better than his sire, prove that he could be human again, even if it meant he didn't feed as often as he wanted to. Hunger was nothing new.

Gabriel patted Stephanos' arm. "Be well, my friend. I'm off to America. When I'm ready, I'll send for you."

He didn't know where that was, nor did he care. After so long, he finally had a home of his own. Something that was his. And Isla.

A rush of memories spanned years: Isla laughing, eating at a table while talking with Stephanos. She slept in a deep nest of blankets, looking much healthier than she had before. Springs and winters, summers and autumns, they sped by in a matter of minutes. Silver threaded Isla's hair.

Then Gabriel returned, dressed in a boxy brown suit, otherwise looking much the same. He frowned when Isla came to the door way, standing beside Stephanos. "I see you're alive."

Isla fisted the back of Stephanos' shirt. His sensitive ears picked up her racing heartbeat.

While it was good to see his friend after so long, he didn't appreciate Gabriel frightening her. The people in the village did that enough just for living with him. She was kind and deserved none of it from anyone.

He wrapped his hand around Isla's, gently pulling her behind him, and faced his sire. "What do you need?"

Gabriel scowled. "I need you."

"I don't want to go."

His scowl deepened. "That was the deal Stephanos. You get the house and the slave and when I need you, you come."

"But Isla is no longer young. She needs help with the animals and the house."

"She's just food." Gabriel's disdain-filled gaze fixated over Stephanos' shoulder. "I'm your sire. Your friend. We help each other as we always have. And I came a long way to get you. You're coming to America to help me take care of some trouble. It's what you do best. Surely, you're bored here anyway."

"I'm not bored." And Isla wasn't just food.

Gabriel sighed loudly. "Fine. I'll send someone from the village to help your slave."

No one else had set foot in their house since they'd lived there. Isla told him that the villagers called him cursed. They said she lived with a demon. If they'd glimpsed him working outside after nightfall, they might think him odd, but he'd been on his best behavior.

He'd only traveled into the forest surrounding the cluster of buildings where Isla traded for supplies when he felt his control slipping, when he needed more blood than Isla could provide. He was careful and only fed on men there, never in the village. Those men were likely up to no good anyway.

"But the villagers barely tolerate her. They won't come up here to help."

"I said, I'd take care of it. Have I ever lied to you?"

"No."

His sire nodded. "You won't be gone too long, assuming you do want to return once you see the wonders of a more civilized city. The slave will be fine."

He'd never treated Isla like the slave Gabriel insisted on calling her, but they were both owned by the Boros. Resigned to his obligation, and assured that she would have help, Stephanos said farewell to the teary-eyed woman.

Lavina hated the taste of tears. Though she needed to feed, she only lightly grazed on what Stephanos had shown her so far. These were memories he'd want to keep. Bracing for the worst, she waited for the ones he wanted to forget.

Weary and ragged, Stephanos approached the house on the hill. Broken windows and a door that banged open and shut with the wind greeted him. The yard was silent. There was no sign of the goats or chickens. In fact, there were no footsteps outside to be seen at all.

Stephanos called out for Isla, not wanting to startle her. He received no answer but the wind whipping at his hair and clothes. With deep trepidation, he stepped inside.

A shattered bowl littered the floor by the table. One of the benches lay on its side, the other still standing. Mice scurried away. The shelves on the wall were empty. No food stores remained but two ragged, hanging bundles of herbs twisting in the breeze. The smell of home, of the fireplace, of bread baking, soup bubbling, a bouquet of wildflowers, had been replaced with damp rot. The floor near the broken windows appeared to have suffered seasons of rain. Seasons. How long had he been gone?

Stephanos shook his head, hands trembling as he pushed a tangle of hair from his face. Gabriel had kept him too long.

"Isla?"

The desperate sound of his voice was eerily similar to how he'd called for her. Lavina felt the urge to reach out to comfort Stephanos, but didn't want to interrupt the memory playing out between them.

Stephanos pushed onward, up the stairs, pausing his hesitant steps when he came to a moonlit spot on the landing. He looked up to see a hole in the roof. Gabriel had said months, but he'd been gone years.

Isla had been cared for. His sire had said so. Maybe she was elsewhere, had been moved, taken to safety.

The door to his room hung open. His few belongings lay strewn across the floor. His vision went dim, hazy, everything blurred at the edges as Stephanos left that room and went to the other door.

It hung crooked, one hinge ripped from the wall, a hole smashed through the center as though someone had taken an axe to it. Sooty writing covered the walls, but Lavina couldn't read it. Whatever it said made Stephanos see red. His vision narrowed even further. Then he approached the bed. The nest of blankets from his earlier memories was stained rust, sliced, tattered, and torn. So were the leathery remnants of the woman tangled in them. Strands of long dark hair clung to her scalp, but her ruddy cheeks and sparkling eyes were long gone. Broken ribs and the cocked angle at which her upper and lower halves sat, the hollow gap in the scraps of withered flesh that clung to bones, illustrated that the axe had been used there as well.

Stephanos collapsed to his knees, clutching what remained of Isla with great, wracking sobs. And suddenly there was only red.

Lavina feasted on the flickers that followed. A breakneck run down the hill, through the trees, along a winding dirt road, and into a darkened cluster of buildings. A scream cut short. The gurgling of a man choking on his own blood. A woman's terrified face, spattered with blood as the light left her eyes. Children running into the night, hand in hand. A grizzled old man swung his cane only to be ripped open by bloodied hands that looked more like claws. Fangs tore into the throats of men and women. Children wailed in the dark. And then flames.

The flashes solidified into the smoking remains of the village under a pinkening sky. Somewhere in the distance a child called for his mother. Stephanos turned his back on it all and ran for the trees, for soft soil filled with leaves of the years he'd been gone. He buried himself there.

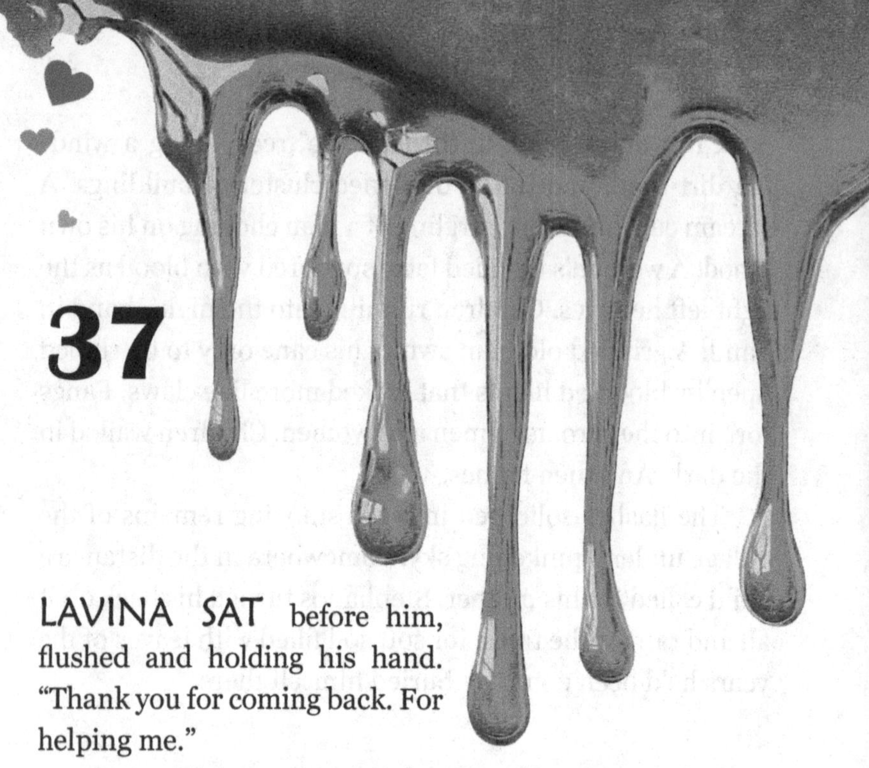

37

LAVINA SAT before him, flushed and holding his hand. "Thank you for coming back. For helping me."

He couldn't survive another loss like the one before. The one he didn't want to think about, yet meeting Lavina's gaze, he couldn't help but remember Isla. He poked gingerly at the edges of his memory of entering the empty house and finding her long-dead body. Sorrow wrapped around him. The anger and rage were softened, distant.

"You didn't take it all? I wanted you to."

"No. She helped make you who you are today. If I take too much, you lose too much. You'll change. I like you as you are."

"Maybe I don't."

With no regard for the blood covering his face and clothes, Lavina wrapped her arms around Stephanos, pressing her cheek against his. "I can help you with that. If you'll let me."

He scoffed. "After you've seen what I'm capable of?"

"Because I've seen what you're capable of, and I don't just mean the violent parts." She sat back and smiled softly. "As long as you only let the wild side out when Vadim needs it, it sounds like you might already have a place here. With his blessing, even, and after knowing first-hand what you can do."

"You would want me to stay?"

Her gaze dropped. "How much did you tell Vadim? About me, I mean?"

Stephanos reached out to wipe away the smudge of blood that had transferred from his face to hers. "That you fed from me. That you were one of us."

Her mouth dropped open. "You lied? You lied for me?"

He shrugged. "It's the truth, mostly."

Lavina grinned. "Yes, I want you to stay. Very much so, in fact." She leaned in but stopped short of kissing him. "I'd also like you to take a shower. While you do that, I'll call Trina and Nathan. We're going to need a lot of help with the cleanup. You said Vadim might be on the way?"

Grabbing her arm, he tugged her closer. "You're forgetting that we had a deal."

"I most certainly did not forget, but I was hoping to have you cleaner and maybe comfortable in bed before you got all blissed out on my blood."

"But I'm very hungry right now." He kept her arm close, staring at the pulse beating on her neck. The compulsion to bite was nearly overwhelming, but he fought it. He'd ripped into her once already. The odds she'd forgive him a second time weren't in his favor. Favor. Flavor. He licked his lips, reliving the glorious taste of her.

Lavina watched his every movement with a wary gaze but didn't struggle. "I'm sure you are. You've lost a lot of blood. However, if Vadim shows up or Fane or Max, I can't exactly answer the door while feeder drunk, can I? And you can't answer it high on me, so either we wait until our impending visitors are taken care of or you call him and tell him everything is under control."

Without hesitation, Stephanos let her go and pulled out his phone with a bloody hand. He'd just managed to wipe his finger off enough to pull up his contacts when the doorbell rang. "Fucking hell."

"I'll go deal with this. Stay put or clean up, whichever you can manage. I'll be back as soon as I can to fulfill my end of the deal." She gave him a quick peck on the forehead. "I promise."

He wasn't sure he could trust her promises just yet. And he'd lost too much blood. Like hell was he letting his meal out of sight. Stephanos shakily got to his feet and stumbled his way over the body and into Lavina's bedroom. Following his bloody tracks in her thick carpet, he made his way out into the hallway, one hand on the wall to steady himself as he went, making more work for Trina later. She wasn't going to like him much after this.

Out in the foyer, Lavina answered the door, her voice carrying thanks to the hard surfaces. She wouldn't have answered unless it was necessary, or someone she knew, not with all the blood and bodies in the house.

Her sudden, shrill tone put him on high alert. He grunted, quickening his staggering pace. He hadn't come back to help, only to lose her now.

A heavy thud spurred him onward. Lavina swore. So did someone else in a muffled voice. Something shattered on the tile floor, echoing throughout the house. The sounds of a struggle followed.

Isla, caught unaware, had passed from this life in her bed. Lavina wasn't going down so easily.

Blood was again openly seeping from the multiple bullet wounds in his side by the time he made it to the foyer. Stephanos pressed himself against the wall where he could survey the situation and catch his breath.

Lavina stood over Gabriel with the jagged shard of a broken vase in one hand. Blood dripped from its pointed tip. Gabriel on his back on the floor clutched his neck, blood oozing between his fingers.

"I said, get out," she hissed, breathing hard. Hair in disarray and shirt ripped from the neck to shoulder, she had never looked more beautiful.

"You idiot women keep thinking you can have him, but he's mine." Gabriel got to his knees, keeping one hand on his neck.

For as wounded as he'd been, he must have fed heavily to be healed enough to be out and about. Then again, there was no telling what shape he may have truly been under his clothes. Stephanos watched Gabriel carefully, noting the stiffness of his movements.

"You don't own him anymore, asshole. We don't do slavery here."

Gabriel lurched to his feet. "He owes me a debt."

She held her ground, glaring at him. "If he ever really owed you anything, he's paid that off long ago. Leave."

"Not until you release him to me."

Lavina laughed ruefully. "I'm not holding him. He's a free man, and he's not here."

Stephanos couldn't believe that she was lying for him again despite what it had cost her last time Gabriel had invaded her apartment. He leaned forward a little further to keep them in sight.

They circled each other slowly, each keeping their distance.

"I'm not blind, woman. I'm well acquainted with his handiwork." Gabriel pointed to the bloody remains of the first body Stephanos had ripped through upon entering the house.

"No, you're deaf. I said, he's not here. He left after tearing through the men you sent to kill me. Vadim isn't going to like that, by the way."

A smug smile bloomed on Gabriel's face. "Last I heard, you lost favor with the overlord of Northchester. I'm guessing he'd be glad to have you gone. He might even consider it a favor."

"Your intel, like your morality, is outdated." Grip firm on the shard, she advanced, driving him backward step by step toward the door.

Gabriel seemed to suddenly realize what she was doing and scanned the room, likely looking for a weapon of his own. Instead, he spotted Stephanos. His brows rose, and he grinned.

In his current condition, Stephanos wasn't going to be of much help to Lavina unless he let go of what little humanity she'd helped him regain. Wounded animals fought to the bitter end.

Lavina cast a worried glance at Stephanos and then placed herself firmly in Gabriel's path. What the hell was she doing? She was going to get herself killed. He hobbled forward, even more determined than before to prevent that from happening.

"You lunatic!" Gabriel screamed. "Do you have any idea what you've done? These men had families. This is going to cost me a fortune to keep quiet. You're going to owe me for the rest of eternity!"

Lavina thrust her empty hand in the air, snapping her fingers. "Hey, asshole, we're not done here."

Gabriel stopped short when she didn't move. He grabbed her shoulder to shove her aside. She didn't budge.

"Tell me about how you found Stephanos when he was buried underground," she said, her voice soft, hypnotic.

His sire's motion slowed, his face going slack, eyes half-lidded.

Fascinated, Stephanos watched Lavina feed. So that's how she did it. No pain, no blood, just compulsion and proximity. He moved in closer while they were both occupied. To avoid interrupting her, he came around behind Gabriel where he could easily grab his sire when she was through.

Her eyes darted around, yet not appearing to see him at all. Her fingers twitched, but otherwise, she remained still. He very much wanted to know what she was seeing in Gabriel's memory. His mind supplied his side of events with softened edges and none of the terror. What emotion was she siphoning from Gabriel?

Minutes ticked on while the two of them stayed locked in a trance. Upright and on his feet, the momentary burst of adrenaline subsided with his inactivity. His side began to burn again, and his hands trembled. The scent of blood was heavy on the air. He was so hungry. Vampire blood didn't taste good, but Gabriel's neck was right in front of him, bare and defenseless. Blood was blood to the starving. He bared his fangs, inching closer.

A loud rumble outside caught his attention just before he sank his teeth into his sire. Unable to deny the urge, he

allowed himself the consolation of a quick lick at the oozing wound there. Sour but wet and nourishing all the same.
The lick became much more. He gulped greedily.

Another rumble outside. Slamming metal. Car doors,
his brain distantly informed him. He needed to stop, to
break Lavina's trance before she was discovered, to deal
with his maker and whatever this new threat might be, but
he was so...hungry.

The front door slammed open, smacking Stephanos
in the shoulder, spinning him off balance and propelling
Gabriel into Lavina. The two of them toppled onto the tile.
Stephanos stumbled sideways and into the wall, knocking
a framed landscape photo off. Glass shattered. Metal frame
pieces clattered across the floor. Fane and Max raced into
the foyer, nearly tripping over Gabriel and Lavina.

Vadim strode in behind them, taking in the chaos with
a scowl. "What the hell is going on here?"

Max headed for Gabriel, hauling him off Lavina.

Fane approached Stephanos warily. "You're not looking
so good, pal."

"Not feeling so great." Everything hurt, and his hurried
slurps of Gabriel had barely taken the edge off his starva-
tion. He needed Lavina right now.

But she wasn't moving.

Stephanos limped to her side and crouched down. Had
the interruption in her feeding left her dazed or had she hit
her head? Carefully feeling the back of her scalp, he was
relieved to find no blood because he might have started
licking his fingers, and that would have earned him strange
looks for sure. He held her head on his lap.

Her eyes slowly flickered open. "What?" she uttered
shakily.

"Our visitors," he explained.

Gabriel had recovered much faster, pulling and straining to escape Max's hold.

"Explain," Vadim demanded.

"He's the one covered in blood." Gabriel glared at Stephanos.

"Lavina?" Vadim prompted.

"Gabriel sent these men to kill me. Or kill Stephanos. Probably both of us." She made a passing effort at a shrug but winced and rubbed the back of her head. "Stephanos took care of them. Thankfully. And then you three barged in."

"Unsubstantiated lies. She has no proof that these men were sent by me." Gabriel wriggled his shoulders, still trying to escape Max's grip.

Vadim surveyed the damage and the two bodies visible from the foyer. "Lavina, do you have any proof that he acted against you?"

Stephanos answered for her, "I followed them from Gabriel's estate."

What he really wanted was a mouthful of hot blood, preferably Lavina's and to sleep for a few days. Having to explain everything was not on his immediate agenda.

Fane quirked an eyebrow. "Do you make a habit of following people who are leaving Gabriel's estate? That sounds like harassment."

Stephanos sighed. "I was headed there to talk to him when I spotted this lot, armed and riled up, piling into two vehicles parked in his driveway. Knowing Gabriel wasn't currently working for you," he said to Vadim, "I figured they couldn't be up to anything good, so I followed them."

"And thank goodness he did, or I'd be dead by now."

Lavina worked herself up to sitting. She smiled at him. "Now, if you don't mind, we need to have a few minutes alone with the madman of the hour before you take him away to do whatever you want for his disrupting the peace in Northchester."

"Is that so?" Vadim regarded her with suspicion. "Forgive me, Vina, but it would appear neither of you is up to the task or mindset of restraining Gabriel and ensuring he is returned to me in the same condition as when he left."

Seeing Lavina preparing to get to her feet, Stephanos also stood, though he wavered on his feet. Vadim wasn't wrong.

"I only need a few minutes," she said without as much conviction.

Vadim shook his head.

Gabriel laughed. "What are you going to do, let Stephanos bleed on me? You have nothing. You are nothing and you always will be."

Steel returned to Lavina's voice and spine. She dodged around Fane and strode over to Gabriel to jab a finger into his chest. "Just like Stephanos is to you?"

"What are you raving about, madwoman? Stephanos and I are friends. I made him."

"You *owned* him," she spat in his face. "You treat him like you still do."

Lavina stepped back, running her hands over her hair and shaking out her arms. She slowly turned to regard Max, Vadim, and Fane, before locking her gaze onto Stephanos.

He watched her swallow. Her nostrils flared, gaze wavering for a moment before offering him a slight nod. "Perhaps it's time to rip away a few lies between the five of us."

"Six, you ignorant—"

"Oh, shut up, Gabriel. You won't live out the day if I have anything to say about it," Vadim said.

Lavina grinned. "As I was saying." She beckoned Stephanos closer.

He shuffled to her side, wondering if she really meant what she'd said about the lies, because that hadn't gone so well when she'd bared the truth to him the day before. If any of them reacted worse than he had, she was mostly on her own. What little remained of his strength was keeping him on his feet and not much more.

"You sure about this?" he asked.

She gave him a wavering smile. "For better or worse, right?"

"I'm pretty sure that's a marriage vow, not a throw fate to the fucking wind kind of statement."

Lavina chuckled under her breath and then quickly sobered. "Before the three of you joined us, I was asking Gabriel to recount how he came to rescue Stephanos after he'd been buried alive for a substantial number of years."

"Sixty-seven years," Stephanos clarified. The prospect of learning the truth made him lightheaded and giddy. Or maybe it as the blood loss.

Gabriel shook his head, entirely unimpressed. "You asked no such thing. The man gets overzealous with his feeding, works himself into a blood frenzy, and inevitably, it gets him into trouble. I do what I can to help him stay ahead of his weakness. I've had to come to his rescue countless times. Just like I did when those men captured him and buried him alive. Tell them, Stephanos. Tell them how I always save you."

"You have. Eventually," he admitted.

"The timing is the thing, though, isn't it?" Lavina asked, tapping Gabriel's chest.

The fabric under Max's fingers puckered from the pressure being exerted to hold Gabriel in place. Stephanos was glad he wasn't the one having to hold his sire back.

"What are you insinuating, Lavina?" prodded Vadim.

She turned to regard Stephanos, gazing at him for a long moment and then taking a deep breath. "He left Stephanos to suffer for sixty-seven years until he needed him again. As he had countless times before, I'm guessing. Keeping your *friend* on the back burner until you needed a killer again, weren't you?"

"I would never!"

Vadim and Fane watched Lavina and Gabriel quizzically. Max was too busy keeping his charge under control to track Lavina's hints at her methods.

Stephanos flew through his memories, recounting each time he'd been detained, captured, or imprisoned. Shortly after each one, he'd been given tasks. "You were keeping me busy, making me feel useful," he whispered, using the same words Gabriel had spoken. "You were asking me to do what I would have been doing all along had I been by your side," he said more firmly.

Gabriel nodded. "Exactly that. I would never wish you harm, my friend. You helped me."

Lavina scoffed. "Wish him harm? You were the one to turn him in!"

Stephanos couldn't break his stunned stare at Lavina. That couldn't be true.

"That's absurd," Gabriel shouted.

"That's the truth."

Vadim shook his head. "Lavina, come on, the whole

truthsayer thing is a ruse. My ruse, specifically."

She ignored him, giving Gabriel a forceful slap on the chest. "I saw it plain as day in your memory, asshole."

Fane's eyes went wide, his mouth dropping open.

"You had Stephanos followed, knowing the recent tasks you'd given him had left him craving immense amounts of blood. You didn't want to sacrifice your staff or purchase the number of humans it would take to wean his appetite back to a manageable level. It was easier, as it always has been, to tuck him away somewhere until you had need of him again."

"Don't listen to the witch, Stephanos. It's always been you and me."

Her voice rose. "I'm not a witch!" She shook her head and pressed her eyes shut for a moment.

When she opened them again, she was back in control. "Always, except when it was inconvenient to travel or establish yourself in a new place with the ravenous killing tool you'd created. The tool being a man you exploited to further yourself. Always, except when hiding him could be used to your advantage. When the man you keep calling your friend was nothing more than... What where your words? A crumb to offer the rabble?"

Gabriel tore his fuming gaze from Lavina to drill into Stephanos. "You're not buying any of this, I hope? You've always been a simple man, but surely even you can see she's trying to drive a wedge between us. Women do that. You know how they are. Just like that slave I gave you. They only want to dig their claws deeper into you, to have you all to themselves."

Vadim studied Lavina, his brows knitted and a scowl on his lips. "And why would she want that?"

Stephanos tensed, ready to leap to Lavina's aid with whatever strength he had left. "Because she feeds on us," he offered, spelling it out for them. "But never with harmful intent. Think about what you've told me. Are each of you better off, having spent time with Lavina?"

"You tricky bitch." Fane grinned. "That's why we never saw you feed, yet you were robust as could be."

"What do you take?" Max asked over Gabriel's shoulder.

"Fear, pain, anger—anything dark, really. It tastes the best." She turned to Vadim. "I took too much from you. I'm sorry. Staying with you too long changed you more than I wanted it to. I was selfish and didn't want to leave."

"Didn't want to leave?" His voice boomed through the high-ceilinged foyer. "You ripped my heart out, woman."

She bowed her head. "It was for your own good. Had I stayed longer, I would have whitewashed you completely. I couldn't do that to someone I loved, no matter how good you tasted."

Suddenly, Gabriel was free. He barreled toward Lavina.

Max grabbed at thin air, reaching for him.

Stephanos tried to leap forward, to rush to her side, but he'd stood in one place too long. His feet dragged across the floor like a sleepwalker in slow motion.

A hundred emotions flickered across Vadim's face as he absorbed what Lavina had said. Fane seemed to be doing the same, neither of them making a move to stop the deadly force with his hands out, going for Lavina's throat, his fangs bared.

Her reach was longer. She punched him in the throat. He dropped to one knee, gasping and gagging.

Lavina leaned down with one hand on his shoulder

to look him in the eyes. The compulsion in her voice was so heavy, Stephanos felt it, and he wasn't even her target. "Let's talk about Isla. Tell me how you looked after her when you took Stephanos away."

The three other men watched raptly as she and Gabriel locked themselves in a memory invisible to the rest of the room.

38

BEFORE TAKING the moonlit walk up the road to Stephanos' house, the one he'd gifted along with the half-dead slave, Gabriel stopped in town. He asked questions, innocent at first, just a man passing through, having a pint to get the lay of the land. Then he asked the few lingering occupants of the inn who lived in the big house at the end of the lane.

"A witch and her demon lover," was the unanimous answer.

He was glad to hear Stephanos had managed to rein in his feeding to avoid capture. A manageable appetite would make their traveling with him easier. The lover part of that though, he didn't like that at all. He'd left Stephanos here too long, allowed him to get too comfortable, but he'd been distracted with all America had to offer.

"You can look at the witch, she's pretty enough, but don't let her hear you speaking ill of her. She'll curse you," said a man with a pipe.

A brawny man with a thick dark beard spoke up, "Her demon pet comes out at night and roams the forest and the fields. Keeps the bandits and thieves at bay. We find their bloodless bodies in the morning light."

"Don't you fear the demon will come after you?" Gabriel asked.

"They been up there cavorting in dark magic for years but it never done harm to one of us," said the man with the pipe.

Gabriel shared his eye roll with the watery beer in his mug before surveying the room. He took a long drink and set the empty mug down. "That you know of. Are you aware that the demon drinks blood? Drinks *your* blood? He can drink from you but not take enough that you'd notice. He can make you forget you ever saw him."

The room fell silent. All eyes focused on him.

"You've been feeding a demon for years and never even realized it. What if I told you I could lure the demon away?"

The brawny man shook his head, a hint of a smile on his face. "You could do such a thing? You're but a young lad, not much muscle on you even."

Deep in Gabriel's memory, Lavina fed gleefully on the anger the man's doubt brought to a boil in her prey's mind. She might have dealt with being older than most vampires she'd ever met, but she'd never considered the inadequate woes of a pampered young man perpetually locked in at twenty.

Gabriel drew himself up. "I can take care of him tonight. For a price. I've done it before. Quite successfully, I might add."

"Is that so?" the big man said good-naturedly. "What's this price then? And what about the witch?"

"Yeah, what about the witch? She cursed my wife," called a man from the back corner.

"And my boy! He's never walked the same since the day the witch bought cloth from him at the market. Twisted his spine right up," added another man.

Gabriel grinned. This routine got easier every time he used it. Or maybe he was just that good at manipulating people, he thought proudly.

"When I lure the demon away, the witch will be unprotected. Go in just before dawn, when she's weakest. Don't give her time to speak. Quick, clean strokes will take her swiftly from this world and set you all free."

"And who gets the house? You?" asked the smoking man.

"That house is cursed now and forevermore, tainted by black magic. Take what you will when you kill the witch, but do not set foot there again."

"And your price?" prodded the brawny man.

Gabriel considered what these poor farmers might have to offer and named his fee. "In the dark morning hours, you will find the witch alone in her bed. The demon will be gone. Heed my words and you will all be free."

The men cheered and excused themselves to gather up his payment. Gabriel asked the innkeeper for a loaf of bread and a wedge of cheese to take with him. He patted his pocket where the vial of poison rested. Stephanos may have brought the slave back to life, but this would take her out of it easily enough. Who could resist fresh baked bread?

Within half an hour, Gabriel hefted his paltry palm-sized pouch containing a good portion of this village's wealth and his poisoned gift for Stephanos' slave. Scotland was too far away to be useful. He'd have to find a closer place to stash his thirsty pet once he'd ripped his way through the men standing in Gabriel's path to success. Confident he had this safe haven erased, he gathered up his things and headed up the winding path on the edge of town.

Filled with revulsion, Lavina pulled away from Gabriel's memory. Any other time, this would have been a satisfactory meal, but she'd felt Stephanos' love for Isla in his memories, the deep sense of loss he still carried with him to this day. She knew the victim, and that ruined her appetite.

Not taking any chances and needing to vent, Lavina slapped the man on one knee in front of her, full palm, across his face with all her might. Still in a daze from her trance, he fell to the floor, blinking slowly.

"Fane, Vadim? Perhaps one of you could take a turn restraining him?" she said.

"Lavina? What did you see?" Stephanos asked, though his tone made her wonder if he really wanted to know.

Seeing Vadim watching Lavina raptly, Fane took control of Gabriel, keeping him on the ground. Max loomed over them, ready to help if necessary.

"That's what you did to me?" Vadim asked.

"The process yes, not the slap." She faced the man she'd hurt with her shoulders squared and prepared to take whatever his anger might bring to the surface. The truth did hurt sometimes. Sometimes physically. But doing so lifted a tremendous weight from her conscience.

"To all of you," she admitted.

"Lavina," Stephanos prodded with desperation.

"You're going to want to sit down. In fact, you should do that anyway. You look like you could blow over any second." She was surprised that no one stopped her when she darted over to one of the decorative straight-backed chairs against the wall and placed it behind Stephanos.

After checking to make sure Gabriel was contained and Vadim was doing nothing more dangerous than staring at her like she had a third eye on her forehead, she recounted what she'd seen in Gabriel's memory.

Fury lit Stephanos' face like a flare. "You poisoned her?" he screamed, shooting to his feet faster than she thought possible, given his condition. "You kept me away for years knowing she was dead the day after we left? You let me think…" he sputtered.

For the first time since Gabriel entered the house, he appeared truly afraid. He did not struggle in Fane's grasp. If anything, he looked like he wanted to hide behind him.

Lavina stepped in front of Stephanos before he toppled over. Rage would only carry him so far. "I know it's little consolation, but the poison likely put her to sleep and she died quietly before the violence ever entered the house. She would not have suffered."

Stephanos' whole body shook. Seething and blood-splattered, he appeared to embody the demon Gabriel had named him to be. "You killed Isla! The one person you let me have. The one person who loved me even as the monster you created."

His fingers curled stiffly into claws. His fangs shone brightly in the well-lit foyer, bared and clearly thirsting to sink into flesh, no matter how sour the blood might be.

Lavina rested her hand on his shoulder, trying desperately to get him to look at her, but he was too focused on the vampire in Fane's grasp.

"Isla is not the only one to love you even as you are," she said calmly. "Stephanos, you have the truth. You are free. He cannot harm you ever again."

"I want to kill him," he declared around the exposed fangs that made him sound more animal than man.

Lavina turned to Vadim. "I'd say that's his right, but it's your city and your rules."

Vadim threw his head back and laughed.

Stunned, Lavina's heart beat erratically. Should she run? Was this the point where the truth of what she was and what she'd done had soaked in enough? Was Vadim going to explode in a fit of wrath that would surpass Stephanos'. Fear lit in her, igniting every nerve and pore. Regardless of the danger in front of her, she turned her back to Stephanos and placed herself against his blood-soaked chest. The devil she knew was safer than the one about to blow.

Her fear must have been a strong enough scent to break Stephanos' single-minded fury. He wrapped his arms around her and made a low growling noise deep in his throat that she could feel more than hear.

"You're a fucking therapist," Vadim said between guffaws. After a moment, he wiped his watering eyes and wound his outburst down to a chuckle. "We speculated so many options to explain the changes we all experienced around you, and the lack of ever seeing you feed. The times we'd catch you awake before we were, so many strange coincidences you always had excuses for." He wagged a finger at her. "You're a smooth one, Lavina, but once we all started talking, it was clear something was off about you."

"I'm not a therapist," she huffed, attempting to will her shoulders to stand down from their scared-stiff attention.

"Oh, honey, you are," Fane said. "We've all benefitted from talking to you. And hell, look at the man behind you. You talked him down like a pro."

"Hardly." She pulled gently away from Stephanos,

grateful for his support, but needing to stand on her own for a moment. Needing to catch her breath in this whirlwind going on around her.

"Not that our sessions were consensual," Max grumbled.

Fane snorted. "How many non-consensual meals have you consumed, hypocrite?"

Max shook his head. "How many more of you are there?"

"My mother was like me. I've never met another. I'm guessing they try to stay under the radar like I do."

Vadim eyed Stephanos. "You lied for her. You knew the truth of what she is?"

"Yes. She told me. Came clean on her own."

Being judged, having them talk about her while she was right there, made her back itch. However, there wasn't much to say. 'A girl's gotta eat' wasn't the most compelling defense. They needed to work this out on their own.

Holy shit, maybe Vadim was right.

The four of them huddled over Gabriel. She understood why they did, but it was the where that made her grimace. Letting that vile man know everything only gave him ammunition against her. Vadim had better be letting Stephanos at him once this conversation was done. She sat in the chair she'd dragged over and let them deliberate in hushed voices.

"I say we off the bitch," Gabriel said loudly over their discussion.

Vadim gave him a sharp kick in the ribs that seemed to shut him up. At least, as far as she could make out. Gazes darted furtively in her direction more than once. Stephanos' and Vadim's voices rose enough that she knew things were getting heated. She clutched the sides of the seat, tapping her nerves out with her fingertips on the underside of the chair.

Then the huddle broke. Fane hauled Gabriel to his feet. The five of them faced her.

"The agreement is this," Vadim stated, giving Stephanos one last annoyed glance. "You will remain here in Northchester, and the four of us will keep your secret. You will not sell any of your blood drug. That's my territory."

"You are no longer required to provide it to him either," Stephanos said, glaring at Vadim.

That explained the raised voices.

Lavina nodded, relieved the secret of her blood was safe with Stephanos. "Agreed. No problem."

"I will provide you with an office, and you will take clients," Vadim stated. "You may take your own, but priority will go to the ones I send you until I am satisfied with their results."

"I don't know as I'm actually qualified for that. I'm sure there's licensing and degrees."

He gave her a deadpan stare. "I will make sure you have what you require to pass inspection. The condition of all of this is twofold."

"Okay?" She perched on the edge of her seat, waiting for something terrible to fall into her lap.

"You will only feed with consent outside of that office."

A readily available food source wasn't at all terrible. "Agreed."

He held up a hand. "Not so fast. Your first client will be Gabriel, and you will wash him clean as can be."

"Wait, you're not going to kill him?" She looked from Stephanos' dark glower to Vadim. Even Fane and Max didn't appear happy about this decision.

She reevaluated the topic of the heated discussion.

"He is a prominent member of Northchester's vampire society," Vadim said. "If I make him disappear, there will be fallout. You know that I'm not in a financially secure place to deal with that at the moment."

"But he knows about me!" she blurted, no longer able to contain her frustration.

"Stephanos explained that you blur memories, not remove them entirely? That you dull the emotions in them?" Max said.

Lavina nodded hesitantly. "That's true, but—"

Max held his hands out, offering Gabriel to her like a gameshow prize. "Then I suggest you have a session immediately and dull his excitement over your revelation."

"You keep that bitch away from me!" Gabriel struggled in Fane's grasp.

Stephanos bared his fangs, grumbling profanities under his breath.

"Fine, but we need him conscious. There's been enough bloodshed tonight," Vadim conceded.

"Not quite." Stephanos strode over and punched Gabriel in the face. Blood poured from his nose. "Now we're good for tonight."

Max snickered.

Vadim sighed and shook his head. "Go on and let's get this over with. The sun will be up before we know it. I have a bed to get to before that happens."

"You're keeping him contained? For at least a while? I'll need time to work on him. Taking too much too fast could scramble his brain."

"That would be a shame." Fane shook Gabriel by the arms he held twisted behind him.

Lavina rose and stood before the man she now despised more than ever. He might be a meal that she would have otherwise found highly desirable, but now, he was nothing more than a heaping platter of kale. Nutritious, but there was no joy in it.

When she finished, she stepped away to find Stephanos beside her. He leaned closer to whisper in her ear. "I can't stay on my feet much longer. I need you."

The oblivion of the feeding daze would wash away the foul taste Gabriel had left behind. She took Stephanos' hand in hers.

"Do you need assistance with the cleanup?" Vadim asked.

"Nathan and Trina are on their way to help with that. If you wouldn't mind taking the bodies, we can handle the rest. I have a feeling you're more equipped for making men disappear than I am," she said.

"We can do that."

Stephanos leaned heavily on her, his hand cool to the touch.

"Max, perhaps you could assist Fane with moving the bodies to the trunk? There's a tarp in the back. Always good to be prepared," Vadim said.

Fane nodded to the man he held. "What about him?"

"We no longer need him conscious."

While Max took care of Gabriel with a gusto that gave Lavina great satisfaction, Vadim continued. "Yes, I will keep him for a week or so until you have adequate time to dull a few important memories. We'll start with the vital ones and work from there."

Stephanos cleared his throat. "Would you mind clearing his estate of those kids he feeds on? They are not there by consent, only by necessity and threats."

"That does indeed violate my rules. Noted and thank you for the information." Vadim smiled. "In fact, that gives me a valid reason to confine him a little longer. Even better."

Fane and Max had hauled two men out already and were on the second pair when Vadim approached Lavina.

"Do you mind?" he asked Stephanos.

"I need your bed. Join me soon?" Stephanos asked, not hiding his desperation.

"I'll be right behind you. Go on." She grimaced to see him walk so slowly, holding the wall as he limped away.

"You really care for him?" Vadim asked.

"Of course. I cared for all of you."

He reached out to cup her cheek. "Even me?"

"Especially you, but I went too far. Some of your personality traits have come back over time, but I don't want to do that to him. Learn from my mistakes, you know?"

"I was a mistake?" he asked softly.

"The mistake was mine, not yours."

He nodded, brushing his thumb over her cheek. "I wouldn't be where I am today without you. I meant that before, and I'm sorry I lashed out at you. It was just..."

"I hurt you. I get it."

"I'm glad you told me. And them." He nodded to Fane and Max. "You'll be safer with all of us behind you. And your talents will—"

"Come in handy?"

"Very much."

Lavina gently slipped away from his hand. "I don't know how I feel about being used like that."

"Stephanos will have a place too. No ill will to either of

you. I promise."

"I feel I should get this in writing," she joked.

He didn't laugh. "I'll draw something up tomorrow."

"Thank you." She kissed his cheek, feeling more at peace than she had in a very long time.

He smiled and then took a step back.

Fane and Max came back in after loading out the last of the bodies. Max took Gabriel's feet while Fane took his arms. They hauled the unconscious vampire out. Lavina would have been happy to never see him again, but they would be seeing a lot of one another for a while.

"I'll, uh, leave you to it then." Vadim followed them out the door, closing it behind him.

Lavina reached out to lock it just as the door opened. "What did you forget?" she demanded, her patience gone.

Trina grinned. "Hello to you too."

Nathan came in behind her, carrying their bags. "Evening, ma'am."

"It's wonderful to see both of you, truly, but I really need to get to my bed."

"Does there happen to be a certain vampire in it?" Trina winked.

"A wounded one, yes."

"Does he require a feeder?" Nathan asked, pulling out his phone.

"Not tonight, but thank you. I'm afraid you have a lot of cleaning to do. And repairs. And painting. What a mess." She spared a moment for the sad state of her cozy home. "Perhaps call Rosa and ask her to take a few more days off until this is under control. The boys don't need to see this mess."

"Will do. We've got this. Go on." Trina nodded toward

Lavina's room. "We'll try to keep the noise down out here."

"Don't worry about it. I have a feeling we'll both sleep like the dead." Lavina headed to her room, trying not to see the blood spatters, dented walls, stained carpet, and disarray of all her things. Exhaustion washed over her with every step.

With her bedroom door locked behind her, she approached the bed and the wounded vampire resting on top of the comforter.

He cracked an eye open. "I didn't want to ruin your sheets."

"I appreciate that. Let's get you fed."

Lavina snuggled in beside Stephanos, pulling her hair aside to offer him an unencumbered path to the vein he was eyeing up now that they were alone. Minutes later, sweet oblivion took them both away from the horrors of the night.

39

STEPHANOS WOKE with Lavina in his arms. His body still ached, and it would be another feeding or two before he was back to his full strength, but he felt fantastic.

Gabriel was no longer a danger to Lavina. He had the freedom to make a home here and a job offer. He might even have friends given some time. More importantly, he'd happened across a woman who cared enough to give him the truth even at great risk to herself. He planted a kiss on her warm cheek, not surprised that she was still sleeping. Last night had been long and terrifying for both of them.

He carefully slid off the bed and went to take a shower. The water hitting his barely healed wounds made him wince, but being clean further improved his mood. He reached for a towel only to land his hand on Lavina instead.

"Mind if I join you?"

"Not one bit." He shuffled to the back of the shower to give her the full stream of steaming water.

She picked up her shampoo, but he took it from her, taking his time to wash her hair and then the rest of her. He was about to reach for the towel again when she turned around and pressed her wet, naked body against him.

She eyed his hand on the towel hanging just outside the door. "Are we done here?"

He closed the door. "I don't think so."

"Good. Feeling fed enough to enjoy yourself?"

"I think I can manage that, but I will need a full feed tonight."

"I'll get Trina on it. Or, better yet, if you want, we can load the app on your phone and I'll show you how to use it. About time you take control of how often and from whom you feed."

"I would love that. And you."

She grinned. "You too."

The hot water ran out before they were finished, making Lavina shriek when the frigid stream hit her back mid-orgasm. "What awful timing!" She laughed as he carried her to bed.

"I'll make it up to you."

"I have no doubt of that." Her laughter quickly turned to moans as he made good on his word.

Around midnight, they emerged from the bedroom, dressed and prepared to handle whatever life threw at them next, side by side.

Lavina's phone dinged. "At least he waited a few hours." She scanned the text from Vadim, letting Stephanos guide her to the kitchen where they sat next to one another at the island.

"Will you need the car this evening, ma'am?" Nathan asked from his chair at the table. He tucked a finger into his book and waited patiently for an answer.

"Not tonight, but tomorrow, according to this novella of a text, Stephanos and I both have jobs to attend to. I'll see about hiring a second driver, someone for you to train, so you don't have to work the late nights anymore. How does that sound?"

The old man hesitated a moment, hurt flashing over his wrinkled face before fading into a deep sigh. "If that's what you wish, ma'am."

"What I wish is to see your smiling face every evening when I wake. Perhaps for a shopping run now and then. I will have an office to decorate and a somewhat professional wardrobe I'll have to maintain, after all. And book recommendations. And you know Trina needs your guidance, and that new driver will take some breaking in. You're just the man to do it all. Until you're ready to retire, that is. On your own terms, but I do wish for you to enjoy yourself. You deserve that."

Nathan nodded. "Thank you, ma'am. I appreciate your retirement package, really, it's just... I've been here so long I have nowhere else I'd rather be."

"Once I'm settled, we can explore some options." Lavina turned back to Stephanos. "It seems my office will be the empty apartment above The Jackyl, where Vadim held Nathan. He wants to keep me close in case either of you gets nervous about anyone he's asking me to see."

"I approve of this."

"It's not exactly a legit therapist's office," she grumbled.

"You're not exactly a legit therapist."

Lavina harrumphed. "Fine. Vadim would like you to report in tomorrow evening for your first shift at the club so you can also oversee Gabriel's first official appointment with me."

"I also approve of that. Though you're quite capable of defending yourself, having someone else around just in case the odds are against you would make me feel better."

"It sounds like you and Vadim are on the same page then."

He studied her, catching the hint of annoyance in her voice. "And you?"

Lavina sighed. "I'm somewhere in the same book. I need a little time to settle into the idea of having a job. I've been fortunate that I haven't had to work, in, well, a very long time."

"Is it work if you're helping people?" he offered.

"It's more the having to show up every night, having appointments, keeping records, having to juggle multiple people and how much I take from each one. It all feels over-whelming."

Stephanos glanced at Nathan, who was sitting there quietly, watching both of them like an eager student begging to answer the teacher's question. "Perhaps what you need is a familiar face to help you manage those things. Someone who knows what you are and what you do, that you trust. Whom I trust to notify me immediately if you need help. Someone like Nathan."

Lavina grinned. So did Nathan.

"We start tomorrow, ma'am?"

"We do. Our hours will be sundown to midnight."

"Very good. If you'll excuse me, I should pack a few things to brighten up the place."

After the old man had departed with a surprisingly springy step, Stephanos regarded Lavina's beaming face. "I was thinking, perhaps, I could be your late-night driver. If you'd be willing to teach me?"

"I would love to, but to be honest, Trina might be the best teacher. I could use a little brushing up on the rules myself. We could do that together?"

He nodded. The thing he'd been thinking about in the shower before she'd joined him reared up with all the talk of Lavina having to settle into her obligations with Vadim.

She set her phone down, eyeing him with a raised eyebrow. "What is it?"

"I don't want to do what I did for Gabriel anymore. Not even for Vadim. He made it quite clear that's what he wants, and I'm sure it's all outlined in his message to you. A message he didn't send to me."

Lavina sucked her lips. "I don't think he meant to leave you out. It's just, you're not the savviest person with phones. We'll work on it. Like the driving," she offered brightly.

"Sure, but what I'm trying to say is I don't want to have to manage my feeding frenzies if he sends me after more than one person. I have a hard enough time as it is. I want to learn to manage myself on my own, like I had started to do when I lived with Isla."

Lavina nodded. She rested her hand on his arm. "What other therapist have you been seeing? I'm jealous right now."

"I like this." He gestured around them. "You, this house, Northchester. Feeling human again. I don't want to screw up and make trouble for you or Vadim."

"What do you propose?"

"I want to learn more about what Trina was trying to get me to do, diagnosing illnesses by tasting blood. I can help that way. Do you think Vadim would accept that instead?"

"I think I will *make* him accept it." Lavina grinned. "I'm

sure he can find something in that service that will benefit him. You may have to work at the club in the meantime to satisfy his terms though."

"You'll help me? Let me know if I'm getting out of control?"

"Absolutely. Now let's get started by getting you set up so you can feed yourself as needed. First, you'll need to download the app. Go to—"

Feeding was the last thing on his mind at the moment. Even with the house in only semi-recovered shambles, all he had eyes for was the woman in front of him. He kissed her. "Show me later. If we have to work tomorrow night, we're spending this one in bed."

Trina wandered in, glancing around. "Oh, there you two are. Have either of you seen—"

Stephanos narrowly swerved to miss Trina with Lavina's legs as he carried her back to the bedroom. "Sorry," he threw over his shoulder, never slowing down.

"At least you're dressed this time," she shouted after them.

Lavina had already shoved the soiled comforter onto the floor earlier. He tossed it outside the door and locked it. There were benefits to having staff, and he was going to enjoy not being one of them for the first time in his life.

"Whatever will we do with the rest of the night?" Lavina asked, already pulling off the hoodie she'd donned. Her yoga pants hit the floor a moment later.

"The same thing I'd like to do every night for the rest of our lives." He pulled the last of his clothes off and slid on top of her between the layers of thick blankets and satin sheets.

"I approve of this." Lavina laughed, her fangs tangling

with his.

He didn't even care that they weren't real. She'd sunk her teeth into him in so many other ways, and he loved all of them.

**If you enjoyed this book,
please consider leaving a review.
They are much appreciated.
Thank you!**

About the Author

Jean Davis writes an array of speculative fiction and plays with chickens. She has written short story collections, a space opera series, stand-alone novels, children's books about her chickens, many projects that aren't yet finished, and a lot of pages that you will never see.

When not ruining fictional lives from the comfort of her writing chair, she can be found devouring books and sushi, weeding her flower garden, or picking up hundreds of sticks while attempting to avoid the abundant snake population that also shares her yard. She lives in West Michigan with her musical husband, an attention-craving terrier, and a mostly friendly flock of fluffy fowl.

Read her blog and sign up for her mailing list at www.jeandavisauthor.com. You can also follow her on Facebook and Instagram @JeanDavisAuthor, and on Goodreads and Amazon.

www.ingramcontent.com/pod-product-compliance
Lightning Source LLC
Chambersburg PA
CBHW011924050726

47591CB00009B/2335